THE WITCHING TIME

THE WITCHING TIME

Jean Stubbs

ST. MARTIN'S PRESS ✠ NEW YORK

ISBN 0-312-19367-x

First published in Great Britain by Victor Gollancz, an imprint of the Cassell Group

First U.S. Edition: October 1998

10 9 8 7 6 5 4 3 2 1

To Felix, who built me a writing room

ACKNOWLEDGEMENTS

These characters and their county do not exist, and the events happened only in my head, but I owe a debt of gratitude to the following people for their generous help and good counsel.

Ian Atlee and the staff of Helston Branch Library who suggested and obtained many books on witchcraft; in particular, *The History of Witchcraft and Demonology* by Montague Summers; *Magic* by David Conway and *Witchcraft* by Pennethorne Hughes.

Ali Muirden who gave me a copy of *Persuasions of the Witch's Craft*.

Gretel McEwen who introduced me to *Dreaming the Dark* by Starhawk, and *Women Who Run with the Wolves* by Clarissa Pinkola Estés, with tapes; and whose home inspired the original idea of 'Howgill House' and its surrounding dale. Robin and Gil Brookes whose toyshop in Swan Yard gave me the idea of the Catwalk.

Kevin and Helen Gilbert who shared their knowledge of bell-ringing without stint, and gave me a video of the casting of Solomon – the Great Spurr Tenor bell – at the Whitechapel Bell Foundry, and its subsequent arrival at St Buryan Church in Cornwall.

John Dunstan, Bob Hickman and the bell-ringers of Crowan Church, who invited me to attend a practice peal and view the tower.

David Thorne, editor of *The Ringing World*, who very kindly sent me a copy of the magazine, a *Ringing World Diary* and *The Ringer's Handbook*.

Frances Meeks, my nursing adviser, who produced an amazing assortment of pamphlets on community services.

Gil Fox whose glorious millinery sparked off the notion of 'Crazy Hats', and who gave me valuable background detail.

My agent, Jennifer Kavanagh, for encouragement and enthusiasm.

ASSEMBLY

ONE

London, October

The candles were burning well now, pushing back the dark, creating pools of shadow beyond the refectory tables.

'We'll sit here,' said the woman who had introduced herself as Rhoda Ford, and she set her sherry glass down with a triumphant little smack. 'We have a good view of the top table from here.'

Imogen was not listening.

'What a lovely idea,' she said, standing dutifully behind the plain chair, 'to light the room with candles.'

Momentarily they had gleamed through her personal sadness, and her eyes mirrored their reflections as if she could not have enough of them.

'They lend atmosphere to the occasion,' said Rhoda. 'This was originally a medieval hall, badly bombed during the war, but restored later. We've been using it for the annual dinner since 1952.'

Candle flames glittered in her spectacles. She was no longer a fellow guest at the Scarcliff Old Girls' Reunion but a prefect imparting information to a junior.

'You haven't been here before, have you?' she asked, guessing the answer, conveying censure even before she heard it.

Imogen shook her head.

'I come every year,' said Rhoda Ford righteously. 'Every year.' She reminded this negligent ex-pupil of a cardinal rule. 'We mustn't let the side down, must we?'

Imogen's little flare of pleasure died. Building up her former confidence, learning to say yes to life, was a slow, sorry business, taken one step at a time. I wish I'd never come at all, she thought. But she would not allow herself to slip back.

'There must be hundreds of Old Girls on the register,' she protested. 'It wouldn't be feasible for every one to come every year.'

'No, of course not. But each of us should do her bit now and again.' Sportingly, she gave Imogen a chance. 'Perhaps you live too far away?'

In Imogen's head, Fred said, *Tell her to get stuffed.*

'Kingston,' said Imogen rebelliously.

'Kingston, Jamaica?'

'No, Kingston, Surrey.'

'Oh dear me,' cried Rhoda Ford archly, playfully. 'I can see you've been slacking. We must bring you up to scratch.' Reading Imogen's expression aright she changed course. 'Even if no one is here from your time it's worth coming just for the company. We have awfully interesting members, you know. That's Claudine Masham talking to Dr Friar, the President. She was a secret agent in the Second World War. Awarded the Military Cross. She must be well over eighty by now.'

Rhoda Ford lifted one hand in greeting to Claudine Masham and was ignored. She identified half a dozen other distinguished members and waved to them also, with much the same result.

You've picked the rotten apple in the barrel, said Fred.

I didn't pick her. She picked me, Imogen answered him mentally.

The tongue and eyes of the inquisitor were busy.

'When were you at Scarcliff?'

'From 1973 to 1982.'

Rhoda Ford made a swift calculation in her head.

'So you'll be about thirty?'

'Twenty-nine.'

Why are you putting up with this old bat? Fred asked.

'I was there during the war,' said Rhoda. She lifted her steel-grey head high, inflated her bosom, remembering. 'We all had to pick potatoes one day a week. Doing our bit for the war effort.' Then, unfairly, for Imogen was not about to speak, 'Hush! Dr Friar is going to say grace.'

Standing beside and beyond them, along the polished trestle tables, sixty other members of the Old Girls' Club bent their heads, listened to familiar words, and prepared to eat familiar food.

Windsor soup. Lamb and cabbage. Rice shape and stewed fruit, Fred prophesied.

He was not entirely wrong, but sherry and wine were also served.

As the chairs scraped back and chatter resumed, Rhoda Ford began again.

'They were the best days of our lives.'

Speak for yourself, said Fred, since his widow remained silent.

Imogen thought, This was a great mistake. In a moment, I'll tell her I feel ill. That I have been ill for a long time. That this is my first evening out since my husband died. That I'm sorry but they must excuse me . . .

The door at the end of the hall was being opened discreetly, and its opener might have slipped in unobserved had not the drawling hinges announced her. Every head turned to see who had arrived late. It was Ceres who surveyed them with smiling dismay: a plump and comely Ceres in her middle forties, disguised in a good tweed suit and camel-hair coat, polished brown brogues: wheaten hair coiled round her head, celestial blue eyes concerned. As she saw the evening uniform of dark silk dress and pearls she began to laugh nervously and apologize all round, taking this roomful of strangers into her confidence.

'Oh dear, how smart everyone is! Do forgive me . . . only up for two days and so much to do . . . I brought a dress with me but didn't have time to change.'

The elderly secretary laid aside her napkin and came forward to greet and guide this dilatory guest. She addressed the delinquent in hushed tones, as if they were in church.

'Mrs Brakespear, isn't it? Miss Wareham as was?'

The newcomer's voice was hurried and penitent.

'Yes, that's right. Terribly sorry . . . realized I was running late . . . made the mistake of taking a taxi that got stuck in a traffic jam.'

Here she laughed again, slightly breathless with the rush and anxiety. 'Like the Red Queen I run faster, faster, just to stay in the same place!'

From the far end of the hall Imogen could not see the stranger clearly nor catch all her words, but the tone and delivery were familiar and lightened her darkness. She watched and listened intently.

As always, when his widow stirred to life Fred retreated into silence.

Mollified, the secretary was saying, 'It's always wise to allow at least half an hour extra for any journey across London. But here you are and we're delighted to see you. You'll find the cloakroom outside on the right, clearly marked. I'm afraid that the only two seats left are at the end of this table near the door. Mrs Donnelly − Netta Curtis as was − is also late.'

Forgiven and accepted, Alice Brakespear spoke cheerfully now.

'Oh, I don't mind where I sit, Miss Healey. Is anyone here from my time?'

'Without consulting the list, I can't say, but we have a good cross-section of members this evening, and we can socialize afterwards when they serve the coffee.'

The ex-Geography mistress returned to the top table, smiling on all, to show that Scarcliff, though keen on punctuality, was also gracious to those at fault.

But Alice Brakespear, eager for company, hung her coat on the back of her chair and even stood on tiptoe so that she could see more clearly. Her eyes scanned the candlelit room, and in the instant that they rested on the still pool of Imogen's watchful face a flare of recognition lit between them.

Alice gave a gasp of delight and immediately began to weave her way politely but purposefully down the hall, murmuring, 'Pray do excuse me!' to each waitress and table as she went. Imogen jumped up so quickly that her chair fell over. And every head turned to see who had caused the commotion.

'Mrs Brakespear has evidently found a friend,' Miss Healey said.

The feeling of a pair of arms enfolding her was the thing Imogen most missed about Fred. The sense of *déjà vu* was even stronger. For in this way, with little cries of maternal affection, had Alice comforted her when Imogen first came to Scarcliff at eight years old, bereft of both parents. As form mistress to the first-year pupils, Alice became Imogen's adored guide and mentor. She left Scarcliff to marry when Imogen was a willowy teenager, and promised to keep in touch. But time and circumstance intervened and Alice was too busy living her daily life to write regularly. Besides, she was not a natural correspondent, preferring to deal with people directly. Gradually communications dwindled. She moved and did not give a forwarding address. Imogen no longer needed a surrogate-mother. The relationship faded away.

Now the past was resurrected, for once again Imogen was bereaved, and once again Alice had appeared to console and strengthen her.

I shall stay for dinner after all, she thought, because Rhoda Ford can no longer oppress me. And after dinner, when we have coffee and mingle, I can tell Alice that lightning does strike twice in the same place, that I have lost my whole world for a second time. After dinner, I shall tell her about Fred.

But Alice did not intend to wait until pale brown coffee was served.

'You must come and sit with me at the end of the table near the door,' she cried. 'We need to talk.'

Mindful of her bridling neighbour, Imogen said reluctantly, 'But I'm sitting with Miss Ford – who has been so kind.'

Liar! said Fred. *Coward!*

Alice's eyes were her best feature: of an excellent blue, they shone with kindness. Now they looked from her friend to the stranger and back again: assessing, understanding, regretting this companionship.

'Oh, I'm so sorry. I hadn't realized you came together.'

12

Rhoda Ford had been silenced only for the moment. She moved into the fray, teeth and spectacles glittering, and staked her claim to Imogen.

'We didn't. We haven't met before. But we hit it off from the beginning and we're getting on famously. So . . .'

So that was that. First come, first served. Perhaps, out of charity, Rhoda would have invited the latecomer to take coffee with them afterwards. They were not to know because Fred said, *Speak up!* and Imogen came to life.

'Oh, but I'm sure you'll understand when I tell you that Alice and I are *very* old friends, who haven't seen each other for years, and we simply must talk.'

'But they've served your soup!' Rhoda Ford cried.

Imogen flowered.

'I'll take it with me,' she said. 'If you'll excuse me.'

Then she and Alice smiled at each other and on Rhoda Ford, who was thinking that this was, quite frankly, a bit thick.

'So nice to have met you!' they cried in unison, and walked down the room: Imogen carrying her plate carefully so that it would not slop.

The secretary, glancing up at the clock, said to the president, 'I don't think that Mrs Donnelly, Netta Curtis as was, will be coming after all. But I am not in the least surprised. As a girl she always lacked any sense of time or place. And her cheque – to use the vernacular – *bounced*.'

Alice lifted her spoon, gave Imogen a long deep blue look, and said, 'You first.'

Fred was alive for Imogen once more, and life suited him so much better than death that it seemed doubly sad he had left it so young.

'We met in Manchester in the rain, eight years ago,' she said. 'Both of us had been . . .'

Bumming around, Fred suggested cheerfully.

'. . . exploring different careers and acquiring various skills. I was beginning to earn a living in – handicrafts . . .'

Hats. Crazy Hats!

Alice said loyally, instantly, 'You were always so clever with your hands.'

Why not tell her the truth?

Not all at once, Imogen replied.

'. . . and Fred was preparing the ground for a personal business venture.'

You mean Magical Toys for Adults?

Imogen did not respond to this, because she knew that above all else Alice was a sensible lady, not really into magical things, and it would be

13

wiser to tell her the truth in stages. She remembered a game they had played at a school party, which afterwards they learned was a symbol of their imagination. Given a horizontal line they had to create a quick picture. Imogen had drawn a broad road vanishing into infinity whereas Alice drew a five-barred gate. But being a good sport she laughed as much as everybody else when the game was explained.

'And while he established himself he worked in catering,' said Imogen. *Frying hamburgers in a downtown diner.*

Imogen had preserved her virginity for reasons of shyness, shrewdness and lack of true opportunity. In a sexually vibrant age she was as old-fashioned as a cottage rose. She was looking for love, which seemed to be in short supply, but she did not intend to be seduced or bullied into anything less. So hearing a young man's voice hail her, in the dark of early winter evening, she quickened her pace. The rain, which had been lying slyly in wait all afternoon, now pelted down in reckless abundance. She pulled her coat collar higher, kept her face averted from the doorway in which he stood.

He hailed her again.

'Hey, Miss! Miss! You in the red raincoat. Come in out of the wet!'

She hurried on, and with terror heard him hurrying behind her.

'I've got an umbrella!' he cried.

She scanned the street ahead. She was not alone. Though head down and scurrying for shelter, the inhabitants of this sopping black city would surely protect her if she screamed?

Armoured by that thought, she stopped, turned and faced him.

He was a pleasantly plain young man of medium height with a long jaw, a good nose, a wide mouth and eyes of different colours: one green, one blue. His was a clown's face, and when he smiled or laughed it was in the way of the clown: childlike in its glee and holding an inscrutable sadness. But the sadness, she learned later, was not in himself but in his fate. He was destined to die young.

'I've got an umbrella,' he repeated, smiling.

He was so innocent, so vulnerable, so ridiculously light-hearted, that she knew he could be trusted, and smiled on him. So he laughed, and held his streaming black shelter high to accommodate her.

'You're a long lass!' he remarked, as they stood shoulder to shoulder.

'There's no answer to that – apart from yes!'

'I bet you thought I was trying to get off with you!' he said, and laughed again.

She laughed with him, and said yes, she did.

'Well I was,' he admitted. And added, 'But even if I hadn't been I'd have offered you a share of the umbrella.' He said, 'My name's Fred. Fred Lacey.'

'Imogen Roper.'

They stood in the teeming rain, and he changed hands on the umbrella in order to shake hers.

'Are you going anywhere in particular?' Fred asked.

'I was looking for somewhere cheap, good and plentiful to eat.'

'I know a place. I work there actually. But I'm off duty at the moment,' said Fred, offering her his arm. 'Let's go together, shall we? Do you have to be home at any particular time?'

She was too proud to reveal the poverty of her social life.

'No, I happen to be free this evening.'

'I suppose you live with your parents?' Genially.

'Why should you suppose that?'

'You give the impression of being protected.'

She laughed again then, but not in amusement.

'My parents died when I was eight and I live alone in a bedsitter.'

He squeezed her arm and said, 'Sorry.'

Then gave her a brief autobiography.

'My parents never married. They're both journalists, high-powered stuff, working abroad in different places. Neither of them had or have time to spare for me. I was an unwelcome accident, brought up at first by my mother's parents and then sent to boarding school. They all tried to make something of me but it hasn't worked. I've failed at all the things they wanted me to do. Now I'm going to be me.'

They linked arms and matched their pace, stride for stride. The streets were emptying. The rain was a backdrop which left the stage free for them.

Imogen said, 'I was an only child too. My parents were killed in a car accident which I survived. Oh, I'm not an abandoned orphan. Uncle Martin, my father's brother, has always looked after my finances, and I'm festooned with relatives. I can stay with any of them, at any time. They're kind and well-meaning, but curiously impersonal. So I take care of myself.'

Fred halted them both and they stood face to face while the rain poured down on his umbrella, and sent little streams cascading from each point on to whatever portion of them remained outside its perimeter.

'I would take care of you,' said Fred.

His first kiss was a solemn promise. His second kiss was a question.

Imogen moved away from him, shaken. 'We don't know each other,' she said.

He nodded, acknowledging the brevity of their acquaintance.

'I happen to have fallen in love with you,' he said humbly. 'My intentions are honourable, and everything's above board.' He felt in his raincoat pocket and produced a card.

They moved to a street-lamp so that she could read it.

Fred Lacey, it read. *Maker of Magical Toys for Adults.*

'Magical Toys?' Imogen said, entranced.

'For adults. Adults are only children in disguise. They need toys, too.'

'It's a wonderful idea.'

'The only thing is — the toys take a long time to make.'

The child in Imogen possessed a good business head.

'So how do they sell?'

The child in Fred did not know what business meant.

'Not very well, actually. That's the trouble. Only now and then. And some of them are very big and come very expensive. You could call them Crazy Toys! They're elaborate complex structures, with stories and games attached to them that you have to play out. Fortunately, my landlady believes in me and she lets me store them in her attic.'

Imogen scrutinized his card again. His address was in the poor quarter of the city, 'c/o Mrs Eileen Bradshaw'.

'My landlady,' Fred explained. 'She cooks an excellent hot-pot on Monday nights if ever you'd like to drop by.'

'Thank you. That sounds lovely,' said Imogen absently, thinking of his sales. 'But wouldn't it be wiser to use a good covering address? Success invites success, you know. Humility invites the boot.'

'Oh no,' said Fred, with the utmost faith. 'This shows that I'm poor but honest. She was unconvinced and he asked, 'What do you do?'

'I've rented a workroom in Deansgate. It costs an arm and a leg, but I go without other things. Here's my card.'

Someone who knew about art and marketing had designed this, severely black on white with a sophisticated logo, and the two words *Crazy Hats* scrawled fantastically across it.

'Effective *and* expensive!' Fred observed, eyebrows raised.

He surveyed her with increased respect.

'Uncle Martin arranged for me to use some of my capital to start me off.'

'You make truly crazy hats?' Fred asked, intrigued.

'I make *amazingly crazy hats!*' Imogen cried, released into her own world.

16

'I thought hats were out of fashion.'

'It's a luxury trade,' she admitted, 'and each hat is individually designed and hand-made. But the price matches the effort. I'm becoming known, and I get by.'

'So we're both young, mad and penniless, with wonderful futures ahead of us?'

'Yes. I suppose we are.'

'Couldn't be better,' said Fred. 'I don't suppose you've fallen in love with me, by happy chance. Have you?'

His tone was inconsequential, his meaning serious. She considered him seriously.

'I don't fall in love easily. In fact I take time even to make friendships. But I like you. And you make me laugh.'

'It's a fair start,' said Fred. 'Stick around while you get the hang of it.'

Despite everyone's sound advice they married two months later on a wet Saturday morning in a register office. Their families sent cheques and good wishes but did not turn up. Fred's landlady and her husband acted as witnesses, and gave them the kitten, Polly, as a wedding present.

They were so much in love that they hardly noticed the lack of guests.

Imogen stopped, a little shamefaced at the length of her recital.

'And then?' Alice prompted kindly.

Seven happy years? Fred prompted.

'No, I've run on long enough,' said Imogen. 'I want to know about you, Alice.'

'Oh, still a clergyman's wife.' Cheerfully. 'I could hardly be anything else, coming from a family of churchmen, could I? Born to serve!'

'A born carer,' Imogen corrected gently.

'Well, well. You always had a charitable turn of phrase. We've been married for fifteen years now and we have two sons, both away at boarding school. I'd hoped for a larger family, but it wasn't to be.' Trying not to mind. 'Still, that's perhaps as well. We've moved around quite a lot. Our first living was in Gloucestershire. We had a Georgian house in a lovely old-fashioned village.'

Her lips moved as if twitched by an unwelcome memory.

'Hal is a man of principle and he stands by his convictions,' she said. 'Of course, I wouldn't have him any other way, but he does tend to lack diplomacy. I'm afraid he upset a number of important local people, and finally the Church moved him on. In fact this is our third parish. We're living in a North Country market town called Langesby. Rather bleak and run down, but there are some lovely houses in the old quarter. Hal is the vicar of St Oswald's, which used to be a prominent church, but the building is in a poor state and the congregation has dwindled. Still, he enjoys a challenge, and he's made the town think about the church instead of taking it for granted . . .'

She was pensive for a moment, then her face relaxed, her smile returned. 'Anyway,' she said in a rush of confidence, 'we have a very exciting time ahead of us. It will be four hundred years next July since Langesby received its fair charter, and the town is celebrating the event with a whole week of festivities. Market stalls and side-shows and roundabouts and entertainments of every description. We expect it to be a great tourist attraction – and in these hard times we hope it will be. Naturally, Hal is taking this opportunity to raise more money for the church, and I'm always involved in his projects, so we shall be busy . . .'

Her eyes clouded slightly at the prospect, then came to rest on her friend. She brightened again.

'But here I am, chattering away, when we should be thinking about *you*. Are you sure you've convalesced fully? You seem very quiet and withdrawn. And you say this is your first evening out, and you've been home for a month? My dear Imogen, that's no way to start a new life. What you need is to be taken out of yourself, given a sense of purpose. You must come and stay with us. You must come soon.'

'No, no. It wouldn't be fair. You have far too much to do,' said Imogen, afraid of effort and change.

'That's part of my job,' said Alice, and then with rare insight, 'and part of me, too, I expect. I seem to attract responsibilities.' She mused on this for a while and then recovered. 'It's no trouble. I'm used to having extra people in the house. And you're a special person, Imogen, and special to me, and I feel we've been brought together again so that I can help you.'

The prospect of solving Imogen's problems caused her to forget her own. Her eyes sparkled. Her mouth was purposeful.

'Yes, you must come to us. We'll put you back on your feet again, and set you on the right road.'

Why can't people leave me in peace? Imogen wondered crossly. And how should they know if their road is right for me?

Aloud, head bent, fiddling with her coffee-spoon, she said, 'I'd love to come, but I can't possibly leave Polly. She's our cat – my cat. She's very special too. And she's been in a cattery for ages while I was ill. It had such a bad effect on her. I daren't leave her again.'

'Bring her with you,' said Alice. 'We have cats of our own. She'll run along with the rest of them.'

'I think that might prove difficult . . .' Imogen began.

But Alice, who welcomed all waifs and strays, said briskly, 'Nonsense! You're only sitting and brooding on the past down here. It would do you a world of good to get away from London. Meet new people. Make new friends. There's no time like the present for making a start . . .'

She took out a small businesslike diary. It seemed to be extraordinarily full, and Imogen breathed again, but only for a minute.

'Now let me see . . .' Alice mused, biro poised over the pages. 'Yes, we seem to be free at the end of this month . . .'

TWO

Hallowe'en

The train was grumbling and mumbling through the industrial landscape, on iron rails between iron girders across an iron bridge. Telephone lines skimmed by, telegraph poles trod on each other's heels, ran up and vanished. Now came signs of an approaching main-line station: balding embankments planted with dusty shrubs, concrete sheds with rust-red doors, captive papers blowing on wire-mesh fences, a long black ripple of railings, buildings of black-red brick.

Many rails were crossing each other's paths, merging, twisting, winding and turning in this direction and that. Carriages waited in sidings. The grumbling became grinding. A scalloped roof of dingy cream appeared, heralded by a broad iron-grey curve of platform. Faces flitted slowly past. Slower and slower yet.

From the opposite platform an InterCity train began to glide sedately towards London and Imogen was consumed by a desire to leap out, run after it, board it, and return to her familiar void. Instead, flanked by a large suitcase and an overnight bag, holding the caged and enraged Polly, she remained immobile.

Her train had stopped. Pressure, both physical and emotional, built up behind her. Voices enquired, explained, urged her on.

'Why doesn't she get out?'

'Perhaps it's the wrong station.'

'Come on, love, we haven't got all day!'

'No, it's her luggage. She can't manage all that luggage.'

'Would you mind moving, madam?'

Snap out of it! said Fred.

Shaken into action, she tumbled herself, her bags, and Polly on to the platform. In her head her personal demons began to chant *It's the wrong station.*

'Are you all right, dear?' asked a different voice. 'Can I help you?'

She panicked now at the prospect of dealing with a stranger's sympathy, of having to reveal her inadequacies.

'Yes, yes. I'm all right. Thank you. My friends are meeting me.'

She stared round for help, and there was Alice, standing some yards further up the platform, looking wonderfully handsome and country lady, and behind her towered the unknown quantity of Alice's husband, in the shape of a tall man with horn-rimmed spectacles and a high balding forehead, who stared gravely over his wife's barley-gold crown of hair. He was not wearing clerical garb or a collar. His air was vigilant and his bearing upright. Had Imogen not known he was a vicar she would have guessed him to be a military man of some standing.

'There are my friends!' Imogen cried, and gave a despairing wave.

They were hurrying towards her, and Imogen began simultaneously to thank the stranger and welcome them. She was aware that she babbled to no purpose, and that Hal Brakespear's sharp grey eyes were noting this fault. But Alice's goodwill could encompass a critical husband and an absurd friend without being disturbed by either.

'Imogen, this is Hal,' she said proudly, and stood back, smiling on them both. Imogen's hand was taken and shaken firmly, and an authoritative voice said, 'Welcome to Langesby. We've been looking forward to your visit.'

The words were hospitable but sounded formal.

Attracted by a toneless howl, Alice cried, 'Oh, is that dear creature in the basket the famous *Polly*? Hello, Polly!'

'I shouldn't touch her if I were you,' Imogen warned nervously. 'She's been there since breakfast and she's feeling scratchy.'

Hal said briskly, 'Shall we go, then? We have half an hour's drive ahead of us and I expect you'd like your tea.'

Lifting both bags as if they were weightless he marched ahead.

The station car park, which overlooked the city, was high and windy and cold. Here a palatial old Rover was parked slightly askew, as if the Brakespears had arrived late. It needed washing, but beneath the sprays of mud, the veils of dust, its colour gleamed a rich dark blue. Inside, the same combination of opulence and neglect prevailed. The grey plush upholstery was shabby. The leather hand-straps looked as if a dog had gnawed them.

'How very luxurious,' said Imogen, quick to praise.

'Hal's brother gave it to us when our old car broke down,' said Alice. 'It's rather grand for a vicar, but so comfortable and spacious, and it runs beautifully.'

'Hobson's choice. It drinks petrol,' said her husband in his dispassionate manner. 'I shall change it as soon as I can for something more economical.'

Alice passed over this remark, and Imogen guessed that their marriage was peppered with such small-shot and this was how she rendered it harmless.

'You must sit in front with Hal and get acquainted,' said Alice generously. 'I'll take the cat basket.'

'No, Alice. You two sit in the back,' said Hal. 'I'm sure you have lots to talk about.' He remembered something, and addressed his wife. 'We must discuss the question of Stephen Proctor later.'

'If you don't mind,' said Imogen, sliding into the ample solitude of the back seat, 'I think it best if Polly and I sit here by ourselves and draw breath quietly. We're both feeling a bit shattered.'

She could tell that Hal was relieved by this decision, and as both husband and wife began immediately to speak of Stephen Proctor she drifted off into another daydream.

This was the poorer part of a North Country city. The detritus of urban dwelling. Abandoned cars, piled high like bright crushed sardine tins. Concrete walkways. Rusting corrugated iron sheds on vacant lots. Waste ground littered with the rubbish children used in play: plastic milk crates, a rubber tyre hanging from a leafless tree. Writing on walls, the graffiti carefully blocked in. Fire escapes on the sides of old black buildings. A brown canal overhung by dank warehouses. An Odeon cinema. Church spires. A timberyard. A derelict terrace, windows and doors boarded up, some vandalized.

Then came a new housing estate. Red-brick boxes climbing a hillside. New trees planted in their protective casing. The road broadened into a motorway. City and suburbs were left behind. Blue and white signs, seen in the distance, came close, were passed, became the information of a few moments ago, and they were out into the open country.

Sky and light were different here, and space abounded. Hills curved, valleys dipped, stone walls traced the boundaries of fields. The landscape seemed to be far below the washed blue arch, like a scene in a glass snowstorm. And from the corner of one field rose the shimmering tulle scarf of a rainbow.

'There!' Alice cried, as if she had personally ordered its appearance. 'There's a welcome for you! And just over the brow of this hill you can see Langesby in the distance. We're almost home.'

★   ★   ★

Langesby had dignity of a grimy stolid sort and, as Alice had said, there were some lovely old buildings. Handsome stone houses on the outskirts, now converted to council offices and business premises, bore witness to the former affluence of its mill-owners. The main street, though given over to the usual shops and stores, a Chinese takeaway and an Indian restaurant, still had its cobbled market-place and covered market hall, and a fine old hostelry at the far end called the Ram's Head. And Church Street, into which they turned at the top of the town, had been preserved in eighteenth-century elegance.

In its prosperous past Langesby, gratified with its achievements and untroubled by doubts, had sorted out life on earth and paid a deposit on heaven. Now, gripped by recession, losing its faith in God, the royal family, the country and the economy, civic confidence had dwindled, and an air of uncertainty hung over the town like a miasma.

'There's the church!' Alice cried, in pride and chagrin.

St Oswald's was an austere edifice of great age and unusual character. Conceived on a grand scale by a visionary bishop, it had been an unlucky enterprise from the beginning. The weight of its soaring spire on a sandy foundation had caused the building to tilt slightly, with consequent distortion. The effect was both impressive and unsettling.

'It may look a little odd but it's quite safe,' Alice assured her, as the car rolled graciously past blackened stone walls, dank with moss.

'How old is it?' Imogen asked.

Hal spoke up. 'It's an architectural patchwork. Founded in the twelfth century. Rebuilt in the sixteenth with subsequent additions.'

'The vicarage is mid-Victorian,' Alice said, and endeavoured to summon up enthusiasm. 'Very well built.'

It was also very large and fanatically symmetrical, with a broad bay window on either side of a gabled porch, two tall first-floor windows which opened out on to miniature terraces, and four porched attic windows above them. Lawn and flowerbeds were equally balanced and surrounded by rhododendrons. Split by its gravel driveway, the house could have been identical twins.

'How imposing!' Imogen remarked, thoroughly daunted.

Alice sighed as if every begrimed stone lay on her heart, but said gallantly, 'Oh yes, we have lots of room.'

The front door was opened by a short stout lady with tight white curls all over her head. She bore a strong resemblance to Harpo Marx but Alice introduced her as 'My Right Hand, Vera!' and immediately made use of this right hand by placing the cat-basket in its keeping.

24

'This dear little cat is called Polly, Vera, and she's rather shy. You needn't worry, Imogen. Vera knows all about cats and she'll have this one eating out of her hand in no time. And now, you must be exhausted after your long journey,' said Alice, as if her friend had flown in from Beirut. 'I'll show you to your room first and you can see the rest of the house later.' Then, raising her voice slightly and infusing it with a command, 'Hal will take up your bags . . .'

He had been walking off to his study absent-mindedly but wheeled round at once, picked up the luggage, and strode ahead of them. Where-upon Alice said gratefully, as though he had thought of this himself, 'Oh, thank you, darling.'

The hall was high and sombre, with a Victorian tiled floor and stained-glass windows. As they mounted the wide staircase Alice said to Imogen, 'I've given you a room on the top floor, so you'll be self-contained and quiet and private.'

Does she go there sometimes, and close the door on her daily life? Imogen wondered, registering the words 'self-contained and quiet and private'.

Yes, said Fred. *Even the most energetic generals need to rest between battles.*

The staircase now divided on to a extensive landing, and against one wall stood an immense doll's house, silent and secretive behind its lace curtains.

'That was mine,' said Alice, slightly out of breath, 'when I was a little girl. It's been in my family for nearly a hundred years. Passed down from first daughter to first daughter. I was hoping . . .' She did not pursue the hope but ended quickly, 'I'll show it to you later.'

'We turn to the left here,' Hal proclaimed, for Imogen's benefit. 'These used to be the servants' quarters. The stairway is narrow and has a low archway. As you're taller you'd better mind your head.'

They emerged into a corridor full of chocolate-brown doors.

'The bathroom is opposite, next to the linen cupboard. I should leave the landing light on at night, if I were you, so that you find your way about.'

'Here you are, and we hope you'll be very comfortable,' Hal announced, in his punctilious manner. He set the suitcases down in the middle of the room, said to his wife, 'I'm sure that you and . . .' He had forgotten her name. Alice prompted him. 'And Imogen – of course – want to talk about old times, so I'll have tea in my study. Oh, by the way, George Hobbs may be dropping in on his way home. When do we eat?'

'Between seven and half-past.'

'Good.' He remembered their guest. 'Then I look forward to meeting you again at supper . . . Imogen,' he said formally, and stalked off.

Alice explained to the universe, 'Hal has a lot on his mind at the moment.'

Since there was no answer to this statement Imogen simply smiled and nodded and then, with interest, began to inspect her new shell.

It was a long low attic room with oak beams, polished wooden floorboards and a carpet that had once been brilliant and was now a gentle ghost. The woodwork was painted white, the walls papered in tender grey and ivory stripes, and adorned at regular intervals with Alice's watercolours. A bowl of chrysanthemums glowed on a chest of drawers. A tray of tea-making equipment gleamed on a table by the bed. An electric fire sat with its wire wrapped cosily about it, like a silver cat with a furled black tail.

Yes, this is her personal sanctuary, said Fred, echoing his widow's thoughts.

Alice read her friend's face with pleasure and affection.

'I can tell you like it. I knew you would. It's a good place to recharge one's batteries. I want you to feel at home here. You don't have to stand on ceremony with us. Just retreat to it whenever you want to. Rest. Relax.'

The voice spoke to Imogen's bones, as it had always done: compelling certainly, not to be opposed or denied, but nevertheless soothing, reassuring, upholding, protecting: the voice of the mother she had lost too early. As the afternoon light waned, softening objects, stealing into the senses, Imogen felt at one with the past they had shared.

'Another nice thing about this room,' Alice continued, 'is that the windows face in opposite directions – Goodness, it does grow dark early at this time of the year. I'll switch the light on in a minute. Come over here. This window looks into the back garden.'

Short and tall stood closely: Alice's rounded arm linked Imogen's slender one. Imogen's sleek dark head inclined towards her friend's barley-coloured mound.

'Those are our hens, next to the clothes-line,' said Alice, 'and you shall have a new-laid egg for breakfast. Beyond the washing and the hen-house is the orchard, which produces a wonderful local apple called Cockcroft's Marvel. The rest of the garden is mostly lawn with a border of perennials, to make life simpler. The Youth Club act as unpaid gardeners.'

The lawn stretched ahead of them, a dim and ghostly green.

'And from this side' – leading her friend towards the other window – 'you have a bird's eye view of Langesby and the dale. Rather obscured by mist and poor light at the moment. Lovely on a clear day . . .'

Out beyond the chimneys and rooftops of Langesby the dale was becoming insubstantial, but on a hill some distance away, nine jagged fingers pointed up into the evening sky.

'Oh, what are those?' Imogen cried, pointing.

'Just an old circle of standing stones over at *Haraldstone*,' Alice answered. She stressed the name slightly as if it were a place of ill repute, and her breezy tone alerted Imogen, telling her that this subject was not to be discussed. Stubbornly, she pursued the matter.

'I'm fascinated by stone circles. When Fred and I went to Brittany we drove down to see the standing stones of Carnac. But I felt there were too many of them. I prefer places like Avebury. More intimate.'

'I can't say I know a great deal about any of them,' said Alice dismissively.

'Has the circle got a name?'

Alice answered reluctantly, 'It's called the Listening Women.'

'Why?' Interpreting Alice's expression she begged, 'Please tell me why.'

'Oh, some superstitious nonsense about a group of women dancing on the Sabbath and being turned to stone.'

'What are they listening *to*?'

Alice made an impatient little movement of the hand that Imogen remembered. She was putting something away from her which did not meet with her approval.

'One version says that the wind is telling them stories. Another says that they were witches and they're listening to – to the Devil. But you needn't pay any attention to either of them.'

'But it's a lovely idea – the wind talking and the women listening.'

Alice's tone conveyed that she was fond of her friend but thought she was being rather silly.

'Oh, well. It's an ancient pastime – hearing words from the wind in the chimney, and finding pictures in the fire. And now I must run downstairs. Tea will be ready in half an hour, and you and I can have it by ourselves in front of the parlour fire. We're dining in style tonight, by the way.' This was said with pride. 'Our friend Dr Timothy Rowley, a retired headmaster, has offered to produce a play for us during the Festival Week, and Hal needs to discuss it with him, so this seemed a good opportunity. I promise you won't be bored. Tim is a great conversationalist and he likes pretty women – in the nicest possible way, of course – so he'll adore *you*. You might like to put on your best bib and tucker . . .'

She did not wait for, nor expect, an answer: already walking away, her mind on the coming tea. Her voice floated back at Imogen.

'I've put out towels for you. Let me know if you need anything else.'

*   *   *

27

Standing in her slip before the dressing-table mirror, brushing her hair, listening to the wind testing the acoustics of the chimney, Imogen experienced a blissful illusion of security. Time was suspended here, and though suffering and death existed they would not darken this moment. She was aware that Fred had temporarily subsided into the silence of which he was now a part. He, who had always been a chivalrous and perceptive man, left her alone when she was content, and charged to the rescue during times of minor or major crises.

'Recovery,' her counsellor had told her, 'is a long halting process, and we all have to get through it as best we can. But some day, I promise you, you won't need Fred any more. And when he's gone you'll begin to live the rest of your life.'

THREE

Alice could not help thinking that Imogen had never come to grips with real life. As an eight-year-old orphan, she had at first kept herself apart, politely but stubbornly refusing to merge with the school's *esprit de corps*, which in her tragic circumstances was understandable. But even when she came round she was inclined to be odd: talented in many ways, lovely and lovable, but also self-willed and unpredictable. At twenty-nine she had apparently not changed. Her marriage to Fred Lacey, for instance – though no doubt a nice young man, and it was shocking that he died so young, poor soul – had been rash, luckless and penniless. Their way of earning a living sounded a hand-to-mouth affair: two children playing at housekeeping. Their cat, who had already made a mess in the kitchen coal scuttle, was another disappointment. From the fuss Imogen made about her, Alice had expected an exquisite feline with a long pedigree, but quite frankly the animal was in no way distinguished, and contrary-minded into the bargain.

Then there was always the niggling suspicion that Imogen lived in some world of her own and only paid lip service to this one. That was acceptable as a symptom of grief, but might it not be a sign of an undisciplined nature and a rebellious spirit? What her friend needed, Alice felt, was a mature and worthy man and a proper purpose in life, and she intended to provide both.

Imogen, coming downstairs, chic in a blackberry velvet trouser suit and antique silver earrings, met her hostess carrying a tray full of tableware in from the kitchen.

The dining room was large, imposing and cool, despite four radiators and an open fire in the grate. Leaves had been taken out of the heavy, handsome dining table to render it small enough for an intimate supper. The cloth gleamed with starch. Glass and silver glittered. Two branching candlesticks, charged with tall pale columns, waited to illuminate the occasion.

'Goodness, how elegant! How grand! How busy you must have been!' Imogen cried, appreciating both effect and effort.

'You look very elegant yourself,' said Alice, pleased, 'but we're not at all grand. We're the poor relations on both sides of well-heeled families. We inherit their cast-offs, and they give us little luxuries which we couldn't afford.'

It was certainly a long time since the table linen embroidered with a W for Wareham, and the cutlery still faintly traced with a B for Brakespear, had been new; and none of the glasses matched, though they were beautifully cut.

'I see that we're dining by candlelight,' said Imogen, smiling at her friend, 'and I do so love it.'

'So do I.' Alice glanced at the clock, but for once time was on her side. Tranquilly she resumed her task. 'George Hobbs came about a quarter of an hour ago. They shouldn't be very long now.'

The study door opened and Hal strode across the hall and stood on the threshold of the dining room rubbing his hands. He began his news with an explanation as if he guessed that it might not be entirely welcome.

'You know how helpful George always is? Well, directly he'd finished work this evening, he came over from Haraldstone to give me the latest news of the bell tower. He hasn't eaten yet,' Hal continued, 'and it's getting on for seven o'clock. Miserable sort of night to turn a man out again without so much as a drink.'

Alice's face seized up. She regarded her husband fixedly. Guiltily, he did not return the look. His tone became more hearty, more confidential.

'I expect he lives on fry-ups and takeaways. You know how these bachelors are. So your home cooking would make a nice change. I suggested he stay to supper, but he won't accept until he knows it's all right with you.' And in reply to her stiff automatic nod, he hurried off saying, 'Thanks, Alice.'

In the silence that Imogen did not know how to break, Alice struggled with herself, wanting to be loyal, but her sense of injustice would burst out.

'Well, if that isn't typical of Hal! I don't ask much of him. This was meant to be a special occasion, and now he's spoiled it. But why should I be surprised at that?' Alice demanded of a spotless napkin. 'The surprise would have been if he'd allowed my arrangements to stand!'

She folded the linen square emphatically into a bishop's mitre and set it down on a plate edged with worn gilt, talking to herself all the while.

30

'Oh, I've nothing against George personally. He's a decent person, and a gifted man in many ways – though I do feel he should have done more in life than carpentry and wood-carving and bell-ringing. A good wife would have sorted him out and put him on the right road . . .'

There comes that right road again. I wonder where it is? Imogen thought.

'. . . but he keeps himself to himself, so he's hardly an asset on a social occasion. I shall probably spend the evening coaxing him out of his shell instead of enjoying you and Tim.'

Imogen moved forward and put one arm round her friend's shoulders, and one cool young cheek against the flushed middle-aged one.

'Oh, don't take any notice of me,' said Alice tremulously. 'I'll be all right.'

Imogen said, 'Of course you will. And I don't mind anything or anyone at all, so long as I'm here with you.'

Alice recovered herself.

'You're quite right. That's what matters. And it's not a crisis. There's plenty of food. I only have to lay another place at the table.' She faltered for a moment. 'I'm not being mean, Imogen. It's just . . .' She became breezy again. 'Well, well. Mustn't grumble. Would you like to hold the fort while I dash up and change? Hal will be in soon to offer you a drink and introduce our unexpected guest.'

A shabby but beloved image rose in Imogen's mind.

'Is Polly . . . has Polly . . . ?'

Alice spoke cheerily. Life was not behaving well. She chose to ignore it.

'Settling in nicely. She's eaten most of her food and drunk some milk, and Vera's buttered her paws and let her out to explore the garden. And she's making friends with the other cats. Nothing to worry about.'

Imogen guessed that this was a white lie meant to set her mind at rest, and she had much to worry about. Polly loathed other cats. Most probably the perverse animal had made a mess on the doormat and hidden up a tree.

She stood near the fire, rubbing her arms for consolation and warmth, feeling displaced, and wishing they were both safely back in London.

Hal must have been forewarned, even subtly but firmly threatened, about his behaviour towards Imogen. He strode into the room alone, rubbing his hands and affecting a tremendous interest in this unusual guest: an interest that the uneasiness of his glance and the staged welcome of his

31

voice denied. Imogen realized at once that her blackberry velvet trouser suit and dangling silver earrings were not his style.

'Well, well, well. That's a – remarkable – outfit,' he said.

'Kind of you to say so.'

'Singular shade of . . .' He was instantly lost. 'Is it purple or navy blue?'

'It's called blackberry.'

He turned his attention to the bottles on the sideboard.

'I don't pay much attention to clothes and colours,' he said honestly. 'Alice has been quite annoyed about it on occasions. Now what would you like to drink? Sherry – sweet, medium or dry? Gin? Whisky?'

She needed a double gin, but out of her depth with him and his background she played safe.

'Dry sherry, please.'

He filled a small glass to the brim with pale gold liquid.

'Help yourself to crisps and things,' he commanded, measured a generous whisky for himself, sat down, took a satisfying swallow, and searched for a suitable topic of conversation. 'So what kind of hats do you make?' he offered.

'All kinds from romantic to eccentric.' Her smile was diffident. 'I carried on my business under the name of Crazy Hats.'

His grey gaze measured her and found her puzzling.

'In what way – crazy?'

'Because they aren't sensible,' she answered candidly.

She spoke up for herself and her craft.

'I don't make hats to keep women's heads warm, or to be conventionally smart. I create them to suit the client, the event for which they're worn and the time of year. Fantasy hats with flowers, sequins, lace, chiffon and veils. Baker boy hats sewn with peacock's feather eyes. Highwaymen's hats with plumes. I want the women who wear them to feel beautiful or impudent or daring. I want to give them a new vision of themselves – a new dream.'

'Ah!' said Hal. He realized that she was perfectly serious, and could not comprehend why she should be. 'Can you make a living at that sort of thing?'

'Oh yes. And I did for seven years. Nothing wonderful, but quite adequate. Enough to live in modest comfort. But I haven't done any work since Fred's . . .'

Don't walk round the word or disguise it with euphemisms, say it naturally and factually, her counsellor had advised. In that way you tell yourself, as well as your listener, what has happened. It will save you both

32

embarrassment, and by admitting the situation you learn to accept it.

'. . . since my husband's death. But when I get back to London I shall start a new life.'

Hal crossed his legs and considered one black polished shoe. He would have liked to ask if this bereavement had curbed her evident frivolity and turned her thoughts in a more serious direction, but Alice had forbidden him to discuss Imogen's loss or to criticize her craft. So he temporized.

'And how had you intended to begin?' he asked.

His tone suggested that he required a sensible answer, and brought out a former imp in her.

'I expect,' said Imogen, keeping her face and tone smooth, 'that I'll create an especially crazy hat.'

Alice, coming downstairs, dressed in a sister-in-law's discreet finery, prevented them from estranging each other further. But she had not forgiven her husband, whom she addressed with an airiness that was patently false.

'What's happened to George? I thought he was joining us for dinner.'

Hal's reply should have been conciliatory. Since he had forgotten his transgression it was not.

'He went back to the church for something. He'll be along soon.'

'I just wondered,' said Alice, with a chilled smile, 'whether you might have mentioned that this was a dinner party, and he had gone home to change?'

Hal dismissed this remark with good-humoured indifference.

'Don't be ridiculous, Alice.'

The doorbell saved the situation, and from the genial way in which Hal cried, 'Ah, here he is!' and hastened to admit him, Imogen knew that the two men were allies, and perhaps Alice resented this as much as the intrusion.

They heard Hal laugh and saying, 'What? Tim as well? Come in. Come in.'

A rich voice answered, 'My dear fellow, we may arrive together but I assure you that we came separately. I am no longer young enough to ride pillion on George's splendid motorcycle.'

Alice's face shone. Her mood changed. All, it seemed, would be well.

'You'll simply *love* Timothy!' she said, squeezing Imogen's fingers, and as he came into the room she cried, 'Tim, this is my especial friend, Imogen Lacey. Imogen – our distinguished friend, Dr Timothy Rowley.'

That was a good name for a short, stout, twinkling gentleman, who kissed Imogen's hand and held it for an appreciable moment, while gazing up into her eyes with evident admiration. He was smartly but some-what rakishly dressed. A crimson striped bow-tie offset the quiet good taste of his grey suit, and he flaunted a crimson handkerchief in his top pocket.

Stepping back like a courtier, he spread out his arms to indicate the effect of blackberry velvet and silver earrings, and murmured, 'Charming! Charming!'

Fond of women but doesn't let them come too close, Fred observed.

In complete contrast, the long brown fellow introduced as George Hobbs wore blue jeans and a crew-necked sweater. The formal splendour of the ladies and the dining table did not perturb him. He gave Imogen a pleasant smile and a brief handshake, and showed no further interest in her. He had an independent jut to his jaw and a straight gaze. He stood at his ease, and when offered a choice of aperitifs he answered, 'I'd rather have a beer, if it's no trouble, Alice.'

'No trouble at all,' said Alice distantly, who had expected no better of him.

Tim assessed the drinks and asked for 'some of that excellent old East India sherry from your discerning brother'.

A gourmet, Fred remarked.

'George has come with great news for us,' Hal began. 'They're taking down the bells next week, so we can begin rebuilding the tower – and Tim, I've had an excellent idea about raising funds . . .'

He seemed about to launch forth in detail but his wife interrupted brightly: 'Hal, dear, Imogen is a stranger to these matters and will be in the dark if you don't explain the situation. Just briefly. While I get the beer from the kitchen.'

'Ah. Yes. The situation,' he said to himself, momentarily checked. 'Well, Imogen, George is the captain of the tower – the man in charge of the bell-ringing. And St Oswald's is notable among other things for its peal of bells. Do you know anything about bell-ringing? No? Well, I can't go into that now, but George will tell you all about it. In fact I'm sure he would arrange to show you over the tower and explain everything some time during your stay here – wouldn't you, George?' He turned to Imogen and said, 'You'll find it most interesting.'

'I'm sure I shall,' Imogen murmured.

Her tone suggested amusement, resignation and disbelief. Tim chuckled. George Hobbs gave her an enigmatic glance. Hal continued his lecture, unaware.

'To cut a long story in quarters, as they say locally, St Oswald's has been falling down for years, and no one has done anything about it. When I first arrived here, George came to see me, and convinced me that our priority was to restore the bell tower and overhaul the bells . . .'

Alice reappeared, sighed involuntarily, smiled resolutely and said, 'Your beer, George. Nice and cold.'

'. . . so I consulted experts,' Hal went on, as if she had not spoken, 'and discovered that the cost of restoration and renewal would be around £80,000. I made that a priority, and over the past few years a small group of us has been busy raising money in every way we could, despite,' this uttered with tremendous contempt, 'a large uninterested populace, a hostile town council, and an unhelpful parochial church council – and I'm glad to say we have worked wonders.'

'Wonders!' echoed faithful Alice. 'Darling, could I have a dry sherry?'

Automatically he poured a glass while continuing to talk, and handed it to her.

'But we are still short of our financial target, and I've had a brainwave about that which I want to discuss with you this evening, Tim.'

'My dear Hal,' said Timothy Rowley, smiling and urbane, 'I shall be fascinated to hear it, but at the moment I am consumed with curiosity about this engaging young lady. May I ask how long you are staying here, Imogen?'

Alice answered for her.

'As long as possible. In fact I'm hoping to persuade her to leave London and set up a modish little shop in Langesby. I've thought it all out,' said Alice, pleased with herself. 'She can live with us while I help her to find a suitable place.'

Hal was nonplussed. Imogen looked down Alice's right road with misgivings.

'And what might that modish little shop sell?' Timothy purred.

Imogen opened her mouth to speak.

'Exciting hats,' said Alice. She neither knew nor cared about hats and had never seen any of Imogen's, but loyalty was her watchword. 'Langesby needs exciting hats.'

Hal remarked unhelpfully, 'I don't think Langesby will be interested in a luxury trade like millinery. This isn't a rich town, and we're deep in recession. Besides, women don't wear hats these days.'

'They will wear Imogen's hats,' said Alice, daring him to contradict her. He seemed about to challenge this but she would not let him.

Taking Timothy Rowley and George Hobbs into her confidence she said, 'I know Imogen won't mind my telling you that she suffered a grievous loss early this year, and has only just recovered from a nervous breakdown . . .'

But I do mind, I do, Imogen thought rebelliously. It's not their business to know. Nor yours to broadcast it, come to that.

'. . . and what she needs is a new outlook and a new beginning. So I want everyone to make her welcome.'

'You have only to introduce her,' said Timothy courteously, 'and they will open their arms and their hearts.'

Alice patted his hand, smiled on her guests and moved away, saying to her husband over one shoulder, 'Do look after everyone, darling, while I serve up . . .'

'Can I help?' Imogen asked, with more politeness than sincerity for she was annoyed.

'No, no, my dear. Special visitors are not allowed to help.'

'If you'd like me to fetch and carry for you, Alice, I'm your man,' said George, stating an honest intention.

She hesitated, but he was not yet forgiven.

'No, I can manage nicely, thank you.'

'Wonderful Alice!' Timothy murmured, which seemed to amount to assistance.

Hal, contemplating an inner vision, did not offer his services. Food, in his experience, was something that appeared at regular intervals as if by divine decree.

FOUR

Alice's cooking was good, plain and plentiful.

It would make all the difference, said Fred, if she'd puréed that leek soup and decorated it with cream and chives . . .

Imogen had earned their daily bread and butter, and Fred's meagre sales were supplying occasional jam, until that great day arrived when he earned a fortune and they could live on cake. For Fred, no doubt about it, had a dash of genius, and all things were possible. Meanwhile he was an excellent house-husband who made a little art of cooking for them both. They had worked together contentedly in their cramped quarters: he whistling softly as he chopped and garnished; she in an ongoing reverie, transforming dreams into money.

Spooning up his soup, Timothy said to Imogen, 'I'm delighted to hear that you might enliven Langesby with yourself and your exciting hats. Do you – or did you – have your own millinery establishment?'

His tone was conversational but his glance direct, and Imogen sensed that he was building up a picture of her, seeking information.

'No. Investing my capital in a business was a financial risk I felt unable to take,' she answered frankly. 'I preferred working at home and selling to individual shops. It gave me a certain freedom that I need. I can't create anything' – this comment was aimed at Alice – 'when I'm being organized and tied down.'

Timothy did not miss the allusion.

'The artistic temperament,' he observed, with benevolence.

The room was warmer now, the flames flared red and gold, the pool of candlelight lent an air of intimacy to the moment.

'I think I should explain to this charming stranger,' said Timothy, making a little bow to Imogen, 'that I have two loves in my life. Education is my beloved spouse, and the theatre my adored mistress to whom I devote my retirement. I give advice and guidance on school play productions, and I am writing a book on amateur theatricals. These occupations take me away from home periodically.'

'I love the theatre, too.'

She would have expanded on this, and Timothy was ready to listen, but Hal plunged into his personal fray.

'Tim, I've had an excellent idea – and I hope you're going to back me up.'

'Do tell us,' breathed Timothy Rowley, reaching for the salt.

A man of portly build, he had a fine high forehead, a Roman nose, a precise mouth, slightly protuberant blue eyes, and a shock of thick white hair. He smiled a great deal, and his voice was the voice of an actor: rich and deep and expressive. His appetite was excellent and his remarks appreciative, though from the professional way he sniffed the wine and looked questingly round the table, Imogen suspected that he usually dined far better than this. Life must have been good to him, for he radiated ease and benevolence, was easy with the men, courtly towards the women, and well disposed to all. Yet his *bonhomie* was a cloak for shrewdness. The mouth smiled and ate and drank, the resonant voice praised and expostulated, the wit beguiled, but the eyes watched and assessed.

A first-class manipulator, said Fred.

Hal was holding forth.

'Our present policy of selling pencils, mugs and tea towels, begging grants and donations, and placing a box prominently by the church door, is a slow business. Now I believe that I could raise a loan for the remaining few thousand pounds privately, so that St Oswald's will be in good working order by July. But this sum, and the interest incurred, would have to be repaid within a certain period.'

Alice laid down her spoon. Her eyes beseeched her husband, but he was not looking at her. He spoke well, in strong measured tones.

'Let us be frank. Langesby's motive in celebrating its charter is not a matter of local pride and historical importance but an excuse for making money for the town. Morally, I detest this materialistic age, and so far I have fought it, but I now believe that in order to survive the Church must move with the times.'

He turned to Timothy.

'When you suggested giving a play to benefit St Oswald's I was both touched and grateful. But if I am to redeem a substantial loan then we need to think further than a production which manages to scrape enough money together to cover its expenses and relies on family and friends for support. We need something unusual – I know it will be of high quality – which draws in a wider audience and makes a substantial profit.'

A short silence followed. George Hobbs spooned up his soup. Alice and Imogen glanced at each other and then at Timothy, who now acted as spokesman.

'My dear Hal, as always your worthy schemes prove to be wider and deeper than one had imagined. *What a charming idea!* I thought, when we talked of this originally, and I envisaged it – though perhaps a little more ambitiously – pretty much as you described. But a church play designed to bring in the shekels does rather remind one of the moneylenders on the steps of the temple!'

Alice nodded. Imogen and George listened intently. Timothy rolled smoothly on.

'There is a further consideration, my dear Hal. As you say, the main function of the Langesby Fair is to fill public as well as private coffers. The council will not mind your making a few hundred pounds and pocketing the lot. I believe,' turning to Alice, 'that this is the case with our good friend Philip, who hopes to raise funds for a gymnasium at Prospect House?'

Alice seemed flustered, but said, 'Yes, I believe so' to Timothy, and, 'I'll explain about Philip and Prospect House later', to Imogen.

'I understand,' Timothy continued, 'that the council was perfectly amicable about his modest target and wished him the best of luck. But, my dear Hal,' turning to his host, 'if you are talking in terms of a few *thousands* then I think you'll be expected to pay a percentage of your profits like all the other traders.'

Alice and George nodded agreement.

'I see no reason why I should finance the council when they have obstructed me from the outset,' said Hal. 'I have no intention of concealing anything. I shall inform them and the Festival Committee of this project and my hopes for it. But I shall refuse to pay on principle.'

Alice's smile was one of fixed despair, and she looked round for help.

Timothy cleared his throat and came to her rescue.

'A production of the quality you envisage will be a costly, risky business. Indeed, some of the costs and risks cannot even be anticipated. In the end you may find yourself no better off.'

In contrast to the other man's cultured voice and circumspect approach, George Hobbs struck a forthright North Country note. He had relished his soup, and now accepted a second helping, holding out his plate to Alice.

'Besides, Hal, you've upset too many councillors already. And councils, like elephants, never forget. It wouldn't do to provoke them.'

Hal gave a quick deep snort of contempt.

'And although I believe in keeping the council's hands out of the Church's pockets,' George went on, unperturbed, 'it's no good being honest and above board with them. They're not bothered about moral issues. They're out to win – and you've got everything to lose.'

Alice, alarmed by this speech, said, 'George is right, Hal. I think you should drop the whole idea.'

Her husband took it in his stride, replying coolly, 'I shall do no such thing!'

There was a short silence before Timothy Rowley spoke.

'Then I suggest that you approach the question diplomatically, plead Church poverty, and ask for a charitable dispensation.' Humorously: 'Offer them riches in heaven in return for a small concession on earth.'

'Give them a finger and they'll take an arm,' Hal cried hotly. 'Surely the Church is a special case?'

Timothy Rowley finished his soup, and lifted a hand in smiling protest as Alice offered more. His answer was playful, balanced.

'At one time the Church wielded immense political power and could call any tune it pleased and tell someone else to pay the piper, but it can't push its luck nowadays. And I would respectfully remind you, my dear Hal, that you have already pumped every source of public goodwill dry, and your congregation – though devoted to you – does not grow appreciably larger.'

Hal's colour rose.

'In short, you refuse to back me?'

'I didn't say that. Like all your friends, I wish St Oswald's well, and will do everything in my power to help you. But I do advise you, my dear fellow, not to take further risks nor to lay yourself open to your enemies.'

The conversation was temporarily stopped by the plates being collected and the main course brought on.

She should have popped a china bird on top of that steak and kidney pie, said Fred, *and sprinkled parsley on the potatoes.*

Rosy with distress, Alice gave out bounteous helpings while Hal poured liberal measures of red wine and headed for fresh controversy.

'I've been thinking what kind of entertainment would be suitable,' Hal said. 'I was involved with the Early English guild plays when I was at college, and found them very impressive. The York Cycle. The Townley Cycle. We produced some striking effects for *The Creation and Fall of Lucifer* and *Doomsday*. And we toured the city in wagons, stopping at certain points to rattle our money-boxes. The donations, I might add, were liberal.'

Timothy laid down his knife and fork and deliberated, mouth pursed.

'I am familiar with the plays, of course,' he replied slowly, 'which are deeply impressive, as you say, and fascinating to both historian and scholar, but I can't imagine them drawing huge crowds here. Langesby is not a cathedral city. The festival is strictly secular. And it is tempting Providence to travel about in wagons, during what we English laughingly call our *summer*. If it rains you're sunk.

'No, my dear fellow, since you intend to make money you must please the populace. The average family on a day out in Langesby will be looking for entertainment, and if they are to watch a play they want a comfortable place to sit, laughter and tears, and good value for their money – no thank you, Alice my dear, not another morsel . . .'

Hal was affronted, and sounded it, though the warning about rain did remind him of many a sopping vicarage garden party.

'I suppose, by entertainment, you mean *Hello Dolly* or *Sailor Beware?*'

'No, actually, I do not,' said Timothy. His tone, though silky, was a reprimand that silenced Hal.

'I was thinking of a play which would echo the era we are celebrating,' he continued. 'An Elizabethan drama, for instance, with a strong storyline, a happy ending and plenty of comedy – even farce – to liven it up.'

'What are you recommending?' Hal asked, convinced but displeased. '*As You Like It*? That won't draw the crowds.'

'A little too long and obvious for our purposes, perhaps?' Timothy purred, head on one side. 'But here comes a Queen of Puddings – and I do love my pudding. Allow me to ponder while I savour it.'

The earthenware dish was deep and wide. The meringue had been whisked high into white and golden peaks. The scents of raspberry jam, hot sponge and egg custard brought back memories of childhood.

I wish I could have some, said Fred.

There followed a reverent silence, as they tasted and appreciated the pudding.

Then Timothy finished his last spoonful, looked up thoughtfully, and cried, 'Ah, now I remember a *captivating* play!'

You didn't need to remember it, Imogen thought. You've probably had it in mind from the beginning.

'A "pleasant conceited comedie" as they called it. "A scarce and curious piece." Written by a highly underrated playwright. But then, with Shakespeare and Marlowe glittering centre stage, what poor hack in the wings

41

could hope for a gleam of recognition? I speak for George Peele and *The Old Wives' Tale.*'

'Never heard of either of them,' said Hal dismissively.

Timothy Rowley's tone and smile remained good humoured, though his gaze was implacable.

'I don't suppose many people have, but it would fit your bill perfectly in many ways. It combines the ingredients of a fairy tale, a fable, a morality play, a pantomime, a dramatic comedy. Call it what you will. There is plenty of scope for theatrical effects such as you describe in the guild plays. And it will appeal to both adults and children.

'It's length – or brevity – also commends it,' Timothy went on. 'It is a one-act play – say an hour, all told. So you can give *two* evening performances as well as a couple of matinées, price your seats slightly cheaper in consequence, and bring in the crowds. Audiences will be attracted by the thought that they are getting quality entertainment at a bargain price.

'It is, of course, written in sixteenth-century English but with a little skilful editing you could overcome any difficulties in that direction.' Humorously he added, 'I am prepared to help you over that *style!*'

He laughed at his own pun, and then became serious again.

'Still, if you are not interested in the idea, my dear Hal, I can return to the tranquil groves from whence I came, with no offence taken nor – I trust – given?'

Meaning, Imogen translated, either you accept my choice or lose my services. And she watched both of them with renewed interest.

A seasoned fighter always knows when to retreat.

Hal hesitated only for a moment before saying, 'Naturally, I bow to your professional judgement. But I shall need to read the play before we go further.'

A skilled manipulator is always gracious.

'So you shall,' Timothy purred. 'Fortunately, many years ago, I resurrected it as part of a course on Elizabethan drama, for a group of mature students, so I have a number of photocopies. It will be my pleasure to lend them to anyone who is interested. I shall also need to test the Langesby waters, to make sure that we have a clear field, and to involve talented friends who are prepared to work for nothing. In short – I must hold a meeting for general discussion.'

'You can hold the meeting here,' said Hal. 'Arrange it with Alice.'

'I think,' said Tim gently, 'that we need not impose upon Alice again so soon. If we meet at my place, about four o'clock, my housekeeper will be delighted to offer afternoon tea – such an elegant institution, and a dying one, alas.'

'What a lovely idea!' cried Alice sincerely. Enjoyment without responsibility.

'Yes, Tim. Much appreciated,' said Hal automatically. He was already thinking of something else, and added, 'Oh, and talking about cost-cutting, you can have the use of the church hall for rehearsals and performances rent-free.'

'The church hall. How very kind!' Timothy said fervently, but murmured to himself, 'An admirable building in its way, no doubt. Still, one has misgivings.'

Hal was not listening. Surprisingly, George spoke up.

'I don't want to push myself forward, Dr Rowley, but hammer, nails and elbow grease are my middle names, and I'll do anything I can backstage.'

'How very kind of you!'

'And when I was at school I used to be the odd-job man for our pantomime.' He emerged from the shell that Alice had deplored, and became animated. 'I could turn my hand to anything. Lighting, scenery, noises off, special effects, you name it. Right up to leaving at eighteen. I can't act for toffee but I've always enjoyed the theatre. Then life took over. Like it does. Not enough time. But I was . . . anyway they used to say I was . . .' He guttered out. 'Mind you, it was a while ago.'

Timothy's smile was all-comprehending.

'You are too modest to tell me that you were jolly good at the job?'

'Well – in a way. Yes, I was good,' said George. He grinned. 'I was bloody good!'

'You're hired!' said Timothy. 'No pay. No union. Far too much work. An unfair amount of responsibility. Hours unspecified. How does that sound in your ears?'

'I'll shake hands on it!' said George. And literally did, across the dinner table.

The others laughed. The atmosphere lightened.

'I know you're a busy man, George,' said Timothy, 'but if you can spare an hour or so you may care to join my tea party. I think you will find it interesting.'

The invitation was delivered with respect. George accepted it in like manner. Hal was delighted. Alice pleasantly surprised. Imogen amused and observant.

'Theatre talents run in families, you know,' said Timothy. 'I have a feeling,' with a sidelong look at George, 'that our doughty lady of the dales, Mary Proctor, would make a splendid Gammer Madge – the old wife who tells the tale.'

'You'd never persuade Mary to set foot on stage,' Alice said outright.

'I shouldn't be too sure of that,' said Timothy. 'She was a fine amateur actress in her younger days. You forget, my dear, that all of you' – gesturing gracefully round the table – 'are newcomers. Mary and I were born and bred and have lived all our lives in the dale. I saw her in quite a few local plays when I was a boy.'

He looked enquiringly at George Hobbs, whose colour had risen.

'What's your opinion, George? Do you think the lady might agree to a meaty part as narrator in an Elizabethan comedy?'

George said cautiously, 'She might, if you went about it the right way.'

'We need a sympathetic messenger. Would you, I wonder, be so kind as to have a word with her?' Timothy asked, 'Good. I thank you. I shall distribute copies in the next day or so, and give you one for her.' Then he cried, 'Ah, cheese! And a local cheese at that. Clever, clever Alice!' And concentrated on matters of the stomach.

FIVE

They drank coffee in the parlour, which was small and comfortable. Hal made up the fire. Alice brought in the candlesticks. In the mild light they looked upon one another as if under a benevolent spell of enchantment. No longer obsessed by the state of the bell tower, the iniquities of the local council nor the financial aspects of play production, Hal touched upon lighter topics, addressing himself principally to Imogen in order to please his wife.

'It must have been rather daunting to be plunged into the deep end of Langesby politics this evening,' he began affably. 'I hope you didn't find us all a bit much.'

'Oh, no. I swam to the surface quite happily after a while,' Imogen answered, impishly grave. 'Not drowning but waving.'

He was puzzled, but Timothy, overhearing her remark, laughed and pulled up his chair to join them.

'Imogen is a slyboots!' he affirmed. 'My first impression was of a shy charmer. Later I realized that there was "a chield amang us taking notes".'

Still puzzled, Hal said, 'But Imogen makes funny hats.'

She imagined the funny hats: floating round his head, concocted from crêpe paper, used for a party, crumpled up and thrown away. They bore no resemblance to the creations which transformed a housewife into the stuff of dreams.

'Not *funny*,' she replied indignantly. 'I said *crazy*, not *funny*.'

'There's a world of difference,' said Timothy, forestalling Hal's next remark. He turned to Imogen, asking, 'Tell us what else you have done.'

'I wanted to be an actress,' she admitted, and saw by the gleam in his eyes that he had been hoping for, or expecting, just such a revelation. 'I didn't manage that. But I was assistant stage manager to rather a good repertory company for two years, until I changed my mind.'

'Alice didn't tell me that,' Hal said, amazed by yet another frivolous revelation.

'Alice doesn't know. I only told her about the hats.' She glanced at Timothy and said mischievously, 'I thought one crazy thing at a time was enough!'

Timothy laughed aloud.

'Do you understand what I mean by a slyboots?' he asked.

Before he could comment on this Alice paused in her conversation with George, lifted a hand for silence and said, 'I think that's the riders. Can we listen for a moment?'

In the obedient hush that followed they could hear the distant trot of hooves, the faint shouts and calls and whoops of many voices.

'Yes, there they are!' Alice cried, illuminated. 'I must fetch the tray.'

George, who seemed to have come out of his shell without her assistance, said firmly, 'I'll carry it.' And followed her through to the kitchen.

Hal's explanation to Imogen was amiable.

'The local children go "trick-or-treating", but the Hallowe'en riders are rather special and Alice always makes a fuss of them.'

Timothy said, tongue in cheek, 'Yes, we know how to celebrate unholy festivals in style here.' With a dramatic flourish of one arm, he intoned, 'On this ungodly night our witches and warlocks ride.'

Alice returning, followed by a laden George, said vivaciously, 'Such nonsense! Take no notice of him, Imogen. It's a delightful little custom, where young people dress up and collect for charity.'

She was flushed and excited, talking too much, as Hal opened the front door in welcome.

Even the weather had paid tribute to All Hallows Eve, forming a misty backdrop to the group of ponies that stood before the vicarage door, heads tossing, hooves restless on the gravel. On their backs, eyes gleaming through their masks, grimly cloaked and hatted in black, sat ten riders.

'Come along,' said Timothy, bringing Imogen forward, 'you must see what evil spirits we can conjure up in Langesby. This is witches' country, you know. That's one of the reasons why I chose *The Old Wives' Tale*.'

'Infernal worshippers of Satan,' Hal intoned, and they gave him an ironic cheer, 'refreshments are available, but only when we hear the witch cry. Make it a good one. We have a guest here from London, who would like her blood chilled.'

The leader lifted one hand, and the troupe hushed. The hand descended, and immediately the riders threw back their heads and gave three long unearthly calls that brought up the gooseflesh on Imogen's arms.

'Ai-yee. Ai-yee. Ai-yee.'

Hal applauded, well pleased. Then Alice was on the doorstep, handing out steaming mugs of blackcurrant cordial and wedges of home-made gingerbread, while George held the tray. Nine of the riders removed their masks, revealing the youthful faces of four boys and five girls in their middle teens. The leader gave the reins of his pony to one of them, came forward, still masked, stripped off his black leather gloves and kissed Alice's hand with reverence.

So that's what she was thrilled about, Fred commented.

'Imogen,' Alice cried, turning to her, 'this is someone you must meet.'

Bowing over her outstretched hand, he said softly, intimately, 'I am Lucifer, son of the morning.'

Pale eyes gleamed through the slits in the mask. She was tall, but he was taller, with the build of an athlete and a physically imposing presence. He held her hand for a few moments longer. His voice aroused something in Imogen that had long slept. Her fingers tingled at his touch. The flesh rose again on her arms. She shrank from him, was drawn to him, thought him beautiful.

Then he stood back, pulled off his mask, and revealed a pleasantly attractive man in his late thirties, with thick fair hair still bleached from the previous summer. His gaze was frank and amused, his tone genial.

'Nothing so grand as Lucifer, I'm afraid. Merely Philip Gregory, at your service.'

'Oh, Phil, you *are* absurd!' said Alice, all indulgence. 'This is one of our local celebrities, Imogen. Phil, this is my special friend, Imogen Lacey, of whom I've spoken.'

'Imogen,' he said, lingering on the name, and bowed to her.

Then he laughed at Alice and kissed her cheek, and accepted a mug of cordial. The laughter was warm and spontaneous. He was eminently likeable.

'Celebrity indeed! Alice, you do talk the most delightful nonsense.'

He thinks as much of himself as she does, Fred remarked with unaccustomed sourness.

Perhaps he had noticed the *frisson.*

Unmasked, the night riders lost their mystery and the event became affable and prosaic. The nine youngsters were polite in a curiously old-fashioned way, responding only when they were addressed. But Hal moved among them, familiar with all, and there was talk of a Youth Club dance, of Bonfire Night and Christmas carol singing, of a guitar concert in the church. This vicar might be at odds with the hierarchy, but he was on good terms with his juvenile flock. And after him came Timothy Rowley, with his air of benevolent authority. They were a little in awe of him at first, but gradually he charmed them.

Leaving George to butle, Alice linked arms with Imogen and Philip and drew them away from the crowd.

'Phil,' she explained to Imogen, 'lost his wife in very sad circumstances some years ago, and came here to – well, not to forget, because one never does, nor should, but to make a new life – as I'm trying to persuade you to do.'

She squeezed Imogen's arm. Feeling it stiffen, she hurried on.

'Phil runs Prospect House, which is a most wonderful home for young offenders. In fact, I believe these are your good boys and girls, aren't they, Phil?'

He spoke with affection.

'All my youngsters are good,' he said. 'They've just been treated badly. These –' indicating the respectful group of riders – 'are the ones who can be trusted in the outside world. Very soon they should be rejoining it.'

'Phil opened Prospect House four or five years ago, having started with nothing but a dilapidated old building and a need to care for young people,' said Alice, full of pride. 'You *will* invite Imogen to look round the home, won't you, Phil?'

'I shall invite you both as soon as possible Name your day.'

'Phil should have been in the honours list last year, but somebody put a spoke in that wheel. Jealousy, of course, but I should like to know who it was.'

Philip Gregory interrupted her, flattered but slightly impatient.

'My dear Alice, you're far too charitable. I'm the most selfish man in existence, and I don't give a fig for honours.' He turned to Imogen. 'I have an empathy with young people, particularly young people with problems. I was fortunate enough to be able to finance my experiment, and to find so many supportive friends – for example the local stables, who donate a certain number of riding lessons at Christmas, and allow us to use their ponies free of charge on Hallowe'en.' He shrugged, smiled, lifted his shoulders in deprecation. 'I'm simply enjoying myself,'

Raising his voice, he called, 'Drink up, you lot. We must be on our way,'

He donned his mask and held out a box for offerings. 'It's for Save the Children fund this year,' he said factually.

One by one the vicarage party deposited pound coins in the collection box, which was bound in black crêpe paper and decorated with white runes.

Imogen, looking up into pale eyes which once again glittered through the slits of a mask, shivered involuntarily.

48

'You're cold, my dear,' said Timothy Rowley. 'Come back into the house.'

She felt him to be sympathetic towards her, and confided in him.

'Not cold. Suddenly afraid of something for no good reason. Were there truly witches here at one time?'

The others were standing side by side, waving the riders off.

'Good-night! Good-night! Good-night!'

Timothy said, taking her arm and leading her indoors, 'Are you not acquainted with the history of witches?'

She shook her head.

'They were the healers and midwives of their communities, worshippers of the old religion, with special knowledge of herbs. The reasons for giving them a bad name were both political and sexual. Call a woman a witch and you could execute her. The wretched old creatures who were intimidated, tortured, drowned, burned or hanged – thousands of them in this country alone – were generally victims of superstition and hatred. This feminist age is shedding a kindlier light upon them, but the fears they still rouse are deep and ancient. Mention the word *witch* and you awake strong emotions. Witness your little shiver just now, and your feeling afraid for no good reason.'

The long weird halloo of the riding troupe echoed faintly in the distance.

'Ai-yee. Ai-yee. Ai-yee.'

Imogen said uneasily, 'What would happen if anyone refused to give the riders money?'

'Nothing, of course – apart from being regarded as mean of spirit and pocket. But no one would dream of refusing. Superstition holds fast. People would rather give, even if they laugh at themselves and the custom, simply because they still *are* slightly afraid and wish to propitiate the devil's disciples.'

Hal came in, rubbing his hands, partly from cold, mostly from satisfaction, saying, 'There, Imogen, you've witnessed one of Langesby's medieval customs.'

'I was about to tell her,' Tim Rowley continued, 'how the Church persecuted members of the old religion, called witches, in order to establish Christianity as the new religion.'

'That's a loaded argument,' said Hal, brought up short. 'I don't condone the torture of heretics, and I agree that the Church has been guilty of some heinous acts in the past, but in order to plant new seeds you must clear the ground.'

'And clear the wise women away?' Timothy observed.

'More coffee, anyone?' Alice asked brightly, checking possible controversy.

Firelight, candlelight and their hostess prevailed, but only for the moment.

Turning to Imogen, Timothy said in his bland, pedantic way, 'Witchcraft is one of my hobbies. I have the honour to be President of the Langesby Magic Arts Society, and I give a paper now and again. But it is an academic interest, I hasten to add. I am too mindful of the powers of darkness to court them.'

'Yes, indeed. Evil must not be regarded lightly,' said Hal, very serious. 'It has a way of slipping in at the back door. And though I don't doubt your integrity, Tim, nor that of your Society, this is an age of unbelief. Too many people have given up on God and are looking for easy answers elsewhere. The present-day fascination with magic in all its forms is as dangerous as drug-taking, and can corrupt the strong as well as the weak. Look at all these strange new sects.'

Timothy replied coolly, 'But you can't place every unorthodox belief under the heading of magic and damn it altogether. There is white magic as well as black, and all shades of grey in between.'

In an attempt to lighten the atmosphere Imogen chose the wrong subject. Vivaciously, she said at large, 'I'm so intrigued by your stone circle. Is it simply decorative or do people observe pagan rites hereabouts? I mean, it's Hallowe'en. Shouldn't they dance round, or something?'

A gleam of amusement lit George Hobbs's face. 'Oh, don't you know about . . . ?' he began, but Hal cleared his throat and took charge of the conversation.

'I believe we still have some sort of witches' coven in the dale, but no one takes them seriously. It's a free country. If a group of silly middle-aged women choose to dance on Haraldstone Hill under the full moon they're welcome to do so.'

Alice also dismissed the local coven.

'Oh, they're not the genuine article at all. And thank goodness for that. We don't want real witches in Langesbydale.'

Flustered, Imogen proceeded to compound her error.

'I don't know about witches and their beliefs, although I've studied lots of religions. You see, I feel at home in any sacred place. Church, chapel, mosque, synagogue, Quaker meeting-house, even pagan circles like Avebury. And Fred and I went on a Buddhist meditation weekend once, and it was absolute bliss. Quite a jolt to come back to the everyday world. But I haven't yet felt that I belonged to any *particular* religion.'

Hal said, 'Really, there's no need to explain.'

Yet she felt compelled to explain, and Timothy's smile encouraged her.

'I'm not an atheist or an agnostic or a non-believer or an unbeliever. I'm just not committed. I suppose you could call me a seeker.'

'A seeker,' said Hal, and said no more.

Alice did not know how to redeem the situation but Timothy's smile remained benign.

'Fascinating,' he murmured. 'Well, my delightful seeker, I differ from our good host and hostess on this subject, and give you a word of warning into the bargain. If you pursue your religious studies here you will find that witchcraft, both black and white, is still practised in the valley, and the genuine article – to quote Alice – is still with us. Be very careful how you approach it.'

The silence was absolute.

George Hobbs looked at the clock, put his empty cup carefully on the table, and said, 'I don't want to break up the party but I have an early start tomorrow.'

Timothy's resonant voice echoed him.

'I, too, must take my leave. I am at the mercy of my excellent house-keeper, who insists upon waiting up for me!' He held Alice's hands and kissed her cheek. 'We have been entertained most royally. Thank you, my dear, for a truly memorable evening. I shall send someone round tomorrow with a copy of *The Old Wives' Tale*. I think, when you both read the play, that you will be as enchanted with it as I am. And I shall ring you as soon as possible to arrange my little tea party.'

He turned to Imogen and bowed in courtly fashion.

'Do not imagine for a moment that I shall allow you to escape. I look forward to your opinion of the play, and also to giving you tea one day next week. Mrs Housam is noted for her cinnamon toast.'

'Oh, I *love* cinnamon toast!'

George Hobbs shook Alice's hand heartily and spoke sincerely.

'I thank you for a grand meal, and the Queen of Puddings was rightly named.'

Hal was now conversing earnestly with Tim Rowley, and only Imogen heard what was meant for Alice's ears alone. George's colour rose: the only sign that this laconic man was sensitive.

'About this evening,' he said in a lower voice. 'I didn't mean to keep the vicar so long, and when he invited me to stop to supper he wouldn't take no for an answer. It was lucky for me, and I ate like a king in consequence, but I never meant to inconvenience you.'

Alice's reply was spontaneous and contrite.

'There's no question of inconvenience. We were delighted to have you. You must come again some time.'

George took her at her word.

'Thank you, I should like to.'

Walking through the hall, Timothy Rowley clasped Imogen's arm and spoke confidentially in her ear.

'You have no idea how fortunate it is that you happened to arrive here at this particular time. Alice is a serendipitous lady. She brings people together, quite by chance, and the most unexpected and delightful things happen to them in consequence.'

In a sudden lift of spirits, Imogen felt that she had been right to come, that Alice was the messenger who would show her the way.

'Fred believed in serendipity. My husband. My late husband. There!' Realizing. 'I'm speaking naturally about Fred for the first time since his death.'

And I said *death* quite naturally, too, she thought.

Timothy's expression was compassionate. He drew closer.

'When one is recovering from bereavement, it is of the utmost importance . . .' he began.

But the importance was lost because George Hobbs was hovering.

'Sorry to interrupt you both, but I wanted to say good-night. I part company here and go out the back way. I left my motorbike in the yard, and my helmet and gear in the kitchen.'

'Ah! The famous motorcycle,' said Timothy. 'An old Harley-Davidson, isn't it?'

Imogen's interest was aroused. She would have liked to comment, but the men did not notice.

George said proudly, 'Yes, and I rebuilt it myself. Well, I'll be off. Here's my business card, Dr Rowley. It's got my telephone and mobile numbers on it, and there's an answering service, so you'll be able to reach me any time.' Encompassing the group with a wave of one arm, he cried, 'Good-night, everybody!' A few minutes later they heard him roar off into the dark.

Hal, who always found it difficult to part with the day and its ongoing concerns, said, 'Tonight being Hallowe'en, I'll double-check the church locks.' He disappeared into the mist.

Timothy was the last to leave. He would always be the last to leave, wringing the ultimate drop from the occasion, needing to have or to be given the final word.

52

'Good-night, sweet ladies, good-night, good-night.'

Then Alice closed the door, and she and Imogen stood there yawning like fools, too tired even to discuss the evening.

' "Sufficient unto the day are the evils thereof," ' said Alice. 'Let's leave the dishes until the morning, and go to bed.'

But between one yawn and the next, Imogen had to say, 'I'm sorry if I upset anyone, but there was a lot of thin ice around, and occasionally I fell through.'

Feeling mellow, Alice answered openly.

'It wasn't your fault. I'm afraid Tim was being very naughty this evening. He adored you, of course. I knew he would. And he was showing off in front of you. Playing power games with Hal. Teasing George to ask a favour of Mary Proctor. Being provoking about witches. In that sort of mood there's no stopping him.'

Imogen, intrigued, picked out one point.

'What's the connection between George Hobbs and Mary Proctor?'

'It's only a rumour so I shouldn't repeat it – and a very old rumour at that, because George must be in his late thirties. Oh, I might as well tell you. He's supposed to be Mary's illegitimate son. How that can be I don't know, since Mary was married before the last war and there are older children than George. But they say she had him adopted as a baby, and brought up outside the dale. Then years later he came back to find her, and stayed on here. Neither Mary nor George has ever acknowledged any relationship, and no one would dare ask either of them. But George goes there for his Sunday dinner and keeps an eye on her, and Mary will sometimes listen to George when she won't give a hearing to anyone else. In a quiet way, they seem to be devoted.'

'I think that's rather touching.' Imogen was surprised.

'Oh, there are more tales to tell about Mary Proctor than that! But I'll take you to meet her next week. Which should be quite an experience. And now, my very dear Imogen, we must go to bed.'

They linked arms like the old friends they were, and went upstairs together.

Imogen's mind would not sleep. Lying between chilled sheets, it tumbled and tossed in remembrance until she slid out of bed, clutching her rubber hot-water bottle, and looked through the window over Langesbydale.

The night was veiled in mist, so perhaps she only imagined the flickering glow of a Hallowe'en fire on the hill where the Listeners stood.

SIX

Bonfire Night

The days passed rapidly. Caught up in Alice's schedule, swept along in Alice's wake, Imogen had no time for thinking, only for doing as she was bidden. Even Fred was overwhelmed by the constant bustle and seldom spoke. For Bonfire Night was following close upon the heels of Hallowe'en and Imogen was conjuring up a guy out of rags and straw and making him a dashing black wool moustache and beard. At the far end of the vicarage lawn a vast pile of fallen boughs and old boxes was mounting, ready for the night. And Hal, revealing a surprisingly boyish streak, had accumulated a stockpile of fireworks and intended to give a dazzling display.

'We shall be quite a big party,' said Alice. 'Friends and neighbours with their children. More people for you to meet. I did ask Philip, but they have their own bonfire. Still, he's invited us both to tea on Tuesday, so that will be nice for you.'

'Yes, indeed,' said Imogen, quelling a twinge of doubt, a tremor of desire.

As Alice was observing her closely, she changed the subject.

'Do you always live at Red Queen speed? You know – *Faster! Faster!*'

'Oh come, it's not as bad as that!' Answering the telephone, dealing with a query from Vera, scribbling a memo to see somebody about something, wondering what to cook for supper. 'You're used to working quietly by yourself. Being a vicar's wife is a different game altogether. Which reminds me, Vera always helps me out on these occasions. Perhaps you'd like an afternoon off?'

The prospect elated Imogen, but she had to say, 'Are you sure?'

'Oh, quite sure. We're used to managing by ourselves.'

'Then I'll go for a walk. I used to be a good walker.'

Out of London, down to Epsom, and over the downs with Fred. Swinging along, sometimes hand in hand. A rucksack on his back contained sandwiches, a thermos of coffee and two plastic raincoats. If they found a fine and private spot they might make love and walk on again, smiling inside and out.

'Yes, go for a walk,' said Alice. 'The dale is delightful at this time of year.'

Yes, come for a walk, said Fred, surfacing.

The weather was crisp and dry with bright blue sky and cotton wool clouds. Gusts of wind stripped the trees and piled their autumn rags into corners; whirled her skirt up over her knees and blew imitation blushes into her cheeks. Battling against it, Imogen was both exhilarated and irritated. She pulled an emerald velvet beret well down on her head, dug gloved hands deep into the pockets of her long black overcoat, marched through the surging waves of air to the outskirts of the town. There, looking over the vast counterpane of Langesbydale, she saw the grey listeners on their hill, and beneath them a sprawl of houses sheltered by trees. HARALDSTONE FIVE MILES, the signpost told her.

She hesitated for a moment, knowing that Alice would disapprove. Then, obeying an inner command, took the first step towards them.

Fred strode forward with her, joking, whistling, singing.

'*Where have all the flowers gone?*' he sang cheerfully, who had gone with them.

The wonder of being alive possessed her. Forgive me! she begged of him. She tugged off her cap, and let the wind unravel her knot of dark hair and send out fluttering strands like messages. She lifted her face and felt life blow on it. The fingers beckoned. An answer to some question she had not been able to frame lay before her. Onward she went, to hear it.

The nine listeners towered above her. Crudely hewn by centuries of weather, they resembled the visions of a sculptor who had not yet released them from the stone, so leaving her free to imagine them: old bent women, long slim girls who had once danced like flames, mothers with children. She wandered from one to another, touching the rough surfaces tenderly with her fingertips, making acquaintance with them. But the wind was up again, giving orders, harrying, hustling, and on Haraldstone Hill the gusts were so fierce that they snatched her breath. Locks of hair stung her mouth and lashed her cheeks. One especially boisterous blast almost threw her to her knees.

She sat with her back to the wind and rested against a mother-and-child. In the state between sleeping and waking, it seemed to her that the tall stone prickled with energy, and the ground beneath the coarse tussocks was alive as if some great engine throbbed and turned in the depths below. For some time she allowed herself to be lulled, while the wind blundered and blustered among the quiet figures. Dignified, patient women, they were waiting until it blew out so they could be at peace among themselves. She sat and waited also, placing her palms directly on the restless grass: listening without ears, seeing without eyes.

She woke up cold and confused, looking round for the companions who had watched while she slept. There was no one. The light was failing. The squall was over. The women had reverted to stone. The engine of the earth had stopped. And Fred had gone.

Oh, he'll be back, Imogen thought. She jumped up and beat life into her arms, stamped warmth into her feet, and looked down on a toy-sized Haraldstone.

An experienced eye could have traced its origins from primitive hamlet to industrial village. But Imogen was not an historian and she saw Haraldstone in skeleton form, with limbs of minor roads branching out from the spine of its main street; fingers and toes of lanes stretched out towards the solitary farms on the fells, and a skull full of shops.

Yes, there you are, she thought. As if it had been waiting for her to recognize an old friend.

Her watch said 4.05. Her stomach said *Time for tea.* Her head said *It'll soon be dark. Get down there and be quick about it!*

So she did as they told her.

Haraldstone was lighting up when she entered the main street. Blocks of modest terraced houses faced each other: solid little two-up two-down affairs, brick-built with slate roofs, sash windows, a small fenced garden at the front, and a small concrete yard at the back. At the end of each block was a large double-bay-windowed house. A few of these bore a brass plate to indicate the presence of some professional person: doctor, dentist, chiropodist.

Each block had been given an old-fashioned street lamp, once lit by gas but now by electricity. These were freshly painted a rich dark green with the decorated base picked out in lemon.

At the far end the shops had been built to provide fully for this small community and, though tactfully modernized, their Victorian aspect had been maintained. It was all so clean and tidy, so self-aware and on display, that Imogen was reminded of a museum. And like a museum Haraldstone kept regular and early hours. At quarter to five on a Saturday afternoon it had nothing to offer her apart from viewing. Still she walked and looked and absorbed the place, fascinated.

A café, the Copper Kettle, whose symbol was its sign, exhibited the works of local artists on its walls; but a waitress was already clearing the round tables, covered in peach-pink cloths, and a solitary customer was paying her bill. A fish and chip bar stood in shining silence, bearing a notice that said FRYING AT 6 P.M. A hairdressing and beauty salon called Jon and Deirdre had already drawn down its blinds. Either closing down or about to close were Helme's Ironmongers; a health food shop named Back to Nature; a general stores with modest premises and tremendous ambitions advertising itself as Hunwick's Supermarket; a greengrocer's, a baker and a butcher: all family concerns clearly established in the nineteenth century.

She was turning back to look at the shops on the other side when she saw an arched passageway whose sign read THE CATWALK. Going through it she found herself in a small cobbled court. These buildings, of older origin, had possibly been the original village shops before Haraldstone became part of the industrial age. Here were the specialists: a shoemaker, a weaver, a silversmith, an old-fashioned sweet shop, a *pâtisserie*, and unexpectedly an Italian restaurant called Mario's, which boasted an Egon Ronay recommendation, AA and RAC stars, and accepted certain credit cards. Finally Crafty Notions sold everything from silver earrings to fringed silk shawls, all quoted as original and hand-made, and its window was dominated by a wonderfully imaginative patchwork quilt.

Imogen stood and stared for a long time at the bedspread in which local colours and contours were used, producing something indigenous to the place in which they were made, until she became aware of a round high-coloured face staring back at her. On being seen, the face immediately disappeared from its station. The door opened a few inches, a bell jangled, and a throaty voice asked, 'Are you interested in the quilt?'

The voice was seductive. The person to whom it belonged was not: a stocky little middle-aged woman with glossy dark eyes, dressed in what appeared to be a selection of garments and beads from her own shop.

'Absolutely fascinated. But I'm not buying, just browsing.'

The door opened wider.

'Would you like a closer look? I can take it out of the window. It's worth looking at.'

Intrigued but reluctant, Imogen repeated, 'Truly, I'm not thinking of buying it.'

'Come and look anyway. I like people who like what I make.'

'I thought the shop was closed,' Imogen temporized.

'Always open to those who show interest in my wares.'

Hesitating still, Imogen said, 'I really ought to be getting back.'

Yet she found herself inside the shop: betrayed yet again by her own good manners, stammering an explanation.

'I'm staying with friends in Langesby. I've been walking through the dale. Such a lovely day. Though windy. Particularly up on the hill. I was hoping to have tea here before I started back again, but it's later than I thought . . .'

The woman only came up to Imogen's shoulder and yet she dominated. Her ample flesh was smooth and tight, glistening with health and good eating. Her unruly hair had attempted to go grey and been dyed a resolute black. Her lustrous eyes rolled eloquently as she talked.

'But me no buts. Let me take your coat. Oho! Smart coat. Snazzy hat,' she said, reading the labels, feeling the material. 'London made? I thought so. Yes.' She peered up at Imogen. 'You're tired, whether you know it or not. You're one of those that shows it under the eyes. Come and sit down.'

'But I must be back before seven . . .' Panicking.

'There's a 5.30 bus from the stop outside Hunwick's Supermarket which goes to Langesby. You'll be there by six. You can wait here for half an hour and catch it. I'm Sadie. Sadie Whicker. And your name is?'

'Imogen Lacey.'

'Imogen! Suits you. The poignant type. You take your sorrows to heart. Golden lads and girls all must, eh?'

Like chimney-sweepers come to dust, she finished. Like Fred, who had done.

'So you've been roaming the hills, Imogen? Did you see our stone circle?'

'Yes. Amazing. I fell asleep actually, sitting up against one of the stones. They look like people.'

'Oh yes. And powerful still.'

'My back tingled when I leaned against one. And the ground felt alive.' She stopped herself and said briskly, 'I must have dreamt it, because it was all very normal when I woke up.'

Sadie had evidently decided they were friends.

'Then stand in front of your bedspread, Imogen, and weave a dream or two into that. I'll bet you're a great dreamer. Night *and* day. Go ahead, handle it. It may look delicate but it isn't.'

Imogen stroked it: pliable, padded, soft. The design was abstract and asymmetrical. Vigorous undulating lines, shading from deepest cobalt to palest baby blue, indicated sea below sky. Beneath it, fluid shapes of copper, green and beige suggested fields, some ploughed by fine brown stitching. This yellow tadpole might be a crop of rape or mustard: that sepia figure a tree driven by the wind; these greenish-black digits on a hill standing stones. And then the design, seeming to run freely from left to right, stopped short a few inches from the edge and turned tenderly back upon itself, disclosing another land and another sea behind it. A sleeper might lie beneath this quilt at night and fall to dreaming of it, as one meaning slid into another and made a third, with others beyond.

'Have you lived here long?' Imogen asked absently, contemplating this eccentric inner world.

'Seven or eight years. The longest time I've stayed anywhere. I'm restless by nature. The quilts are the only part of me that hold stillness. My mother made quilts. She was an American, born in Philadelphia. Quaker country. Wonderful history of patchwork there. I can't remember the place because we left when I was four years old. She had divorced my father by then, married again and moved on. Divorce, marriage, quilts and moving on was the story of my mother's life. I don't know where she is now, but she taught me my craft. I use the traditional designs as well as my own. My bride's throws sell like hot cakes. The one you can't take your eyes off is an original, inspired by the dale.'

'Yes. I can see that. It would be quite different inspired by Langesby.'

Sadie made a scoffing noise.

'Langesby's too smug to inspire me. We're closer to nature out here. Older. Tougher. Rougher. And a hell of a lot more interesting. Don't just look at the quilt. Feel it. Wrap it round yourself.'

She scooped it from the stand, spread it over Imogen's shoulders, clad her in earth and sea and sky, watched her relax and become an Imogen no one knew, including herself.

'You must have it,' said Sadie decisively. 'It's yours.'

Imogen tried to picture this acquisition in some future bedroom of her own that would be minus Fred, and felt a traitor to be choosing it without him. Nor would it have been his choice. Unconventional in his work, he preferred the traditional at home.

'But it's so very large,' she offered, as a detraction from its merits.

'You can sleep under a big quilt just as soundly as under a small one. Or,' with a jocular wink, 'find a nice warm man to sleep under it with you.' She meditated on Imogen. 'Yes. You'll be attractive to all sorts of men. The dark lady of the Sonnets. Careful, though. You could tempt the wrong sort. Something vulnerable about you. You might draw a

Bluebeard! And even the best of them will want to have, hold and protect – though with that mouth and chin you could probably protect *them*.'

Imogen laughed, warming to her, and stroked the yellow tadpole that could be a field of mustard.

'But there I go,' said Sadie, watching her, 'talking as if you're on your own, when you've probably got a heap of lovers.' Smiling, curious.

Imogen said, drawing the quilt up to her chin, 'I had a lovely husband but he's dead.'

'Oh. Sorry. Putting my fat little foot in it.' She was instantly contrite.

Imogen gave a swift nod, accepted the apology, dismissed the subject. Smoothing the material, feeling the warmth and lightness, coveting its earthly-heavenly tones, she asked, 'How much is this?'

'Two hundred and twenty pounds. Two hundred to you. It may seem expensive,' Sadie added defensively, 'but there's hours of work in it and I have to make a living of sorts.'

'Oh I understand that very well,' Imogen answered. 'I'm self-employed in a luxury trade, too. It isn't the way to become a millionaire.'

'I knew it! I knew we had lots in common. Here, let me take that from you. What do you do?'

'I make crazy hats,' said Imogen, and grinned. She pointed to the emerald velvet beret: 'That's one of the more sober ones. In fact it had a couple of giant daisies on the band but I took them off. I thought it was too much for a country walk.'

Sadie burst out laughing. She laughed from the belly like a female Falstaff, hands on hips, frizzy dyed hair thrown back, thick lips stretched over teeth that had been excellent and were still good.

'Well, I'm damned,' she said. 'I've been thinking that we need a hat shop here.'

They assessed each other, wondering whether to explore this possibility. Sadie glittered with hope, but was moving too quickly for Imogen, who began to retreat.

Concentrating on the bedspread, she said, 'I can't promise to buy this, but could you hold it for a couple of days while I check my account?'

'I'll hold it for you any old how,' said Sadie cheerfully.

She folded it away with layers of tissue paper in a large square box, across whose lid CRAFTY NOTIONS was printed like cross-stitch. Her movements were quick, neat and sure.

Over her shoulder she said, 'If you don't mind drinking herbal tea you can have a mug of nutmeg and orange spice with me.'

Her glossy brown eyes enticed.

Imogen, who had been yearning for strong Assam with perhaps a hot buttered teacake, said, 'Oh, please don't bother. I—'

'No bother. I'll put the kettle on,' said Sadie. She shooed a vast black Persian cat from an easy chair. 'Off, Tarquin! Sit down, dear. I won't be five minutes.'

From the kitchenette, whose genial disorder Imogen could glimpse through the doorway, she called, 'Are you staying in Langesby long?'

'I don't know yet,' Imogen called back, inspecting hand-knitted sweaters. 'I thought I'd just be here for the week, but then I was roped in for the bonfire tonight. Half the town seems to be going to it. We're invited out to tea on Monday and Tuesday, and Wednesday evening is arranged, and Alice keeps fixing things up, and so it goes on.' Mesmerized by Tarquin's yellow glare, she broke off to say, 'What an astonishing cat this is!'

'Do you like cats?'

'Oh yes, I'm a cat person. So was Fred. I have a humble tabby,' said Imogen, 'about half the size of this splendid creature. But deeply loved.'

'Cats is cats is cats. I wouldn't be without one. So your friends are throwing a big bonfire party? Have they got children?'

'Two teenage sons away at boarding school. I haven't met them yet, but Alice wants me to be a constant visitor. So no doubt I shall.'

'D'you like children? I mean, *honestly* like them.'

'In a detached way. Yes. And I can revert to childhood with very young children. Play games. Create paper hats. Crayon things. Make up stories. Read to them. Enjoy their company. But I'm not a born mother like Alice.'

Sadie reappeared with two Denby mugs, one blue, one green, both chipped. They had been rinsed beneath a running tap and Imogen suspected tide-marks beneath the glowing red-gold liquid.

'That sounds like me,' said Sadie. 'I've never been a mother. Didn't know what a mother ought to be. Mine was hardly ideal. I suppose I didn't feel adequate enough to perpetuate the myth. Not the maternal sort.'

Nor the domestic sort, Imogen thought, amused rather than critical. 'I don't know *what* I am,' she said honestly. 'Fred and I never got that far.'

'Fred being your late beloved? I didn't go in for husbands either,' said Sadie, sitting with her sturdy legs apart, poking her tea-bag down to deepen the colour and strengthen the mixture. 'Can't do with a man around all the time. And men forget the courtship bit so quickly. At first you're Venus, and they're strewing roses at your feet. But give them three months and you find yourself standing over the stove every night cooking their supper, while they read the evening paper and grunt if you ask them a question. The men are still very patriarchal up here, you know. Their mothers run round after them as if they were the sons of God, and they expect their wives to do the same. Anyway, I'm between men at the moment. They don't breed them as tough as they used to, unless, of course' – and here she looked up, shyly, slily – 'it frightens them when they hear rumours that I'm a witch.'

Imogen stared back at her for several seconds, teaspoon poised, and then spelt out 'W–i–t–c–h?'

'W–i–t–c–h,' Sadie repeated. She was reassuring. 'A white one, not a black one. Not that they know the difference.'

'But of course you aren't a witch,' said Imogen, and paused. 'Are you?' Her dismay and Sadie's fading smile destroyed their rapport.

'I wouldn't have mentioned it,' said Sadie stiffly, 'if I hadn't thought you were a friend of ours.'

'A friend? Of witches? I've never even met a witch! Before,' she added. Sadie shrugged.

'You'd been up there with the listeners. Between the worlds. You felt the power. You understood the quilt. You thought you were telling me too much, and stopped.' As Imogen could not think of a reply she said impatiently, 'All right, then. I made a mistake. Stupid of me.'

Imogen was silent, looking down at the herbal tea she no longer wanted to drink.

'I'm not going to turn you into a toad or anything,' said Sadie derisively. 'Anyway, that's a rubbishy notion, put about centuries ago by men in authority who wanted to get rid of us by fair means or foul – and preferably foul.'

She was angry with Imogen, but mostly with herself, and rattled on, trying to establish a new footing.

'I'm surprised I've stuck to men, to be honest. They're an unsatisfactory lot. I prefer women for company and friendship – but I couldn't be a lesbian. Nothing against them, mind. How about you?'

'Me?' said Imogen, unprepared. 'I've never thought about it. Oh – I like men. I suppose. At least, I liked Fred.' She corrected herself. 'No, I loved Fred. Liked him *and* loved him.'

Then she let him go.

'I've never met a real witch,' she said dubiously. 'Do you cast spells and . . .' her eyes wandered to the great black cat winking on the hearthrug with satanic eyes, 'belong to a – is it a – coven?'

63

Sadie gave a self-conscious laugh.

'Not a full coven – that's thirteen witches.' She tried to be funny, nonchalant. 'There aren't enough of us around here to make up a baker's dozen.'

Imogen heard Alice say dismissively, *Not the genuine article.*

'Yes, we cast spells. Good spells. Trying to put things right for someone in bad health or bad circumstances. We make herbal potions and medicines – again, to help, not to harm. *Do as thou wilt, and harm no one.* We meet once a month and celebrate all the festivals.'

'Up there in the circle? With the Listeners?'

Reluctantly, 'Yes, when the weather's good.'

'I thought I saw a fire on the hill at Hallowe'en.'

'You did. That was us.'

Hal's voice scoffed, *Silly middle-aged women dancing under a full moon.*

Imogen could not take it so lightly.

'Witches aren't alien creatures from another planet, you know,' said Sadie. 'We're human beings. We come from all walks of life and most of us lead ordinary lives. Of course there are bad apples in every barrel, but who can say different? There are all sorts of witches. Some of them are loners, like the old witch I know locally. She's the right sort. With all the old wisdom.'

Imogen said with difficulty, 'I'm sorry if I misled you into thinking I was a – a witch-friend. Naturally I shan't betray your confidence.'

But she was keenly aware of betraying Alice and Hal, who would strongly disapprove of this association. She managed to finish her herbal tea and stood up.

'That was delicious.'

Sadie studied her closely, spoke persuasively.

'You could cultivate a taste for the esoteric if you'd let yourself. Have another.'

But Imogen said, 'I think I'd better catch that bus now. I'll be in touch about the quilt some time on Monday. Would you give me your telephone number?' Her thoughts were panicking, finding reasons to end this acquaintanceship.

Because two hundred pounds is a lot of money, however wonderful the quilt is, and if I come back to Langesby again it would be too embarrassing to be friendly with a witch. I'll ring her up on Monday and say that I'm sorry but I can't afford it after all, and how lovely it was to meet her but I'm going to back to London sooner than I thought, and if ever I'm this way again etcetera . . .

Sadie looked uglier, stockier, coarser, swarthier: eyes opaque. Imogen was tall, thin, white, sharp, fearful. They shut each other out, and took refuge in the roles of saleswoman and customer.

'I'll give you a card,' said Sadie, all efficiency, 'but you do understand, don't you, that if I haven't heard from you by Tuesday midday I shall have to put the quilt back in the window?'

'Yes, of course. But I shall ring you without fail on Monday morning,' Imogen replied, and added falsely, 'It depends on the state of my bank account.'

They both knew what decision she had made, and why.

At the door Sadie gave her one more chance.

'I felt the quilt belonged to you, and I wasn't mistaken about that.'

But Imogen, catching sight of headlights in the dusk that would rescue her from the wiles of the sorceress, cried, 'Oh, there's the bus. Thank you for everything. I must run.'

The door shut behind her with a scornful sound, the bell jangling in derision, as if she had given the wrong answer.

SEVEN

Monday

Halfway between Langesby and Haraldstone, in a secluded part of the dale, the Mount was built in the early Victorian period before elegance gave way to the baroque. Timothy Rowley had been born in that house, spent most of his boyhood there, returned for regular visits in his maturity, maintained it after his mother's death, and had now retired to it. Apart from the introduction of a few modern conveniences, he had altered nothing. Such a place was both shelter and showcase. Behind its tranquil exterior, in its atmosphere of polite restraint, Timothy could charm people into thinking him a delightful if eccentric old academic. It masked the passions that possessed him, the devious plots and traps he laid in order to gratify them, and the means by which he achieved them. Here his deepest secrets were in safe keeping, while outwardly he remained a highly respectable and respected citizen of Langesby.

Alice and Imogen were the first to arrive, bearing apologies from Hal, who had been detained at the last minute and was following as soon as he could.

'Let us hope that he is not detained too long,' Timothy soothed, taking Alice's tweed overcoat.

You don't mind a bit, Imogen thought. You'd rather he didn't come anyway.

Timothy received her stylish coat with a smile, twinkled at her swaggering beret, now complete with giant daisies, and when she revealed herself in a jade skirt and tangerine sweater, cried, 'What a bird of paradise you are!'

'Yes, very colourful,' Alice echoed doubtfully.

He turned to her and spoke lower, in confidence.

'I'm glad you arrived early because I wanted to warn you that I have had to invite Our Friend.'

Alice's face conveyed not an atom of friendship.

'It could not be helped,' Timothy explained. 'You know how difficult it is to part her from Philip anyway. But, that problem aside, I had to know what was happening at the dramatic society.' Turning to Imogen, he said, 'I'm afraid you're going to get another lungful of Langesby politics, my dear. So remember that waving rather than drowning is the motto!'

Imogen smiled at his joke, and did not care anyway. She was in the privileged position of an outsider whom no one could harm. She intended to enjoy herself.

The drawing room in which they sat could have been a stage setting for a play in the 1920s, and the lady of the house was at one with that time. A portrait over the fireplace showed her in an oyster-coloured satin evening dress, sitting on a crimson ottoman. She was turning towards her audience: dark hair shingled, dark eyes enigmatic, fine red mouth smiling, twisting a long pale rope of pearls round long pale fingers.

Timothy introduced her to Imogen with the reverent words, 'My mama in her prime', and received compliments on her beauty with deep personal satisfaction.

Recalled to his duties as host, he cried, 'Ah! There's the bell again!'

With a mischievous sparkle at Alice he added, 'Who knows? It might even be Hal!' and hastened away.

It was not Hal, but the other three guests had arrived together.

Listening to their voices in the hall, corn-coloured head held a little to one side, Alice said *sotto voce*, 'I can hear George – and Phil – and I'm afraid you're going to meet Edith, which was inevitable sooner or later. I should warn you . . .'

The caution went no further because a handsome woman with prematurely white hair walked into the room as if she owned it. She was wearing a plainer and more expensive version of the Langesby ladies' winter tweeds. Her fine wool suit was beautifully tailored, in subdued colours, and at the neck of her silk shirt she had pinned a splendid cameo. Even as she smiled, her ice-green eyes disparaged Imogen's vivid plumage.

'Now do I spy a fashionable Londoner?' she cried.

No one could have found fault with that remark but it did condemn, and Alice's introduction was edged.

'Edith, I would like you to meet my *gifted* friend Imogen Lacey, who designs, creates and sells the most exciting hats. Imogen, this is the *busiest* lady in Langesby – Edith Wyse.'

A cold white hand touched Imogen's hand and withdrew.

Ignoring the flash of unseen swords, in came Philip, smiling and urbane, to convey that disturbing tingle; and in came George, with a mumbled greeting and a reticent nod.

Edith and Alice maintained wide tight smiles. Imogen experienced an inward bubble of amusement.

'Should we, do you think,' Timothy asked Alice, 'allow Hal another few minutes' grace?'

'No, I think not. He did say not to wait tea for him.'

'Ah!' Timothy's smile had never believed that Hal would come. He spread his arms to embrace the company. 'Then, my dear friends, let us indulge ourselves.'

Afternoon tea at the Mount was, as Imogen had been told, a rare treat. Timothy's elderly housekeeper provided paper-thin cucumber sandwiches as well as hot muffins, cinnamon toast and scones. There were fluted dishes of home-made jam, a honeycomb dripping nectar, and a jar of Gentleman's Relish. She had baked a cardamom seed cake with a sickle of candied peel piercing its high gold crust, and a Dundee cake symmetrically studded with whole almonds. Small embroidered napkins were provided; the china was fine and garlanded with roses.

Timothy helped her to carry everything in, and it was evident that this ceremony delighted them both. She even provided him with a silver caddy lined with cedarwood, and he made quite a ritual of unlocking it, measuring out the tea, boiling a spirit-kettle and warming the silver pot.

While Timothy fussed over the cups Edith opened the conversation.

'Do tell me about yourself, Isabel. It is Isabel, isn't it? Oh. Imogen. So sorry. Never can remember names. In what way are you talented – other than selling exciting hats? I'm so interested!'

Alice interposed, flushed in defence of her charge.

'She's creative in *every* way. She excels in handicrafts. She can draw and paint beautifully. She can sing and dance. At school she was a splendid little actress – and such a mimic! Do you remember, Imogen, making us all laugh?'

'I'd forgotten,' Imogen replied, refusing to explain or defend herself.

Philip gave her a smile of complicity and involuntarily she smiled back. Edith moved in, frosty and composed, to tackle Alice.

'What we really need in these circumstances isn't talent so much as general usefulness. A dogsbody – as Philip would say!' With a scintillating glance at him, because his eyes were on Imogen. 'In any case, the interesting jobs must naturally be offered to local people who have important connections.' She addressed Imogen point-blank: 'Now if you can manage a stall or draw plain signs and placards I can find you plenty to do.'

'I doubt that I shall be here,' Imogen replied coldly. She was regretting her incursion into their world.

Timothy Rowley reprimanded the lady mildly but firmly.

'My dear Edith, you are giving Imogen a very *parochial* impression of Langesby. We welcome and have need of talented people, whether they are based here or not.'

Philip Gregory's remark was affable but also pointed.

'Besides, you already have an army of volunteer helpers, my dear. You don't need to shanghai any more.'

'Goodness!' Edith cried, throwing up her hands in mock dismay. 'I was merely pointing out the difficulties of employing Imogen's astonishing talents.' She glided into a glacial silence, accepting only one cucumber sandwich, and having to be persuaded to a sliver of cardamom cake, which she tested with the tip of her fork, frowning.

After these initial salvos, the conversation was pleasant and of little consequence until tea was over, when Timothy became businesslike.

He had, he told them, rubbing his hands, twinkling over his half-glasses, been highly diligent in the past week; and he ran over the programme of his activities as he opened a great green-backed folder, on which was printed large and clear:

THE OLD WIVES' TALE

The progress of this theatre project reminded Imogen of the tale of Solomon Grundy. Timothy had proposed the idea on a Monday, distributed copies of the play on Tuesday, inspected the church hall with Hal on Wednesday, consulted with George Hobbs on Thursday, made several telephone calls on Friday, re-read the play and taken further notes on Saturday, and collected all the information together on Sunday. Today, he said, he was inviting opinions and suggestions. But Imogen felt this was a matter of form. He evidently saw the production so clearly in his own mind that they could surely only agree and be absorbed, or disagree and be explained away – and thanked, of course, for Timothy was always courteous.

'*Should* we begin?' he asked.

The polite query suggested that someone was missing. Alice apologized again.

'It seems that Hal will be unable to come after all.'

Timothy shrugged and smiled, settled back into his armchair.

'No matter, my dear, no matter. Your excellent husband has already done his bit by lending us the church hall for rehearsals as well as the performance. But I regret that he missed a good tea, and we shall miss his invaluable judgement!'

'Well, no, actually,' Alice confessed, bringing forth a little notebook. 'He jotted down one or two comments in case he wasn't able to come.'

'How very thoughtful,' Timothy purred. 'We shall consider them with interest. Now, as you all know, the Friends of St Oswald's have been discussing ways of raising money for the church funds, and Hal came up with the idea of a play, to be given as part of the July festivities. He was kind enough to ask my advice on this and we discussed the project last week – deciding on *The Old Wives' Tale.*'

Here, Alice hesitated over Hal's first comment before crossing it out.

'I then took the liberty of sending copies of the play, together with an explanatory note, to certain important people who could be of inestimable assistance,' said Timothy amiably, missing nothing. 'I include, of course, those present, and I should like to have your general reactions.'

He looked benevolently round, awaiting the first response. It came from Edith.

'Before we go any further,' she said, showing all her teeth, 'I wonder – do Langesby Dramatic Society know about this play of yours? I mention the fact because they are the town's official drama group.'

Alice interposed, saying, 'Naturally, Hal has already taken into account the fact that the LDS produce their plays in spring and autumn, and the festival will be held in the summer.'

Edith's appetite, starved of tea, sharpened on controversy.

'Then I think I should mention – though in the strictest confidence because it isn't common knowledge yet – that Langesby Dramatic Society are also considering a play for the festival.'

Timothy pursed his lips. Philip looked embarrassed. Alice made little shocked murmurs of protest about their usual production being in April.

'Oh, they can postpone that until July,' said Edith.

'And then give another play in October?' Alice said incredulously.

'They can move the autumn production nearer to Christmas. It will require some adjustments, but the festival was an opportunity not to be missed.'

She smiled into their silence, aiming her information in darts.

'Knowing their reputation, we can expect a highly polished production. A three-act play. To be held in the town hall. Tickets at cinema prices, and half the profits to go to the Town Fund. It's a pity' – to Alice – 'that Hal didn't think of mentioning this to me beforehand. I could have warned him off. But I'm sure you'll be able to do something else instead. A choir recital, for instance.'

As St Oswald's choir was no more than adequate, and on occasions less than that, Alice mentally pawed the ground on her husband's behalf and prepared to charge to his defence. But Timothy Rowley placed one pacifying hand on her arm and gave Edith Wyse his full and most courteous attention.

'How fortunate we are to have you with us. I had heard nothing of this.'

'It has only been proposed recently.'

'Ah! Do you know how many performances they intend to give, and when?'

She was delighted to tell him.

'As you know, it's usually three evenings – Thursday, Friday and Saturday, with a matinée on the Saturday – but they think of putting it on for the whole of the festival week. And of course, being our *established* dramatic society, they can call upon a tremendous amount of local support. The *Langesby Chronicle*, county newspapers and so on will give them full coverage. And the mayor and mayoress and local VIPs will be invited to the opening night.'

Alice simmered, lips compressed, but Timothy kept his plump well-manicured hand on her arm and spoke with lofty mildness.

'If our production is as good as I intend it to be, I believe I can rummage up a professional theatre critic and persuade a few important theatre names to attend the opening performance. I also have some small influence in certain sections of the national press. So the local bigwigs and local newspapers will hardly pass us over. In which case "St Oswald's Players" – as we may call them for easy reference – will command equal, and possibly superior, publicity and prestige.'

He had shaken Edith, but her next words were designed to chill his enthusiasm.

'Call your players whatever you please, but they haven't as yet been recruited, and you'll have to look for them elsewhere. I mean, this is only a small town, and all the *good* amateurs are in the Langesby Dramatic Society.'

Timothy explained, as to a recalcitrant pupil, 'Personally speaking, I would most sedulously *avoid* directing local amateurs with an established reputation. They are often bursting with self-importance and lacking in what one might term *plasticity*. I have had many years' experience, my dear, with major school productions, and found genuine talent waiting only to be discovered and drawn forth. I believe I can find a cast which – directed with intelligence and inspiration – will *eclipse* that of Langesby Dramatic Society. So I think we shall "have a go", as they say.'

Edith's green eyes could have turned him to stone. Alice was delighted. George grinned. Philip sighed. And Imogen divined a deep satisfaction in Timothy.

'There will be an open audition, of course,' he continued, 'but I shall also be looking close to home for our actors and actresses.' He astonished Imogen by saying, 'I could wish that our charming visitor here were indeed settled in Langesby, because I sense that she would make a perfect Delia – the lady under the Sorcerer's spell. And in our friend Philip – whose hidden talents interest me even more than his outward ones – I believe we may have an ideal contender for the Sorcerer himself – Sacrapant.'

Philip's colour heightened. He looked down at his hands and made no answer.

Edith cut in: 'I think you're going to have great difficulty in making the play and the players understood. It's simply a childish fairy tale. A romp. And if you're hoping to produce a show-stopper then the speeches will do that – in quite the wrong sort of way.'

Alice crossed off the second comment on her list, and sighed.

'I can visualize the production so well.' Timothy murmured, looking into the middle distance. 'The present difficulty of comprehending Shakespearian English is the result of too much television, too many video games, and not enough reading. But I can find a solution without editing a word. Some twenty-five years ago, I saw *The Taming of the Shrew* in San Francisco. The producer had placed a semicircle of players round the edge of the stage, who mimed their reactions to events. It added another dimension to the play, was beautiful and illuminating and remarkably simple.'

He leaned forward and said engagingly to Philip, 'Those youngsters of yours, whom I had the good fortune to meet on Hallowe'en, were so well behaved and entered so splendidly into the spirit of the occasion. I do hope, my dear fellow, that you will allow them to play the parts of my mimes?'

Philip relaxed, smiled, and said, 'It's good of you to think of them. They'll enjoy doing that.'

Edith's little laugh tinkled with ice.

'My dear Timothy, it's extremely brave of you to risk your reputation in this way, and I'm sure your production will be highly intellectual, but do you really think anyone will pay a penny to watch a one-act Elizabethan farce?'

Alice crossed out Hal's final comment, and sat back, routed.

Timothy remained cool, though his eyes were hard.

'This *farce*, as you call it, is a delightful piece, full of wit and humour, comedy, romance, mystery, magic and effects aplenty. Oh, he knew his audience, did Peele – pray God we know ours as well!

'Yes, Edith, I believe it would be a rare attraction, and singularly appropriate for the occasion. And if you are asking me whether I will back it against the usual worthy production by Langesby Dramatic Society, the answer again is *Yes!*'

She was not yet defeated.

'There's another point,' she said. 'Considering that the church hall is the only community centre in Langesby, I'm surprised that it's so readily available. You'll have great difficulty fitting in rehearsals with everything else that goes on there.'

'I dare say,' said Timothy smoothly, 'that we shall manage somehow.' And he smiled on her. 'Tell me, my dear, do you happen to know if Langesby Dramatic Society has made its choice for the festival?'

'Not as yet,' Edith admitted. 'They're divided between a Terence Ratti-gan and an Emlyn Williams.'

'*French Without Tears*? or *Night Must Fall*?'

His irony was lost on her. She answered seriously, 'No. *The Deep Blue Sea* or *The Corn is Green*.'

'Powerfully popular stuff! Still, neither of them should queer our pitch.'

Edith's eyes glinted.

'On the other hand, they may consider a period play. They do them so beautifully – a Pinero or a Wilde . . .'

Has she told them that a minor Elizabethan masterpiece will be taking place at the other end of the town? Imogen wondered. And then answered herself. Yes, of course she has. She's carrying tales to both sides, and Timothy knows it. He's using her as an informant and a conveyor of information.

'A company of some quality,' he was drawling, 'but their choice of play does tend to linger in the *drawing room*. I'm surprised, with their reputation and backing and the various talents they can call upon, that they haven't tried something more *ambitious*.'

Edith took aim.

'Such as?'

He fumbled, pursed his lips, laughed, gasped. *Caught out!* his expression read, but Imogen did not believe it.

'Heavens above, my dear Edith, how you do drop on a fellow. Oh, I'm not suggesting Beckett or Pinter. But something more *modern*. More *astringent*. A complete change of mood. A reflection of the age and this part of the country. Plater's *Close the Coalhouse Door*, for instance? If they *must* have a period play how about Greenwood's *Love on the Dole*? Anyway –' with a gesture of his well-kept hands, a shrug of his shoulders – 'the Lord knows I have enough business of my own without presuming upon theirs.'

He dismissed the subject, but left Edith thinking about it.

Clearing his throat, looking at them brightly over his half-glasses, he asked, 'Now how do the rest of you feel about the play? Isn't it something of a gem?'

Yes, they thought it – unusual – with great possibilities.

Edith had to say, 'I found the humour very laboured.'

This time Timothy went on the attack.

'Would it be fair to observe, my dear, that apart from a cultural interest your knowledge of the theatre is not especially profound?'

She disliked this assessment but could not argue with it.

'*Laboured*, I think you said?' Timothy persisted.

She would not give in.

'Yes. The opening scene, for instance – I can't see amateur actors coping with that. Professionals might make it more amusing, of course.'

He was watching her over his glasses, half-smiling. His reply was enthusiastic, as if she had said exactly what he wanted her to say.

'You are absolutely right, my dear Edith. Amateurs would indeed *labour* that scene. And my next note concerns that very problem. I suggest that, though we offer an open audition – which is only fair – I should bring in one or two people I know well, to take small parts that would otherwise be – as our forthright friend Edith says – *laboured* . . . unless anyone objects to the idea?'

No, they did not object.

'I am sure that some of my old pupils will be only too delighted to oblige me. In fact, I have made a few telephone calls that may prove fruitful.'

He's cast the play in his mind already, Imogen thought.

'You are quite happy with that notion?' Timothy asked, eyebrows raised.

Oh yes, they were happy to leave it all to him.

Imogen did not feel the need to answer directly. After all, this was nothing to do with her. She was merely a guest who had been invited out of politeness. But she no longer agreed with Alice's assessment of Timothy: *You'll adore Tim. Everybody does. He's such a darling. Of course, being an elderly bachelor and set in his ways, he has his little foibles, and his friends understand that, but he's a perfect pet.*

Imogen thought him less than perfect and far more than pet. She was drawn to him, felt a certain trustfulness towards him, as if he might have been her father, but guessed that he intended to have his own way and to lead while others followed. She would also have applied this judgement to Hal, but whereas her host announced his intentions openly and galloped ahead, Timothy was bland and devious, pursuing his goals adroitly but just as ruthlessly.

She became aware of his slightly protuberant blue gaze and gave him her quick sweet smile, intended to placate, but he shook his forefinger at her.

'A chield's amang us taking notes!' he said once more.

'What nonsense,' Alice replied indulgently. 'You don't know Imogen. She lives in a world of her own, and is probably thinking of something else entirely.'

'She is a slyboots,' said Timothy, very positive. 'But let us return to our play. Next on my agenda is the name of the company. I am open to suggestions on this point.'

On this, Imogen thought impishly, but not on any other.

'Certainly not the St Oswald Players – which gives a very *parochial* impression,' said Edith. 'It says quite clearly, "This is a group of well-meaning amateurs who belong to the local church".'

Timothy said persuasively, 'Ye-es? And what would you propose?'

She shrugged. He turned away from her and addressed the others.

'We need something lively, evocative and pertinent to the occasion.'

'The Festival Society,' George offered, and was instantly crushed by Edith.

'That wouldn't be ethical! It sounds as if you're representing the theatre in Langesby, whereas you're only a temporary group with a one-off production.'

'Here today and gone tomorrow,' Timothy observed softly. 'We entertain you for a while and then depart. Life in a nutshell. Well, well. Let us forget the occasion, since Edith is so sensitive about local feelings, and think of the company.'

'What about the Strolling Players?' Alice ventured.

'A little too perambulatory, my dear,' said Timothy kindly.

'The Troubadours!' Philip offered.

'A shade too jolly, and suggestive of strumming?' Timothy remarked gently.

Edith cried contemptuously, 'Oh really, Phil! You'll be proposing the Jolly Minstrels next!'

'Then let us think of some name sympathetic to the era of original production,' said Timothy. 'For instance, the first performance was given by the Queenes Majesties Players, though that is far too grand a designation for us.'

Edith drawled, 'Why don't we consult our multi-talented visitor?'

'Oh no, I couldn't,' Imogen protested. 'I don't know anything about it.'

But Timothy put his hand on hers and smiled into her face, saying, 'Yes, my dear. Give us a good resounding title.'

His white, plump, effeminate hand transmitted surprising energy and power.

Resounding, Imogen thought. *Bells. Chimes. Peals. Peele's . . .*

She said as if the name had been there all along, 'Peele's Players!'

'You show talent,' he said quietly. 'Peele's Players! A compliment to the playwright. Lively, evocative, suggestive of the age. Peele's Players!' He was triumphant, turning upon his adversary. 'Any objections, Edith?'

'Since I am having nothing to do with it, why should I object?'

The others tried the name over and smiled and nodded.

Alice said proudly to Philip, 'I told you how clever she was!'

'Then as we are agreed on this point,' said Timothy, giving Imogen's hand a pat and returning to his notes, 'shall I write that the motion was adopted unanimously? Good. Henceforth we shall be called Peele's Players!'

Imogen experienced a few moments of bliss. She had named the company.

Timothy permitted himself a little fun.

'Time to hear Hal's comments, I believe. Alice?'

'Oh, they were very slight. They've all been answered.'

'Good. George, my friend?' George looked startled. 'Has our friend Mary Proctor read the play, and will she be our Old Wife who tells the Tale?'

'Yes, she says she will, as a matter of fact,' said George, surprised.

'Goodness!' Alice cried. 'I would never have believed it.'

'Oh, I thought she might,' said Timothy, gratified by Mary Proctor's acceptance and his own good judgement. 'Please give her my warmest thanks and regards, George. My dear Philip,' rousing him, who sat, hands clasped on his knees, head bowed, 'I should like you to think seriously about taking the role of Sacrapant.'

Edith simmered, and seemed about to speak, but Timothy cut across her. 'Now let us come to the bones of the enterprise.'

He meant to control, but not to drudge.

'I wish to keep the official side of the business to the minimum. I can combine the roles of producer and director, and chair any necessary meetings – we shall keep them to a minimum – but we need a secretary and a treasurer.'

Alice said automatically, 'I will do what I can, whenever I can, Tim, but Hal and I are having a garden fête in aid of the Church Fund, and I know that the organization will depend on me because he has so much else . . .'

'My dear!' he said, almost reproachfully. 'I had no intention of burdening you. Nor of imposing on Edith,' as she opened her mouth again. 'I know how hard you ladies work already.'

He smiled and paused.

'As we all know,' purred Timothy, 'Edith is a leading light on the Langesby Dramatic Society Committee, so it would be invidious to divide her loyalties.' He gave the little cough preparatory to an announcement. 'Nevertheless, we have reason to be extremely grateful for her invaluable guidance so far.' He bowed in her direction, 'Thank you, Edith.'

Used and discarded, Imogen thought. She would have liked to giggle.

'Now, Alice, my dear,' persuasively, 'I know that you can conjure up any number of willing helpers. Would you bear in mind that I need these two confidential and responsible – though not onerous – posts filling? Good. That is all I ask.'

He returned to his notes.

'Meanwhile I have many commitments, here and elsewhere, so I shall not be starting work before January, and rehearsals will not begin before March.'

He ran down the list, talking aloud to himself, ticking off points.

'One. Hal is most generously letting us have the church hall rent free, but we must provide materials for scenery and costumes etc., so we have to tackle the question of money-raising and sponsors.

'Two. George is taking care of the stage management side, and will bring in any necessary assistants and supervise them. No worries there.'

'Three. I must look around for a wardrobe mistress, someone with knowledge of theatrical costume, and hope she can find people who will sew for us.

'Four. Catering for refreshments? I don't doubt that Alice knows umpteen good Langesby ladies who would gladly take that task upon themselves. All posts are voluntary and unpaid, of course.

'Hm, hm, hm. That seems to be all for the moment.'

He took off his glasses, swung them gently in his fingers, smiled upon his audience.

His dismissal was brief and courtly.

'I think I have troubled you good people long enough. I thank you all for giving up your valuable time to come here this afternoon.'

EIGHT

Tuesday

They drove to Prospect House in the dilapidated little vehicle that Alice called her 'runabout'. Judging from its age and condition Imogen would have thought running was beyond its powers, but Alice dealt firmly with its disabilities and drove with a confidence that the engine did not merit.

'The Rover is really Hal's car,' she confided. 'This one is much more convenient for driving around locally. In any case the Rover would be no use to me. It isn't a lady's car. So heavy to handle.'

Philip's hostel was a building of bleak simplicity standing in its own grounds a mile outside the town. Considerable trouble had been taken to make it look as much like a family home as possible. The glossy noticeboard did not state it to be a detention centre for young offenders, but simply said PROSPECT HOUSE. PRIVATE PROPERTY. NO TRESPASSING. In the process of softening and brightening its aspect, Virginia creepers had put out tendrils over the flat grey stone front. The front door had been painted a beatific blue. The unblinking windows had cheerful curtains. But the garden walls were high, the heavy iron gates were locked, and Alice had to ring an old-fashioned bell-pull to gain entrance.

Philip himself walked down the gravel drive to let them in, very much at ease in his own kingdom, making a joke of turning the great key as if it were a stage prop. He kissed Alice on the cheek, shook hands with Imogen, and smiled on them both.

'This way, ladies. I'll show you round first and we'll have tea later.'

He began the guided tour by saying, 'We're not a large community. We can house about two dozen young people of both sexes, aged from twelve to sixteen. Their crimes range from soft drugs to amateur prostitution and petty theft. They come from poor backgrounds. None of them is violent. I would call them sinned against rather than sinning, and public nuisances rather than malefactors. They've been up before the magistrates so often that the police are tired of arresting them. Detention centres are overcrowded, and I provide a halfway house for minor offenders. Since I own the premises and run the show myself, and as we are partly self-supporting, the authorities are grateful. They keep a stern eye on us, but so far we seem to have passed muster.'

'Passed muster indeed!' Alice said, ever ready with the right reply. 'This man, Imogen, is the nearest thing to a saint that you are likely to meet.'

'Oh come, Alice,' said Philip with his glint of humour. 'I'll put my hand on the Bible any day you like and swear that I'm not.'

He spoke directly to Imogen.

'As I tell everybody, my motives are selfish at bottom. I do this work because I want to, and because it gives me a reason for living.'

'Philip went through a very grim time some years ago,' Alice translated.

'That part of my life is behind me now,' he said decisively. 'And they aren't bad kids – simply misused, misunderstood and misled. We reckon to make something of them, though they do tend to disappear for good when they leave us – no Scarcliff reunion dinners!' With a smile at Imogen: 'My staff is small and I rely largely on voluntary help and local goodwill. Edith is my mainstay. She puts in a lot of time with the youngsters and they respect her . . .'

Respect or fear? Imogen wondered.

'How Edith does love to help out!' cried Alice, unable to bear this. 'She has a finger in all the local pies. Her energy is quite alarming.'

Philip's smile was amused and tolerant.

'She is not the only busy and public-spirited lady I know,' he said courteously. 'You two have more in common than you might think.'

Imogen glanced at him, but his face remained pleasant, impassive. Alice was silent, wondering whether she had been complimented or reproved.

They walked along milk-white corridors with dark blue runners. The surface of the walls and the paintwork gleamed faintly. Everything was very clean and uncannily quiet. Philip, who had seemed so promising on previous occasions, now positively flowered.

'We'll start from the top and work down. Our youngsters are employed with handicrafts in the afternoons,' he explained, as they walked on. 'They earn good money this way. Part of it is pocket money, the rest goes towards their keep. They're particularly busy at this time of year. We make a grand occasion of Christmas. Give them a treat that none of them – I can say that, hand on heart – has ever known. The ingredients for cakes and puddings are provided by a local supermarket and we bake them here. A local farmer gives us a couple of turkeys. A local nursery donates their largest tree. And the presents come from St Oswald's congregation and other good souls – organized by Alice. I give the youngsters as much outside freedom as I can, and the degree of freedom depends entirely on them. Occasionally – inevitably, I suppose – my trust is betrayed.' His face darkened. 'But we don't do badly on the whole.'

His smile returned as he added, 'And once they realize that good behaviour and trustworthiness equals treats they respond remarkably quickly. Under our supervision a select group are allowed to join the church carol-singers on their Christmas Eve round, and to see the local pantomime on Boxing Day.'

He paused and asked, 'Where will *you* be spending Christmas, Imogen?'

She had not thought that far ahead, and was framing a noncommittal reply when Alice said, 'She's going to stay with us, of course – aren't you, my dear?'

She squeezed her friend's arm, but Imogen remained mute and unresponsive.

'Anyway, that's what we hope,' Alice said quickly, reminding herself that Imogen could be moody.

Quickly, smoothly, Philip replied, 'I'm sure we all hope that.'

The awkwardness passed.

Continuing the tour, he said, 'Here are the dormitories. They have their own rooms, as you can see. The boys are on one side of the house, the girls on the other. Personal privacy and personal space are luxuries none of them has known.'

They inspected cell-like cubicles: each of them immaculate, with a neatly made bed and an identical striped cotton cover. They approved spotless bathrooms and showers. They descended the stairs and admired a large sitting room supplied with a television set, and a dining room with two trestle tables laid for tea. They looked into the kitchen and greeted the cook. Finally they went down to the basement.

'This is our indoor recreation area,' said Philip. 'We cleared it out ourselves, cleaned it up, decorated it, and partitioned it off. The equipment has been generously donated by local firms and individuals. As you see, we have table tennis, darts, various board games, a somewhat basic gymnasium which we are gradually building up . . .'

The gymnasium was warm, but its white stark walls and glaring lights chilled Imogen, its dangling ropes and hard benches seemed forbidding, and she had never liked rooms without windows, however well lit. But obedient to his enthusiasm she said, 'I think it's remarkable!'

'And this is our workshop – also in the process of being improved, but again reasonably well equipped.'

The youngsters were working silently and intently on various projects, under the supervision of a vigilant middle-aged woman, who brightened up when she saw her visitors.

'This is one of my cherished helpers, Mrs Slater,' said Philip, with a special smile for her.

Imogen shook hands with this new stranger, but Alice, who knew everyone, said jokingly, 'I think you and I have met before, Margery!' And both ladies laughed.

Philip's stance was easy, his tone friendly, as he addressed his charges.

'Hello, you lot!'

They struck up a polite chorus of 'Hello, Mr Gregory!'

'Everything going well?' he asked.

Mrs Slater answered for them.

'We're having a lovely afternoon, Mr Gregory. Aren't we, everybody?'

A few shy murmurs of agreement.

Imogen looked on the countenances of these young offenders and found them human, if lacklustre.

'Nearly four o'clock,' Philip said, and ushered the visitors to his private quarters on the first floor. The two rooms and an office were decorated and furnished as plainly, and kept as cleanly, as the rest of the home.

'I can't promise you such an elegant tea as Tim gave us yesterday,' he said, 'because we all eat and drink the same things, and we can't afford fine china.'

Beaming with sincerity, Alice said, 'That doesn't matter a bit, and we don't care anyway, and well you know it!'

'Yes, of course I do,' he said, and laughed. 'I'm only showing off!'

His candour was refreshing, was part of his charm, and he engaged in a subtle courtship of both women. He delighted Alice by teasing her, conveying admiration from a respectful distance. He kept Imogen physically aware of him with the touch of a guiding hand under her elbow, his closeness, his smiles, his glances. His charm even extended to the plain girl who wheeled a trolley into the sitting room.

'Ah, bless you, Connie. What would I do without you?' Shining on her until she departed, pink and pleased. Then, deferentially, 'Alice, would you like to pour?'

They ate substantial scones with commercial jam and slices of crumbly fruit cake. Tea came from a blue earthenware pot. Alice praised everything too much. Imogen hardly spoke. And Philip chatted easily but observed her closely.

'You should have seen this building when I first came here, Imogen. It was almost derelict, and the garden had run wild. I believe Alice may have told you that I lost my wife in tragic circumstances? This was followed by a series of harrowing experiences which are best forgotten. It was one of the unhappiest periods of my life. I sold up and left the place we had lived in, took a solitary walking holiday to recuperate, spotted this old pile, bought it for a song, and worked on it more or less single-handed until Alice rounded up a little army of unpaid assistants.'

He mocked her gently, while his eyes expressed devotion.

'If you were a Buddhist, Alice, instead of a Christian, I would suggest that one of your previous lives was spent as the leader of a press-gang!'

They laughed at this remark, and he smiled mischievously.

Yes, I do like you, Imogen thought. I do. And this is a marvellous achievement.

Yet despite the bright colours and light furniture there was a frigid air about the place which mystified her. Perhaps it was the broad bare face of the building, with its rows of narrow windows, that paint and creeper and pretty curtains failed to disguise.

It lacks warmth, she thought. Too ordered. Too hygienic. It needs a few flowers, a scatter of magazines, a little kindly carelessness.

As if in answer to her unspoken comments, Philip said, 'I've done my best to make the home look cheerful rather than clinical, but of course there are bound to be restrictions when you're housing two dozen adolescents with serious problems. We can't dispense with locks and bolts and other safeguards. And health comes before beauty. So tell me, Imogen, what are your impressions?'

She fended off the question with another, feeling her way to an answer.

'Was this a private house before you bought it?'

His answer was frank and regretful.

'I wish it were, but then I shouldn't have been able to afford it. It used to be the Old Langesby Prison.'

He looked at her anxiously, and Imogen saw that his interest in her went beyond sexual attraction. He wanted them to understand each other, and she glowed with a return of life that had nothing to do with reason, because she still felt uncomfortable here.

'No one would guess that,' she said diplomatically. 'You've transformed it.' Truthfulness forced her to add, 'But I'm surprised to find your youngsters all so . . .' she transformed *subdued* into 'polite.'

'Why? What did you expect?' he answered, laughing at her. 'A bunch of hooligans hurling missiles?'

She laughed with him and rephrased her remark.

'No, of course not. I meant, I was impressed to see how . . .' – what was an acceptable expression for people without a will of their own? – 'how tranquil and contented they were.'

Because I would have expected them to be talking while they sewed and sawed and painted, she thought. Otherwise, the handicrafts might be mail sacks, and the basement a treadmill.

'Tranquil and contented?' a voice cried on a rising note. 'What praise, Phil! What more could you ask?'

The door had opened and Edith walked in, beautifully costumed and coiffured, teeth gleaming on the company.

'Alice and – is it Imogen? Imogen, of course! How nice to meet again so soon.' And she held out a cold white hand to each of them.

She brought tension with her. Though Philip remained affable his easiness had vanished. Alice bristled, and Imogen felt uncomfortable.

'Tea, Edith?' Philip asked, but she refused.

No, thank you so much. She had had tea at home. In Church Street. She had been to a committee meeting earlier that afternoon, and simply dropped in for a chat with Phil. She didn't mean to intrude. Indeed, she had no idea that Alice and Imogen were coming here.

Imogen detected some resentment in this last remark.

'You must both come to tea with *me*,' she said, to Alice. And to Imogen, 'I'm fortunate in owning one of the prettiest houses in Langesby. Early Georgian. I know you would love it.'

She settled down in an armchair and smiled round on them.

Imogen reflected that Edith being amiable was even more petrifying than Edith on the warpath.

'What a fascinating meeting that was yesterday,' she went on. 'I adore Tim and Hal, as you know, but I do think they're on a wild-goose chase with this peculiar little play. And – naturally I didn't say anything in front of George! – but what an extraordinary idea to ask Mary Proctor to take a leading part.'

Alice, who secretly concurred with both remarks, said stiffly, 'Oh, Tim knows what he's doing, and Hal backs him absolutely.'

'Well, we must all hope that Tim has chosen wisely. And it certainly shows how broad-minded you and Hal are. Most of the church people I know would steer clear of a play about black magic, and they certainly wouldn't concur with casting a genuine witch for the part of the wise old woman.'

Alice flushed. Philip compressed his lips. Edith, in seeming innocence, addressed herself to Imogen.

'I do apologize for chattering away when you don't know what I'm talking about, so let me explain. Langesbydale was famous for its witches, and the old tradition lives on. There is still a family in Langesbydale who have carried on witchcraft from mother to daughter right through the female line. And the present incumbent – though possibly the last – is the worthy Mary Proctor.'

'That sort of remark is quite out of place, Edith,' Alice cried indignantly.

Edith insisted. 'But everyone – apart from our dear Imogen, of course – knows that she's the local wise woman of the dale, and her great-grandmother was the last witch to be hanged in Langesby market square. It's no secret.'

'Oh come, Edith,' said Philip uneasily, 'you shouldn't retail local gossip.'

Alice said, trying to keep her temper, 'Mary is a strong character, like many of the old dalesfolk, and has her own way of doing things, but that doesn't mean she's a witch.'

Edith was quite amazed.

'Surely you must have heard tales of unauthorized midwifery, rustic medicines and ointments, healing spells and other peculiarities.'

'Mary is *not* unauthorized,' Alice insisted. 'She was a fully qualified midwife who worked for the local health service and delivered two generations of the dale's babies.'

Edith was enjoying herself.

'When I say *unauthorized* I mean that she has a superstitious hold on the expectant mothers in the dale, who would rather consult her than their doctors or the local hospital.'

'I happen to know from Vera, who lives in Tofthouse,' said Alice, now thoroughly angry, 'that the consultations are minor ones. Homely remedies for morning sickness and suchlike. Mary charges nothing and there is no question of superstitious fear. The dalesfolk simply, and quite rightly in my opinion – and in Hal's opinion too – respect nearly fifty years of experience.'

'But I heard that she has delivered babies *since* her retirement.'

'My dear Alice, my dear Edith,' said Philip, attempting to pacify them. 'Mary Proctor is a person whom everyone holds in high regard . . .'

Alice said, in a high trembling voice, 'I believe I can both refute and explain that particular accusation, Edith. When we first came to Langesby

I was seven months pregnant and we had not had time to make friends. The move had been fraught, I wasn't feeling well, and Hal had to go away almost immediately for a couple of days. The only person we knew was Vera, who had acted as housekeeper to the previous incumbent. Because of my condition and the situation we asked her to stay overnight, and this was fortunate because I went into premature labour.

'There was an influenza epidemic at the time. The doctors were run off their feet and all we could get were answering services, with advice on how to deal with the flu and instructions to leave a message. On her own initiative, Vera sent for Mary Proctor, and Mary came at once. She organized everything and everybody, bullied an ambulance and a bed out of the city hospital, and took me in.'

Imogen instinctively, guessing the end of the story, clasped Alice's hand and glared at Edith.

'They weren't able to save my little daughter, but they saved my life, and I shall never forget what Mary did,' Alice added, slightly hysterically. 'It was a desolate, terrifying time for me and she was my good angel.'

She rounded on Edith, saying, 'And that was not unauthorized mid-wifery, nor witchcraft, nor a superstitious hold over anyone. That was what I call Christian charity and compassion.'

Her face was ravaged. Too much had been revealed.

Imogen rose, helped Alice to her feet, and said without compromise, 'I think we should be going home now. Goodbye, Edith. Thank you so much, Philip.'

Leaving Edith behind, without a demur on her part, for she had gone too far, he escorted them to the gate in silence. There he kissed Alice on the cheek in apology, and managed a personal message aside to Imogen.

'Look, I'm sorry about all this. I have tried, but I can't seem to find the right time or place to get to know you. Let me take you out for dinner where we can talk properly.'

'Thank you,' she replied, coolly, 'but I don't know how long I shall be staying.'

And yet, the invitation drew her, and perhaps her final glance offered him some hope.

'Tell me,' she said to Alice, as they drove back to the vicarage, 'what's the relationship between Edith Wyse and Philip Gregory?'

Recovering from the grief which had silenced her enemy, Alice answered with biting emphasis.

'Hal and I call her "The Widow Wyse". "Black Widow Spider" would be more like it! Apparently the late Mr Wyse was old and rich, so now she's looking round for a young husband. She's years older than he is, and the moment she set eyes on him she stuck her claws into him. It would need a hatchet to separate them now – or a lovely young wife for Phil.'

'How you hate her!' Imogen observed.

Alice checked herself; became contrite.

'I know I should be more charitable. Hal manages to dislike her without making it personal, if you know what I mean. And I do try to be objective, but Edith makes it so difficult . . .'

'She makes it impossible,' Imogen said, and laughed. 'I don't like her either.'

'No one does, apart from Phil. And everyone – except Hal and me and Tim – is slightly afraid of her. Phil is such a wonderful man that it drives me wild to see him tied up in that way. He devotes himself entirely to those youngsters, and I know they need him, but he ought to have a private life too. He's still only in his thirties. He should remarry and have children of his own. And don't think that I haven't tried to find someone for him, and to get him out of her clutches!'

Alice's driving and her expression made Imogen afraid for their safety. 'Car coming!' she warned, just in time.

Alice swerved without blenching, ignored the reproof of a horn blast and a furious V sign, and carried on talking and speeding.

'I must have introduced him to a dozen – well, not a dozen, but you know what I mean – two or three eligible youngish women. And the moment he becomes interested, Edith makes it so difficult for them both – well, you saw her this afternoon – that they give up. That *vampire*' – with tremendous force and reckless cornering – 'would suck the life-blood out of any man!'

She swerved into the vicarage drive and brought them to a sudden halt.

Well, I'm damned! said Imogen to herself, shaken twice over.

Alice did not attempt to get out of her runabout immediately, but sat in sorry contemplation.

'What I don't understand,' she said, thinking aloud, 'is how such a kind, intelligent, attractive man should allow himself to be eaten up in this way. He *is* attractive, don't you think? And so masculine! So healthy and normal and frank. Oh, I know Edith makes herself indispensable at Prospect House, but a wife could do as much and *be* far more.'

Why, you're in love with him, Imogen understood. Not in a gnawing desperate way, because your commitment to Hal would save you from that, but in a *wouldn't it have been lovely if we'd met earlier?* sort of way. You won't lie awake at nights yearning for him, but you'll plan, just as wives in ancient China planned when they reached the age of forty, to choose him a mistress, a substitute for yourself, who will keep him in the fold and fulfil him at the same time. And then the wife you've chosen, like the mistresses they chose, will be as indebted to you as he is to Edith. And you will have won. And Edith will have lost. Now which is more important to you, I wonder? That Philip Gregory should be happy or Edith Wyse should be vanquished?

She remembered Philip's smile, and his comment: *You two have more in common than you might think.*'

She liked him for perceiving the situation and dealing with it so gently. Yes, he was kind and intelligent, attractive, masculine, healthy, normal and frank, but what appealed to Imogen most were his flashes of self-knowledge and the way in which he parried Alice's attempts to present him as a saint.

Then her instinct for self-preservation came uppermost. Whoever committed herself to Philip must surmount the twin barriers of Edith the Evil and Alice the Good and dedicate herself to his life's work, and that was a fearsome undertaking.

NINE

Wednesday

'Have you come by yourself, then?' George Hobbs enquired, as Imogen appeared head first through the open trapdoor. He spoke with some chagrin. 'I thought the vicar was bringing you.'

The small square bell chamber was reached by way of ladder stairs and he held out his hand to assist her. His clasp was warm, firm and impersonal. Imogen was not interested in him either, but she disliked being passed over.

'He won't be long,' she replied briskly. 'The telephone rang as we were leaving and he told me to come on ahead.'

'They can't leave him alone for five minutes,' said George in disgust. He decided that he must show some courtesy to this unwelcome visitor. 'Well, this is it,' he said stiffly, in the tone of a guide who is not used to showing people round. 'This is where the bell-ringers come on Saturdays, or did. And one of them being ninety-two, he might not come again!'

The day had been fine, cold and bright, and the little room was full of evening sun. Above her, Imogen could hear the church clock keeping stately time, as it had done for over two centuries.

'These are the ropes,' said George unnecessarily.

Six blue and green striped ropes were looped up on a metal chandelier of hooks which hung from the ceiling. Motes danced in the dusty air. A long stained-glass window in the wall of the building, irradiated with the last of the light, cast jewels on the wooden floor. A plain glass window opposite enabled the ringers to look down into the body of St Oswald's while screening the congregation from noise.

'This might interest you,' said George hopefully, pointing to a notice on the side wall.

She walked round him to read a brief history of the bells.

                    Isaac Dashfield of Shropshire cast us all 1725
                    Inscriptions
TENOR   My tongue shall Extol the Lord   37 cwt
VI   Blessings on This Church   20 cwt
V   They Shall Prosper that love Thee   13 cwt
IV   John Rush gave me Voice to Praise   13 cwt
III   Peace to this Parish   8 cwt
II   In memory of Marie Arthur 1720–1724   7 cwt

The notice stabilized something in her that had been adrift since Fred
died. There was sense and beauty in the world, after all. Bells had been
cast and named, had rung in or rung out the most important events in
local lives for over two hundred years, and extolled a religion nearly ten
time as old themselves.

'"John Rush gave me Voice to Praise,"' Imogen read, under her breath.
And aloud, over her shoulder, 'They sound like people talking about
themselves.'

'They're a damn sight easier to get on with than most people,' said
George Hobbs. 'They do what they're supposed to do and they don't
make trouble – unless you trouble them.'

His hand moved towards one bell rope, touched it, and retreated.

'You might like to sit here while you're waiting,' he said, and dusted
the wooden window-seat with his handkerchief.

Imogen settled down and observed the coloured lozenges of light
advance and retreat, shorten and elongate over the backs of her hands. She
would have been content to sit in silence, and so would George, but he
felt it incumbent on him to make conversation.

'How are you finding Langesby, then?'

'Oh, I'm – enjoying it.'

'How long are you staying?'

'I'm not sure but I've got lots of things to sort out at home.'

She had no home to go to and there was nothing to sort out, but she
could hardly stay on indefinitely, and Polly's daily visits to the kitchen
coal scuttle were becoming a talking point. Besides, life at the vicarage
was rather like living in a railway station: a constant coming and going of
people, bent on their different purposes and asking for directions. Imogen,
used to long quiet working hours, was chafed by lack of privacy and
oppressed by Alice's good intentions. Furthermore she felt uncomfortable
with Hal, and guessed he would be relieved when she was gone. This
evening, for instance, had begun awkwardly, and now through no fault

of her own she was bothering George Hobbs, whom she observed to be going through the motions of civility whilst wishing he were elsewhere.

He said abruptly, 'Do you know anything about bell-ringing?'

'I'm afraid not – but I do love to hear a peal of bells . . .'

'There's a lot more to it than that,' said George in his forthright fashion.

It sounded like a snub, though he had meant it as a beginning. Silence threatened to oppress them once more.

'What I meant to say was that there's an art to bell-ringing,' he began again, in desperation. 'It's not just a question of pulling a rope. I was sixteen when I started, and it opened a whole new world for me . . .'

He began a monologue while she pondered future plans. His conversation and her reflections ran through and over each other, with the occasional clash of recognition as speech met thought.

. . . If I could find a new place to live it might spark me into life again. If I cared about a place I could set root there. I've never had any roots . . .

'There's a camaraderie among bell-ringers, as you might say, and you can count on it anywhere you go. I could tramp this country end to side – and I have done – and in any tower I introduced myself, they'd give me a rope. "Take hold!" they'd say, as if they knew me. Which, in a way, they do . . .'

. . . Hal Brakespear judges me without knowing me. He thinks I'm frivolous, not worthwhile. But when I'm fully myself, I can perform a sort of magic with women's hats. And I was magic for Fred and he was magic for me, both in ourselves and in our work . . .

'Bell-ringers don't have to be members of the Church. I'm what you might call an uncommitted believer myself. I know there's something grand out there, but I don't know what it is. Mind you, some of the vicar's sermons can strike a spark in me. Now *he* believes, hook. line and sinker. If they burned him at the stake he'd die believing, and tell them a thing or two before he went.'

. . . I believed in Fred. And he believed in me. But I can't find anything to believe in any more.

Imogen sat with her hands in her lap, looking at and through George Hobbs, half hearing, half smiling, and he thought what an excellent listener she was. Most women would have interrupted him long since. The last of the sun, and their conversation, both wordless and spoken, held a certain mellowness.

'What I do know,' said George, 'is that on Sundays, when I'm ringing, I ring with the best of me, body and spirit, and it adds up to something worth hearing, and perhaps that's what it's all about.'

He stopped, aware that she had somehow betrayed him into revealing a secret corner of himself.

'What I mean to say,' he finished curtly, 'is that bell-ringers are a good crowd.'

Purposeful footsteps trod the gravel, marched across the slate slabs, mounted the wooden stairs. Hal Brakespear's balding head rose above the trapdoor, chin thrust out, glasses glinting.

'Sorry about that,' he announced. 'I'm fighting both corners at once, having problems with Mary as well as the health authorities.'

'Is Stevie being turned out of Bethesda?' George asked.

'Yes, I'm afraid so. Another casualty of the present system.'

As if Alice were at his elbow, saying, 'Darling, Imogen will be in the dark about this . . .' he tossed an explanation in her direction.

'Mary Proctor's youngest son. Mentally disturbed. Twenty-eight years old. They're releasing him into the community – meaning into the care of his aged mother and an overworked district nurse – with a regular prescription of tranquillizers.'

'Poor Mary,' said George. 'Not that she'd thank me for saying so.'

Hal's tone and aspect changed. He was at ease with George.

'No, she wouldn't. She'd probably bite your head off to prove that she still had some of her own teeth! It's a pity those children of hers don't do something for her. She worked hard enough for them, by all accounts, and the husband was no good either.'

'They all live too far away,' said George, 'and though Mary needs money as well as moral support she'd neither ask them for it nor accept it.'

With surprising insight, Hal said, 'It's partly her own fault, you know, George. She's an admirable woman, but she must be difficult to deal with at close quarters. I expect the husband, and eventually the children, had to get away from her in order to lead their own lives. Take Stephen, for instance. Alice and I are doing our utmost to help her and she sabotages every move we make.'

George gave a shrug and a short sharp sigh.

Imogen lit up. 'Like Mrs Patrick Campbell,' she said, and quoted, ' "A sinking ship, firing on her rescuers".'

'Yes,' said Hal abruptly. 'And we all do it. One's worst enemy is one's self.'

Imogen wondered unkindly whether he applied this truth to Hal Brakespear as well as to lesser mortals, and if so whether he intended to improve the situation or merely to comment upon it.

'Anyway,' he said to her, 'if you want to see the bells we'd better hurry up about it before the light falls. George and I need to talk, so you won't mind going home by yourself afterwards, will you? It's only down the lane.'

Before she could reply, George, who had been assessing her black-and-white check trouser suit, said abruptly, 'You're too smart to go up aloft. It's a mucky old place. And I'm not sure you should go sightseeing, with the condition it's in.'

Quite suddenly she lost patience with the pair of them, and with her present situation as an unwanted dependant. She spoke with a fierce honesty that had been lacking in life-since-Fred, and in a tone that they had never heard.

'I was told that if I wore old clothes I could see the bells. These *are* old clothes and I *want* to see the bells. And no,' turning on Hal, 'I don't mind going back by myself. I came by myself, if you remember, and I do know where the vicarage is.'

They may be tired of me, she thought, but not half as tired as I am of them. I won't have people patronizing me and organizing me and misjudging me. I shall go back to London as soon as possible, and I certainly shan't be coming here for Christmas. Nor am I putting Polly in a cattery while I share one of Uncle Martin's deadly festivities. She's had enough grief already with my breakdown and this visit. No. Polly and I can share a roast chicken and spend Christmas by ourselves. If she is all I've got then I'll stand by her. And the Brakespears can do what they like with their Elizabethan play, and their idiotic festival, and their local politics, and their gossiping tea parties. I'm having nothing more to do with any of it – or them – ever again. In fact, I'm going to lead my own life.

She gave voice to her thoughts. 'And I shall be leaving on Saturday.'

George looked sideways at her, surprised by information that she had chosen not to volunteer earlier.

'Alice didn't tell me you were going!' said Hal, taken aback.

'She doesn't know yet. I shall tell her this evening.'

Imogen's dreaming air had vanished. She would have liked to be a dragon, and roar and breathe flames. Instead, she sounded grateful and was being ironic.

'You've both done more than enough for me – sorting me out and putting me on the right road – and it's time I stood on my own two feet again. And as Alice has made arrangements for tomorrow, and I shall be busy packing on Friday, if I don't see the bells now I shan't get another chance.' She weighted her argument. 'And you did suggest the idea in the first place.'

95

Her mood was painfully apparent to both men. They exchanged glances which said that when a woman was being unpredictable it was best to humour her.

'Oh, well, in that case we mustn't disappoint you,' said Hal heartily. 'George was only thinking of your safety, you know. And Alice would never forgive me if you had an accident.'

'Right you are, Miss Lacey!' said George, amused. He was quite prepared to fulfil this whim since it would evidently be her last. 'If I lead the way, and the vicar comes behind us, you'll be safe in the middle. There's dry rot in the floorboards. When we get up top just keep your eye on me and watch where I step.'

The tower was claustrophobic and smelt of ancient dust. In the twilight the bells were luminous presences, and Imogen made silent acquaintance with them. There they were, from little Marie Arthur to the imposing tenor bell, dumb of tongue for the moment, but waiting to Extol the Lord.

George laid a loving hand upon him.

'This is Great Isaac,' he said. 'This is my bell.'

Imogen's natural gentleness returned.

'Is he named after Isaac Dashfield, who cast him?'

'I wouldn't know,' said George mildly. 'He was named a long while ago.'

Smiling on him and Great Isaac, she said spontaneously, 'I feel just the same way about the bells as I did about the quilt.'

'Oh, what quilt is that?' Hal asked politely. He was feeling relieved that she would soon be gone, and conscience-stricken lest her sudden departure had anything to do with his lack of empathy.

Imogen clarified her statement.

'I saw a quilt in a crafts shop when I walked over to a place called Haraldstone on Saturday. I've just decided to buy it – if it's still for sale.'

Hal was not interested in the quilt and said, 'Oh, George could tell you tales about Haraldstone. He's got a special stake in Haraldstone, haven't you, George?'

The long brown man stood patiently, looking away from him, saying nothing.

'George is something of a visionary. He sees order where everyone else sees chaos,' Hal continued, thoroughly enjoying his own joke.

George said drily to Great Isaac, 'I'm restoring Crossdyke Street chapel.'

'Not as a place of religion but as a future home and workshop,' said

Hal. 'The chapel has been standing empty for years, and was neglected for years before that, so you can guess what condition it's in. And he's virtually camping in the place while he rebuilds it, despite its reputation and some rather strange neighbours. A hardy fellow is our George – and in more ways than one.'

'What was that you were saying about a quilt, Miss Lacey?' George asked her, restive at being the subject of conversation.

Imogen would have preferred to talk about the chapel but saw that he would not. He was an odd man, an unexpected man. But she had always trusted oddity and the unexpected.

'It was just a feeling I had,' she explained, not caring whether Hal liked it or not, nor what he thought of her for voicing her inmost reflections. 'The quilt means a great deal more than it is. And these are the same,' indicating the weighty silent shapes. 'They mean much more than they are. They're – numinous.'

Hal said, in genial puzzlement, 'Well, perhaps when they're all in working order you may like to come back here and join our merry band of ringers – eh, George?'

George said, speaking to her naturally for the first time, 'We'll put a rope in your hands whenever you care to turn up.'

He reached out and touched the tenor bell gently.

'We'll have them all ringing again,' he promised, and smiled at Imogen. He changed the subject. 'So you found your quilt in Haraldstone? Was it in a shop called Crafty Notions? Ah! I thought as much.'

'It's growing dark. Time we were on our way,' said Hal, whose personal concerns were always more fascinating to him than anything else.

But George continued to speak to Imogen in a friendly, teasing tone.

'Haraldstone is witches' territory, you know. You might have a few weird dreams under that quilt of yours.'

Hal, making his way down the ladder, giving Imogen orders and warning over one shoulder, said, 'Rubbish, George. I have nothing against women of a certain age making fools of themselves if they want to, but don't pretend there's anything more to it than exhibitionism and a great deal of superstitious nonsense.'

TEN

Thursday

Alice accepted Imogen's decision to leave with surprise but few protestations. Possibly Polly's regular visits to the coal scuttle had something
to do with that. Also the vicarage guest list was filling up, and other waifs
and strays were waiting to be sorted out and put on the right road. Imogen's
room would be needed, and for the time being Imogen herself had become
yesterday's good cause.

'Remember that this is only the first of many visits,' Alice said positively
over breakfast. 'We expect you to come for Christmas.' She commanded
her lord. 'Hal! Hal! Wouldn't you love to have Imogen for Christmas?'

'What? Oh, yes. Why not?' he answered from behind the *Daily Telegraph*.

'Hal, dear!'

The balding head and horn-rimmed glasses appeared over the top of
the paper. Alice's eyes stabbed him. He summoned up a welcome.

'We should enjoy having you with us.'

Imogen's excuse was conveyed as skilfully as Alice's invitation.

'That would have been lovely,' she replied, telling a half-truth, 'but
Uncle Martin has already asked me to stay with him. He and my aunt
were always very good to me, and since she died he is so much alone. I
really don't feel I can—'

'Oh, quite right, quite right,' Hal cried, relieved. 'Christmas can be the
loneliest festival in the year for old people.' He sensed his wife's displeasure
and added quickly, 'But you must come next Christmas. We insist!'

'Mary Proctor is a great character,' Alice explained. 'You may find her
slightly forbidding at first, and like all northerners she tends to be out-
spoken, but at heart she's pure gold. She was married to a drifter, who
left her with a brood of children to bring up single-handed, and they've
all done well, except for poor Stephen – and that isn't his fault – but we
really must try to make her see sense over the question of having him
home. I'm sure we could stop it if only Mary would co-operate.'

They were trundling down the dale in the runabout, and Imogen listened with a smile, as she had done in her schooldays. For Alice had made up her mind and was determined that everyone should agree with her.

'He's never been dangerous,' Alice continued, 'though on the other hand his behaviour could be – well – a trifle disturbing . . .' She paused for a moment. 'Of course, all this happened long before we came here, but when you're in touch with people daily, as we are, you soon learn the local history. Apparently, he was an object of derision at Haraldstone school, poor thing, and finally he refused to go there. Mary's youngest daughter was still at home and Mary was still working as a midwife, and they looked after him between them. But as a teenager he would slip out of the house and roam round for miles. Sometimes he'd stand at school gates or at the edge of playing fields, watching the girls.

'No one ever accused him of making a nuisance of himself – indecent exposure or anything of that kind – but the girls and their parents naturally felt uneasy. There were a number of complaints, and that's when he was put into Bethesda. Mary kicked up a terrible fuss, but she was in her sixties and the daughter had left home by then, so part of the reason given for putting him away was that she couldn't cope. Which is why it is so hypocritical of the authorities to decide that in her seventies she is perfectly capable of doing so.'

They glided over a humpbacked bridge, turned left and parked to one side of a steep lane. A rowan tree, brilliant with berries, grew beside the gate. A pen full of ducks greeted them jubilantly.

'Mary's ducks,' said Alice unnecessarily. 'We'll walk down to the house. The lane isn't an easy place for turning, and the engine doesn't like hill-starts.'

Howgill House was a long, eccentric building, with three descending slate roofs, four chimneys, two front doors, one hay-door, seven windows, and a ramshackle glass greenhouse tacked to the near end. A dry-stone wall divided it from the lane, which Imogen now realized was not a public pathway but part of Mary Proctor's estate. Fields ran up and away on all sides. At the back, sycamore and ash provided shelter from the wind, another rowan tree tossed its berries, and grey willows pored over the running stream. The local stones with which the house had been built were wet with recent rain, gleaming blue-grey, beige, honey, umber, chestnut. The house itself stood in silent contemplation, holding and keeping secrets, and Imogen loved it.

'How much of all this belongs to Mrs Proctor?' she asked, indicating the rising land.

'An acre or more. Watch the mud! It's far too big for Mary to run these days, but she'd never admit that. She loves this place, just as she loves Stephen, and what Mary loves she holds and won't let go.'

The paint was flaking but geraniums burned in the windows.

'At first sight it looks like three adjoining cottages,' Imogen observed.

'That's exactly what I said when I first saw it, and Mary told me its history,' Alice explained, picking her way. 'The far end – the two-up two-down part – was built in 1830 and used to be an inn called the Howgill Arms. Then a generation later they extended it – that's the one-up one-down bit. And finally they added a stable and hayloft for the horses, which is now a store room. But it went out of fashion as an inn and became very run down. Mary's father bought it as a bargain price and did it up for her as a wedding present. He was a builder.'

Stone steps led down to a paved walk in front of the house. Alice took them carefully, one at a time.

'Mary only uses one front door. She keeps the other one locked. It's very lonely out here, and at her age that's not a good thing, but she's so independent.'

At eleven o'clock on a watery November morning the isolation of Howgill was marked. Mary Proctor's nearest neighbours were lone farms, barely visible through the mist on the fells. Her only contact with the outside world was the solitary road from Langesby.

'Still, we do what we can for her,' said Alice. 'In fact I have a nice surprise in store. I persuaded meals-on-wheels to call today.' She looked at her watch. 'They come about twelve, I believe, so we've plenty of time to talk, and then she can enjoy a good hot dinner.'

This idea pleased her immensely. Her plump little gloved hand lifted the knocker and rapped twice, softly, imperatively, to be answered at once by a dry North Country voice.

'It's not locked, and I'm taking the loaves out of the oven. You'd best come in.'

The front door opened directly into a large square kitchen with a stone-flagged floor, and the first impression was that of plenty. The air was compounded of delicious smells: the scent of stored apples, dried herbs and flowers, freshly ground spices and newly baked bread. A wide rack of clean ironed bedlinen had been hoisted up to the ceiling. A scrubbed deal table stood in the centre of the room, its complement of plain chairs pushed against it. There were open shelves of preserves, a glass-fronted cupboard displaying pots and potions, and a dresser stacked with blue and white china. Mary's rocking chair had a velvet patchwork cushion on its seat which reminded Imogen of Crafty Notions. On the hearth, in front of the black-leaded kitchen range, lay a winking tortoiseshell cat suckling four tortoiseshell kittens. Mary Proctor herself was tall and spare and strong, wearing a clean flowered overall over a black wool dress, her hair drawn into an old-fashioned bun.

She was a striking old woman and must have been a handsome girl in her prime, but her flaming red mane had turned sandy white, freckles fought with wrinkles for supremacy, and age had dimmed a magnificent pair of sea-green eyes. Still, she stood erect and held her head high, and though plaid slippers comforted her feet, black lace-up shoes stood by the door, highly polished and ready to wear.

Altogether, Imogen could not have thought of a less suitable candidate for meals-on-wheels, and asked herself whether Alice had blundered.

Mary's voice changed, became cordial when she recognized her visitor.

'You'll excuse me if I sounded a bit sharp, Mrs Brakespear, but I thought it was that Matty Hardcastle. She's got nothing else to do but wander round the dale, knocking at folks's doors and wasting their time. The other day I gave her a fresh baked bun with her cup of tea, and she picked all the currants out of it and threw them on the fire. And all she said was, "I never did like currants"! What do you reckon to that for bad manners?'

'I'm afraid poor Matty knows no better,' cried Alice, automatically charitable towards the infirm and unfortunate.

'I reckon different,' said Mary. 'She's brighter than she makes out. She needs straightening up, in my opinion. Well, come on in.' She looked keenly at Imogen, saying, 'And who's this young lady you've brought with you?'

'A dear friend of mine, Mrs Imogen Lacey, who has been visiting us.'

Imogen came forward smiling and would have shaken hands, but Mary was easing the last hot loaf on to a wire tray beside its companions. Now she looked directly at Alice.

'You've always got somebody staying with you,' she said. 'If I didn't know you better I should think you were afraid of your own company.'

Her straight gaze and humorous tone removed the barb from this remark, which Alice chose to treat lightly.

'Mary always teases me about our visitors,' she explained to Imogen, who was wondering whether some truth underlay the remark. 'And how are you, Mary?'

'I've been worse,' she said tersely. 'Pull two chairs forward and sit yourselves down by the fire. It's a cold morning.'

She did not ask them whether they wanted tea but filled a big black kettle from the brass tap and set it on the range. They waited while she warmed a brown pot, fetched three cups and saucers from the dresser, and put six digestive biscuits on a plate. Only when they were sitting together, sipping a strong brew, did she ask briefly, rocking to and fro in her chair, 'So what's all this about?'

Alice began delicately.

'Mr Brakespear and I have been thinking a great deal about the question of Stephen leaving Bethesda . . .'

'It's about time he did,' said Mary outright. 'He should never have gone there in the first place. The lad may be no more than ninepence in the shilling but he's never harmed a living soul and never would.'

She put down her cup and poked the coals in the grate vehemently to emphasize the statement. Her face was set and stern.

Imogen, glancing round covertly, saw that Mary's possessions, though still serviceable like their owner, were as old and worn as she. The impression of abundance was due to the strength of her spirit and the labour of her hands, but Alice was impervious to such fine points.

'It isn't a question of his harming anyone. Mary. As you say, he wouldn't do that, and in any case he's on a strict medical regime . . .'

'Drugged to keep him half alive. That's what you mean, isn't it? I'm a trained nurse, remember. I do know what goes on.'

'Mary, we all realize what a wonderful person you are, but Hal and I think that it will be too much for you to look after Stephen.'

Mary Proctor spoke fiercely.

'He's my son. And I've got nobody else to care for. I'm a daleswoman, Mrs Brakespear, and until they retired me I brought two generations of the dale into this world. I've worked hard all my life, but now I'm old and poor nobody wants me. I'm on the scrap heap. How would you like to wake up every morning, with nothing to look forward to – bar dying?'

Alice's honest blue eyes acknowledged the justice of this attack, yet she persisted in the course she and Hal thought right.

'Mary, I do understand how you feel, believe me.'

'And you can believe *me*,' Mary retorted, 'when I say that my mind's made up.'

This reaction had been anticipated during private pillow talks at the vicarage, so they had thought out the next step. Alice gave way on one argument in order to win another.

'Well, perhaps we can find a middle course and bring about the change gradually,' she suggested. 'Supposing that Stephen came home just for weekends at first? And then, if all goes well, you can increase the amount of time he stays with you.'

'Bethesda said nothing to me about that,' Mary said, watching her closely.

'No, I know they didn't,' Alice replied, glancing away, 'but we could put the idea forward, and Hal can be very persuasive and effective.'

About as persuasive and effective as a blow on the head with a heavy instrument, Imogen thought, and suppressed a smile.

Mary gave a short sharp sound, something between a scoff and a laugh.

'Mrs Brakespear, Bethesda want to get rid of Stevie. They want him to go soon and they want him to go for good. You can take it from me that they won't be bothered with half-measures, no matter what the vicar says.'

'But surely, as a Christian institution, they won't refuse an appeal to their humanity . . .'

'Oh, of course they will!' said Mary contemptuously. 'Let me tell you something, Mrs Brakespear. It isn't love and Christianity that makes this world go round, it's money and self-interest. The truth of the matter is that somebody high up has told Bethesda to pare its costs to the bone, and that's exactly what they intend to do, whether anybody likes it or not. So you may as well save your breath to cool your porridge.'

Alice made another effort.

'Well, of course, we can't promise anything but . . . Mary, my dear, look at the practical side – and this is the second important matter we should raise – Howgill House, snug and welcoming though you make it, is very isolated. There are no amenities nearer than Langesby, and buses are infrequent. And then, you have always kept yourself to yourself – in a private way, I mean, not in your public capacity as a midwife – so apart from the community nurse, who else will call? What will Stephen do with himself all day?'

'There's plenty to do,' said Mary vigorously. 'He can feed the hens and ducks, and help me round the house and in the garden. There's plenty to do.'

'But you will have to be with him all the time. He cannot – this is no criticism of Stephen – be relied upon to do anything without supervision.'

'That won't bother me. I've looked after folk all my life.'

'But he's been used to having lots of people round him, and various recreational facilities to keep him occupied.'

'Well, if all else fails,' said Mary sarcastically, 'he can watch the television in the parlour. I hadn't got a television when he was little.' In vindication of this extravagance, she said, 'And don't think *I* bought it! It wouldn't bother me if I didn't see it from one year's end to the next. My sons and daughters gave it to me as a present when I retired – and that was more to do with salving their consciences than caring about *me!*'

She stood up to indicate that the interview was over. 'You need say no more, Mrs Brakespear. I appreciate that you and your husband mean well, but my mind's made up. Bethesda don't want Stevie, and I do. So that's that.'

Despite this warning, Alice was about to make a final effort when a small green van slithered down the lane and came to a halt. The sound of voices and a brisk banging and clashing drew Mary first to the window and then to the door, upon which a portly woman in a green uniform was about to knock.

Alice's conversation became fragmented.

'Oh my goodness – it's only half-past eleven, I haven't had time to tell – Mary dear, I was about to mention – I thought it might help if . . .'

'Meals-on-wheels, dear!' the green lady cried confidently.

Mary gave Alice a look which said, Judas! and barred the entrance of this intruder, who was trying to walk past her into the house.

'I'll just bring these in, dear,' said the green lady, of the covered dishes.

'Oh no you won't,' Mary said. 'I haven't invited you. And I'm not your dear. You'll stop where you are.'

The green lady had dealt with awkward customers before. She lifted the cover. 'Braised liver, cabbage and mashed potato, dear,' she offered enticingly. 'With jam roly-poly and custard to follow.'

'Put that lid back on and let me tell you something!' Mary commanded. 'Can you smell the bread in my kitchen? I baked those loaves this morning. I bake every week. I'll lay a pound to a penny that you buy yours sliced from the supermarket.'

The WVS lady may have been misjudged, but her open mouth did not correct the impression.

'I cook a good hot meal for myself once a day,' Mary continued, 'and I mean a good one. That cabbage –' pointing to a pale disheartened mound – 'has had all the goodness boiled out of it. And the liver's curled at the edges.'

The green lady hesitated. Then, catching sight of Alice in the background, she said in a gush of relief, 'Oh, Mrs Brakespear, perhaps you can persuade—'

Mary said clearly, in a message to them both, 'Nobody will persuade me to do anything I don't want. I didn't ask you to call and I don't want you to come back. Is that understood?'

Alice was saying, 'Mary dear, I'm terribly sorry. Terribly sorry, Mrs Kean. All my fault, I'm afraid.'

The green lady lifted her chin an inch to show that she was undefeated, and without speaking to either of them returned to the van. The driver shrugged at her and mimed good-natured despair. She ignored his sympathy. He shrugged again, banged the doors shut, and backed the van cautiously and with difficulty out of the lane.

Mary remained where she was, arms folded, unforgiving, by the open door. She was waiting for her other visitors to leave. Imogen gulped the rest of her tea and stood up. She was sorry for everyone concerned, and yet she wanted to laugh.

Alice, very pink, and busy with her gloves, said, 'I'm sorry if I've offended you, Mary. I was only trying to help.'

Mary did not reply at once, but as they sidled past her she delivered the *coup de grâce*.

'I know you acted out of kindness, Mrs Brakespear, but it isn't the road to heaven that's paved with good intentions, it's the road to hell. Think on.'

'I do beg your pardon,' Alice said stiffly. 'I didn't mean to interfere.'

Mary Proctor merely nodded her head, and repeated, 'Think on.'

Then she shut the door behind them.

They were nearly home before Alice recovered herself sufficiently to break a mutually embarrassed silence.

'I know that Mary must seem abrasive on first acquaintance, but I can tell you from experience that she's pure gold at heart – oh, pure gold!'

ELEVEN

Friday

Haraldstone was wide awake at half-past ten on the following morning when Imogen sat in one bay window of the Copper Kettle, drinking excellent coffee. The watercolours on its walls were surprisingly good. She could hardly ask the waitress why a small café in an unimportant village should have such high standards, but she did wonder. Her half-hour of procrastination over, she paid her bill and walked resolutely down the street; past the shining fish and chip bar which was beginning to heat its fryers; past Helme's Ironmongers and the health food shop named Back to Nature; past the minuscule Hunwick's Supermarket, the greengrocer's, the baker, the butcher, and the hairdresser and beauty salon where Jon and Deirdre worked on a client apiece. She turned down the passageway into the Catwalk and stopped in front of Crafty Notions.

Her quilt was no longer in the window, which was devoted this week to brilliant sweaters, captivating bobble hats and multicoloured wool scarves. She tried to peer through the gaps in the display, but could not see it anywhere. Finally she inhaled a deep breath of courage, and on the exhalation opened the door and was announced by the jingling bell.

A customer had asked to look at something on the top shelf, and Sadie Whicker was saying, 'I'll just get the steps' when Imogen seized the opportunity. She strode forward, reached up two long arms, brought down the box, and presented it in a graceful gesture of reconciliation.

'What it is to be tall!' said Sadie, knowing, accepting, beaming up at her.

Through the partly opened kitchen door Imogen could see a plume of steam spouting from the kettle and two mugs standing by, complete with brightly tagged tea-bags. Someone was evidently expected, but she did not intend to stay long.

Sadie said to the customer, 'These are the only silk scarves I have left. I'm waiting for more to come in, but I doubt they'll be here in less than a week. Will you be staying that long? No? Well, have a ponder on these.

If you'll both excuse me for a minute . . .' And she whisked away.

While the customer considered colours and patterns, Imogen scanned the quiltless shop.

Sadie was back again, glossy eyes roguish.

'I can't make up my mind between the sage and the violet,' said the customer.

'Take your time,' said Sadie placidly. 'There's all the time in the world, you know.' Over her shoulder she said to Imogen as if a question had been asked, 'Yes, your quilt's ready for you.'

In the instant that Imogen's mouth opened slightly and Sadie lowered one eyelid, she knew that her return had been a foregone conclusion, and that the second mug was awaiting her mid-morning arrival.

The customer, intent on the box of scarves, said laughing, 'Oh, I can't decide. I just love them both. I'll be crazy and have both of them.'

'The best decision in the world,' Sadie answered smoothly. 'It's always nicer to have both. Twice as good, in fact. How would you like to pay? Yes, American Express will be fine. Thank you. I won't be a moment.'

The huge black cat lying on the basket chair yawned majestically and stretched out an unhurried paw. The customer became ecstatic, hands uplifted.

'Oh, my word, I didn't see *you* back there. Aren't you gorgeous?'

Two yellow slits acknowledged the compliment. Then he closed them and yawned again.

Imogen said, 'He's called Tarquin.'

'But what a wonderful name! And doesn't it suit him? Hello there, Tarquin!'

The cat turned his back on her and went back to sleep.

'He's got no manners this time of day,' said Sadie blithely, offering the semi-transparent slip. 'He's a night-lifer!' The customer laughed again. 'Now if you could sign here, please. Oh, what lovely handwriting. Nowadays everyone scrawls. I know I do. You'll be delighted with the scarves. They're Milia Godden designs, hand-blocked and original. Natural colours, of course. She makes her own dyes. I'm slipping my card into the bag in case you come this way again. Yes, these little carriers do look striking, don't they? A very talented young man designs my logos and so forth.'

Her remarks were addressed as much to Imogen as to the customer: friendly prods and pointers in the direction she thought right. Still sensitive from being organized by Alice, Imogen was careful to draw the line between her needs and other people's desires, but in this case they appeared to coincide.

'We have a lot of craftspeople in this village, particularly in the Catwalk, and every one of us is self-employed and still managing to keep afloat. I always say that we may not be rich but we lead rich lives. There we are, then. Enjoy the scarves. I hope to see you again, some day, so I'll say *au 'voir*, not *adieu*! Not at all. Thank *you*.'

The doorbell echoed her farewell.

Imogen, who had been rehearsing explanations and apologies all the way from Langesby, decided that none was necessary, and smiled instead.

Sadie held out both hands and Imogen shook them.

'How about the mug that cheers?' Sadie asked. 'Strawberry spice today.'

'Thank you, I'd love to, but I've already been cheered at the Copper Kettle. By the way, they have some rather good watercolours for sale.'

'Frank Hedge and Beth Lawler. They live together. Both local artists. Shoo, Tarquin! Sit down, Imogen.'

'I can't quite make Haraldstone out,' said Imogen, sinking into the cat's warm hollow. 'I should have thought it too small to generate much money, but the quality of the shops and the number of craft shops is impressive.'

'We all specialize, that's why,' said Sadie. 'Nobody trespasses on anyone else's territory. We're very old-fashioned here. The butcher only sells local meat. The baker bakes all his own bread. The sweet shop sells nothing but sweets. And so on. But we craftspeople take every opportunity that's offered and make a few more for ourselves. You name it – we're there. National trade fairs, local craft fairs, Saturday markets . . .'

They picked up the end of each other's sentences and expanded on them.

'That's how I started Crazy Hats when we left Manchester and went to London to seek our fortunes. Selling from a stall in Camden Lock market. The stallholders became friends. Almost like a family.'

'It's a tight little clique here, too, and we attract regular customers from a wide area. They're our bread and butter. The tourists provide the jam.'

'I produced the bread. Fred made the jam. Not much jam, but always special.'

'The word spreads. Customers tell their friends. We recommend each other. And so we become known. Our names are respected in the craft world.'

'But Alice – my friend – never mentioned Haraldstone as a possibility when we were talking.'

'We have a reputation for being different here. Some people like everything to be the same . . .'

'Alice wanted me to settle in Langesby. She said they need exciting hats.'

'The burghers' wives wouldn't buy them, and if they did they wouldn't know how to wear them,' said Sadie tartly. 'Langesby's too big and too provincial for specialized crafts. A nice curio shop is more the Langesby style. China mugs engraved with pictures of the old town, and a pile of tea towels sporting St Oswald's church spire . . .'

Imogen glanced at her quickly, but Sadie's face was bland.

'Have you seen the Listeners lately?' she asked, black eyebrows raised.

'Oh yes. I came here on the nine o'clock bus from Langesby, and walked up the hill especially to say hello to them.'

'Just hello?' Amused but interested.

Imogen smiled, and answered in the same half-joking manner.

'No. I went to ask them if they would allow me to live in Haraldstone.'

Sadie's expression became inscrutable. Imogen hurried on.

'Fred and I had a flat near King's Cross station, but the lease was running out, and when Fred died and I was ill my uncle sold it for me. I have the capital. And though I've always worked from home I'd be prepared to take on a small shop if I couldn't rent a flat. I wondered – are there any properties to let in Haraldstone?'

'Possibly, but you only hear of them by word of mouth.' With a sly smile.

'What are the rents and rates like?'

'Modest. To match the amenities. And you can take short-term leases. But they aren't in business for charity, even in Haraldstone. Have you got a car? No? Well, we're a long way out, here. You'd have to learn the bus timetable by heart, buy a bicycle, or ride shanks's pony until you found a friend who had transport.'

'You said the Catwalk needed a hat shop . . .'

'Yes, it does. But. Big but. First time out with a shop? And in a strange place?' Sadie wondered. 'You'd be taking a big risk.'

'Fred and I could always take risks, and I believe I can do it again. By myself. For myself,' said Imogen. The statement was also a vow. 'Besides, I've lived in the North Country before. I went to boarding school in Yorkshire and worked in Lancashire. It doesn't seem strange to me. In fact, I feel at home here.'

Sadie said, warming her hands on the mug, 'I'll keep my eyes and ears open.'

'You see,' said Imogen, trying to explain her decision to them both, 'I feel there's something here which is missing in most places. I felt that when I first saw the village – from the top of Haraldstone Hill. And then again when I came down into the main street. It seems – and this may be my imagination, but I feel it so strongly – it seems to have preserved all the old values. Like a museum. Except, of course, blessedly, it's not a bit like a museum because it's a working community.'

Sadie made a sound between a snort and a sigh: derisive but sympathetic.

'Even museums change. Collect dust. Lack funds. Decay. The trouble with Haraldstone is that it won't be allowed to stay the same. Right now, this valley is one of the places that people talk about in hushed voices. Still unspoiled, they say. Then, naturally, they tell their best friends – who tell theirs. Mrs Two-Scarves from Michigan, this morning, will broadcast me – and I hope she does because I have to pay my way – but a gold carriage attracts robbers.

'Haraldstone's days are numbered, Imogen. We haven't seen a charabanc park here yet, but this is a small country and unspoiled places are at a premium. You can bet your bottom dollar that within the next decade the big boys will move in all along the dale, building chic pubs and smart garages and giant supermarkets and stylish housing estates. And that will put paid to all our local shops. The craftspeople will last a bit longer, but we're only human. We can be persuaded to sell out or join in, and some of our ideas can be mass-marketed.

'In fact I've no doubt that, in the end, even the Listeners will be taken over by some charitable body bent on their preservation. As if they needed help! They've lasted long enough without us! Oh yes, I can see it quite clearly, with the wood chopped down to make a car park, and a couple of neat green litter bins, and a nice green-painted noticeboard giving you details of its age and possible use . . .'

Sadie finished off her strawberry spice, lifted her mug in farewell salute, and said, 'Until that Doomsday we're enjoying the benefits of being over-looked.'

They sat in responsive silence. She changed the subject.

'So you're leaving us for the time being?'

'Yes. On the morning train.'

'What are you going back to, and what will you do when you get there?'

'I'm going back to a rented bedsitter, giving it a quarter's notice, and finding out where to rest my caravan next. If not here, then elsewhere.'

Sadie gave her a shrewd look.

'You *have* changed. You were waiting for a miracle when I last saw you,' she observed, 'and they're hard to come by.'

111

'Yes. I'm not sure how it happened but I've decided not to let people take charge of me any more.'

'You've taken charge of yourself again?'

'You sound like my therapist,' said Imogen, smiling. 'Yes, I suppose I have.'

Sadie pulled a long box from beneath a curtained recess and said, 'Here's your quilt. Two hundred pounds, I think we agreed?'

Imogen presented her Mastercard and Sadie admired her signature.

'Two customers in one morning with an elegant hand!' she remarked. 'But then yours *would* be elegant. You like things exactly so. It's a strength and a weakness, like everything else. Perfection needs chaos. Traditionalism needs new blood. That's why you like this quilt. You're law-abiding. It's a rule-breaker.'

Imogen said, writing on the back of an old Crazy Hats card, 'This is my temporary address. If you hear of anything in Haraldstone will you let me know?'

'It'll be a quick phone call if I do,' said Sadie enigmatically. 'I don't write letters. And don't count on anything. Keep your options open.'

'Oh, I shall,' said Imogen. 'I've given life an invitation. Let's see what it offers.'

'That's the way to be.'

To shake hands would be too formal. To embrace would be too familiar. They nodded at each other and smiled in understanding. Sadie had the last word.

'We'll say *au 'voir*, then, not *adieu*. Enjoy the quilt. Good dreams!'

The shop bell jingled as Imogen left. Carrying the box as if it were a precious child in her arms, she crossed the road to catch her bus.

FAMILIARS

TWELVE

January

The church hall, built at the end of the previous century, was an unwieldy building of blackened brick, designed to accommodate any public function from WI meetings and seasonal parties to jumble sales. It managed to provide every necessary convenience while making it inconvenient to use. The two lavatories were located on the first floor up a long worn flight of concrete stairs. The kitchen, if such a description could be used of a crazed glazed sink and a febrile gas stove, was placed at the back of the hall, so that refreshments had to be carried past a long queue of people who had little room to manoeuvre. The stage was a modest platform with steps up either side and mean curtains. Piles of ramshackle folding chairs were stacked against the walls. Dressing rooms were non-existent.

'I've tackled worse,' said George Hobbs philosophically.

'And I've tackled better,' Timothy Rowley replied. 'Far, far better.'

Though dressed for an informal occasion, he was as immaculate as ever, and wore a dashing silk neck-scarf. George, on the other hand, was informal and rather untidy. They were unlike, and yet there was an affinity between them.

'Would you be so kind as to stand at the back of the hall, my dear fellow,' said Timothy, 'and tell me if you can hear me?'

He mounted the platform in a leisurely dignified manner, tilted back his head slightly, surveyed an imaginary audience, and gave splendid voice.

' "How now, neighbour! You look toward the ground as well as I: you muse on something?" '

His delivery was excellent and he must have known it, yet he paused and said humbly, 'How was that?'

'I can hear every word,' said George, impressed.

Timothy's voice dropped to a furtive softness. He cringed and rubbed his hands together slowly as he spoke.

' "I am, as you know, neighbour, a man unmarried, and lived so

115

unquietly with my two wives, that I keep every year holy the day wherein I buried them both . . ."'

George laughed, and Timothy smiled in acknowledgement.

'Every word again,' said George, admiring.

'Yes, the acoustics aren't so bad,' said Timothy. 'In fact better than I dared hope. Thank you for listening.'

'I think it's mostly you, mind you,' said George, coming forward. 'You've done this sort of thing before, I take it?'

'A little. A little. I prefer to direct rather than to act, but occasionally I have taken part, and I flatter myself I have a notion of how it should be done.'

They were pleased with each other.

George, returning to business, said, 'This stage is too small. The actors will be on top of each other.'

Timothy agreed. 'And people always look so enormous on a narrow platform.' He put one finger to his forehead and thought. 'An apron stage would be the answer – don't you think? – with the audience in a horseshoe round it? But we must bear in mind that we can't fix up anything permanent because the hall is in general use.'

'We could improvise an apron stage,' said George, narrowing his eyes to perceive the vision more clearly. 'If they'll give us a day or so beforehand to set it up, and another to clear it away when the play's over. Yes, I can fix that up.' He added, with a little grin, 'What do you think about those curtains?'

Timothy stared disparagingly at the hangings of limp blue rep.

'Personally, I should like to incinerate them. As they are not our property I suggest we roll them up and hide them somewhere. On the other hand, we do need something. What about wings?'

George said, 'No problem. I can knock them up in five minutes. But the hall's a different kettle of fish.' He mused on bad design and worse management. 'The kitchen's in the wrong place, and they should have put that hatch in the middle of the wall.'

'I'm afraid,' said Timothy, as bland as a baby, 'we can do nothing about the wretched kitchen and its misplaced hatch.'

They understood each other. George nodded and spoke tersely.

'I shall need a fair amount of wood. Is the vicar supplying that?'

'I'm sure he will raise funds, or,' with an appreciative chuckle, 'involuntary donations.'

'Then I'll raise an involuntary assistant or two,' said George, smiling. 'The chairs . . .'

Timothy indicated with a beautiful gesture of despair their hardness, ugliness and general inadequacy.

'We can't do anything about the chairs,' said George flatly, in his turn. He gave a wry smile. 'The audience'll have to take their chances on *them* – as well as paying for them.'

'Aching bums!' said Timothy joyfully. Then in all seriousness, 'But we must keep the audience's thoughts on the play rather than their behinds.'

'Advise them to bring cushions with them – or hire cushions out at the door and make another pound or two that way.'

'We must not seem *too* mercenary. I recollect being somewhat *harsh* with Hal Brakespear on that point.'

'And the walls could do with a coat of paint. There's nothing worse than dingy surroundings for putting people off.'

'My dear fellow, let us be frank. The entire place should be demolished, redesigned and rebuilt, but this is not within our compass.'

'We can do a lot with lighting, mind you.'

'Ah yes. And we do *need* to create a totally different atmosphere. This hall tells me somewhat forcibly that it has no vanities – to which I can only suggest that it should cultivate several and as soon as possible!'

'I was thinking,' said George, 'that the vicar has a wonderful means of – I can't quite think of the right expression – screwing things out of people – if you'll excuse the phrase . . .'

'Persuading them to part with far more than they had intended?' Timothy suggested. 'Yes, indeed. His wife is also a skilful persuader but she uses her gift with insidious grace. He is inclined to be precipitate. You were saying?'

'Look how he's scraped up funds for the church. I mean, to collect the best part of £80,000 when nobody's interested you've got to be pretty ruthless.'

'Oh, he is. He is. What a good thing, I always think, that he's on the side of God and the law. Otherwise we should have a master criminal in our midst.'

George was meditating, hands in trouser pockets, head bent, his shoe absently scuffing out a scrap of silver paper that was trapped between two floorboards.

'*He* could get us the chairs,' said George, convinced, 'and the paint. We can't rebuild the hall, as you say, but we could make it a hell of a sight better. And we've got six months in which to do it. What's more, it would benefit everyone else as well as ourselves. Do you think we should put the idea to him?'

Timothy looked closely at his fellow conspirator, and said affably, 'What a thoroughgoing scoundrel you are, George. I'm delighted to know you better.'

George gave a small grim smile to indicate that he felt the same about Timothy.

'Anyway,' he said, picking up the silver scrap, rolling it into a ball and aiming it at a fire-bucket full of sand and cigarette ends, 'I'd best be going. I've taken today off work so I can get on with the chapel lighting, and I mustn't waste time.'

'How is the chapel coming along?'

'In stits and farts, as they say. I've been at it for three years now. I have to earn enough to buy materials, as well as to keep myself. And I'm self-employed, which means that I can't turn a job down. So if I've got the money I haven't the time, and vice versa. And winter means that light goes early, and heating costs more.'

Timothy said, musing, 'A dream is an expensive commodity, but you are privileged to have one. Without a dream, where would any of us be? I admit that I dream of producing this play so well that the playwright will be deservedly acclaimed – and, of course, my humble championship acclaimed with him!'

His following thoughts, spoken aloud, and in complete trust that the words would not be repeated, conveyed how close he and George Hobbs had become.

'Your vision and mine, George, are modest achievable things. Think how wild and improbable some others are. Hal Brakespear dreams of restoring the Christian faith to its original simplicity and St Oswald's to its former glory. His wife dreams that when Hal achieves all this the church authorities will – for some reason as yet unclear – make him a bishop. And then she will become what she should be – a bishop's wife.'

Mentally, he surveyed their circle of acquaintance.

'Phil Gregory dreams of being publicly honoured for his good works, and any past stain – deserved or undeserved – removed from his character. Edith Wyse dreams that if she makes herself indispensable to him he will marry her. What price would you give for any of their chances?'

George shrugged, unable to judge, but doubtful of the odds.

'Desperate and deprived people do not dare to dream, or do not know how to,' Timothy continued, 'and some – like that long slim lass with the sad face – have lost one dream and are seeking another.'

He switched from contemplation to gossip.

'What happened to Imogen Lacey, by the way? Her departure seemed rather abrupt. Phil said she had been invited for Christmas but she never showed up, and Alice has said nothing about her return. So strange when we did our best to make her welcome. I suppose you haven't heard anything?'

'Why should I?' said George laconically. 'If you want my opinion she looked more of a loner than a joiner, to me, and there might have been friction between her and Alice. Very likely it was a question of the irresistible force and the immovable object. I've got the greatest respect for Alice but she will have her own way, and Miss Lacey's got a stubborn chin.'

This was a long speech for George, and having uttered it he seemed to regret it. Amused, Timothy asked, 'Why do you call her *Miss* Lacey? She was a married, or rather widowed, lady.'

George shrugged.

'I don't know. Miss Lacey suits her. And she acts like a single woman. Anyway it doesn't matter now, one way or the other, does it?'

Timothy sighed.

'A pity,' he said to himself. 'I felt she had much to give, once she found herself.'

A short pause. George said nothing.

'Ah well! These delightful creatures think their own thoughts and go their own ways. All we can do is put a blessing on the path they follow, and hope they choose the right one. The pity of it is that they may sometimes judge unwisely, or be outwitted by a partner to the darkness in themselves, if they do not find the right guidance.' He paused for a while, remembering. He said, 'I once knew a girl very like Imogen Lacey. In my youth. At Cambridge.'

Another pause. George stared up at the soiled ceiling. Timothy roused himself.

'Still, that's old history and of no interest to anyone but myself. Let's lock up this mausoleum and return the keys, shall we?'

THIRTEEN

February

'It's the most provoking thing,' said Alice at the vicarage breakfast table, reading Imogen's letter for the second time, 'but she always was impetuous and unpredictable. Hal, will you listen to me for a moment, please? I need your advice.'

He came reluctantly from behind his morning newspaper and peered at her.

'And yet who would have thought this of Imogen? She kept us at arm's length over Christmas and New Year, with a pretty thank-you letter and a seasonal card – oh, and very nice presents I must say, but still . . . And now, without warning, she writes to say that she has taken my advice – which indeed she has not, and well she knows it! – and she will be back here some time this month.'

'Your friend Imogen is coming back here this month?' Hal repeated. He concentrated. This would impinge on him.

He asked defensively, 'You mean – she is coming to stay with us again?'

'No, no. And that's the extraordinary thing. Three months ago she disappeared into the blue with some nonsensical explanation about having *found herself* – that was the phrase she used at the time, and I must say I thought it rather a pretentious expression, although I accepted it, of course. And now she has reappeared just as suddenly, having settled her affairs in a highly secretive manner, without asking for consultation or advice, and presents us with a *fait accompli*. She's packing up and leaving London for good, presumably with that untrained alleycat, and investing all her money in a new business here.'

'A new business?' Hal was mystified.

'Surely you remember that Imogen had a business before her breakdown?'

He delved into the past, produced 'Funny Hats!' and immediately pronounced judgement on it. 'Well, she'll never make a living in Langesby as a milliner. It's a luxury trade and I said so at the time.'

'She isn't *coming* to Langesby. She's renting a shop in *Haraldstone* of all places. Parkinson's Sweet Shop. You know the one. In that little court called the Catwalk. I remarked on the windows being so dusty and wondered whether it had closed. And later on I asked Vera about it . . .'

'I don't remember any sweet shop.'

'Yes, you do. It's near the Italian restaurant where Julia took us for dinner in December. A poky old-fashioned place on the corner. And though you may not remember it, I do. Vividly. Imogen says she's taken it on a five-year lease and it was amazingly cheap. Well, the price might have amazed Imogen but it wouldn't have amazed me. It's probably full of dry rot. Vera told me that the previous owner, old Miss Parkinson, never made a decent living there – and Vera said she knew why.'

He looked longingly at his newspaper, but muttered, 'Oh yes?'

'Vera says that the shops in Haraldstone are run by witches, and they have a sort of freemasonry between them. So if you're not one of them you don't prosper.'

Hal became alert. This comment sounded as though his wife had strayed from the straight and narrow path of truth, and he marched her briskly back.

'Vera is an excellent woman, but prone to gossip rather than to getting her facts right. Does she mean that this sweet shop was the *only* business in Haraldstone not run by a witch?'

Alice had suffered this kind of inquisition before, and murmured, 'Oh dear!' to herself.

'Does she, for instance, include the restaurant where we dined?' Hal continued. 'I must say that Mario seemed like a straightforward Italian Roman Catholic to me.'

'Oh no, not the restaurant . . .'

'And Helme the ironmonger can't be a witch.'

'Well, *most* of the shops, then,' Alice cried, annoyed.

But Hal was in pursuit of accuracy.

'Neither is the butcher nor the baker a witch. They're both bell-ringers.'

'Oh, well, never mind all that,' said Alice, defeated. 'I was simply saying that poor Miss Parkinson couldn't make a living in Haraldstone.'

'Well, there are more likely reasons for that than witchcraft. She might not have been very good businesswoman. The three businesses I mentioned are all family run, and have been there for half a century.'

Alice swam resolutely against the tide of his attention.

'The only way the poor woman could resolve her financial problems was to die.'

Hal raised his eyebrows.

'Of natural causes, of course,' said Alice quickly. 'I am not suggesting for a moment . . . and anyway they're not real witches . . . but still, I should have advised Imogen to have nothing to do with that shop.'

Here she began to read the letter for a third time, and Hal was able to return surreptitiously to his newspaper.

'And who's going to buy hats in Haraldstone?' Alice asked the universe. 'No. In my opinion Imogen has made a grave mistake – not for the first time! – and before she knows it she'll find herself bankrupt among strangers.'

Her crusading spirit and warm heart triumphed for the moment over the wound to her feelings and self-esteem.

'Oh, but we mustn't let that happen. We must do something about it, Hal. Hal! Are you listening?'

'No,' he replied honestly, 'I'm trying to read my paper.'

Still, he lowered the *Telegraph* grudgingly because his wife's judgement had once again gone astray and she must be set right.

'My dear Alice, there's nothing we *can* do about it. If she hasn't asked for our advice it's because she didn't want it. And if she's completed all the legal transactions then there's no point in offering it anyway.'

'But such an old friendship, going back over so many years . . .'

'I'd never even *heard* of this friendship before last October. I didn't know the girl existed until she turned up here.'

Alice corrected him with dignity. 'One may be out of touch for a long time and still cherish fond memories. I remain loyal to old friends.'

He humphed.

'Evidently, she doesn't feel as deeply as you do.'

Alice's tone sharpened.

'So I'm to accept a situation of which I strongly disapprove, and say nothing?'

'Either that or lose her friendship altogether. It's up to you, my dear. I don't mind either way. If you really want my advice, I should send her our joint good wishes, suggest she comes to tea some time, and let it go at that.'

Alice's fear and anger burst forth.

'How can I? Haraldstone is the entirely the wrong place for Imogen. She needs a stable environment, and friends who can exercise common sense and restraint and be a good influence. Haraldstone is full of highly unsuitable people, and Imogen is far too impressionable.'

'You can't judge an entire village by a handful of cranks,' he said. 'I'm sure the majority of them lead ordinary decent existences. Don't forget that George Hobbs lives in Haraldstone.'

'I should hardly call George Hobbs a good influence. He's just as peculiar as the rest of them, in his own way.'

'George is an honourable man who has my liking and respect,' said Hal sternly.

His tone was final.

'As for Imogen Lacey, she is your friend, not mine, you must decide what to do about her, and I'll abide by your decision. That's my last word on the matter.' And he shielded himself from further interruptions with the *Telegraph*.

Alice sat for some moments in silence. Two tears slid down her comely face. She wiped them slowly away and sat looking into her handkerchief before tucking it back in her cardigan sleeve. Then she sighed, folded Imogen's offending letter, slipped it into a pocket of a capacious leather handbag, and began to make up her shopping list.

Good Luck or New House Card for Imogen she wrote at the top of the page, in her legible straightforward hand.

FOURTEEN

Sunday, 27 February

Imogen thought that the birds sang more sweetly at the close of a winter day, but she was in love with her new life and so heard with the ears of love, which can mislead. She had virtually camped at the shop since the previous Monday: cleaning, decorating, planning the layout of the work area, unpacking and arranging her furniture.

Her dealings with Alice had been carefully thought out and her timing shrewdly judged. In order to circumvent kindly interference from the vicarage she had kept the date of her removal vague, and given herself a week's grace before Alice could catch up with her. In all her recent decisions she knew that she had changed the course of their friendship irrevocably. For her mentor, having played a leading role so far, was unlikely to relish a walk-on part as an old acquaintance. And in reply to Imogen's official card, informing her that from the first of March her new address would be as follows, telephone to be reconnected shortly, Alice had sent an ornamental answer to await her supposed arrival.

A rainbow, arching hopefully over a rose-covered cottage, carried the wish that Imogen should be happy in her new home. A brief note, written in her friend's indomitable hand, indicated the degree of hospitality and intimacy Imogen might expect from her in the future, and the gravity of her displeasure.

You secretive little thing! Must recommend your hat shop to all my friends. Do come to tea some time when you have settled in. Love and best wishes from us both.
    Alice and Hal.

Imogen felt sorry, guilty, but mostly relieved.

Yet despite her secrecy, the local grapevine had been busy. A little handful of interested notes, also slithering through the letterbox, showed

125

that Alice had been well aware of her movements and was making no attempt to visit her.

From Timothy Rowley at the Mount:

My dear Imogen,

I thought we had lost you! So pleased to hear that you are settling among us *for good*, as they say up here – and from our point of view it is indeed a good thing!

I do realize how busy you must be, but Peele's Players would love you to attend their first reading, on Monday 7th. Perhaps you might like to come to tea here, at four o'clock on Sunday 6th, when we could chat about this and other things? I enclose a little map because Alice brought you by car the last time, and you may not have realized exactly where I live. It is only a short walk from the 53 bus stop which is on your route, and situated, appropriately, halfway between Christian Langesby and Pagan Haraldstone. As I say, in jest, I do like to keep my options open! Meanwhile I wish you every happiness and success in this new departure.

Yours ever, Timothy

From Philip Gregory at Prospect House:

Dear Imogen,

I'm sorry you missed rather a splendid Christmas in Langesby, but very pleased indeed to know that you will be living not too far away. We had few opportunities to speak to each other on your last visit, and I did feel there was so much more to say. Having uprooted myself after a similar tragedy, and made a new life, I am well aware of the challenges you face and the demands that will be made upon you, but when you feel you have an evening to spare do give me a ring. We can go out and dine somewhere – and talk. As a Londoner you may think that there are no good restaurants north of Hampstead, but I shall be delighted to confound your prejudices. Let us meet very soon.

Edith is here today, helping us, and joins me in good wishes for the future,

Sincerely, Philip

And a succinct note, which had made her pause and think, headed CROSSDYKE STREET CHAPEL.

Dear Miss Lacey,

Just a line to say welcome to Haraldstone. I hear that Jim Buckett is fitting out your shop. He's a good carpenter, but if you run into bigger problems I'm willing to give advice or lend a hand. I know your property well, and used to do the occasional job for the late Miss Parkinson. She was a decent old body, but no businesswoman. I have a feeling that you are.

All the best, George Hobbs

P.S. You'll get a lot of flak about living in Haraldstone, but it's a capital place providing you can keep your feet on the ground and your mind open.

These three personal letters were accompanied by half a dozen civil cards of welcome from neighbouring businesses.

And now the two-month fever of decision-taking, buying, removing, cleaning and arranging was over, there was nothing more to be done. The blank grey stillness of Sunday evening in a northern village closed around her. Doors were shut and residents secreted behind net curtains. Standing at the first-floor window, looking down into the court, the only sign of life Imogen could see was a thin black cat trotting purposefully along the cobbles.

She became aware that she was extremely hungry and probably had little to eat in the house, that she was lonely and Fred was not on speaking terms. His silence had lasted since that first afternoon on Haraldstone Hill. This was a great achievement, as her counsellor had told her at their final meeting, but Imogen also felt it as a personal loss. And yet she was alive again, desirously alive. She exulted in being alive. She no longer wanted to join Fred in oblivion.

An unsure leap, secured with a raking of claws, a nuzzling head and a querulous cry reminded her that she was not entirely alone in the world and someone else was hungry too.

'Oh, *you're* all right,' said Imogen, unpicking Polly from her shoulder, moving away from the window. 'I brought a mountain of tins for *you*.'

While the animal supped and sipped and grunted in lip-smacking satisfaction, she poured a gin and tonic for herself, and wondered what she could do with half a packet of dried spaghetti, marked BEST BEFORE OCTOBER the previous year, and a heel of doubtful cheese which had survived the removal from London. There was only enough bread and milk for breakfast, no vegetables of any sort, one squashed tomato, two hard green apples and a suspiciously soft banana.

'I should have shopped yesterday,' she said aloud.

Shopping had been Fred's job.

'Cooking was your job, too!' she reminded him.

No reply.

She looked through his little collection of cookery books, chose *Great Dishes of the World*, and sat at the dining table to consult the section on pasta.

'Dear God!' she murmured, assaulted by a battery of ingredients and directions. 'Olives, mushrooms, peppers, onions, garlic, dried tomatoes and freshly grated Parmesan? Oh, have a heart!'

She leafed through a few of Fred's favourite recipes, which he had dated and starred according to their merits, and sighed for his gourmet offerings of yesterday. She poured another gin and gave Polly a sprinkle of crunchy cat food. This was the end of the road. She had burned her bridges with Alice and she hesitated to beg favours of Sadie. Old friends were not to assume that she was the same Imogen, and new friendships must be forged between equals. Having found that it was harder to receive than to give, she did not intend to cast herself in a supporting role again.

Still, as the Roman proverb said, a hungry belly has no ears. She wondered whether to swallow her pride, knock on Sadie's door and ask for the loan of a tin of something or an egg, but on looking out of the window she saw that Crafty Notions was shrouded in darkness. Momentarily, she felt herself to be floundering in this new world, though she dared not admit it. With time on her hands she was lost. Fissures of fear were undermining her confidence. She talked aloud to encourage herself.

'So what I really need is a pub which sells hot meals. And first,' she said, of her old corduroy trousers, her stained sweater, her pony-tail of hair bound with a rubber band, 'I must have a shower and make myself look presentable.'

The late Miss Parkinson's property had been built in three storeys with one fair-sized room on each floor. Crazy Hats occupied the ground floor. Above this, attained by means of a hidden staircase on the side wall, was Imogen's kitchenette and living space; on the top floor she had her bedroom and shower.

She dressed with care and flamboyance. She wore the blackberry velvet suit that had caused Hal to judge her worldly, and teamed it with a scarlet wool poncho and heavy silver earrings. She wound her hair into a knot and secured it with two tortoiseshell pins. She hesitated, wondering if she should quite literally cap it all with her latest creation, made in honour of local traditions: a black velvet witch's hat with a silver gauze scarf wound round the brim and a broomstick hatpin stuck dashingly through the crown. If she were to make her mark on Haraldstone and district she needed to advertise herself and her wares. Yet this final act of bravery eluded her. She left the hat in its box.

Feeling alien and self-conscious, she stood on her doorstep, locking up, before turning resolutely to face her new world.

Although its name and sign would indicate a light-hearted attitude towards the opposite sex, the Dancing Witch at Haraldstone crossroads was not used to having its male preserves invaded. Conversation round the bar, dartboard and fruit machines ceased as Imogen pushed open the door and entered. Her appearance as well as her sex told against her.

Accustomed to the indifference of a metropolitan city, she was at once afraid and repelled. Smoke hung on air already stale with the smell of beer, and several hard eyes which had been fixed on her now turned back to the landlord in accusation. He, who had to deal with the public in general, as well as his regulars, adopted an ingratiating, apologetic smile, and called from behind the bar to reassure her.

'Good evening, Miss. The parlour's next door. You'd be best off there.'

Having found their voices, the other men directed her loudly, as if she were a half-wit or foreigner. In the north this can mean both.

'Back into t'lobby, and through t'door on the right, love!'

It was embarrassing to call back to the landlord over their heads, but at half-past seven on a Sunday evening without food, transport or intimate knowledge of the district, she had no choice.

'Is it possible to get a meal here, please?'

They all answered, triumphing in their general knowledge, and in the strength of their opposition to what she was and what she stood for.

'No, love. Not on a Sunday. Nothing hot served on Sundays.'

'The wife,' the landlord offered, jerking his head in the direction of an elderly blonde drawing beer, 'could make you a sandwich. Wait in the parlour, love. She'll be along in a minute.'

'If I could have something on toast and perhaps coffee . . . ?'

'You'll have to ask her. In the parlour, love.'

Defeated, Imogen thanked him and withdrew. The explosion of comment, immediately upon her departure, was evidently not in her favour. Hurriedly, so that she might not hear what they thought of her, she opened the door of the parlour and put her head round it to test the atmosphere. Smelling of cigarette smoke, port and lemon; joylessly tricked out in forest brown and green; and furnished with small ring-marked tables, plastic-covered benches and hard wooden chairs, it was empty.

Demoralized, Imogen sidled into a chair and waited. After a while the elderly blonde came in and announced, hands on spreading hips, 'We only do sandwiches on a Sunday evening.'

'What kind of . . . ?'

'Ham or cheese.'

'Is the ham home-cured . . . ?'

'Tinned.'

'Then I'll have cheese, please. Is it . . . ?'

'Cheddar, and we've run out of tomatoes.'

Let's not be snobbish about this, Imogen thought, as her bile and temper rose. She's no worse at catering than I am. She may have nothing worth eating in her larder, but nor have I.

'A cheese sandwich, please. Is it possible to order a pot of coffee – or tea . . .'

'We don't serve hot drinks on Sunday.'

Imogen bit her lip and thought. She looked up and saw the landlady's eyes fixed on her garb with evident hostility. She decided to appeal to the woman's good nature.

'You see, I haven't had much to eat all day,' she explained. 'I've been busy moving in, and I forgot about food, and left it too late to do shopping.' The silence was self-explanatory. 'I've taken over Miss Parkinson's sweet shop.' The silence deepened. 'If it's too much trouble,' Imogen said in desperation, 'is there anywhere else round here? I just need something on toast and a pot of tea or coffee.'

'Not on Sundays. The café and the fish and chip shop are closed on Sundays.' She stretched the menu. 'You can have a soft drink with your sandwich.'

'Is there anywhere within walking distance – or a bus ride away, perhaps . . .'

'The next bus to Langesby is at half-past eight. There's plenty of places open there, but you'll have to be sharp back. The last bus leaves soon after ten.'

Imogen sat perplexed.

'We're very busy,' said the landlady, finally dropping all pretence of hospitality. 'Do you want anything or not?'

Imogen rose with dignity.

'No thank you, I do not!' she said, and walked out head high, famished. So much for the conviviality of the local pub.

130

At the bus stop she switched on her torch and consulted the timetable. The landlady was right. *Haraldstone. 8.30 p.m.* She consulted her wristwatch: 7.40 p.m., and the night was cold with a raw coldness known only to the north.

I suppose I could start to walk, she thought. The idea depressed her, and the notion of missing the bus between stops immobilized her. She stood doubtfully.

Oh, I'll go back and make do, she decided. At least I can have a hot drink.

She was crossing the road when the sound of a solitary motorbike turning the corner made her quicken her pace. The bike slowed down as its headlights picked out her hurrying figure, and the rider braked with one boot, drew up under a lamp-post just ahead of her, and waited. His visor was down, his face invisible. The dark helmet and gleaming leather clothes turned him into an anonymous creature of the night. Only the two of them peopled Haraldstone High Street, and the village might have been dead for all the signs and sounds of life she could see. Alarm made her hesitate for a moment, then, clutching her poncho to her throat, she crossed the road again to avoid him, and began to run. But where she was running she could not have told, because her shop was in the other direction and only open country lay beyond.

A familiar voice shouted, 'Hey, Miss Lacey. Stop a bit. It's all right! It's only me. George Hobbs.'

Feeling a fool to have panicked, she waited. Straddling his steed he walked it to her side, and lifted his visor to smile on her.

'I'm sorry if I frightened you,' he said. 'I didn't think for a minute what it must have looked like. You can't be too careful these days, can you?'

And now she saw that imagination, and possibly hunger, had transformed the normal into nightmare, because the leather clothes must have been as old as his motorbike, and bought in a second-hand shop or picked up at a jumble sale. Only his helmet was new. His voice was amiable, reassuring. He meant no harm, but because he had scared her, and seen her scared, she was curt with him.

'My name isn't Miss Lacey, it's . . .' His expression was friendly to the point of innocence, and she could not go on. 'Why on earth don't you call me Imogen?' she asked crossly.

He answered prosaically, 'Because you didn't say I could.'

She was still busy getting her breath back, still angry with him and herself.

'Can I give you a lift anywhere?' George asked.

She burst out, 'Only if you know of a decent place to eat. I'm starving. I've had nothing but a sandwich and a tin of soup all day, and when I went to that pub at the crossroads they weren't even polite, let alone helpful.'

'No, they wouldn't be,' he said. 'Particularly with you wearing those clothes. They're not used to fashionable ladies at the Dancing Witch. For one thing they don't like strangers, and for another it's a man's pub.'

'So I was given to understand,' she answered bitterly.

'The nearest place would be Langesby, but the buses aren't all that frequent.'

'They made that perfectly clear, too.'

She was trembling with rage and cold.

'I'm going back to the shop,' she said. 'I shall be quite all right.'

'Here,' said George, 'let me take you back to my place. I can give you something to eat. It'll be cheap and cheerful, mind. Egg, bacon and tomato. Bread and cheese. The vicar gave me some of their apples. And I'll brew us both a pot of tea.'

Imogen struggled with hunger, frustration and pride.

'Go on, take a chance!' George advised kindly. 'I've got one corner of the chapel as warm as toast and I do a good fry-up. I can run you there in five minutes and then run you safe home again.'

Her stomach capitulated.

'Thank you,' said Imogen. 'I should be very grateful.'

'Can you ride pillion?'

'Oh yes.' She brightened up at that. 'Fred – my late husband – had a motorbike.'

'What sort?'

'An ancient BSA.'

'This is an ancient Harley-Davidson. Nothing beats the old bikes. They knew how to make them then . . . hop on!'

FIFTEEN

Crossdyke Street Chapel had never been a cheerful building. Life was too hard, the district too bleak, the Victorian ethos too depressing, to sustain a lively place of worship. But the Victorians had built it strongly and well, and George had a loving eye for its virtues, and an artistic one for its possibilities. His sentences came out in little puffs of breath on the chilled air.

'I'm thinking of this main hall as open-plan living space. At the moment I'm working in here and camping in the back premises – where they used to keep the hymn books and make tea. But by this time next year I'm expecting to live here, sleep in the gallery, and use the back premises as my workshop.'

He walked round, talking, absorbed in his vision, forgetting that Imogen was chilled and ravenous. Politeness prevailed. She wrapped herself still closer in her poncho and summoned up interest.

'The ceiling is a beauty,' said George. 'I shall restore the plaster moulding exactly as it was, and keep the iron chandelier. It's come a long way from its origins, that centre light. Started out with candles, moved on to gas, and graduated finally to electricity. Proportionally speaking, the place is a gem. Of course, the 1850s were a nice period for architecture. Still restrained. Give them another thirty years and they were clapping on the fal-lals and doo-dads. If you like Victorian baroque you're laughing, but for myself I prefer a plainer style. Nothing beats simplicity. I wanted to be an architect . . .'

'Why weren't you?' Imogen felt she had to ask.

'Not much money in the family and my parents had no ambitions for me. In their opinion my ideas were above my station in life, so I had to scale them down. I'm a carpenter by trade – and I don't regret it, mind – but I wanted to be up and about, to meet different people and see a bit of the world. So I went to evening classes, and picked up a lot of other information, about building and plumbing and draughtsmanship, and set up as a general handyman. And I must say I like it. I prefer to work for myself, and live by myself, and of course the old dream hasn't died. In a way I'm being an architect, redesigning this chapel . . .'

His walk round his unfinished kingdom had ended in front of Imogen, and he emerged into reality.

'Here I am, talking, and you're as white as a sheet,' he said, in consternation. 'You must be clemmed. Come on through into the warm.'

The warm, provided by a paraffin stove, was cluttered but immensely comforting. Two primus stoves on a wooden table took the place of a cooker.

'Here, sit down in front of the stove,' said George, contrite. 'I'll have the frying pan on in a jiffy. Kettle first! Instant coffee or tea-bag tea? Tea? Right!'

She spread out her fingers in the heat, and her eyelids drooped. For some blissful minutes she swam away.

'Tea!' said George, and gave her a St Oswald's mug to sip and to hold. The liquid was strong, brown and scalding, as Mary Proctor brewed it.

Their thoughts touched.

'I've put a dollop of brandy in it,' said George, 'to thaw you out. Mary Proctor likes what she calls "a drop" in her cup of tea. I gave her a bottle at Christmas.'

'Thank you,' she said, waking up as the hot liquid and alcohol coursed through her. 'It was such a shock. The hostility at the Dancing Witch, I mean.'

He poured cooking oil into the pan, arranged sausages, bacon and tomatoes round the edge and cracked two eggs into the middle.

'Ah! The pub. Yes, they're a bigoted lot. The beer isn't up to much, either. I never go there. They're stuck in some kind of time warp. I'll introduce you to the Unicorn in Tofthouse, a mile or so up the road. But I warn you that single women aren't really welcome in pubs, up here. The local women go with a friend, or in a group. You're likely to feel out of it on your own.'

'How very odd!'

She picked up his first sentence.

'You have a high opinion of Mrs Proctor, haven't you? I remember, from the way you spoke of her at Alice's dinner party.'

George glanced at her, made up his mind, and answered factually.

'She's my natural mother,' he said, basting the egg with bacon fat.

Imogen set down her mug, amazed that he had decided to confide in

134

her. So, as a matter of fact, was George, but now he had begun he would go on.

'There are rumours but it's not known for a fact,' he explained. 'Mary never had much luck with men. Her husband, Dick Proctor, was no good. He used to go away for a year or two, come back home and fill the cradle, and go off again. He'd not been gone long when my father came to Langesby, and the pair of them fell in love and started courting – on the quiet, of course, because neither of them could afford a scandal, but they thought the world of one another. Mary said those were the happiest months in her life. But the work he came to do was over and he had to leave.'

He turned the sausages over, cut two slices of bread and buttered them.

'What work did he do?' Imogen asked, interested, but finding difficulty in focusing her attention.

'He was an architect, and his name was George. Would you believe it?'

I'll believe anything, she thought, if only you'll feed me!

'Langesby's old indoor market had been bombed during the war. He designed the new one. You should look at it some time. It's not the usual civic architecture. There's imagination in it, and grace.

'Anyhow, there was no future for them together, and he liked his freedom, so she didn't tell him she was pregnant when he left. It must have been the first time Mary ever let go of anybody she cared for, poor lass, and she was in deep trouble. She wouldn't think of an abortion, so she and her sister Florrie Hobbs concocted a story about Dick Proctor paying a flying visit and getting Mary pregnant again. They had no hope that he wouldn't turn up meanwhile and raise hell, but he didn't. He stayed away for eight years, as it happened. There was gossip, of course, but Mary and George had been discreet, and folk respected her and knew she had a hard life, so nobody made trouble.

'She said it broke her heart to part with me, but she didn't feel she could keep me. Dick would know I wasn't his son. I might look sufficiently like my father – which I do – for people to make the connection. She had a houseful of children already, and a job to hold down. Her sister Florrie was childless, and suffering from nervous trouble on that account. And Florrie's husband was a southerner and had been offered work down south.'

He set the frying pan on top of the paraffin stove to keep warm, and poured more tea for them both.

'So they put all these facts together, and when I was born Florrie and

135

her husband adopted me, and left the dale soon after. I knew nothing about it until Florrie died. *He* told me. My stepfather.'

Imogen's mind was on Mary, but her eyes, nose and rumbling stomach were occupied with the contents of the frying pan.

'Funny thing was,' George continued, transferring the food to a blue and white striped plate, 'I liked Mary the minute I saw her, and I'd never felt close to the one I called mother, although she was a good sort. And I did have a decent stepfather – narrow but decent – which was more than Mary's other children had.'

Then he placed a tray of food on her lap and said, 'Eat up!'

Partly out of curiosity, mostly so that he would leave her to pig it alone in peace, Imogen asked, 'So when did you meet Mary?'

'As soon as my stepmother was buried. I'd left home a few years previously and was working in the Midlands. I packed up my traps and came to Langesby for a week's holiday. That was eight years ago. I took lodgings in the town and made enquiries. Mary had retired but she was still living in the old house. So I walked to Howgill on the Sunday morning with a bunch of flowers, knocked on the door and didn't get the reception I expected . . .'

'Don't tell me!' said Imogen, fork uplifted. 'Did she call out that it wasn't locked and you'd best come in?'

'Not exactly,' said George, and chuckled. 'She said, "I'm coming as fast as I can. You needn't knock the house down!" I wasn't used to North Country ways and I wondered for a minute whether to walk off. Then she opened the door, and her hands flew up to her mouth, and she stared at me as if I was a ghost. I said, "I'm George Hobbs", and she said, "I knew it!" She was on her own, but she cooked us a grand dinner, and we talked all afternoon. I'd no one to please but myself and I thought I'd stay in Langesby for a while and get to know her better.

'She wanted me to live at Howgill House, but I thought we'd be better friends apart. So I made myself at home in Langesby, joined the bell-ringers at St Oswald's, built up a one-man business, and looked round for a place of my own. Found this one eventually. Mary says I'm just like my father – a loner and an outlander. But I see her most days. I keep an eye on her. And I'm still here.

'As I said, there are plenty of rumours about our relationship but nobody knows the full story. There's no shame attached to it, but we don't see why we should satisfy idle curiosity. So we say nothing and let them guess.'

Imogen, biting into thick bread and butter, said, 'You've told me.'

'Oh, *you* won't tell anybody,' said George with confidence. 'You're an outlander like myself. Outlanders learn to keep their ears open and their mouths shut.'

She wiped the bread round her plate.

'You're right there,' said Imogen. 'I shan't tell a soul. Not even Sadie.'

'I dare say that Sadie has sussed it out for herself by now,' said George, 'but she won't say anything either. More tea?'

They sat together eating Alice's famous Cockcroft Marvels, which were large and crisp and juicy. Imogen curled up in George's one armchair, replete, eyes half closed with sleepiness and satisfaction.

George asked, 'Any problems with the shop so far?'

'Only the lack of storage space.'

'I expect,' said George innocently, 'that hat boxes take up a lot of room.'

'It's not the hats. It's Fred's toys.' He looked nonplussed. 'Fred. My late husband. He designed toys for adults.'

'Oh yes?' George said cautiously.

'Until Fred died he always found somebody prepared to house them, in an attic or a back room, but when I was ill my uncle collected them up, sold our flat, and put them in storage along with the furniture. Everything arrived together last Monday. I hadn't forgotten about them, but somehow I hadn't reckoned with them, if you know what I mean.

'Anyway, at the moment they're taking up most of the shop floor, and when Jim Buckett comes tomorrow morning we shall have to move them so that he can put up shelves. I don't even know if we can get them on the stairs. And if we do it means crowding my living space. I'm in a quandary. Do you know anyone round here who would store them? I mean, I'd pay rent, but I want them near me and I shall need to inspect them regularly. Right now they're in crates and boxes.'

'How many of them are there?' George asked, intrigued. 'How big are they?'

'Oh, Lord! Let me see. There are half a dozen little playthings for businessmen to put on their desks – not that any businessman I've ever known would do that, but Fred was such an optimist! – and then there are four floor toys, each of them roughly nine feet square.'

'I don't know how you squeezed them into the shop in the first place,' said George, and snuffled with laughter at the thought. 'Could I pop in for a minute to see them when I run you home?'

'Yes, of course. In fact, if you'll just let me finish my apple, we can go now.'

'No hurry,' said George. 'It's only half-past nine.'

'You haven't met Fred's toys yet,' said Imogen, wiping her mouth and fingers. 'They take up a lot of time as well as a lot of space – and they're addictive.'

'I'll go in first and switch the light on,' she said. 'You're liable to fall over them otherwise.'

He followed her in and stood smiling in the doorway, amused by the idea of adult toys, by the sight of so many boxes stacked into such a small space, and by Imogen's sudden animation.

'I'd better come over tomorrow morning and give Jim a hand,' said George.

She was not listening.

'Which one do you want to see first?' she asked, and ran her fingers over the labels of each crate, reading the names aloud. 'There's *The Pirate Ship* – that's about strategy. *The Secret Cave* – terribly Jungian. *The Circus* – just good fun. And *Mr Rumbleton's Residence* – which is truly spooky.'

'You choose – but I'll need a screwdriver to get the top off.'

'I've got Fred's tool-box upstairs. I'll bring it down. Oops! Sorry, Polly. You shouldn't be so sneaky and curious. This is my cat, George. Do you like cats?'

'Yes,' said George, surprised by the animal's lack of distinction. He ventured, 'But I should have expected you to have a Siamese or a Persian.'

She gave him a keen perceptive look. She had not forgotten his description of her.

'You mean, a fashionable appendage to a fashionable hat shop run by a fashionable lady?'

He saw that he had hurt her feelings, and said quickly, 'She's got pretty markings. Silver tabby, isn't she? Hello, Polly!'

The cat allowed him to tickle her under the chin.

'She's nothing in particular, as far as I know, but she's very special to me,' said Imogen, scooping her up and holding her close. 'She was our wedding present from Fred's landlady.'

Remembrance saddened her. George tried to make amends.

'I'll bet she's a good mouser.'

Imogen recovered her sense of humour.

'Only if she's in the mood,' she said honestly.

'Well, she'd better be,' said George factually. 'These old shops are running with mice – and worse. Now, how about fetching that tool-box?'

★   ★   ★

138

Mr Rumbleton's Residence was suggested rather than reproduced: a skeleton of a house, full of surprises. Fred had designed the toys so that the player must take part, and Mr Rumbleton had many a hideous secret hidden in his residence. Imogen unfolded the list of instructions and was immobilized for a moment. Written in Fred's upright hand, they reminded her that he would write no more, invent no more. These were his legacy to life.

George was hovering over the toy, hands in pockets, inspecting the workmanship.

'He was a good craftsman,' he said. And added, grinning, 'And as daft as a brush!'

This homely comment brought Imogen back to the business of the moment.

'Come and sit down.' she commanded. 'You have to sit down to play with it.'

Obediently, he folded his long legs under him and sat by her side.

'Fred finished this toy one Christmas Eve,' said Imogen, remembering, 'and we made bacon sandwiches and coffee and played with it until two in the morning.'

George glanced at her cautiously. Her eyes were too bright. This was delicate ground. Then she smiled directly at him to show that all was well.

'You begin,' said Imogen, 'by ringing the doorbell.'

George put out a long forefinger and pushed the miniature button.

Immediately Mr Rumbleton appeared at an upstairs window and fired a rifle at his visitor.

'Bloody hell!' said George, falling back, laughing. 'What sort of a welcome is that?'

'You haven't begun,' said Imogen with relish. 'Wait until you get down into the cellar . . . !'

Sadie, drawing her bedroom curtains at midnight, looked down on the lighted windows of Crazy Hats, and saw them both sitting on the floor of the shop, playing with Fred's adult toy and exploring a new childhood.

SIXTEEN

Monday, 6 March

'Dear me,' said Timothy mildly, as half a dozen people followed him into the church hall, 'this morgue doesn't improve with acquaintance. Well, well. Never mind, everybody. Peele's Players should be able to create the illusion of space, light and beauty anywhere.'

'We'd be hard pressed,' George observed drily, 'to do that here,' and was gratified when Imogen laughed.

'Believe me, George,' said Timothy in high good humour, 'I mean every word I say. Ah, here are two other potential illusionists.' He went forward to shake hands and murmur appreciation of their coming.

The cast of *The Old Wives' Tale* numbered twenty-three, and the hall door opened and shut every few minutes as more and more of the company arrived. Among the last was Mary Proctor and a thin shambling young man with a perpetual smile. The sound of a car driving away in the distance suggested that the couple had been brought by someone who did not intend to come in.

'My dear Mrs Proctor!' Timothy cried, extending his hand in welcome, and looking in question at her companion.

Mary had come in her best clothes. Her black shoes were mirrors, her black stockings fine nylon. She wore a black cloth coat and a floral silk headscarf, but in deference to the cold March evening she had topped this outfit with a deep-fringed grey wool shawl such as mill-girls used to wear. In full command of herself, she held out her hand to Timothy.

'Good evening, Dr Rowley. This is my son Stevie.'

She read his expression and her own stiffened.

'He's living with me now, and I can't leave him by himself.' As Timothy continued to look dismayed, she said firmly, 'I'll make sure he's no trouble. But if you can't be bothered with him we can always catch a bus and go back home.'

Given no choice, Timothy welcomed them.

'*Delighted* to see you both. Did Mrs Brakespear bring you?'

Mary was not one to trifle with the truth, nor to lower her voice.

'Yes, but she wouldn't stop. There's a bit of bad feeling between herself and that young lady over there at the moment.'

She nodded meaningfully in Imogen's direction, and compressed her lips. Imogen checked a smile, and yet, quite irrationally, felt hurt.

'Well, well, well,' said Timothy, soothing. 'These little misunderstandings do blow over. My dear Philip! Delighted to see *you*. Oh, and Edith, too! I thought you would be looking after Prospect House this evening, my dear, while the master was away – or overseeing the Langesby Dramatic Society. To what do we owe this honour?'

Edith showed her teeth to Timothy in greeting, but her eyes were on Imogen as she answered, 'We left Mrs Slater in charge this evening and the dramatic society don't feel the need to start rehearsals so early. They've decided to do *Love on the Dole*, by the way.'

'So I heard. A worthy choice.' Blandly.

Seeking for chinks in his armour, she said, 'They wanted a play with weight and purpose to it. Costume dramas really are rather old hat.'

'And so is the expression *old hat*, my dear Edith,' he replied swiftly. 'And though it is extraordinarily *kind* of you to come and observe our humble efforts, I don't see how you can be of any help. But by all means stay for *this* evening,' and he stressed the time limit.

He consulted the clock on the wall, which had stopped. Tutting, he took out his fob watch.

'There are a few more to come, but we have time yet.'

George was saying to two young men, 'Can you lads help me to stack some of these chairs against the wall? We shan't need all of them. They must have been playing bingo in the hall last night.'

'They *were* playing bingo here last night,' Mary Proctor told everyone roundly, 'and that fool Matty Hardcastle won two pounds fifty. I always thought it was a daft game, and now I know.' She produced two children's comics and a packet of cigarettes from her shopping bag. 'Stevie, you go and sit down and read.'

'My dear Mrs Proctor, I really don't want people to *smoke*,' Timothy protested.

'It'll only be Stevie,' said Mary firmly, 'and he'll sit at the back.' She looked Timothy in the eye. 'He's got little enough. It's not much to ask.'

'Oh, very well,' said Timothy, defeated, and wandered off saying to himself, 'but this does complicate matters . . .'

'Don't you worry,' George said to him in a confidential tone. 'I'll settle

Stevie over there, near the window, and find him an ashtray. He's not a heavy smoker. He'll only have two or three.'

'You're a tower of strength, my dear fellow,' said Timothy, patting his shoulder. Then, *sotto voce*, 'but surely *someone* would look after the poor soul for a couple of hours?'

'It's difficult. He hasn't been home long and he won't go to anybody else at present, except me. And though Mary doesn't take any nonsense from him, it really needs a man to deal with him. He's strong, you see. He could frighten a woman without meaning to.'

'Merciful heavens!' said Timothy, and was fortunately distracted by the entrance of an extraordinary trio.

Three young men in their twenties, wearing striped school scarves, and school caps far too small for them, lined up in army fashion as soon as they saw Timothy, clicked their heels, grinned, and said in a chorus, 'Good evening, sir!'

'My dear fellows!' he cried, hurrying over to shake hands. 'Your sense of humour and occasion never changes. From what *museum* have you lifted these extraordinary garments? Nowadays, you know, even at *our* old school,' this was spoken with a hint of incredulity, 'the boys dress as they please, and the democratic institution of a *uniform* – to my immense regret – has flown out of the window . . .'

As they laughed together, the rest of the company stood apart, glancing at each other with guarded eyes. Timothy had cast a wide net. Imogen recognized the small contingent from Haraldstone: Deirdre and Jon of the salon, Jinny of the health food shop, and two of the St Oswald's bell-ringers. They exchanged nods and smiles. The rest were Timothy's connections, managing to convey that they had belonged to the same school, although at different years, and reminding Imogen of the foreigners-but-family atmosphere at Scarcliff Old Girls' Association. Then Timothy came forward, bringing his ex-pupils with him.

'Let us not stand on ceremony!' he cried. 'I dare say you are all feeling slightly strange at the moment, but if you have the talent to act you have the talent to mingle socially. We begin at 7.30 prompt, which gives us all five minutes in which to show what we are made of. Let us take advantage of it.'

As if he had wound up a set of clockwork toys, everyone began to talk vivaciously to someone they did not know: apart from Edith who smiled coldly, and Mary Proctor who could not be bothered with such nonsense.

Philip made a kindly point of chatting to Stephen first, then gave Imogen a wave and made his way to her side. Edith steadfastly followed, and conversation was necessarily stilted.

'My dear Imogen, how wonderful to see you again! I had hoped to hear from you,' he said, 'but that isn't a reproach, simply an expression of personal disappointment. I expect you've been busy. How are things going with you?'

She felt the usual mixture of pleasure and tension in talking to him, heard her voice sound too high, too blithe, and laid the blame squarely on Edith.

'I'm terribly sorry, but this is the first time I've been anywhere or seen anyone since I arrived.' Untrue. 'Everything is going splendidly so far, and Crazy Hats of Haraldstone opened today.'

She noticed that she brought in the name of Haraldstone with a touch of defiance whenever she met anyone, but Philip did not blench.

'With banners, bunting and a brass band, I hope?'

She laughed naturally, then.

'Nothing as grand as that. It's true that I did think of holding open shop, as it were, and offering a glass of wine and a 10 per cent discount, but I had to give up the idea. More than three customers is a crowd in a tiny place like that. So I've just made the window as glamorous as possible and advertised in the *Haraldstone Gazette* and the *Langesby Chronicle*.'

'Was the glamour executed by your glamorous self?'

'Yes, it was, actually.'

Edith, who had smiled throughout this exchange, now said, 'Of course, I remember Alice telling us how talented you were. A Jill-of-all-trades, if one may coin the expression. I'm sure she's given you lots of good advice, and been a tremendous help and support to you over the past months.'

Imogen allowed Fred a few seconds to say *Bitch!* and then said it mentally for herself.

Aloud, she answered, 'Alice's advice is always good. I think she must be the most helpful and supportive person I know.'

Not a palpable hit, but an extremely neat evasion. Philip, who had been maintaining an air of good-humoured detachment, now gave Imogen an amused smile, and Imogen smiled back, feeling a little flash of triumph and of kinship.

'I think that single women are so brave to start a business on their own,' Edith drawled. 'It must take so much self-confidence – or rashness – to risk losing everything, and have no one and nothing else to turn to – unless, of course, one has a private income, in which case there is no risk at all.'

144

'I've never thought about failure,' Imogen replied, refusing to give her any information. 'Whether you call that rash or self-confident I wouldn't know.'

Philip now cut in before Edith could reply.

'Do I take it that you are joining Peele's Players as well as naming them?'

'Yes. Despite my vehement protestations, I am to read the part of Delia.'

'Tim has a wonderful knack of getting his own way,' said Philip. 'I didn't want to act at all, let alone play the part of a wicked magician, but he leaned on me so heavily that it was easier to give in.'

'Yes, there is something implacable about his charm.'

Timothy had ascended the dusty stage, and George was calling them all together, clapping his hands.

'Quiet, everybody, please.'

Timothy ceased to beam on them benevolently. On stage, he seemed to grow in stature, to bear himself splendidly, and his voice rang out in the dull hall.

'My dear friends. Thank you all for coming. I think I can say quite safely that no one will have wasted his or her time by being here. I believe that everyone has a copy of the play?'

A scattered chorus of assents.

'And I hope they have read and inwardly digested it – if not learned their parts?'

Again assents, and some laughter.

'Good. This will be an informal meeting to acquaint us with *The Old Wives' Tale* and ourselves. At the moment I am the only person present who knows everyone else, but I do assure you that by the time we have rehearsed together for a few weeks you will all be fast friends – united in hatred of your producer and director!'

More laughter, and cries of 'Nonsense!'

'I confess, to those of you who do not know me well, that I am a terrible taskmaster,' Timothy continued, with an agreeable smile.

'Hear, hear!' from his old pupils.

'I intend this play to be an outstanding production. You know, of course, that the result of our efforts will be restore the bells of St Oswald's church to full peal?'

Yes, indeed they did. A stirring note to that effect had accompanied each copy.

'What goal could be more worthy?' Timothy asked, with extended arms.

The response was warm and spontaneous.

His tone now became jocular, but his intent was serious.

'I warn you all now that you will be expected to give of your best, and to believe in this project with all your hearts. And I beg you sincerely, if you have any doubts whatsoever as to your ability to learn your parts to perfection, to attend rehearsals even in extremity, and to do exactly as I ask – please to let me know at once, and you will be released from your commitment without prejudice.'

They were all listening, and inwardly scorning the notion of release.

'To leave us would be a pity,' he continued, 'but the greater sin would be to go along with us for a period of time – and *then* yield to faint-heartedness and fall by the wayside. In that case, grievous wrath will descend upon your hapless heads!'

They applauded him tremendously.

'Good!' Timothy cried. 'I now declare the company of Peele's Players open – and the reading will begin. I should like us all to be on first-name terms.' He caught sight of Mary's flat green gaze and added, 'unless of course you would rather not. But my name is Tim, and that is how I should like to be addressed.' As he came down from the stage he said, 'George, none of your materials has arrived as yet, and you have nothing to occupy your talents tonight. Will this be terribly boring for you?'

'No. I'd like to listen. I'll go and sit with Stevie.'

'George, you are a man of *oak!*' Emphatically spoken. 'Mrs Proctor, I should like you to sit by me. Imogen, my dear, I should like you on my other side. Antic, Frolic and Fantastic,' to the three men who had appeared in school caps and scarves, 'I'll have you opposite, where I can keep an eye on you . . .'

He placed everyone in a particular seat for a particular reason. The play was as clear in his mind as if he had written it himself.

He's waited years to do this, Imogen thought. How curious that it should come together for him now, towards the end of his life, all mixed up with St Oswald's bell tower and the fourth centenary of Langesby Fair.

'I know you are familiar with the lines,' said Timothy, 'but you must remember that your future audiences are not, and this is late Elizabethan English complicated by scraps of Latin. I will give a couple of *for instances*. In the second speech Frolic says, "As I am frolic *franion*". A franion is an idle fellow, but few people will know that. So you must roll the word out, accompanied by a wink – say – or some gesture which indicates that you are a frivolous chap. And then translate *O coelum! O terra! O maria!* by pointing to the sky, the earth, the sea – George, could you make a

146

note, by the way, that we need a hint of sea in the backcloth? – Where was I? Oh yes. And all puns must be clearly delivered, so that the audience get the point. Fantastic's pun, for instance, "a dog in the wood, or a wooden dog" – the wood-in-dog could be separated into syllables, or repeated. He could even address the audience. I don't mind a little extempore. In short, you three clowns can ham it up gloriously. You are there to provide the laughs. That's why Peele sent you on first.

'We then meet Clunch the blacksmith, who is an honest fellow and will get his laughs by being unintentionally funny. Gerald, you have done much of this nature in the past, so you know what I mean?'

The middle-aged man who nodded agreement must have been a pupil forty years ago, and Imogen marvelled at the length and strength of Timothy's attachments.

'But Gammer Madge, the blacksmith's wife, is a very different person. She seems friendly and humorous, but the way she narrates her story shows you that she is the archetypal wise woman, the teller of tales, the repository of history. The play may be amusing but its roots are dark and deep. There is a great deal more about Madge than meets the eye. Now, Mrs Proctor . . .'

'You can call me Mary, if you like,' she said graciously.

'May I really? Thank you,' Timothy replied.

'But I shall call you Dr Rowley, because that's what *I* like.'

Some hidden amusement among the younger members of the cast.

'I quite understand. Now, Mary, I know you have had considerable experience in the past, but I'm not looking for Shakespearian acting. I want you to be yourself, as if you were living four hundred years ago, sitting in your rocking chair by the hearth, telling the audience an old story. That may sound easy,' he said to the company at large, 'but is extremely difficult – as Mary knows.'

He had drawn her fire. She replied almost shyly, 'I'll do my best.'

'Delia's lover, and her two brothers, are straightforward, heroic parts. I chose you three, Ian, Simon and Ken, for good voices, good looks, and the ability to wear a pair of tights with distinction.'

The young men grinned at each other self-consciously.

'The play abounds with clowns of one sort and another, who hold up the plot from time to time, to provide entertainment and please the motley. Melancholy Lampriscus, Huenebango – the choleric gentleman with the two-handed sword! – vociferous Corebus and truculent Wiggen. Make the most of these parts, but leave the farce to Antic, Frolic and Fantastic. We don't want all the comedians to sound alike. And Deirdre and Jinny

147

the two daughters of Lampriscus should be wryly amusing rather than openly funny.'

'The serious parts for the men are played by Erestus, who must change from an old man to a bear and back to his normal shape: the Ghost of Jack – true hero of the drama – who has humour as well as wit, but must restrain it. And Sacrapant the magician, a man of charismatic charm and profound evil.

'Venelia, the young madwoman, is an interesting part, but without words. One of Lampriscus's daughters could take both parts. Delia, the bewitched heroine, whose rescue is the central issue of the play, has paradoxically a small part with little scope. She is simply beautiful and submissive, first to Sacrapant and then to her lover. But I have great hopes that Imogen will make more of her, and also convey the magical solitude of her situation.

'Finally we have walk-on characters and groups of people: Harvest-men, Furies, Fiddlers and so on. In some cases we can double up. In others, I believe that Philip has some of his youngsters raring to help out. But until you all know your parts, and know the play well, we shall manage without them. For this evening, I shall be reading these minor characters, or indicating that a group of people arrive to sing and dance and so on.

'And now, having given you a notion of what I'm driving at,' said Timothy briskly, 'I should like you to read straight through, without further interruption from me. Afterwards, perhaps we can have a general chat over coffee and biscuits, George! Would you be kind enough to time the play?'

The three clowns began with a robustness which startled the rest of the cast, and made Timothy raise his eyebrows and give a sniff of appreciation. Not to be outdone, Clunch the blacksmith dealt with them equally robustly, and Mary Proctor came in strongly as Gammer Madge. Whether the playwright intended her to be an uncompromising North Country-woman is doubtful, but that was her reading of the part, and Timothy gave her an approving nod when she finished. The brothers were charming and ineffectual. Erestus powerful and sad, Lampriscus unconsciously funny.

'We are cutting the Harvest singers!' Timothy cried. 'Enter Huane-bango!'

Whereupon Huanebango blustered and boasted magnificently, swearing to kill the magician and rescue and marry the king's daughter. At one point he set down his copy of the play to brandish an imaginary two-handed sword, which raised laughter among his fellow thespians and a scattering of claps.

But it was Philip who silenced them. He became the sorcerer. His pleasing appearance, and even his pleasing voice changed, as he confided that his mother was a famous witch who had taught him her cunning, and that he abducted the king's daughter not only because he loved her, but because she could restore his youth. For though he seemed young he was in reality an old and crooked man.

'Thus by enchanting spells I do deceive those that behold and look upon my face.' Then he looked straight at Imogen as he said, 'How now, fair Delia! Where have you been?'

Imogen replied with a voice outside herself: soft and bewitched, like a sleepwalker called upon to speak. And when they had finished their exchange both of them smiled at each other, delighted and surprised by this empathy.

The Ghost of Jack, played by one of Timothy's older pupils, then upstaged everyone, and was congratulated as he finished. There was more gleeful clowning, and more laughter from the cast. At intervals Timothy cried, 'Cut the song and carry on!' or read a minor part or stage directions with great gusto, or called out to George, who was sitting with a school exercise books in his hand, alert and interested, 'Make a note of Venelia breaking the glass and blowing out the light, will you, George? Because that's the high point of the play and the end of Sacrapant!'

Delia was discovered asleep, and Imogen awoke to find herself delivered from the enchanter and restored to her lover.

'Slight hiccup here!' Timothy cried. 'Peele wanted the audience to suffer a little longer. Make it sinister, Ghost of Jack! Turn the tables on the joyful couple!'

As Imogen accepted death she found herself near tears, so like it was to the moment when she realized that her life with Fred was over.

'Then farewell, world! Adieu Eumenides!'

'Beautifully done, Delia!' Timothy murmured. 'Now, happy endings, everybody! Cut the last two speeches for the moment. Just a notion.'

Gammer Madge had the last word. Putting down her script she addressed them as simply and directly as if they had knocked on the door of Howgill House.

'But come, let us in: we will have a cup of ale and a toast this morning, and so depart . . .'

There was a long pause as Peele's Players looked round at each other with new eyes, while Timothy unfolded a pure white handkerchief and wiped his own.

'What do I need to say?' he asked, and ended with self-mockery. 'My judgement in this, as in all other matters, has been perfect!'

George lifted his arms above his head like a victorious fighter and cried, 'Well done, everybody!' Stephen jumped up and down, and laughed and clapped far too long because they had aroused and gratified the child that he was.

Mary Proctor said sensibly, 'That'll be enough from you, Stephen Proctor, thank you. Now if anybody's got a box of matches I'll light that gas and put the kettle on for a cup of tea. I reckon we've earned it.'

Alice did not appear at half-past nine to pick up her passengers, but had detailed one of her many helpers to play the chauffeur: she made Alice's excuses, and escorted Mary and Stephen to her waiting Mini. Their departure broke up the meeting. Evidently Imogen remained unforgiven in this quarter, though popular in others. As George summoned her to the motorbike he was intercepted by Timothy.

'No, no, my dear fellow. You brought this lovely lady but I shall take her home. It's cold weather to be riding pillion.'

SEVENTEEN

Imogen was smiling inwardly when she slid into Timothy's glossy limousine.

'Do I gather you have enjoyed yourself?' he asked, glancing sideways.

'I have indeed.'

'I'm delighted to hear it. I have been feeling terribly guilty since I persuaded you to be Delia. After all my importunity, to find yourself with a somewhat sugary part and fewer than a dozen speeches might well be construed as an insult.'

She shook her head.

'You read her quite beautifully,' said Timothy, satisfied, 'as I knew you would.'

Imogen's smile was her reply. He cleared his throat, watching his head-lights leave the intimate huddle of Langesby and enter the open country, picking out stone walls and the solitary road.

'I also thought that Philip did remarkably well as Sacrapant.'

She nodded.

'You respond to him most movingly in the play, which is interesting, because in real life I have the impression that Philip is seeking to find favour with you, but you are holding back.'

She did not reply. Timothy talked on affably.

'A fascinating man but something of an enigma. One wonders whether he will ever overcome that tragic business of his wife.'

A little of Imogen's happiness evaporated.

She asked, 'You mean being involved in her death?'

Timothy gave a small cold smile.

'Where did you hear that malicious report?'

'What report?'

'Ah! Forgive me. You mean being *preoccupied* with her death?'

'Yes. I mean – like I was with Fred. Unhealed.'

He kept his eyes on the road ahead.

'Strange how the truth will out, and in all innocence. You knew, of course, that his wife committed suicide?'

Imogen sat up and stared at him. He glanced quickly, stealthily, back.

'I'm sorry. I thought Alice would have told you.'

'Alice isn't on speaking terms,' said Imogen stiffly.

'No, not for the moment, but she'll come round. I thought she would have disclosed his history when you were staying with her. Since she was pushing the two of you together, one would have thought it only fair to give you all the facts.'

Imogen did not answer.

'Dear me. I do seem to have put my foot in it!' Cheerfully. 'Oh well, I won't bombard you with all the details at once. Briefly then, the late Mrs Gregory killed herself. No doubt about it. And yet there were whispers that Philip was somehow involved in her death. The whispers grew loud enough to persuade the police to conduct an inquiry, but they found nothing and Philip was declared innocent.

'It is now five years since she died, and he has put some hundreds of miles between himself and his old home, and earned an honourable name in Langesby. But mud still sticks. Do you remember Alice saying he should have been mentioned in the honours list for his good works, and wondering why he was not? Well, my dear, there is good reason for that. Public honours are only bestowed upon the publicly spotless – and poor old Philip is spotted like the 'pard!'

Timothy parked in a side-street near the Catwalk and switched off the engine. 'I will confess,' he said, turning to her, giving his roguish chuckle, 'that I am hoping to be invited in for whatever you drink at this time of night.'

Now what is he about? she wondered. More revelations? The news of Philip's wife had been unpleasant.

Aloud, she replied airily, 'Of course you are invited.'

The arches of window light transformed the pavement from grey to gold, and she stood for a moment letting them play the alchemist with her leather boots. Her disturbance faded. Love and happiness repossessed her.

She said blithely, 'You know that we opened this morning, don't you? Tell me, Tim, what do you think of my shop?'

The letters of *Crazy Hats* were painted like gold feathers, flying up into an arch and plummeting down again. In the main window, five slender silver stems of different heights rose from a ground of grass-green velvet, each crowned with a hat for spring. They were simple in shape and design, and Imogen had carried the spring motif through the hats: a cloche of taffeta violets, a straw boater decorated with a daisy chain, a child's Easter bonnet shaped like a daffodil, a purple crocus turned upside down and topped with a perky stem, a dashing Robin Hood hat with a feather. She had trimmed gloves to match them.

'Delightful!' Timothy cried sincerely.

A discreet card in one corner said that Imogen specialized in exclusive designs for important occasions.

'The front window is Me, and may take time to sell,' she explained. 'My bread and butter stock is displayed in the side window.'

Civilly, he walked round to inspect a collection of berets, caps and tam o'shanters, gloves and neck-scarves, to which Imogen had added individual touches. Timothy pronounced them delightful also, and then returned to gaze again at the major display, standing with his hands clasped behind his back, rocking slightly on his heels.

'I have such fond memories of cloches,' he said, pointing to the taffeta violets. 'My mother wore them when I was a small boy. There was one I liked in particular, of rose-coloured velvet. And she had a drawer in her dressing-table devoted entirely to gloves. In those days a lady did not think of herself as suitably dressed for outdoors unless she were smartly hatted and gloved.'

He turned to Imogen, saying, 'I don't wish to sound like Hal, but do women really wear hats these days? I only see them at weddings, funerals, christenings and garden parties.'

'Yes, young girls will buy and wear hats, providing they're reasonably cheap and eccentric. And that's a good sign. Because older women are then encouraged to buy a more conservative version of the same design. Hats are coming back into fashion. You'll see.'

She opened the door and a bell tinkled welcome. Polly jumped down from the counter where she had been waiting, and mewed an enquiry.

'I live on the first floor,' said Imogen, 'and this is my companion.'

She picked up the cat, who kneaded her shoulder in an absorbed fashion.

The living room was softly lit and simply furnished: the room of a single woman with little space and not much money. But there were two easy chairs by the fireplace, to show that she welcomed visitors, and Timothy sank into one of them, murmuring, 'How gifted you are! Like George, but in a different way, you have an eye for effect – you have seen his designs for the chapel, of course?'

'I've seen the chapel, too.'

He ruminated.

'But will you be able to make a living, my dear?' he asked gently.

'I sincerely hope so. I'm trying sidelines. Quick sales for cheaper items. Once they've bought something customers can be tempted to look at other things.'

She opened a small box and unfolded the tissue paper to reveal a black taffeta rose.

'The French call these artificial flowers *fantaisies*. They are to wear on a lapel, a hat, a bag, a belt, a sash – or whatever. I'm finishing a dozen of them in different colours before I display them next week.'

'Most elegant,' Timothy murmured reverently.

'Crazy Hats is getting the best of me at the moment. I've pared my expenses down to the bone. I live by myself. And the evenings are all my own.' She touched the rose before replacing it in its tissue nest. 'This is how I spend them.'

'You are an astonishing young woman.'

His slightly protuberant blue eyes wandered round the room and came to rest on Fred's photograph.

'A good strong face,' he observed. 'Your late husband?'

'Yes. That was Fred.'

'A good name, too. I like the old English names, and I notice that they – like your hats – are coming back into fashion. Ian, who read the part of your stage lover this evening, has two small daughters named Lily and Rose.'

'You amaze me. He looks too boyish for fatherhood.'

'He will be close to thirty, but doesn't look his age – and neither do you.'

Polly, who had been watching Timothy from a distance and needling the carpet in deep thought, now trotted purposefully towards him and jumped on to the arm of his chair. Imogen set down his coffee cup and offered to dislodge her.

'No, no. Let her stay,' said Timothy. 'I like cats. I would have one, but unfortunately my housekeeper is physically allergic to them.'

He patted his knees to indicate that Polly might sit, which she did, stepping down with the utmost delicacy, purring in anticipation.

'I'd say that you were honoured,' said Imogen, 'if I didn't know Polly. She can be lethal with her claws, and I have the scars to prove it. Shoo her away if she doesn't behave. And now tell me,' she said, sitting down in the other chair, 'why are you so intent on producing *The Old Wives' Tale?*'

Timothy lifted his eyebrows. His countenance was unfathomable. He tickled Polly under her chin and she purred louder.

'Why do you ask?'

'Because – though I hate to sound like Edith – I wouldn't describe it as an ideal play for amateurs, and it will be very difficult to bring off.'

He was silent, pursing his lips, looking down, stroking the cat.

She elaborated.

'At Alice's dinner party you said that you preferred to direct inexperienced actors, but those friends of yours whom I met tonight were very experienced. Amateurs they may be, but amateurs of calibre. And then again,' she ran on, as he continued to court the cat, who closed her eyes in ecstasy, 'although you were supposedly forming a local dramatic society you chose very few local people – and they all came from Haraldstone. The majority of the cast are your former pupils who live quite a distance from Langesby.'

'I held an open audition,' he said stiffly, 'inviting anyone interested to attend. I admit that I had marked down the part of Delia for you and Sacrapant for Philip, otherwise there was no favouritism, and I heard everyone out. But I am not accepting people simply because they live in Langesby. They also have to show capability, so I augmented the cast with others whom I considered most suitable.'

His attitude and his tone confused her. She had intended a friendly conversation and encountered hostile defence.

'Oh, I wasn't questioning your motives in choosing the cast,' she said hurriedly. 'Of course not. I just wondered why you were prepared to go to so much trouble with a minor play. I mean' – she was floundering now – 'I'm not an expert but I've had a good education and some experience of the theatre, and I never heard of George Peele before you mentioned him. I'm sure hardly anyone who comes to see it will have heard of him either . . .'

Timothy held up an authoritative hand, and silenced her.

'My dear girl, I believe I said at the dinner party that Peele's reputation was vastly overshadowed by those of Shakespeare and Marlowe. You are asking me if he is worth the effort. Well, I will admit that he has not worn as well as his great contemporaries. He seems slightly old hat – as our friend Edith would say. He creaks a bit. But I can trim him a little, here and there. Tonight was merely the reading. We glanced, as it were, at the map of Peele's country. The journey lies ahead of us, and depends on our enthusiasm, courage, stamina and wit.'

Imogen remained silenced. He continued to fondle Polly.

'And since you ask why this play is so important to me I will attempt to explain. The heavens are not illuminated solely by the sun and the moon. There are also thousands of stars, some brighter than others I grant, but they all shine radiantly and deserve our admiration. Peele is one of these. Why I should have chosen Peele, rather than half a dozen other Elizabethan playwrights, I cannot say, but he and I formed an alliance at Cambridge half a century ago. I have studied him closely, and I should like to see him applauded by a modern audience, even if it is only for a week's festival in a North Country market town. And he has another claim to our attention. The first performance of *The Old Wives' Tale* was given in 1595. So we shall observe the fourth centenary of the play as well as of Langesby Fair.'

He paused, and added, 'Does that satisfy you?'

Imogen nodded, though she was never sure of Timothy, who had many layers. She remembered herself as hostess.

'Would you like some more coffee?'

He had tired himself out, or perhaps she had tired him. He looked old, but the usual stately courtesies tripped off his tongue.

'No, no. I thank you. The coffee was quite delicious . . .'

Fred would have described it as just about drinkable.

'. . . but I fear I must forgo the pleasure of your company, and of this charming creature, and be on my way.'

He lifted the cat gently from his knees and set her down.

Imogen knew she had somehow transgressed. Her cheeks were pink with trouble. Fearful of spoiling this new friendship, she fetched his overcoat and helped him into it.

'I've offended you,' she said directly, 'but you must know that I didn't mean to, and that I'm sorry.'

He stood for a moment, pulling on his leather driving gloves, brow furrowed. Then he smiled at her.

'You have ruffled my vanity, Imogen, though that does not matter, but in questioning my judgement you also roused my doubts. This play, like Bloody Mary's Calais, is engraved upon my heart. To follow one's instinct is sound. To follow one's heart is perilous – and may be a grave mistake. Let us hope that I chose wisely.'

She was still more penitent, following him downstairs with a consoling shower of words, a little rain of good reasons why the play should be a sensation.

At the door she asked him, 'Will you forgive me? Are you still angry with me?'

156

He kissed her on the cheek.

'My dear Imogen, there is nothing to forgive. And I am angry only with myself.'

He raised one hand in a gesture of farewell, which was theatrical yet touching. And as she knew that he liked to have the last word, she did not say anything in reply, but kissed both hands to him and smiled her good-night.

EIGHTEEN

Saturday, 18 March

All the shopkeepers in the quiet conclave at the back of Haraldstone High Street were friendly with each other, but the craftspeople formed an intimate group of which Imogen now found herself a part, and Sadie presided over them.

Winter was their hibernation period, when they replenished and augmented their stocks, rethought their strategies, planned forays into the outside world of trade fairs, and reckoned their profit and loss. Consequently there was time for some amicable visiting between the shops. Customers took precedence, but when they were absent Imogen did not expect to drink her morning coffee or afternoon tea by herself. And she laid in a selection of herbal sachets for those who preferred their drinks without caffeine.

In its first weeks her advertising and the novelty of being a London milliner, however humble, aroused much interest in Crazy Hats, but these people were looking not buying. Her modest sales of gloves and berets did not even provide bread. Her front window display remained the same. Like all the other traders, she sat tight and waited, and hoped for an Easter benison.

'Thank God for Mario's,' said Sadie, as they sat together sipping nutmeg and orange spice, and keeping an eye on her shop opposite. 'If that restaurant wasn't here we'd be completely dead in the winter. He may not keep the same opening hours but at least his customers have to walk past our windows, so they know we exist. His food's good, too. Have you tried it?'

Imogen said, 'Not yet,' and felt guilty.

She should have added, I'm being taken out to dinner there this evening, but then Sadie would want to know by whom and she was reluctant to speak about Philip Gregory.

Sadie's eyes were sharp and knowing.

'You should persuade one of your gentleman friends to wine and dine you.'

Imogen tried to lead her away from the subject.

'What gentleman friends might those be?'

'George Hobbs?' Wagging her finger. 'I saw you both sitting on the floor at midnight, playing one of those games out of the crates. Very romantic!'

There was no one quite like Sadie, Imogen thought, for firing arrows until she hit some target. She gave an uncomfortable smile.

'George is just a friend. No, he's more than that,' being honest, 'he's a *real* friend. He saved my bacon — or rather, fried my bacon — that first Sunday I was here. I was starving and he cooked supper for me. And he's housed all those crates in the chapel gallery, so I can go and inspect them from time to time.'

'Oh, very convenient,' said Sadie, with a jocular wink. 'That little arrangement should suit both parties. He's the right age for you, too — which is more than I can say for the other suitor. Mind you, Tim Rowley has a lot to offer, and those May and December matches can be very happy.'

This time Imogen's smile broadened.

'Sadie! You can't be serious. He's a father figure if ever I saw one.'

'You're a big girl now,' Sadie chided. 'You don't need a daddy. You need a husband to love and hate, and fight and lean on, and to share your bed and life.'

'Why are you so anxious to pair me off?' Half-laughing, half-annoyed. 'You've made it perfectly clear what you think of men and marriage. If they're not good enough for you why should I be saddled with them?'

Sadie was at her most roguish.

'Because you're different from me. Whether you know it or not you came to Langesby hoping to find Love-of-my-life Number Two — which makes me think that perhaps you caught a glimpse of him when you were staying with your friends there, in November.'

Imogen frowned and went faintly pink.

'By the way, aren't these friends of yours coming to see you now you're settled?'

But Imogen was not to be teased or prodded further. She rose slowly and gracefully, stood looking out of the window, and found a solution. Two elderly ladies had wandered into the square and were reading Mario's menu. She opened the door and walked over to them, smiling.

'If you're hoping for lunch I'm afraid Mario isn't open before seven in the winter months – but if you'd like to look round our shops my friend and I would be delighted to help you.'

She indicated Crafty Notions with her right hand and Crazy Hats with her left, smiled to show them that she did not mind which decision they made, and returned.

'I think you may have customers,' Imogen said, as the two ladies hesitated and then meandered politely towards Crafty Notions, where a star-studded white and silver quilt was displayed in shimmering splendour.

Sadie set down her mug, brushed the biscuit crumbs from her flowing gown, and picked up her cloak. A sale was unlikely, but always possible, and she dared not lose the opportunity. She grinned up at her tall friend with great good humour.

'I'll tell you something about yourself which you might not know – or might not want to admit,' she said. 'You're artful!'

Imogen grinned back at her, eyebrows raised.

'I do know, and I've been told before. Call it my defence if you like,' she said. She speeded the departure, tongue in cheek. 'Oh, look how *fascinated* they are by your Easter bride's throw. Do you suppose either of them could be thinking of marriage? After all, it's never too late!'

Sadie gave a snort of disbelief, but trotted briskly across the cobbles to lure the ladies in.

Imogen had not experienced this feeling of a head full of bubbles and a queasy stomach since she was first in love with Fred, and she stared at her mirror image, fearful lest the agitation showed. She reassured herself by talking aloud to Polly, who was contemplating this other person in the glass with suspicion, and ignoring the strange cat who appeared to be sitting on the bed behind her. Imogen's mouth made exaggerated shapes, up, down and sideways as she applied liner and raspberry pink lipstick.

'You know as well as I do, Poll, that it would be an obstacle race from start to finish. First base, Edith. We detest each other and she won't give up without a war. Say that I win, and make it to second base – Alice – and she forgives me. I then have to avoid being swallowed whole again. Suppose that I'm able to be friendly with Alice without losing myself, and I reach third base – Philip. However wonderful he is – and I think he could be – it's a question of love me, love my Life's Work, and the truth is, Polly' – finishing with lipstick and beginning with mascara – 'that I don't suit his way of life. I mean, Polly, be honest, can you see me as the matron of a home for young offenders?'

The image in the glass opened its bright pink mouth, closed its dark-lashed eyes, and burst out laughing. Polly mewed indulgently and needled the bedspread.

'Exactly. So why am I acting like a schoolgirl with a crush on the headmaster? Oh!' For she had been trained to observe herself. 'Is that how I think of us? Master and pupil? How very weird! I must be careful.'

Nothing more remained to be done. She was as fine as she could be. She gave the image in the glass a conspiratorial smile.

'So I'm going to have a lovely evening out, Polly, and I've no objection to a warm friendship or a hot flirtation – but that's as far as it goes.'

She was very pleased with herself for having reached so objective and sophisticated a conclusion. Her satisfaction was immediately dispelled when the doorbell rang and the bubbles and queasiness returned.

Philip was as exhilarated and nervous as she: standing there, defying a bitterly cold evening in a light overcoat, his fair head smooth and hatless. A box of chocolates was tucked under one arm, a bottle of champagne under the other, and he held a bouquet of tulips and daffodils.

'Come in, come in!' Imogen cried.

She closed the shop door. They stood opposite each other and could not stop smiling. He was mocking himself, as he often did.

'I had no idea what to bring, so I brought the lot!'

'Oh, what luxuries!' she cried. 'But you're taking me out to dinner . . .'

'This isn't *instead*, it's *as well as*.'

He began to hand out his bounty.

'Chocolates – don't know whether you eat them or not . . .'

'I do. I pig them. That's why I never dare buy them for myself.'

'Flowers . . .'

'Adore them. Always.'

'I thought we could put the champagne on ice and drink it afterwards?'

'Marvellous idea. I'll do that at once. Come up for a moment.' Over her shoulder, mocking him in turn, she asked, 'Are you intending to drive home?'

'With extreme care, and no faster than thirty miles an hour. In fact, I drive better when I'm slightly drunk than when I'm sober.'

'Tell that to the breathalyser.'

She put the bottle in the refrigerator, the flowers in water.

'In any case, it will be worth the risk,' he said deliberately.

Lightly she asked, 'Dare I offer you a pre-dinner drink?'

She had bought a bottle of gin in his honour.

'Better not. Let's start drinking and talking at Mario's. I'm so very – I can't describe how delighted I am to see you,' he said.

162

Their mockery vanished. She looked at him, looked away, and was rescued by signs of life in the restaurant below.

'Mario is opening up. Do let's go,' she said. 'We shall be his first customers.'

From her living-room window Sadie watched them walk the few yards across the cobbles together, arm in arm, laughing. She drew the curtains, and was thoughtful for a long time.

This was quite different from the courtship of Fred. To begin with, Imogen and Fred had barely enough money for necessities, so their romantic evenings were spent in the dusky intimacy of a suburban Indian restaurant, where they chose the cheaper dishes and went back to Fred's landlady for a pot of tea afterwards.

Here, in an atmosphere of brilliantly contrived intimacy, Mario produced food at a price corresponding to its excellence. Whereas Fred, in his youthful poverty, would have pored over every item, hoping to find something he could afford, Philip handed back the menu without a glance and said to the waiter, 'This is a special occasion, and both of us enjoy Italian food. What do you recommend this evening?'

No one had ever asked Fred if he wanted so much as a glass of house wine, because they knew it would be a waste of time, but Philip received the wine list as of right, consulted it at length, and chose a bottle which drew a look of respect from the waiter.

'Would you like an aperitif?' Philip asked Imogen, 'or are you happy to start with the wine and stay with it?'

'I should prefer the wine.'

'Good. So should I.'

The preliminaries over, he cast a net of charm and gradually drew her in. The person in Imogen watched the process and remained detached. The woman allowed herself to be captured.

As the meal began Philip introduced himself, giving her a brief autobiography. His had been a privileged background: devoted parents, private school, public school, university. He sketched his subsequent career, which began gloriously as one of the youngest headmasters in a private school, and ended ignominiously as a suspected murderer. He blamed no one for this, least of all his wife. In fact he took the blame for her death upon himself.

'Kay was a wonderful woman, a beautiful, highly gifted and generous person, and everyone loved her,' he said, 'but she kept things to herself and brooded on them. I hadn't realized that she was in a state of clinical depression, and needed more attention than I could give her at the time. I was – I admit – driven by ambition. In fact, I see glimpses of my younger self in Tim Rowley. Had I remained a bachelor I should very likely have ended up as he did: retired, revered and respected. But I married Kay, and we had a loving and passionate partnership.'

His smile was so open, and his tone so light that there was no sting in his next remark.

'I sense that Tim is not driven in the same way, and he isn't interested in women except as friends.' He added swiftly, 'You know that, of course, or I shouldn't have mentioned it. And there was never a hint of scandal, not even the suggestion of a homosexual relationship, throughout his entire career. So he was either exceptionally discreet, unusually chaste or – as I believe – of a naturally cool temperament. Anyway it doesn't matter. A person's sexual proclivities are his or her own affair, and remembering my own student escapades – on both sides of the fence, I must admit – I am the last man to cast a stone . . .'

His leisurely voice was suggestive of secrets as yet untold. His expression assured her that he was being honest because she was worthy only of the truth. His eyes assessed her reactions to each statement, and his perception then adjusted it to her liking.

The main course being sampled and appreciated, he turned the conversation on to Imogen, who had nothing to confess apart from contented love and cruel bereavement. Fred did not shine, she noticed, in retelling. His image seemed unaccountably dull, and she skimmed over his toys for adults which might sound silly. It took an unsophisticated man like George Hobbs to play one of Fred's games and delight in it. So she did not explain and Philip did not press her.

They had finished the bottle and he ordered another, then raised his glass, smiling.

'To your beauty and your innocence!'

She enquired, with some hauteur, 'Innocence?'

'Yes,' Philip said. 'The rarest and most wonderful of all qualities. Particularly these days. I have ten girls in Prospect House, aged between thirteen and fifteen, who should be peeping over the parapet at life with wide eyes, and wondering what it's all about. But they were born in a pit of degradation, and not one of them is innocent.'

'Surely you can't mean that I'm ignorant of the squalid facts of life?'

'I wouldn't be so stupid. I don't doubt that you've read about the world's evils and observed a few at first hand, but I doubt that you've experienced any of them. If so, they haven't touched you. My girls are emotionally – and sometimes physically – scarred by their experiences. The best I can do for them is to help them to come to terms with their past and move on to some sort of future – though how they cope with life when they've left me I seldom know. Prospect House is not the equivalent of Scarcliff Girls' School. They were never those girls, and they don't come back for pleasant reunions, like you and Alice!'

Imogen's smile in reply to this mild joke barely reached the corners of her mouth. She had freed herself from Alice's patronage at the cost of their friendship, and the knowledge hurt.

Philip saw that he had touched a nerve, and his voice changed.

'I expressed myself clumsily. I wanted to say that to be with you is as refreshing, as life-giving, and as life-enhancing as water in a desert.'

She was moved to silence, and sat head bent and self-conscious, turning the stem of the wineglass round in her fingers. At once he changed the subject.

'What shall we have for dessert? Something wicked, dripping with cream and chocolate? Exotic pastries? Sinful cakes?'

'Thank you, but I've eaten quite enough – and I don't like sweet things.'

He refilled her glass.

'I'm sure you like fruit?'

She acknowledged that she did.

'They have exquisite fruit desserts. Can't I tempt you?'

The water appeared as if by magic with a three-tiered trolley, reeling off a list of luscious sweets, and finally recommending the cheese board. Imogen succumbed to pineapple drenched in kirsch and topped with mascarpone. Over this course they spoke of Prospect House and Crazy Hats and she relaxed. Her tongue and inhibitions loosened by wine, she thought aloud.

'We couldn't be more different, could we? Your work is useful and unselfish, mine is luxurious and purely personal. And though I'll argue my case any time, I know that hats are on shaky ground compared to housing deprived children.'

'Surely that's part of the attraction between us? At least, it is as far as I am concerned.'

He was waiting for her to admit her attraction to him but again she drew back. Had Fred been there he would have said, 'You're half-pissed, love. Watch yourself and shut up.' As he was not, some inner guardian said it for her.

Smoothly, Philip altered course.

'But I remember your telling me, at Prospect House, that you like to

165

make women feel good about themselves. So you contribute beauty to an ugly world.'

'What a graceful way of putting it. I wish I'd thought of that. I once tried to explain myself to Hal, and he gave me a bleak reception.'

'Ah, well. Hal is a good man by nature and profession, and keeps his eyes on the straight and narrow path. As an ordinary human being I like to wander down interesting side lanes and look all about me. But to return to you — aren't the arts and crafts necessary in a different way? At their simplest they give pleasure. At their best they can sustain and enlighten. Mere existence is not enough for mankind — or womankind either. We can't live, in the truest sense, by bread alone. We need wine and roses too. I provide my youngsters with the basics, but it's recreation that makes their lives worth living — the public festivals and private celebrations or, very occasionally, the discovery of a personal talent . . .'

You are a clever and handsome and persuasive man, Imogen was thinking, as she smiled and talked back. She was riding high on atmosphere and alcohol but a sliver of common sense remained. She put her hand over the top of her wineglass when he tried to fill it again.

'You're not going to help me out?' he asked.

He carried his wine well, and finished the bottle while she mentally checked her condition. Her face felt hot and she sensed that her thoughts were jumbled and her speech might match them. So she encouraged him to talk of himself, while she drank black coffee. His voice floated towards her and floated back. She smiled and nodded and looked attentive, gradually regaining clarity. They had taken the evening at a leisurely pace, and were among the last customers when he asked for the bill.

Now pray God I don't sway when I stand up, Imogen thought. And then pray God I don't wobble when I walk.

Both prayers were heard. Philip helped her into her coat. His hand was under her elbow. They made a creditable exit together. Mario himself bowed them out and said he hoped to see them again.

She concentrated on negotiating the cobbles and worried about the question of asking Philip in. After all, he had wined and dined her lavishly and his champagne was waiting in her refrigerator. But she could drink no more this evening. He would have to take the bottle back with him or return to share it another time. The question of civility remained. The least she could do would be to offer tea and conversation, though she could no longer think of anything to say, and knew that the act of bringing cups and saucers and boiling water together would be an effort. Even before that she had to find the key, and the clasp of her handbag was stiff.

'Here, let me help you,' Philip said.

He unlocked the door and glanced round, smiling, frowning. The upper windows of the court were all lit, their curtains drawn back. Fragments of private lives could be glimpsed: a woman picking up a magazine, a man leaning over the back of an armchair, talking. The headlamps of cats gleamed from the shadows. Philip's mockery was strained.

'You live in one another's pockets here, it seems. I hope no one was watching. They'd think I was robbing you.'

'Nonsense!' she answered absently.

As the shop bell jingled, Polly leaped from the counter, mewing crossly, and bolted upstairs.

'Oh dear. She's angry with me for going out,' Imogen cried. 'What a tyrant!'

She made up her mind to be honest with him.

'Philip, I can't drink champagne on top of everything else, I'm afraid . . .'

'Nor can I,' he answered promptly. 'The champagne can wait for another time. At least, I hope there'll be another time.' He asked, with some trepidation, 'You will let me see you again, won't you?'

She saw that he was unsure of her and himself, and her confidence grew. He was on his best behaviour, as Fred had been in the days of their courtship. The comparison with Fred warmed her.

She said, 'Provided you don't expect the same standard of cooking, I'd love to invite you for a meal here with me.'

His face shone with relief and pleasure. He hesitated, then held out his hand and said 'Good-night.' The hand shook slightly, and as he turned away he stumbled on the cobbles, and made an exasperated sound under his breath.

'Are you all right?' she asked, feeling kindly towards him.

'I think I've had rather too much wine,' he admitted. 'I'm not used to living it up in the evening. A mug of cocoa and one of Connie's rock-like buns are my usual nightcap.'

His tone was light but his face was troubled. The man about town had gone, and left behind him the keeper of Prospect House. Now she was concerned only for his safety.

'I think you'd better have some black coffee. For the road.'

He was embarrassed, anxious to be no trouble.

'No, no. Truly. I shall drive according to the book.' His sense of humour surfaced. 'I'll probably be arrested for making a suspiciously good job of it!'

He could have said and done nothing more reassuring than this. So often he had seemed perfect. Alice might feel at home with saints, but Imogen did not. As Fred once said, when she lost her temper with him over a botched business deal, a few minor imperfections were necessary in any human being.

'Don't be ridiculous. Come inside,' Imogen said, firm and at her ease.

Polly was not to be so readily appeased. She perched on top of the bookcase, hissed at Philip, and refused to come down.

'I'm afraid I'm allergic to cats,' he apologized, 'and they seem to know it.'

'How does your allergy express itself?'

He sneezed twice in reply, apologized again, and wiped his eyes and nose. Polly growled softly and lashed a meagre tail.

Busy setting up the percolator, Imogen replied, 'Cats are contrary creatures. Usually, when they know someone doesn't want them, they make straight for the reluctant lap.'

Still, she took pity on his watering eyes and shuddering sneezes. Lord, to think she had ever been doubtful of him. She lifted the cat down.

'I'll shut her in the bedroom,' she said, feeling brisk, bright and capable.

Polly would have preferred to stay and be a nuisance, and her squalling resistance lasted some minutes. By the time Imogen returned Philip had recovered his equilibrium and was drawing the curtains, shutting out the watchers in the court.

'I do hate to be overlooked,' he said. 'Don't you?'

His distress had vanished. He glittered. His smile was complicit. We know what we know, it told her.

She smiled back uncertainly.

'There seems to be a conspiracy to prevent our being alone together,' he said, and walked towards her, hands outstretched.

Disturbed, attracted, she held out his coffee: a frail barrier. The moment hung between them in expectation, and hung and hung and would not be denied.

The sound of a motorbike split the silence of the courtyard, and stopped noisily in front of Crazy Hats. The moment wavered. An instant later Imogen's doorbell demanded that she attend its summons immediately. The moment evaporated.

Annoyed, Philip cried, 'Who on earth? At this time of night?'

'No idea. But I must answer it,' Imogen replied hurriedly.

She pushed the cup into his hands and ran down the stairs.

George stood on the doorstep smiling, taking off his helmet.

'Oh, it's you,' she said, and was both relieved to see him and annoyed with him. She echoed Philip. 'What on earth do you want at this time of night?'

'I've got some important news for you. Good news. Can I come in for a minute?'

He followed her up the stairs talking.

'I wouldn't have bothered you if the lights had been out, but I saw you were up, so I – oh, sorry!' – as he caught sight of Philip – 'I didn't realize you had a visitor. Good evening, Mr Gregory.'

Philip set down his cup untasted and said, 'Good evening, Mr Hobbs.'

'Am I interrupting?' George asked, looking from one to the other.

'Oh, no,' they answered in unison. Philip added, 'I was about to leave.'

'Philip took me out to dinner tonight,' Imogen explained. 'To Mario's.'

George raised his eyebrows and smiled.

'Best Italian restaurant in the county, in my opinion,' he said. He turned to Imogen. 'I came to tell you that someone's made an offer for one of Fred's toys. A very good offer.'

Transported, Imogen clapped her hands, gave a little gasp of disbelief, covered her mouth, spread them out in wonder, gasped again.

'Which one?'

'*The Circus*. Well, it's straightforward fun, isn't it?'

'What wonderful news!' Philip cried.

His voice, his expression, the words, were exactly right. Still, they sensed that he was nettled.

'Yes, isn't it?' said George, taking the words at face value. 'Of course, knowing Fred, it isn't surprising. He's dead but he won't lie down, as they say up here.'

His tone was affectionate and could not have offended or distressed anyone, and he was as delighted as Imogen.

'I expect you feel that you know Fred as well as I do,' he said to Philip.

Philip gave a noncommittal smile.

'Have you seen his toys?'

Philip was reaching for his overcoat and answered, 'No, I haven't had that pleasure, as yet.'

'Well, I've been living with them,' George continued good-humouredly. 'I'm housing them for Imogen, you see. I expect you know that. The first evening that Imogen introduced me to them we played *Mr Rumbleton's Residence*. And I must confess that I've played with the others since . . .'

'Good Lord,' Philip cried, 'it's nearly midnight. Time I relieved poor Edith.'

169

So Edith had been youngster-sitting while he did his courting, Imogen thought. She found the idea strange and unsettling.

'I'll just stay another few minutes, Imogen. If you don't mind,' said George, 'to sort out the details.'

'I'll see you out, Philip,' Imogen said, conscience-stricken.

At the door she thanked him, shook both his hands, and kissed his cheek, to show that she appreciated the evening and his company.

'Sorry about the interruption,' she said, though she was glad, glad, glad. 'We must arrange a return dinner. Meanwhile,' flippantly, 'I'll practise cooking my one party dish!'

He was recovering from the double setback of George and Fred. He retained her hands and spoke intimately.

'You know perfectly well that I'm not coming for the food.'

She kept her tone light.

'I'm relieved to hear that.'

He smiled. He knew her. He released her.

'I shall be back,' he promised.

First-floor lights in the court were going out, bedroom lights coming on. Two by two the curtains were drawn. She closed the door and walked upstairs soberly, to find that George had released Polly from her temporary prison, and was making fresh coffee for them both.

NINETEEN

Monday, 20 March

Sadie's smile was covert, her demeanour furtive. Monday morning being slow, if not stopped, with regard to customers, Imogen was re-dressing her front window. Kneeling before her display, as before an altar, she paused in the business of pinning primroses on the green baize ground.

'I'm not interrupting you,' Sadie said, though she was. 'I just wondered whether you'd like to come round to my place tonight. I'm having a few girl friends in. You know them all. We're celebrating the first day of spring and we thought you might like to join us. No hard feelings if you decide against it. Just an idea we had.'

'I don't think I can,' said Imogen, yellow calico primrose in one hand, green-headed pin in the other. 'It's a rehearsal night.'

'It'll be over by half-past nine. We're not meeting until half-past ten, and Mary Proctor will be joining us. We're very thrilled about that. It'll be quite an occasion. So George can't ferry you to and fro tonight because he's taking Mrs Proctor in the van. But I've rung Deirdre up and she says they'll look after you this evening.'

As if I were a musical parcel to be passed from one to another, Imogen thought indignantly. I do hate people making arrangements about me behind my back!

'It'll be a heap more comfortable in their car than on that freezing pillion,' Sadie added, placating her.

Imogen stabbed the primrose in place, and turned on her interrupter.

'And what's happening to Stephen Proctor? He can't be left by himself.'

Peele's Players had resigned themselves to Stephen's presence at rehearsals. Whatever he lacked mentally he made up for emotionally. His laughter at the clowns' antics was unrestrained, his tears over Sacrapant's victims genuine. He stood up and clapped between scenes.

'Oh, he'll sit in the back of George's van with the wood and tools. It'll be an adventure for him. And then he's staying at the chapel with George while we go up Haraldstone Hill.'

Imogen's hand paused over the next primrose.

'Up Haraldstone Hill?' she repeated, bewildered. 'Late at night? In the cold and the dark?'

'We've all got the use of our legs,' said Sadie sarcastically, 'and they've invented something called the battery torch — in case you hadn't heard.'

Imogen looked closely at her friend, who stared jauntily past her.

'It's a witches' meeting, isn't it?' she said accusingly.

'Wash your mouth out with soap!' Sadie retorted in jocular fashion.

'You're going to celebrate the coming of spring in that stone circle?'

'Yes! Yes! And thrice yes!'

Sadie's tone said that she was tired of explaining.

Imogen laughed in disbelief.

'And you're asking me to *join* you?'

'Only if you want to.' Shrugging. 'Not as a member, mind. Just as a friend.'

'And what exactly are you going to do up there?'

With deadpan countenance, Sadie said, 'We're planning to catch pneumonia in our birthday suits, sacrifice a newborn babe, cut a cock's throat, and have a quick leg-over with the devil. Anything in your line?'

'Sadie! I'm being serious.'

Still, she had to laugh.

'I can tell you haven't the stomach for it,' said Sadie cheerfully, seeing she had relaxed. 'So when you get back from rehearsal, just pop in and join us girls for a smoking bowl of infant's blood, and then leave us to our evil devices.'

Sadie's warm, untidy living room bore no resemblance to a blasted heath, and even the oldest of the seven women could not be described as a hag. Mary Proctor was sitting in Sadie's high-backed chair, the place of honour, dressed in what Langesby would have called her 'party frock'. It was many years since the black sateen pleated skirt and jacket had been fashionable, but its quality showed through. She had pinned a cameo, depicting the Three Graces with garlands on a biscuit brown ground, at the neck of her white blouse. A long hard life had etched its map in her face but she held herself upright and her sandy-white hair was neatly garnered into its bun.

The others kept a respectful distance apart and chatted among themselves. The atmosphere was peaceful, the women familiar. Only the purpose of the meeting and the secret identity of the members, hitherto unknown and unsuspected, cast a lurid glow over Imogen's spirits.

Sitting nearest to Mary was Milia Godden, who designed silk scarves.

There was a physical sympathy between them, Imogen thought, for Mary in her thirties would also have been green-eyed, red-haired, handsome and tall.

The two wives sat together. Good-natured little Deirdre from the salon, her hair freshly blow-dried by Jon for the occasion, wore a swirling crimson skirt and tight black jersey. The eccentric artist Beth Lawler, who lived with Frank Hedge in a cottage outside Haraldstone, had chosen a long flowing gown and long flowing jacket in subfusc shades of brown and purple.

Opposite Mary sat the two lesbians, though no one in Haraldstone even hinted at such a partnership. Jinny Mercer, from Back to Nature was young and vivacious, with a wonderful fleece of fair hair. Erica Wolfson the silversmith, was quiet and withdrawn with classical features, her hair twisted into a coil and pierced with a silver pin. They had decided on trouser suits for the occasion: Jinny's heavenly blue and casual, Erica's twilight grey and elegant.

Mentally, Imogen began to create a hat for each of them.

'I don't think introductions are necessary,' said Sadie. 'We all know Imogen.'

Friendly smiles and civil murmurs. Beth Lawler swept her garments aside to make way for Imogen's chair. Jinny whispered in her ear, 'I've got a new line this week. Goat's cheese from Stanwick Farm. Absolutely mouthwatering, plain or toasted. If you're interested.'

Sadie, clad in her usual ethnic garb, clapped her hands for silence.

'We need to be off in half an hour, and it's a chilly night, so what about a nice hot drink before we go? Mrs Proctor? Rosehip, fennel, camomile or apple spice?'

Mary's tone was uncompromising.

'I like proper brown tea,' she said. 'I can't be doing with herbal drinks, except as medicine.'

'Ah!' said Sadie, pipped at the hospitality post.

'I might have known,' said Mary to herself, bitterly. 'I should have brought my tea-bags with me.'

Imogen, who had been hugging her knees and keeping quiet, now spoke up.

'I prefer Indian tea, too, Mrs Proctor. I can nip back to the shop and get it, if you like, if Sadie doesn't mind.'

'Bless you!' Sadie cried, all smiles. 'Do that little thing for me. Everybody else happy with herbal?'

They were. She took orders. Mary's fierce eyes focused on Imogen.

'That's a sensible girl,' she said in approval.

At their first encounter Imogen had been judged the accomplice of Alice and meals-on-wheels. Subsequent meetings with Peele's Players had presented her only as a decorative and vacuous heroine. But this evening, as the lone Assam tea drinker among the Haraldstone witches, she had been found promising.

Spring was coming in with a vengeance. A hard frost bit the ground, and as they toiled up the hill a cruel wind whipped up, as if the elements seemed bent on frustrating their progress. Imogen wondered superstitiously whether Alice's God knew what they were about and intended to put a stop to it, as Alice herself would have done.

The women walked slowly and kept closely together, well wrapped, heads down. Between them the younger ones were carrying miners' lamps, candles, a bundle of wood, matches, paper firelighters, a basket of bread and wine, and a small black cauldron. Reverently protected in their midst, Mary Proctor battled on, chin jutting, nose reddening, an occasional sniff or cough escaping her. Now and then she halted and paused for breath. They kept a tactful eye on her, stopped when she did, and matched their pace to hers.

Fred, where are you? Imogen wondered. I'm trudging up Haraldstone Hill with seven witches, and I don't know how it's happened.

On top of the tor the wind dropped, and they stood for a minute in silence under a great bowl of stars. The moon was riding through floating silver strips of cloud, illuminating the world as far as they could see it. Beneath them the county stretched out for miles on every side, its dwellings dwarfed by undulating fells, its domestic lamps doused, its broad ribbon of river shimmering. The frosty grass crackled under their feet. Before them towered the circle of female stones, their rough grey surfaces sparkling in the moonlight.

Sadie said deferentially to Mary, 'We'd be honoured if you'd lead us, Mrs Proctor.'

Mary nodded.

In Imogen's ear, Sadie whispered, 'You can stay out of the circle and watch, or join in. Please yourself.'

Relieved, Imogen nodded, and was about to stand back when Mary turned to her and held out an imperious old hand. Imogen had no choice, so she took it. The flesh was soft and wrinkled like glove leather; the fingers were strong and held her firmly. Sadie clasped her other hand and squeezed it to reassure her.

They stood for a full minute in silence. Then Mary lifted her head and spoke slowly and softly as if she were telling an old tale which they knew very well but were always willing to hear again.

'The Listening Women have stood here longer than anybody can remember. They've seen generations of people come and go, and they'll see generations more. No one knows who thought of them first, or who brought them here, or what ceremonies or rituals were performed here. Only by laying ourselves open to them, making ourselves receptive to them, by using our intuition and getting in touch with our oldest instincts, can we learn about them.'

She paused for a moment, concentrating.

Then she said, 'I want us all to go back to a time when the stones were young, and to become the priestesses who knew the stones. The earth beneath your feet is that earth. You are those women. Let the power of the earth flow through you.'

They stood for a few moments in silence, hands clasped, eyes closed, faces raised to the starry sky. As if, Imogen thought, it were some evangelical prayer meeting.

Panicking, she wondered, suppose I can't imagine this? Suppose I'm like my aunt? I remember peeping round the door and seeing that earnest High Church lady kneeling down with Uncle Martin's wife and asking God what He wanted them to do that day. They both had notebooks and biros, and the earnest lady was listening to God, with her head held slightly to one side, and scribbling away like mad. But my aunt just knelt there with a peculiar expression on her face, and didn't write anything at all. When they both got up, she said drily, 'I think God wants me to have a day off!' And the earnest lady went away and didn't come back.

Suppose I'm like that? Sadie and the others will never speak to me again, and Alice won't speak to me at all if she finds out about this, and I'll be in disgrace with both sides and have to leave the dale and never come back . . .

They were walking round, hand in hand, within the circle of stones, Imogen miserably aware that far from being a priestess of the past she was simply a cold, uneasy, and conscience-stricken young woman who wished she had never been persuaded to come.

Mary's hand held her inexorably, and Mary walked on, head held high. As they paced, one linked to the other, a fine current ran from hand to hand, and Imogen became aware of the circle first as a shape and then as a movement. Mary stopped and released her and knelt stiffly.

175

'Feel the power of the earth flowing through you,' she repeated, and pressed her palms down on the rough grass.

Copying her, Imogen once again felt the engine throbbing beneath.

'Now lie down and look up at the sky,' Mary said.

She paused between each command.

'Feel your body touching the earth . . . Feel the power of the sky above you . . . Keep those two great powers in your mind . . . Now stand outside yourself and see your body, as it is at this moment, lying between them, and joined to both.'

The frosty earth upheld Imogen, the frosty stars glittered down on her. A frosty moon rode through strips of cloud. Above and around her towered the ancient stones, forming a protective circle.

She was free of fear and of sorrow.

Fred, she thought.

Inside her, a flower of bliss opened.

Returning to the business of living was a slow and difficult process.

Imogen and Beth helped Mary to her feet. Jinny and Erica lit a fire in the cauldron, and they all gathered round, shivering slightly, stretching out their fingers to the flames. Then Mary questioned them, and one by one they described the circle as they imagined it, Imogen thought, listening to them. Words and ideas seemed stilted: culled from a child's history book, expressing personal utopias.

'I saw all the villagers dancing round the stones. The priests blessed them.'

'Everyone was happy. Anything they wished at that moment would be granted.'

'The animals were with them, as they worshipped the goddess, and the animals were sacred to the people. No one was cruel to them.'

All of the women, in ways either subtle or obvious, were connecting the vision with their own lives and crafts.

Erica said, 'They worked images in bronze and put them on the altar as a gift to the goddess Artemis.'

Last of all, Mary asked, 'What did you see, Imogen?'

She felt a little shock at hearing Mary pronounce her name for the first time.

Embarrassed, she answered, 'I didn't see anything. I forgot myself. I was at peace with heaven and earth and life – oh,' remembering Fred, 'and death.'

Their silence accepted her.

Then Jinny asked, 'Is anyone feeling brave enough to strip off?'

The response was unanimous and negative.

'It's too cold for me,' said Sadie. 'Midsummer's Eve will be the time for that sort of caper. You can if you like. The rest of us need to warm up.'

They danced round the fire, if it could be called dancing. Mary was too old and stiff to do more than shuffle. The mature members of the party gyrated with dignity. But Jinny tossed up her arms, tossed back her golden fleece, and gave herself to the moment. Fascinated, Imogen mimicked her movements, sedately at first, and then more easily as she became familiar with them. Together they danced faster and faster. The others gradually stepped back, watching, laughing, and clapping rhythmically. Finally, Imogen and Jinny collapsed on the ground, gasping with laughter like the rest of them.

Quiet again, they performed the ritual.

Mary held her old carved face up to the moon, and the moon transformed it into a dull pearl mask with half-closed glints of eyes. She used the curious chanting tone which Imogen associated with gypsies, and the language was archaic. She spoke of the need to be aware of oneself as a being of flesh and spirit, to bring together the soul and the body, to be ashamed of neither and to nourish both. Then she set tall candles to the north, south, east and west of the circle, and lit them. She invoked old gods. Now they walked outside the stone circle and Erica, who had a dark contralto voice, began to hum softly. One by one they hummed with her.

The sound took possession of Imogen. She could hear it, feel it, in her forehead, along her cheekbones, down her nose, out to her ears. Mmmmm. Louder and louder. Her head was a hive of mad gold bees. Her mouth stung with honey. Her skull was about to explode its sweetness into the universe.

The sound stopped. They were silent again.

Then Mary spoke of the earth goddess and the sky god. In unison, the eight women lifted their arms to the starry bowl and drew the god down to them. They mimed the goddess rising from the depths and standing before him. They made them one, and were themselves made whole.

Emotionally and physically exhausted, Imogen sat round the cauldron fire with the others, while Sadie brought forth the contents of the second basket: a silver-plated chalice, a bottle of red wine from the off-licence, and a baton of French bread from the local bakery. Silently they passed the chalice between them, and drank. Silently they broke the bread and ate it.

Imogen began to cry silently. Tears ran down her cheeks. She was neither happy nor unhappy. She cried as a child cries, easily, openly, with her whole being. Incongruously, the words of the Twenty-third Psalm came into her mind: 'Thou hast anointed my head with oil; my cup runneth over.'

She felt the press of friendly hands, the murmur of friendly voices. No one minded. Everyone understood. When she was drying her eyes the practical voice of Mary Proctor signalled the end of the meeting.

'Well, we'd best be getting ourselves down again.'

They began to collect the props of their ritual together. Winter had gone. Spring was here. Summer would come. All had been made well.

TWENTY

Thursday, 30 March

The advent of spring in this northern climate had not abated the bitterness of winter. A fresh fall of snow at night, followed by a sharp morning frost, made the roads hazardous. But riding pillion behind George Hobbs on their way to rehearsal, the cold biting through her leather boots, nipping her toes and reddening her ears, Imogen was filled with exhilaration. She had tucked an artificial rose in the band of her goggles and it fluttered madly in the wind. On the old Harley-Davidson, speeding along a dour grey road between white fields, she was swept clean of doubts and life became simple. Once dismounted, she faced an increasingly complicated world.

'Do you remember,' she asked George, as she removed her helmet, 'telling me that you preferred bells to most people? Well I prefer *hats* to most people!'

He waited for an explanation, but she straightened the taffeta rose and marched into the church hall, leaving him to shrug and say 'Women!' as he wheeled his motorbike round the back of the building.

The company's honeymoon period had been sweet and brief, beginning and ending with that first reading. Afterwards they began life in earnest. Timothy had worked out all the stage moves in advance, and at the second meeting he imparted them in detail. Notes were written in the margins of scripts. Moves and lines were learned together before the next rehearsal. Individual roles were analysed, motives sought, backgrounds considered, and the entire character laid open to discussion and explanation. He forced them to pay attention not only to their roles but to those of other actors, and his eyes and ears were alert to the smallest lapse in concentration.

'Where is the melancholy countenance of Lampriscus? Does that joyful grin mean that he has won the national lottery?'

'Your sword is dangling like a stick of limp celery. Huenebango. Has your fighting arm grown weary?'

179

'Wiggen! When another character is talking to you *try* to look as if you were interested in what they are saying!'

Imogen found the experience rather like counselling. She was being encouraged to look honestly and closely at herself, in this case Delia's self. She had begun rehearsals in a mood of good-natured resignation. Delia was not a part she would have chosen, nor the sort of girl she would have befriended. This she would not have said, for fear of hurting Timothy's feelings. But, when tackled outright the previous week, she did say that she felt Delia was an Elizabethan counterpart of Faithful Grizel: possessed of a conventional type of beauty, soft-spoken, soft-hearted, loving children and animals, anxious to please everyone and succeeding for the most part, staunchly correct in her attitude towards Queen, Country, and the Church of England, and guaranteed to marry a man of whom her parents approved, whether he was her choice or not.

Having delivered this judgement to the general amusement of the company, she considered she had done her bit. So while Venelia's gestures were being censured she thought about the problem of Philip.

Timothy's voice drifted past her.

'Dreaming, Delia?' he asked.

He always addressed the players by their stage names, to keep them concentrated on their parts.

'Dreaming, Delia!' he repeated louder, and brought her back to earth.

Her wits saved her.

'I was wondering how Delia would survive as a girl of today,' said Imogen.

The reply was glib and Timothy treated it as such.

'Nonsense! I know you, Miss, and your ability to give a credible answer. You were taking a mental walkabout and assuming that I wouldn't notice. Now give me one good reason why Sacrapant should have you in his spell?'

Imogen was finding her relationship with Philip extremely difficult. Off-stage, she refused to budge beyond the limits of friendship, and so far had managed to avoid asking him back to supper. On-stage she immediately succumbed to Sacrapant's charms. Moreover, she was having bad dreams about him, and these, she felt, were telling her some significant truth.

'Well, Delia?' Timothy demanded.

His past career tended to overshadow her present one. The tone was that of a schoolmaster rather than a stage director.

Answer him, the imp Imogen said, *and write twenty times 'I must pay more attention in class'.*

180

She thought aloud.

'Delia's instinct is to avoid Sacrapant. She's afraid of him and she distrusts him, but she's very young and inexperienced. He's probably aroused the first strong physical attraction she's ever known, and she can't think straight.'

'Good,' Timothy said. 'A good analysis. Yes. Delia is an old-fashioned virgin, innocent of mind as well as of body – a rare and unfashionable condition in this sexually orientated age. Does she come under his spell *entirely* because of her innocence, do you suppose?'

Imogen dug deeper.

'I think that she might also be drawn towards him *because* she's afraid of him. She knows he can give her the experience she lacks – whether it's good or bad – and in order to grow she needs that experience.'

Timothy gazed at her over his half-glasses with exasperated affection.

'I see you have been rambling to some purpose,' he said drily. 'Does anything else strike you about this dangerous relationship?'

Imogen said recklessly, 'If she didn't know better she would call it love.'

'How very mature of her! But surely Delia doesn't know any better, and would naturally call it love?'

'Yes,' said Imogen, in confusion. 'Yes, of course she would.'

He gave her a shrewd glance, and turned to Philip.

'Now, Sacrapant. What are your feelings about Delia?'

Philip said, in the easy, frank way which always won Imogen to his side, 'Oh, I'm head over heels in love with the girl. But I fear it may be only for the moment. The fact that I have her in my power will bore me eventually. Like any number of men, I'm sorry to say, I worship the lady until she succumbs to my charms.'

'What a cynic!' Timothy cried, enjoying himself. 'But don't forget, Sacrapant, that beneath that dashing exterior you are an old man, and the lady is giving you an extension of youth and hope. So she means more than casual pleasure.'

Philip's expression was strained. Timothy's was genial.

'Anyway, well done, both of you. You're progressing nicely, and I look forward to the eventual outcome.' In a different tone, 'And now to the clowns!'

The trio straightened up and attempted to redeem themselves as he dissected their performances.

Delia whispered to her stage lover, 'Is Tim always as pernickety as this?'

Ian was amused and sympathetic.

'On the whole, yes. Of course, his old pupils are used to being ground

181

exceeding small in the Rowley production mill, but I admit to finding him a tad more obsessive about *The Old Wives' Tale*. I can't make up my mind whether it's to do with the play or old age.'

Mary made the tea, and Imogen the coffee, when rehearsals were over. Their conversation up to now had been noncommittal, but after Haraldstone Hill Imogen had expected a more intimate tone. It was not to be. So this week she ventured to ask when they were all meeting again, and was unpleasantly surprised when Mary took her to task, speaking in a low but forthright voice.

'I'm going to tell you something once and for all, my lass. You'd be well advised to say nothing to anybody about last Monday night. Folk do a lot of guessing and gossiping without believing half what they say, and so long as they're not confronted with the truth they don't mind. But if you start talking about local witches you'll find yourself cold-shouldered at best and victimized at worst.'

Imogen stammered, 'We did no harm . . .'

'It makes no difference. There's a lot of prejudice about, and a lot of fear, and it runs deep. Be careful what you say, or you might get a brick through your shop window one dark night.'

Imogen stared at her, pale and mute.

'There's nothing to look washed-out about,' said Mary more gently. 'Like you said, we harm nobody, and we've helped many a one. But we've been given a bad name and there's some folk still willing to hang us for it.'

She put her hand on Imogen's arm in a rare gesture of intimacy.

'I'm not trying to frighten you, my lass, but up on Haraldstone Hill we were one thing, and down here we're another. Remember to keep them separate and you'll keep out of mischief. Think on.'

Imogen gave a wooden little nod, picked up the tray, and marched back into the hall, wishing she had never gone with them.

'What's wrong?' Philip asked, as she accepted coffee.

She could not confide in him or anyone. So she smiled and said lightly, 'Nothing but tiredness – and don't dare tell me I look tired.'

Timothy was clapping his hands to command their attention, addressing them in ringing tones.

'A word with you all. It's not too early to be thinking about costumes. I have my dressing-up box at home to help us out, and you will be able to provide the more mundane articles yourselves. But the great news is that I have found a splendid costume designer, and an equally splendid wardrobe mistress – both professionals in their fields, and we are amazingly lucky to have them. They are willing to work their fingers to the bone for us, and give their valuable services free, but we can hardly ask them to finance the enterprise as well. Now may I, on top of bullying you twice weekly, proceed to pick your pockets? Are you prepared to pay for – or provide – materials?'

An amused chorus assured him that they were willing to be both bullied and robbed. Only Mary, Imogen guessed, looked worried about the possible expense.

As if he divined this Timothy turned to her, cup in hand, and said, 'Gammer Madge, you are one of the fortunate members of the cast. I have a costume which will suit you perfectly, and I believe it will need very little alteration.'

Mary's chin jutted at the suspicion of charity, but his tone and expression were so matter-of-fact that she lowered it, took a sip of hot tea, and replied peaceably.

'That's lucky, then.'

But Stephen, sitting in his corner, cried abruptly, 'I want a costume!'

At a distance, silent and half-smiling, he gave the impression of being an ordinary pleasant-looking young man, and Mary always made sure that he was clean, combed and neat. Observed more closely, a vagueness behind the eyes, a slackness about the mouth, and a general feeling that he had to wind himself up in order to speak betrayed his condition, and his gestures gave him away entirely. At the moment they were those of a demanding child. The idea of dressing up had captured his fancy. He slopped his cup down on the floor and began to gyrate round the room, arms outspread, head wagging from side to side, chanting, as a child does, 'I-wanta-cos-tume. I-wanta-cos-tume.'

'Stephen Proctor, sit down and behave yourself!' Mary said sternly.

His mouth fell open, his eyes filled with tears. He shambled back to his corner, turned his chair round, and sat with his back to them, head bowed, hands clasped between his knees. There was an embarrassed and sorry silence.

Timothy said quickly, 'Oh, I'm sure we can find something for him,' and in a louder voice, 'What sort of costume would you like, Stephen?'

No answer. Mary spoke up with rough kindness.

'There now, Stevie, what sort of a costume would you like? Tell Dr Rowley.'

Still silence. She sighed and went over to him, stroked his thin mouse-coloured hair, spoke more gently to the child he was.

'It's not the end of the world, my lad. You were being too noisy, that's all. Speak up when the gentleman asks you to.'

He turned round, streaked with tears, and buried his face in her breasts. The muffled jumble of words could be translated only by his mother.

'He'd like to be a clown,' Mary told them.

The guise seemed appropriate, though everyone was ashamed to think so.

Relieved, Timothy said, 'Splendid. I have a costume at home that should fit.'

Stephen lifted his head and wiped his eyes and nose with his coat sleeve, cheered, but Timothy was thinking of possible future pitfalls.

'I must just make a couple of points, first. You can't dress up until the others do, and that will be some considerable time ahead.' Stephen was disappointed. 'And I'm afraid you can't come on to the stage with them at any time.'

'Do you hear what Dr Rowley says?' Mary asked, giving her son his cue.

He looked up with such an expression of cunning that Imogen was startled. The cunning was replaced by sly knowledge, and then once more fell into vacancy.

'You've got a tongue, haven't you?' Mary enquired in her usual tone.

Stephen nodded violently.

'Then use it. Tell Dr Rowley you'll do as he says.'

'I'll do as he says,' Stephen repeated.

'And what do you say to Dr Rowley for his kindness to you?' Mary ordered.

He answered mechanically, 'Thank you, Dr Rowley.'

'That's right,' said Mary, patting him. 'Now drink your tea and keep quiet.'

Relieved, the Players began to chatter as if nothing had occurred.

'Imogen, my dear,' said Timothy, putting one hand beneath her elbow and leading her a little way out of the crowd, 'a word with you. Have you heard about the Brakespears' trouble? You haven't? I thought George might have mentioned it. I know they confided in him. Ah well, he's a man who keeps his eyes and ears open and his mouth closed, and they are trying to hush things up, so perhaps not. Well, I'm glad to say that Hal is taking things in his usual fighting spirit, but I fear that poor Alice is quite overcome, and was in considerable distress when I saw her yesterday . . .'

Imogen paled and then reddened, feeling that her escapade on Harald-stone Hill had been reported.

'Apparently, she was the first to discover it,' Timothy continued, relishing his news. 'A shocking experience – no, far worse than shocking. Vile. Abhorrent. Obscene. Poor Alice. She was made for the mild, sequestered ways of life . . .'

'Oh, please tell me what's wrong!' Imogen cried, beside herself with suspense.

'She went into St Oswald's to do the flowers yesterday morning and the vestry window had been forced open, and there were signs as if someone had celebrated a Black Mass in the church.'

Imogen inhaled a deep breath of deliverance, which emerged as a conscience-stricken exhalation of, 'Oh, how horrible!'

'You may well say so.' He was watching her closely. 'The results could be far-reaching. There is a vast difference between studying the magic arts and practising black magic. In this age of many beliefs, Langesby has been able to accommodate a number of irregularities. But if people suspect that there is evil afoot they will look for a scapegoat, and Haraldstone has something of a reputation.'

Mary, counselling her to stay silent, had said, *You might get a brick through your shop window one dark night.*

'Has Mrs Proctor heard about this?' Imogen asked with some apprehension.

'I have no idea.' Eyebrows lifting. 'In what way is that relevant?'

Be careful what you say.

Imogen floundered into explanation.

'When Alice and I were having tea at Prospect House Edith Wyse said that Mrs Proctor was a witch and came from a long line of witches.'

His face became impassive.

'I'm afraid Edith amuses herself at times by sowing discord. In that instance she was probably trying to annoy Alice. The admirable Mary Proctor, like her character Gammer Madge, is the proverbial wise woman of the village, and no one would connect her with this disgraceful affair.'

Feeling that he was heading her off, as Mary had done, Imogen was resentful.

'No. But rumours can do a lot of damage, and in the present situation Edith's sort of remark could be inflammatory.'

'And the use of the word *inflammatory* is a mite unfortunate,' said Timothy, a headmaster instructing his pupil, 'though witches are not for burning nowadays.'

He saw that his tone annoyed her, and softened it.

'But I have drifted away from the point. What I intended to say is that poor Alice would welcome a few words of comfort from an old friend.'

'Did she tell you so?' Imogen asked, unconvinced and unappeased.

He was engagingly repentant.

'No. I guessed it. If I am mistaken and you meet with a cool response, I shall explain to Alice that it was all my fault and apologize to you most humbly.'

His smile also asked forgiveness for lecturing her. Her smile granted him absolution.

'Bless you,' said Timothy. 'I'm extremely fond of you, my dear, even though my experience and instinct tell me that you are a highly plausible charmer.'

Without thinking, Imogen said, 'Sadie Whicker – who has a crafts shop in Haraldstone – accused me of being artful.'

'Ah yes. The accomplished and engaging Sadie,' he answered. 'She happens to be the lady who has offered to be our wardrobe mistress. And another of your artistic colleagues – Milia Godden – will be designing our costumes. You didn't know that? Then you are not the only artful person, Imogen, and you may tell them so from me!'

He raised her hand and kissed it, replete with satisfaction as a cat would be with stolen cream. He did so relish having the last word.

Clutching George round his leather waist with both arms, her *fantaisie* rippling in the wind, she screamed in his ear, 'Why didn't you tell me about the Brakespears and that Black Mass business?'

He shouted back, 'They asked me not to say anything.'

She could hardly scream such a delicate sentiment as, 'But I'm their friend and I thought you were mine,' so she contented herself with a stentorian, 'You could have told *me*!'

'Sorry!' George yelled over his shoulder. 'Would you rather I was a top hat?'

She could hear the grin in his words, and bawled back, also grinning.

'Not at the moment. Top hats can't take me home.'

'That's all right, then.'

She wished everyone was as agreeable as George. Still, she reminded herself, he had looked after Stephen while his mother led the witches on Haraldstone Hill, and he knew that Imogen was with them. Yet he had never said a word about it. So what did that make him? A kind son helping out his mother and turning a blind eye to her magical practices, or a witches' familiar who aided and abetted them? Even more disquieting, could he be much more powerful than she supposed? An unsuspected and mysterious force in his own right. *Spawn of Meroe. Dreaded Sacrapant.* Now there lay the heart of terror.

Oh, don't be an idiot, she thought. And then, anguished – Oh, to hell with the lot of them!

George dropped her off at the archway of the court and roared off to Crossdyke Street. Neither of them had noticed the old blue Rover parked in a side-street near the Catwalk. Briskly, Imogen walked down the passage, turned the corner, and stopped.

Two people were standing patiently outside Crazy Hats, staring ahead in silence, waiting for her to come home. Hal's expression had the grim confidence of a Christian soldier marching as to war, but Alice's beautiful blue eyes were grieved, and her shoulders lacked assurance. For the first time, Imogen realized that Alice needed her. The knowledge was both sad and exhilarating. On the instant that they saw each other, Imogen held out her arms and Alice came into their shelter.

'I've heard all about it from Tim,' said Imogen, hugging her, 'and I think it's a disgusting thing to happen to such good people. I was going to ring you up tonight. We must be on the same wavelength.'

'Of course we're on the same wavelength,' Alice cried. Overlooking their past coldness, she added, 'We always have been.'

Hal was slow to follow his wife's lead, and Imogen guessed that the visit was Alice's doing and that he had concurred out of regard for her feelings.

In charge, as she had never been before, Imogen held out one hand while continuing to pat Alice with the other.

Man to man, she said, 'Hello, Hal. It's lovely to see you again. And I'm sorry to hear about that shocking affair at St Oswald's.'

He shook hands solemnly, saying, 'We must expect to be tested and tried.'

Then he cast aside the mantle of rectitude in favour of battle.

'But they don't fool me and I'm damned if I'll knuckle under to them.'

Alice said, drying her eyes on the handkerchief Imogen offered, 'Hal doesn't think it's genuine witchcraft. He thinks it's a put-up job, engineered by someone who is trying to discredit his authority. I know he has one or two enemies . . .'

More than one or two, Imogen thought.

'. . . but I believe it's much more sinister than that.'

Remembering convivial ten o'clock mugs at the vicarage, Imogen said,

'Come in, and I'll make us some cocoa.' And as she rummaged for the door-key in her handbag, 'What do you think of Crazy Hats?'

Alice was instantly contrite. 'Oh, how selfish we are. Talking about ourselves. You've made it look lovely. I knew it as rather a shabby little sweet shop. But we were looking at the windows while we were waiting for you – weren't we, Hal?' A grave nod. 'And I said at once, how talented, how beautiful, how spring-like, how like our Imogen – didn't I, Hal?' Another nod. 'And I love that duchess of a hat with the pale pink roses, and Hal liked it, too – didn't you, Hal?'

'Very – fetching.'

He was trying to please Alice by praising her friend's handiwork. He loves her, Imogen thought. Well, that says a lot for him.

She narrowed her eyes, picturing Alice in the wide panama with parchment roses, and approved the choice.

'You must have it,' she decided. 'No, no,' as they both glanced apprehensively towards the price ticket, 'it's not for sale. It's a present. You were both very good to me and for me, last autumn, perhaps in more ways than you realize. So it's a sort of belated thank-you. You shall try it on, Alice, and if Hal approves – but only if – you shall take it back with you tonight on condition that you promise to wear it whenever you can.'

'Oh, but I ought to pay for it.'

'You are paying for it. You'll be a splendid advertisement for Crazy Hats.'

'Oh, are you *sure*? Oh, I shall be delighted,' Alice cried, overcome. 'Oh, Hal, what do you think?'

He said benignly, 'It's a pretty hat which should become you.'

And so it did.

'Goodness!' Alice said, admiring the rejuvenated goddess in the glass. No longer Ceres but her daughter Proserpine. 'It makes me feel quite young again. I wore a hat something like this when Hal and I first met. Do you remember, Hal?'

He lied loyally, 'Yes, of course. And you haven't changed a bit.'

'It's very much your style,' said Imogen, smiling on them both, adjusting the hat to a more sophisticated angle. 'You know what suits you. Very often people have no idea.'

I sound like Sadie, she thought. Blast her for an artful witch!

'I shall wear it for Easter Sunday and Whit Sunday,' Alice decided, 'and of course, for our garden party in July.'

Hal made a handsome gesture.

188

'Perhaps Imogen would like to share Easter Sunday with us,' he offered.

'Of course she would. Oh, you must, Imogen. We make it such a wonderful festival. Even gloomy old St Oswald's looks beautiful in its Easter garb. We make little bunches of wild flowers for the children to give to their mothers. And we have a lunch party at the vicarage afterwards for friends and helpers. I have to admit that I'm influenced by my mother's ideas. She had such a gift for decorating the church on a particular occasion, and Easter was her crowning achievement.'

Overwhelmed, Imogen said, 'Thank you. I'd love to come.'

She wondered if there was a bus on Easter Sunday which would reach Langesby in time for the morning service.

'We ought to invite Imogen to our garden party, too,' Hal said, capping one success with another.

'She's invited to both,' cried Alice, 'but particularly on Easter Sunday. You will come to see us, won't you, Imogen? We've missed you so much.'

Their hour together was tranquil. The Brakespears did not say anything more about the outrage to St Oswald's church, but concentrated on mending the nets of friendship. They praised everything in the shop and the flat, including Polly who did her utmost not to deserve it. And Hal was on his best behaviour, though Imogen saw his attention wander occasionally, as if drawn to more important matters.

They left reluctantly, at eleven o'clock: exclaiming at the lateness of the hour. Outside, the night sky was clear and the stars brilliant. In the velvet silence of the court not one window showed a light. Not one cat cast its shadow on the wall.

Lingering on the threshold of the shop, renewed, restored, clutching her extravagant black and white striped Crazy Hats box, bound by a black satin bow, Alice said, 'If only life were always like this.'

Then, tenderly, they both kissed Imogen good-night.

DEMONS

TWENTY-ONE

The letter in the *Langesby Chronicle* had been placed tactfully at the bottom of the 'Dear Editor' column.

Dear Sir,

Are the citizens of Langesby aware that the vicar of St Oswald's is concealing a potentially dangerous incident from them? I have it on good authority that some person or persons broke into the church on Wednesday last, and celebrated a Black Mass. Yet nothing has been said, and apparently nothing done about the matter. In a less enlightened age the immediate reaction would have been a witch-hunt, with the perpetrators brought to rough justice. Although no one would condone such a response nowadays, we should be ill advised to ignore the presence of diabolism in our community. God and the Devil may seem old-fashioned images to a sophisticated society, but the truth that they represent is eternal. Evil begets evil. In these godless days, when cruelty and violence of every conceivable kind is committed, why should the desecration of an altar satisfy these criminals? Let the vicar of St Oswald's make light of this affair if he pleases, but the rest of us must be more vigilant and root out the evildoers in our midst. We shall have no one but ourselves to blame if the sanctuary of our church is set at naught, and the town of Langesby held to ransom by some satanic Mafia.

Yours etc.

A Concerned Christian (name supplied)

Alice's voice was full when she read out the offending letter to Imogen and sounded as if she had been crying. She declared that nothing as bad as this had ever happened to them before. Certainly there had been difficulties in past parishes, even unpleasantness, but they had never been subjected to wickedness and vile accusations. And please would Imogen forgive her for ringing so early in the morning, but she didn't want to interrupt her when she was busy in the shop. This was followed by sounds as if Alice were trying not to cry again.

Sitting in her dressing-gown, enjoying a poached egg on toast, looking out on to the empty courtyard, Imogen thought, *Busy in the shop? That will be the day!* Aloud she cried, 'How awful for you both! How has Hal taken it?'

'Oh, my dear – don't ask! We're always up at seven, as you know, and the *Langesby Chronicle* is delivered at half-past, so we'd just begun breakfast when he threw down the paper and – well – *roared* would be the word. Yes, fairly roared with rage. He's in his study this minute, writing to the editor. And he says he'll find out who wrote that letter if he has to turn the town inside out and upside down. I can't eat anything, but I've poured myself a cup of tea, and I simply had to ring you. The pity of it is,' said Alice forlornly, 'that Hal is now convinced that this is a plot to get rid of him.'

'But can they do that? I mean, won't the Church protect its own people?'

'Oh my dear,' said Alice sadly, 'there are enemies within as well as without. You don't know the half of it. Hal has ruffled a few feathers in high places before now. One must believe that right prevails in the end, but I have sometimes wondered whether the Church authorities don't regard him with the same suspicion that police regard vagrants. They will keep moving him on.'

Imogen chose her words carefully.

'Hal's a modern-day crusader who is prepared to fight for his principles, and that makes conventional people uneasy. They don't like disturbing thoughts and they're afraid of change.'

There was a pause while Alice thought this over.

Then she said, 'Yes, I think that's very true.'

Imogen dug back in her memory, fetching up consolation and counselling.

'Besides, you wouldn't have been satisfied with a placid man. You chose Hal because he was remarkable, and provided purpose and excitement in life.'

'But perhaps *he* shouldn't have married,' said Alice sadly. 'Sometimes I feel that he's hampered by having to think of me and the children all the time. He could fight better without hostages.'

They were both silent for a moment or two, feeling, on reflection, that the fate of his hostages had never caused him to change course and was probably a secondary consideration. Then Imogen took up the challenge.

'Nonsense. Think what a lonely, comfortless life he'd have without you. He chose you because he needed you. He can fight all the better from a sound family base, with someone to turn to when things get difficult. Besides, he loves you. So that's that. No use bothering about the ifs and buts.'

Captured sobs and smothered sniffles indicated that Alice was crying again, but more happily.

'You're a good friend, Imogen.'

'You're welcome,' said Imogen sincerely.

She was savouring the luxury of being adviser instead of advised. It was indeed more blessed to give than to receive.

A distant clarion call summoned them both back to a harsher world. Alice said hurriedly, 'Oh, that's Hal wanting me. I must go now, my dear, but thank you for everything.'

'You've done the same for me in the past.'

Alice's voice became stronger. Her tone said that she was being fair-minded, despite all her reservations.

'I should like to think so – just one minute, Hal, dear! – Imogen, a word before I go. You know how much we love you, and that we think your pretty little hat shop is a credit to you . . .'

'Ye-e-es?' Imogen wondered, and feared.

'I'm sure that there's a lot of unnecessary gossip and nonsense talked about Haraldstone – and obviously you've been lucky with your premises, and Vera says that Miss Parkinson who ran the sweet shop was a regular chapel-goer until the chapel closed – but in any case people would realize that you're far too good and nice to be involved in anything disreputable . . .'

Oh lawks! She *has* heard about the meeting on the hill!

'. . . but you will be careful, won't you, my dear? There are some rather peculiar characters in Haraldstone. I'm not saying that they're necessarily bad, but . . .'

'I take your meaning,' said Imogen grimly.

'Of course you do. And I know you wouldn't do anything that wasn't quite . . .'

'Oh, quite.'

'. . . and I know perfectly well that I don't have to warn you, but you're very dear to us both – I'm coming, Hal! – so do take care of yourself, and remember that we're expecting you to spend Easter Sunday with us.'

'I look forward to that,' said Imogen, deflated.

She put down the receiver and thought for a moment.

'And God bless *you*, Alice,' she said aloud. 'I know that a widow earning her crust in a hat shop isn't on the same level as Mother Teresa, but I've just this minute sorted you out and propped you up, and in return you very kindly knocked me down and winded me. Thanks a lot.'

Polly mewed loudly, not in sympathy, but because Imogen was scraping the rest of her breakfast into the pedal bin instead of offering it to her better half.

The morning began as emptily as usual, and if the afternoon was to imitate its predecessors Imogen expected to sell little more than gloves or berets from the side window, and possibly a *fantaisie* or two from the display. She had been living as economically as she could since Uncle Martin – whose financial senses were as keen as his perceptions were dull – had most strongly advised her against drawing further on her capital. After paying the first quarter's bills, only the sale of Fred's toy held starvation at bay.

Keeping a shop was quite different from working at home. She and her premises had to be immaculate and ready from opening to closing time, whether customers called or stayed away. Early on, she had decided against standing idle, while time passed slowly and her overheads mounted relentlessly, so each morning she carried down a tray of materials. On this she made trimmings while she waited, and kept an eye on the window. She no longer had expectations when anyone stopped and stared admiringly, wistfully or hopefully at the main display. So many looked, even for quite a time, and then strolled off. So few came in.

She was creating a rosebud from cream velvet when the shop bell jingled. She slipped the tray on to a shelf beneath the counter and rose smiling, to greet two strange ladies of indeterminate age in sensible felt hats, with not an atom of fashion sense between them.

'Mrs Lacey?' the elder one enquired on a rising note. 'We have been sent here by Mrs Brakespear, who recommends you highly.'

Her tone and accent were authoritative, trained from birth to exact obedience from her inferiors.

Imogen's murmur of appreciation went unnoticed.

'We are the Misses Ritchison of Brockridge Hall.'

As she announced their identity both sisters inclined their heads gravely towards Imogen, and she found herself doing the same to them. This time she remained silent until the elder Miss Ritchison had finished speaking and given her permission to answer.

'We are holding a garden fête next month. Our annual garden fête.'

Her brief pause and questioning look made Imogen realize that she was expected to know of this even if she came from another planet.

'Oh yes, of course,' she said, with the utmost confidence.

The two sisters smiled at each other and then at her, satisfied.

As if Imogen were not present, the elder said to the younger, 'Mrs Brakespear *did* say she would understand.' Then to the subject of her remark, 'So we have each come to buy a hat. One moment!' – holding up her hand, as Imogen showed signs of doing something about this request – 'We wish to look round first.'

'Please do. If I can help you at all you have only to ask,' said Imogen, and retreated in order to give them space and privacy.

There was not a great deal of room in which to retreat, but she made herself as inconspicuous as she could, and assessed them at least as acutely as they were assessing the display.

In Imogen's eyes everyone became a possible hat, but in the case of woollen stockings, well-polished leather brogues and well-worn tweed suits, the options dwindled. Her only hope was to transcend them.

They were gazing, wrinkled mouths pursed, washed-out blue eyes staring, grey eyebrows contracted, at the fanciful, the delicate, the charming, the never-them hats. They consulted each other in voices they did not trouble to lower.

'I think Mrs Brakespear must have been mistaken, Evelyn.'

'Not at all the sort of thing one imagined, Julia.'

'And far too expensive for what they are.'

They turned on, rather than to her, and were about to castigate the world of Crazy Hats when Imogen spoke first in tones that were honeyed but compelling, smiling all the while.

'I am wondering what you will be wearing at your fête? You may well find that I have nothing on display that appeals to you. Perhaps you could describe your dresses to me? I create hats individually, for the person and the occasion, you see. So,' persuasively, 'please put me in the picture.' And before they could reply she added, as if to herself, 'I imagine something long and flowing, in a regal style.'

The word *regal* stopped them in their tracks and spoke to their inmost being, because it was above their status and beyond their hopes. They looked imperiously at each other, and Julia the elder answered for both.

'We are not interested in being fashionable, you know.'

'You create your own fashion. Naturally,' Imogen answered, having arrived on their wavelength.

This time their glances were conspiratorial.

Evelyn confided, 'On important occasions, such as this, we wear our late mother's dresses. Wonderfully well preserved. Such lovely materials. So beautifully made. So graceful . . .'

'. . . so unlike the present day,' Julia finished.

Imogen said, as if she had known them for years, 'Exactly.'

Evelyn confided again, 'But her hats, you see, have not worn so well – the moth in the velvet, the mice in the straw – and when we were talking to Mrs Brakespear last Sunday she showed us the hat you made for her. We thought it rather pretty.' She turned to her sister for agreement. 'Didn't we, Julia?'

'For a vicarage garden party,' Julia warned. 'Pretty, but not . . .'

Imogen dared supply the adjective.

'Not impressive.'

Julia was pleased, but tried to conceal the fact.

'And as you are both much taller than Mrs Brakespear,' Imogen continued, 'you could carry off something more showy. I suppose you wouldn't allow me to see your own hats, would you?' She remembered the criticism of expense. 'You may not need new ones. They might just need refurbishing.'

The sisters consulted each other's faces. Then Julia searched her handbag, brought out a visiting card from a tortoiseshell case with a silver monogram and a broken hinge, and conferred it like a favour.

'You may come tomorrow afternoon between three and four o'clock,' she said. 'We would send the car, but at the moment it is out of service, and good chauffeurs are difficult to find. Have you a car? You have not?' Eyebrows raised. 'Ah well. I believe there are *buses*.'

She conveyed that buses were something other people used, but Evelyn ruined this little conceit by saying, 'The three o'clock bus from here stops at our gates. Ask for Brockridge Hall. It is not a very long walk up the drive.'

Julia's eyes brought her sister to heel and froze Imogen's thanks on her lips.

Sadie had been incommunicado for the past few days, as if she guessed that Imogen was annoyed with her, but this morning she sidled in at eleven o'clock, carrying two mugs of cinnamon and apple tea and two cinnamon crunch biscuits on a tin tray. Her timing was immaculate, though no witchcraft was involved in that. Simply, she watched all the goings and comings in the court.

'Well, well, well,' she said, rolling her eyes, 'so you've met the two

Miss Ritchisons? We call them the Miss Havishams round here. They were both jilted at one time or another and they live in their glorious past. Very top-drawer, but no money. Doubt if they can afford your prices. Still, if you play your cards right, they'll recommend you to their richer county friends.'

Imogen was so far mellowed by the morning's customers as to forgive Sadie for ignoring her, but she would not allow her to slip away unscathed.

'Never mind them for the moment, Sadie. I have a bone to pick with you. You didn't tell me you were going to be our wardrobe mistress. I felt a perfect fool when Timothy Rowley told me last Thursday. To think that you called me artful! And what made you and Milia offer your pagan services free for the benefit of the *Church*, may I ask?'

Sadie made herself comfortable on the edge of the dais, and offered Imogen a St Oswald's mug.

'We've got nothing against the Church,' she said equably. 'We all paddle our own canoes these days. As for Milia, she wants to spread her designing wings – rather a good pun, that! – so she'll probably use this collection as a flight into greener fields. And good luck to her – just as long as she goes on supplying me with silk scarves, because they're one of my best-sellers. As for me, I don't need to tell you that I'm handy with my needle and have an eye for dress. I also happen to enjoy good amateur theatricals, and I'm a great admirer of Tim Rowley. I've been to three of his lectures. He's a big noise – well, *the* big noise – at Langesby Magic Arts Society. And he runs erudite little groups who meet at his house once a month and discuss mysticism and alchemy and all that. It's too intellectual for me, but he's got an open mind and he knows his stuff.'

She pounced.

'Besides, you never told me that those great friends of yours were St Oswald's vicar and his wife. Not that you needed to. I knew they must be ultra-respectable, from the way you acted when you first heard I was a witch. Up and off in a minute, and ditching your lovely quilt into the bargain!'

'Well, that's old history,' said Imogen uncomfortably, 'and I did buy the quilt, and I'm part of Haraldstone now.'

'Yes, and they mustn't have been too pleased about that, either,' Sadie continued, loving to probe, 'because this is the first time they've come visiting. Oh, I don't miss much. I saw them waiting for you outside the shop the other night. I suppose they wanted to confide the wicked goings-on in Langesby.' She added soberly, 'That's a very unfortunate incident.'

'Unfortunate is hardly the word. I should have said it was thoroughly despicable and disgusting,' Imogen replied indignantly. 'And have you read that letter in this morning's *Langesby Chronicle?*'

'No, I haven't. I don't take the *Chronicle*, and nor do you, so Mrs St Oswald must have been on the blower at the crack of dawn.'

'Her name is Alice Brakespear, and she's an old and dear friend.' Very stiffly.

'Oh, we are hoity-toity this fine morning,' Sadie remarked. 'Tell me about this letter to save me looking in my crystal ball.'

Her tone was good-natured, but Imogen felt angry and afraid.

'It was signed "A Concerned Christian". The wretched man didn't even have the courage to put his name to it.'

'Then how do you know it's a man? It could be a woman.'

'Whatever the gender, this anonymous correspondent says we have evil in our midst and should do something about it.'

'Well, it wasn't the work of our little group,' said Sadie hotly, 'if that's what you're thinking – and I'm surprised you've got the gall to imagine such a thing!'

'I know it wasn't you, and I wasn't thinking it. But Mrs Proctor has been very stand-offish with me, and when I said something friendly about our meeting on the hill she shut me up properly.'

'Well, she's in the firing line, isn't she?' Sadie said. 'It's all right for you. You're just an interested spectator, but Mary Proctor is known to be descended from the Langesbydale witches, and even in these enlightened days she'll have enemies – probably a few she's made on her own account, but far more who don't like their idea of her. If someone stirs up the local layabouts she'll be the first to have her windows stoned.'

Imogen sat motionless, warming her hands on the mug.

A brick through the window one dark night.

'Still, we've done nothing to offend anybody so there's no point in crossing bridges before we come to them,' said Sadie, being practical. 'This may be a put-up job, aimed at your friend the Reverend Brakespear. Now there's a troublemaker in the best sense of the word, who's given Langesby – and probably his masters – more than they bargained for . . .'

I have sometimes wondered whether the church authorities don't regard him with the same suspicion that the police regard vagrants.

'. . . I mean, St Oswald's was a lost cause until he arrived. Langesby – and probably the Church hierarchy – expected him to get quietly lost with it. But he came out fighting and upset a lot of little apple carts and made some powerful enemies. He won't go quietly, and if he has to go he'll take a few with him.'

'How do you know all this?' Imogen asked.

'The dale grapevine. I like to keep in touch with events. Still vexed with me?' Sadie enquired cheerfully.

Imogen had to smile.

'No. I'm not vexed. But I am worried.'

Sadie said, at a tangent, 'Milia's been stretching the library van to its limits. They brought her a book on Elizabethan costume last week, and she's designed your costume already. You'll fancy yourself in it, I can tell you. It's a dream.'

Then she stood up, put one hand dramatically on her large breasts and broke into song:

'"A dream for a dreamer."'

'Sadie!' Imogen said with stern amusement, as if she were an elder sister. 'What I would guess to be a mother and daughter are pressing their noses against your shop window. This is the season for weddings, and they have *bridal bed quilt* written all over their faces!'

Sadie disappeared in an instant, leaving her tea things behind her.

Julia Ritchison had assumed that Imogen was at her disposal, and since Imogen had not dared to contradict her, and certainly did not want to miss such an opportunity, she had to ask Sadie to keep an eye on Crazy Hats for two hours that Saturday afternoon.

'There won't be much happening, if anything, and as I'm in trade the Ritchison ladies won't entertain me longer than necessary. So I should be back before five.'

Feeling unaccountably free, she caught the designated bus, alighted at Brockridge Hall stop, walked up the long drive and was received with chilled courtesy. Gradually the sisters' mood, or rather Julia's mood for she dictated the climate of their lives together, changed. Imogen's ease of manner and her spontaneous enthusiasm for the late Mrs Ritchison's wardrobe quite won them over. Imogen persuaded them to dress up, tried various hats on them, sketched half a dozen stately wrecks, and packed up two hopefuls to take home for renovation. Finally, by dint of running all the way down the drive with a hat box in either hand, she managed to catch the half-past six bus back to Langesby and arrived at Crafty Notions to find an aggrieved Sadie nursing an evening whisky.

'All pals together, eh?' that lady enquired, with mock sarcasm. And as Imogen laughed and accepted a drink, 'I never knew a girl like you for collecting incompatible friends. Just don't invite us to the same party, that's all I ask.'

201

Ignoring this advice, Imogen cried, 'Sadie, those two ancient ladies are quite *amazing*. I'm not surprised they didn't marry. They have never grown away from their parents. The house is a museum and it's thick with dust and falling to bits, because they've got very little help and less money. They will keep the library clock five minutes fast, because that's the way Father liked it. Mother was one of those improbable female saints who seemed to abound in pre-feminist days. And they were telling me that the Ritchisons have lived in Brockridge Hall since sixteen forty-something. Father was a justice of the peace, and the Lord knows what else.'

'So were his forefathers,' said Sadie with relish. 'Beef-eating, port-swigging male chauvinists to the last hog. And every man-jack of them relished a witch-hunt, preferably on horseback with a pack of slavering hounds and a crew of demented villagers. Give them a dull Sunday afternoon and some poor old soul was due for a ducking in the village pond. Great-granddad Ritchison hanged Mary Proctor's great-grandmother.'

'Oh dear,' said Imogen, seeing further complications ahead, 'because, although I couldn't call them *friends*, we do seem to have established an amiable relationship.'

Sadie answered crisply, 'Well that's *your* problem. More to the point – how many hats did you sell?'

'None. I'm cleaning and refurbishing two of their own, and I've sketched lots of others. Oh, the ideas they've given me! Oh, Sadie, how I wish I had money to risk. I'd love to create an entire display with a 1910 garden party theme.'

Sadie waited, but seeing that Imogen was lost in this mythical project, asked in a high bright voice, 'And did *you* sell anything while I was away this afternoon, Sadie? Well, yes, thank you for *asking*, Imogen! I sold two pairs of white gloves, one of those children's straw bonnets, three *fantaisies*, and a lady is coming back on Monday because Mrs St Oswald recommended her and she's interested in the Robin Hood hat.'

Imogen woke up, crying, 'But that's wonderful!'

Sadie was unforgiving.

'I should say it was. And I was busy here, too. The season's warming up. You should have seen me dashing to and fro like one demented. *Would you mind if I left you to look at those scarves, madam, while I attend to the lady in the other shop?* Trot, trot, trot. *Sorry to keep you waiting, madam. Oh dear, a twenty-pound note. I'm afraid we're short of change. If you'll excuse me a minute I'll get some from the other shop.* Figaro here! Figaro there! Figaro come! Figaro go! I'll bet I've lost a stone while you were hobnobbing with the gentry.'

202

'Sadie, you're a dream. And I love you.' Hugging her.

'Oh, if I'm a dream you're sure to love me!' Sadie replied sardonically. 'And you've had gentlemen callers, too. They all scribbled love-letters to you. Talk about the dark lady of the Sonnets – she had nothing on you. Naturally, I had to provide the paper. And find the envelopes. And stand around trying to get my breath back, while they thought what to say. And both shop bells going mad at the same time.'

'Who, Sadie? Who came, and when?'

The pugnacious little woman had had enough of Imogen's peculiar taste in friends, and replied briskly, 'You'll find everything on the counter.'

But Polly was sitting on the counter, famished and furious, scattering three letters and a note as she leaped down, making loud protests, and Imogen had to appease the cat's hunger before she could satisfy her curiosity.

My dear Imogen,

I was passing through Haraldstone this afternoon, and dropped in hoping to find you reigning over your salubrious establishment. Alas, you were absent, and the excellent Sadie Whicker tells me that you are taking tea with the Misses Ritchison – interesting ladies, if somewhat *fossilized*. I should like a private word with you, and will telephone over the weekend to arrange a meeting.

I see that poor Hal is now being pilloried in the local press about this wretched Black Mass business. Let us hope that he can clear the matter up, so that it goes no further.

Yours, as ever, Tim

Dear Imogen,

I'd expected to find you in the shop but Sadie says you're out gadding with the gentry. There's some further interest in one of Fred's toys – *The Pirate Ship*. Any chance of popping round some time and having a chat about it? I'm out tonight but here all day tomorrow and in the evening.

All the best, George

My dear Imogen,

I now know the meaning of the phrase 'a fair cruel maid'. Even when I am certain to find you captive among your enchanting hats, you manage to evade me. The thought did cross my mind that your good friend from the shop opposite was hiding you from me, and if I

203

searched the premises I should find you locked in a cupboard. But she folded her arms and glared at me so fiercely that I didn't dare try.

No, I don't mean a word of that nonsense, but I do wish we could meet in some place more pleasant and private than the church hall. Why not Mario's again? The flowers are a peace offering – not that I am at war with you, but perhaps you might be with me?

I daren't even sign myself 'yours' – though I should like to, very much.

Phil.

'Oh, damn the man. Why doesn't he leave me alone?' Imogen cried, magnetized, repelled. And then, 'What flowers?'

Sadie's note, written on a torn bill of sale, said briefly, 'Bouquet in kitchen bucket.' Her disapproval was evident.

He had brought a dozen cream roses set off with gypsophila and fine fern. She lifted them up gently, sniffed their fragrance, touched their cool pure petals, admired their pale perfection. His choice of flower and colour was evident. He thought her beautiful, aloof, untouched. He had called her a fair cruel maid, implying that she was unawakened. Beneath that lay the belief that he could and would awaken her.

She stood for a long time, holding his letter, aroused and disturbed. Fred had made life and love so simple.

TWENTY-TWO

Hal's reply, the following week, headed the 'Dear Editor' column, and had been placed in a special box.

Dear Sir,
   I am not surprised that 'A Concerned Christian' chose not to divulge his or her identity. It is the way of scurrilous letter-writers to stir up trouble without first making sure of their facts, and then to hide behind a benevolent pen name.
   Far from ignoring the so-called 'Black Mass' in St Oswald's Church, which may well have been no more than a vicious practical joke, I informed my bishop immediately and all proper procedures were followed. No useful purpose could be served by making the incident known, but my vigilance has never been in question with regard to this or any other matter and I mean to find the offenders and bring them to justice, so there is no need for your correspondent to inflame public fears and whip up hysteria in this fashion, unless of course he wishes to turn Langesby into the very hell he anticipates.
   Yours, etc.
      Harold Brakespear, Vicar of St Oswald's

Hal's congregation was an extraordinary mixture. Sadie might have said of him, as she said of Imogen, that he made incompatible friends. St Oswald's, over the past half-century, had become a depository for old unwanted clergymen. Put in command, as it were, of a slowly sinking ship, they had kept it afloat as best they could before taking to the lifeboat of retirement.

So when it became evident that the Reverend Brakespear must be moved yet again, someone of sardonic humour or infinite genius, or both, recommended this incumbency as a temporary solution. St Oswald's, he argued, was in such a parlous state of body and spirit that Hal could do it no further injury, and by the time the building became uninhabitable they would have thought of something more suited to his peculiar gifts. It was a waste, certainly, of Alice Brakespear's talents, for she would have ornamented the highest sphere; wherever she went she did great good and was well liked.

They had reckoned without the outrageous whims of fortune. There was the fortuitous accident of Timothy Rowley unearthing a book entitled *The History of St Oswald's Church*, written by a Victorian incumbent and presenting the church in his heyday as a smoke-blackened but dignified and powerful centre of the community. There was George Hobbs's passion for bell-ringing and his commitment to the restoration of the church tower. And when both Timothy and George met their new vicar and found him to be a man of mettle, they separately tempted him with these two projects, and he welded them into weapons for a new campaign.

Hal's first sermon was based on St Matthew, chapter 23, verses 27 and 28, and dwelt upon those who outwardly appear righteous unto men but inwardly are full of hypocrisy and iniquity. He was a splendid preacher and a fine-looking man, and the congregation, swelled far beyond its usual proportions by curiosity, hung upon his words. Afterwards, they thanked and congratulated him, but when they discovered that he meant exactly what he said, and intended to act upon it, their initial enthusiasm vanished and numbers dwindled once again.

From the beginning, he refused to consecrate marriages unless one of the couple was a reasonably regular attendee at St Oswald's. He would not baptize a baby unless he was convinced that the child's parents were church members, and that the godparents actually meant to fulfil their duties. These principles curtailed religious events significantly and reduced church revenues, while also offending some local dignitaries who considered St Oswald's merely as a background for social occasions.

'Yet it should be said in his favour,' Timothy once remarked, chuckling, 'that he is merciful to all corpses, because he feels they are beyond his jurisdiction and should have the blessing of a Christian burial!'

The previous vicar had been fairly High Church, but Hal preferred simplicity and went as low as he could, which annoyed several more. On the other hand he was devoted to King James's Bible and would not countenance the modern version of the New Testament, and so displeased the avant-garde. Finally, he believed that any institution, in order to live and grow, should move with the times and bring in the young. So he built up the Youth Club and introduced a youth slot at the end of the service, where guitar groups improvised on a hymn or played a religious folk song. Again, this met with a mixed reception.

His attitude towards young offenders aroused further disapproval. In theory, most people believed that they should be received back into the community and given another chance. In practice, this did not work. There were not enough jobs for honest youngsters, so why should they employ the dishonest? Respectable citizens were disquieted to think of their teenagers mingling with former transgressors, and possibly future criminals, in the Youth Club. And the sight of the unemployed and unemployable, lounging in sullen or abusive groups on street corners, aroused further concern.

Unperturbed, Hal fought the good fight on every front. He believed that right was on his side, and he did not mind asking, nor even haranguing, some of the very people he had estranged. Over the years he had become a self-made authority on grants, and any charity, trust or council could expect a rough passage if he thought they could be of use to him.

So his congregation, though devoted, was small and motley, and they formed individual groups who kept to certain parts of the church. Imogen, looking round, saw the faithful core of workers who cleaned, polished, swept, arranged and embroidered, sitting in the front rows on the right, opposite the lectern. Behind them were pews occupied by such as the Misses Ritchison, who had always attended St Oswald's and always would, despite confrontations with Hal. Foremost on the left sat the youngsters and their families in whom Hal invested the greatest hope, for they believed in him as well as his God. Behind them Philip and Edith monitored their obedient flock. And at the back an ever-changing troop of young sinners shuffled, grinned, whispered, and sometimes sang bawdy words to the hymns, though keeping a wary eye on the vicar.

The eccentric church itself had been made beautiful. Hal would have sold every scrap of gold and silver if he could to pay for some of his schemes, but Alice and common sense prevailed. So the candlesticks glistened on white damask, and the eagle on the lectern spread glittering wings. Spring flowers, from towering displays and hanging baskets to the small posy on the altar table, glorified the bleak stone. An Easter Sunday sun poured through the coloured saints and dappled the pews, hands and faces beneath them.

'More people than usual,' Alice whispered joyfully to Imogen.

Crazy hats, though not in abundance, were also present, and Imogen was advertising her wares personally in the shape of a cap of giant primroses. Alice preened in her panama hat with parchment roses. And the gallant

207

spring green of a Robin Hood feather could be seen just behind the Misses Ritchison, who were wearing refurbished cloches. Alice pointed them out, quite unnecessarily, and said with a sigh of pleasure that it was all very gratifying.

Also gratifying was the presence of her two sons, home for the vacation. Replicas of their father, they sat on either side of Alice and Imogen, attentive, well mannered and well groomed.

'Of course,' Alice went on, 'we usually have a larger congregation on Easter Day, but I do feel that people are rallying round Hal. I said as much to him, when he was preparing his sermon, and hinted that we should put all thoughts of darkness behind us and concentrate on the glory of the resurrection.'

A slight shadow crossed her face, lest he had not taken the hint and was about to sound yet another blast on his trumpet. Then they all rose, because there he was, lordly in his chiaroscuro robes, announcing the first hymn like a battle-cry: 'He who would valiant be, let him come hither.'

Imogen, singing wholeheartedly with the rest, was harried by her conscience, which had been brought up as Church of England. She shared their joy that Christ was risen, but knew perfectly well that she was not one of them. For her, some great spirit, however named or nameless, permeated the universe, refusing to be bound by race, colour, dogma or creed, eternally celebrating with everyone, everywhere, even revelling in such ephemeral things as hats. But that, as Sadie would have said, was *her* problem.

She reflected that this had also been her problem when Fred died, because she did not know what had become of him: and in any afterlife she could picture him only as a comic element, which made her laugh, which made her cry again.

Hal Brakespear based his sermon peaceably, that fine Easter Day, on Psalm 46: 'God is our refuge and strength, a very present help in trouble.'

The preparation of a cold buffet lunch for twenty-four people at the vicarage had occupied Alice and Vera all the previous day, and caused Alice to rise at six o'clock that morning. Imogen, balancing a plate of chicken and pasta salad in one hand and a glass of piercing white wine in the other, gravitated towards Timothy in order to avoid Philip and was confronted by the person she thought of as the Widow Wyse.

Edith's eyes were as cold as her smile. She assessed the giant primroses and found them wanting.

'What a long time since we last met. Dear me. Is that one of your hats?' she enquired.

Imogen wondered whether the hat was a mistake in itself or simply a mistake on that occasion, and was recruiting an army of doubts when she stopped herself. Why, that's exactly what she wants, she thought. She's putting me on the defensive.

So she smiled and said teasingly, 'I can tell you don't like it, but then it wouldn't suit you.'

Imagining Edith as a hat, she found it a night prowler but translated this into more pleasing terms.

'A highwayman. Ostrich feathers,' she said at hazard. 'You could carry off black ostrich feathers. They aren't as easy as people imagine. Or a close-fitting cap in leopard-skin – though that wouldn't be considered environmentally friendly these days. Fake fur, perhaps . . .'

Edith, looking at her fixedly as if Imogen were mentally retarded, took a sip of wine, made the merest grimace, and said, 'Is your little shop doing well?'

'Very well indeed. I counted five of my creations in church this morning.'

'And are you settling down in peculiar Haraldstone? Have the locals introduced you to their version of witchcraft?'

'I'm settling down well, but the only craft I practise is millinery.'

'What? No midnight meetings? No dancing under the moon?' Edith cried, playfully, pitilessly.

She knows nothing about it. She's just testing the water, Imogen told herself.

'What *have* I been missing?' she answered, matching smile to steel smile. 'To think of all that excitement going on while I catch up with household chores or read a library book!'

'Some people might take these amateurs as seriously as they take themselves,' Edith pursued. 'True practitioners would consider them ludicrous.'

'And where would one find these true practitioners?'

Edith's eyes flickered. Her answer was forked.

'You're obviously a beginner in the magic arts or you wouldn't have to ask.'

But Imogen was not to be put down. She remembered Sadie's assessment of her position. 'I'm not even a beginner,' she said lightly. 'Merely a spectator.'

Edith's eyes were hooded.

'You'd be wise not to involve yourself in any way,' she answered, 'with anyone.'

That means Philip, too, Imogen thought.

She said coldly, 'My dear Edith, I have neither the time nor the inclination to be involved in anything but my shop and the play at present.'

Take that message back! she thought, and made a move to go, but Edith detained her.

'Is the play going well? Phil hardly mentions it, but then he has more important matters on his mind.'

Imogen decided to tell her nothing.

'We're all busy trying to please Tim, who doesn't say anything – apart from the fact that we fall far below his hopes and expectations.' In turn she asked, 'And how is the Langesby Dramatic Society progressing with *Love on the Dole?*'

Like most aggressors, Edith enjoyed the thrust but resented the parry.

'I'm surprised you don't know. Haven't you heard through the Langesby grapevine?' Then she saw further opportunity to put this outsider in her place. 'Oh, but of course, you don't live in the town, do you? It's extraordinary how a few miles make such a difference to culture and communication.'

'I'm afraid we're all peasants in Haraldstone. You must forgive us.'

'Then allow me to bring you up to date,' said Edith, pleased to patronize her. 'They've had an amazing response from friends and helpers. Of course, the town hall stage facilities are excellent, and the Society is noted for its scenery and costumes. The stage set promises to be outstanding. And of course the play rouses northern sympathies, and echoes present-day problems. A very strong choice.'

'Unlike anything they have done before, I believe?' Imogen said, smiling as she remembered how Timothy Rowley had planted the idea.

'And a striking contrast to Tim's peculiar little Elizabethan fairy tale.'

I must find out about Edith, Imogen thought. No use asking Alice. Too prejudiced. Timothy, perhaps? Yes. Timothy.

As if signalled, Alice surged forward on the crest of a hospitable smile.

'Dear Edith! So good of you to come. I'm afraid I must interrupt your little tête-à-tête. Imogen is being summoned by our delightful Dr Rowley.'

Deprived of one possible victim, Edith pounced upon another.

'Alice, dear, what a dreadful time you must be having. So damaging in every way. But I see you have invited the editor of the *Chronicle*. A very wise move, if I may say so. The last thing poor St Oswald's needs is a bad press . . . Anyway' – lifting her glass – 'here's to you and Hal!' She took a sip, gave the ghost of a shudder, and set the glass down, saying, 'Delicious! But a little too *acid* for me.'

Alice could turn, though she continued to smile.

'You surprise me,' she said. 'I should have thought it just to your taste. Perhaps you'll find the red wine more warming. Do try it.'

Imogen grinned, and squeezed her friend's elbow as she went by.

'I shouldn't drink too much of that Bulgarian white wine,' Timothy advised Imogen, taking her aside and speaking confidentially. 'I expect Alice was economizing when she bought it. Nor would I recommend the Portuguese red, the label of which I have examined and found most suspicious. Another bargain, I fear. I refused to touch either of them, and persuaded Hal to give me some of the excellent sherry his cousin sends him at Christmas. But that is not why I asked to speak to you. I wanted to remind you of our rendezvous. You *are* coming on Tuesday evening, I hope?'

He was rubicund and benevolent. His eyes sparkled over his spectacles. He exuded a fatherly affection, a concern for her welfare, and yet Imogen felt she was being pressured.

'I believe you will find our little conversation useful in your present circumstances.'

'And what circumstances are those?' Imogen asked, polite but wary.

'Convalescing after a major bereavement. Thinking of making important changes. It can be a dangerous passage without a good friend and wise guidance.'

He's heard about the witches' meeting, she thought, and he's keeping an eye on me in case I go wrong. I do hate people thinking they know best.

'I am not being patronizing,' he went on, reading her, 'but there are certain facts which you should know before you become too involved.'

She contemplated her glass of wine, but did not drink it. She spoke incisively.

'I am not involved. I am a spectator.'

Her annoyance was evident but Timothy remained urbane.

'But you may not be allowed to remain a spectator. You are not wholly in control of your own destiny. None of us is. And you have already taken the first step in what may prove to be a highly perilous crossing.'

She felt herself toppling, the dark water engulfing her, sweeping her away. But she responded with vigour and a sense of injury.

'Originally, it was Alice's idea that I should come up here to live, but

211

you and Philip were also very persuasive. Are you saying that I shouldn't have taken my friends' advice?'

His tone was soft and intimate but he presented his argument vehemently.

'The only advice you took was your own. You left Langesby rather abruptly, if you remember, and none of us heard a word from you until you turned up some months later, and presented us with a *fait accompli* . . .'

She did not let him finish.

'Yes, and for good reasons. I didn't want Alice to run my life and I didn't want to be embroiled in Langesby politics. In fact, I wouldn't have come back at all if I hadn't seen Haraldstone. And my decisions and my life are my business, as are any friends I make – whether other people approve of them or not.'

He made a little gesture of apology and contrition.

Imogen added more gently, 'I recognized something I needed there – though I don't know what. Call it intuition. It began with Sadie's quilt. Anyway, Fred went there with me, and he left me at the stone circle. I've been on my own ever since.'

'I think perhaps you have misunderstood me . . .' Timothy began. But at that moment his attention was directed elsewhere.

'Forgive me,' he cried, in quite a different tone, 'but I see the editor of the *Langesby Chronicle* being buttonholed by Hal and I cannot allow the poor man to be mauled. I must rescue him.' He gave a little bow of farewell. 'My dear, do, I beg you, come on Tuesday evening. It will be quite informal, just the two of us for a drink and a chat. I regret that, owing to a previous engagement, I cannot collect you from Haraldstone, but at any rate I shall have the pleasure of driving you home.' He patted her shoulder. 'Then may I expect you around half-past eight? *À bientôt!*' said Timothy, and twinkled away crying, 'Mr Bryant! I have a favour to ask of you . . .'

'And I have a favour to ask of *you*,' said Philip, coming up behind her.

As always, in his presence, she chattered to cover her nervousness.

'Oh, Philip, I know I promised to ring you, but I've been so busy. I haven't had a minute to spare since Alice recommended my hats to the Misses Ritchison. Stitch, stitch, stitch! Long past midnight, like Thomas Hood's poor shirt-maker – though not in poverty, hunger and dirt . . .'

'My dear girl,' he answered easily, 'there's no need to give me reasons. We both know that you and I have an appointment to keep some time. I'm simply here to look at you and kiss your hand.' Which he did delightfully.

She drew a quick breath, blushed, laughed, glanced round for rescue, and in her anxiety blurted out the question she had intended to ask Timothy Rowley.

'I've been talking to Edith. How long has she been living in Langesby?' His smile stiffened, and he gave a reply that was an evasion.

'I can't remember exactly. Why?'

She could hardly answer, 'Because I can't think of anything else to say', so she fabricated a reason.

'Oh, just idle curiosity. She seems such an important part of the town that I thought perhaps she was related to an old Langesby family or had married a Langesby man.'

He was still smiling, but no longer bent on charming her.

'I don't know anything about her previous life. She was a widow when we met.'

Edith, even in her absence, had managed to dry up their conversation, and they were both trying to think of a new subject when Timothy bustled back with a grateful, if slightly ruffled, newspaper editor.

'My dear Philip, forgive this interruption but it is a matter of some importance. Mr Bryant would like a private word with our talented Imogen.'

'We seem destined to be separated!' Philip joked, and left her with relief.

Timothy never did anything for nothing, nor without good reason, and the editor was looking as if he had been saved from one difficult situation only to find himself pitchforked into another. But on being introduced to an attractive young woman he unwound perceptibly while Timothy explained his double mission.

'This will be excellent publicity for Crazy Hats, and the *Chronicle* will have an original interview for its Woman's Page.' He observed the impression that Imogen had already made on the editor, and added with benign irony, 'I trust, Derek, that this lady will find favour in your eyes?' Then he beamed on them both, saying, 'And now I must leave you to become acquainted while I have a chat with our remarkable Edith about her various enterprises.'

He departed, rubbing his hands at the prospect.

TWENTY-THREE

Tuesday evening

Timothy's invitations were in the nature of royal commands, and Imogen had no choice but to obey. Still, she was spared a bus journey, because George was going to Langesby that evening. So she rode pillion as far as the Mount and arrived far too early. But Mrs Housam ushered her into the drawing room like visiting royalty, received her helmet as if it were a crown, and though apologies were not necessary she made them as profusely as Timothy would have done. 'It's Dr Rowley's Inner Circle meeting this evening, Mrs Lacey, but it's usually over by a quarter-past eight so you shouldn't have too long to wait. The room is nice and warm, and there's a comfortable chair by the fire and magazines in the rack, but if there's anything I can get for you, do say.'

So Imogen sat and leafed through a copy of *Country Life*, in the room which had not changed since Timothy's mother first filled it with her at-home teas, afternoon bridge parties and ladies' circles, seventy years ago. As time went on she yawned, stood up and strolled round, inspecting the past. Old brown photographs of Timothy-when-young beamed from silver frames. Treasured bibelots were arranged in a glass-fronted cabinet. There was a graceful gilt-edged mirror over the fireplace, and porcelain figurines on the mantelshelf. Curtains were swagged, cushions ruched, lamps fringed, upholstery rich and soft. Small bowls and great vases of fresh flowers stood on spindle-legged tables. This was a feminine preserve on which men did not intrude, into which they must be invited. The late Mrs Rowley's presence was almost palpable and Imogen would not have been surprised if she had swept in shortly, saying, 'I'm *so* sorry, my dear. It seems discourteous of Tim to keep you waiting. But he doesn't realize you are here.'

Imogen stopped in front of an elegant escritoire, and picked up the only masculine object in the room: a handsome leather-bound book with no title. Intrigued, she sat down at the desk to examine its contents.

Lectures given by Dr Timothy Rowley on Magical Practices. She skimmed though the index, amazed at the range and depth of subjects. Master rituals. Correspondence charts. Zodiacal tables. Astral projection. Planetary exaltations. Talismans. Prophecy. Visualization. Demons. Magical recipes. Magical scripts. Healing. High magic. The book had been printed privately, handsomely and very expensively, with sketches and illustrations by the author, and the first lecture was entitled 'The Tree of Life'.

Timothy had drawn the tree skilfully and with great care. Its roots were in the earth, its head in heaven. Exotically named branches spread out on either side, their personal details noted in neat boxes. He had combined the esoteric with the natural. Leaves and grass and sky were indicated in a realistic but childlike style.

'Douanier Rousseau to the life!' Imogen said to herself, amused and intrigued.

She thought the chart extremely beautiful and studied it for some minutes: trying to pronounce unfamiliar names and reading the notes, until the sound of voices brought her swiftly to her feet, and the book back to its place.

The Inner Circle members were lingering in the hall, talking in confidential tones. She recognized voices from Peele's Players. Fragments of conversation, meaning nothing to her at the time, would make sense later.

Timothy was saying, 'Oh, the play is a marvellous opportunity. Self-indulgence as well as bait. And if all goes well we shall be able to put theory into practice.'

A laugh and a quotation from her stage lover Ian: 'So "the play's the thing, wherein to catch the conscience of the king"?'

Timothy: 'If he still has one! But power and timing are of the essence.'

Frolic: 'Or else the lady may not be for burning?'

They all laughed.

Timothy said archly, 'It has been a most illuminating meeting, but I fear I must hasten your departure. I am expecting quite a different lady this evening.' More laughter. 'I thank you all for coming. We shall meet at the Thursday rehearsal?'

Various assents and good-nights. Sounds of the front door opening and closing, of lighter footsteps and a softer voice. Mrs Housam had come to inform him of Imogen's presence.

In a moment Timothy hurried in rubbing his hands, using his mother's words and intonation.

'I'm so sorry, my dear. It seems discourteous of me to keep you waiting, but I didn't realize you were here.'

His appearance impressed her. A spotless white shirt set off his dark blue suit. A pearl pin gleamed in his blue silk tie. His shoes were mirrors of perfection. A crimson carnation glowed in his buttonhole.

'How smart you are!' Imogen said, impressed. 'You look like a prime minister on a state occasion.'

'And you, my dear, are as exquisite as usual!'

He kissed her hand.

'I trust you approved of my newspaper coup on Sunday?' he enquired.

'No, no! No need for thanks. I accomplished two objects in one. Hal was hounding poor Derek Bryant with relentless vigour, believing that he could extract the name of that busybody who wrote the letter. But of course he cannot, and must not. If the *Chronicle* betrays the identity of its anonymous correspondents an important source of local news will dry up. So I took pity on the man – and also saw a use for him. Oh, what an artful dodger I can be!'

'I'm glad that you *are* an artful dodger,' said Imogen demurely, and pleased him.

He was walking about the room, making unimportant alterations to the position of flowers and cushions, humming to himself. He paused by the desk and brushed the book lightly with the tips of his fingers before coming back to her.

'Has George sold any more of your late husband's ingenious creations?'

She gave a little laugh that was half a sigh.

'Yes. And the proceeds will pay for my next quarter's overheads. I'm grateful. He's doing far better with sales than Fred ever did.'

'The artist,' said Timothy graciously, 'is rarely a salesman.' He looked at her keenly. 'Does the money make up for losing them?'

'I don't honestly know. I need it badly, but I have pangs of regret as each toy is parcelled up and borne away.'

'But it *is* what Fred would have wished – what he *does* wish, for the spirit does not die. Your young husband is looking after your interests still.'

She turned away from him, pretending to be interested in a watercolour of Langesbydale, and whisked two tears away with the tips of her fingers.

He glanced at her keenly and wandered over to a side table, saying, 'I usually have a nightcap around this time. Would you like to join me? I favour malt whisky myself. What is your choice?'

'Gin and tonic, please.'

'Then – here you are – and here am I. Your health, my dear.'

They sat for a few moments in silence, while Timothy sipped and drummed his fingers on his knee and murmured 'Ho, hum!' to himself, and 'Where to begin?' Then he cleared his throat and spoke decisively.

'Now, first of all, my dear, anything I say this evening is strictly private and you must not speak of it to anyone at all – no matter how close nor how trustworthy they may be. Will you give me your word on that?'

She compressed her lips and nodded.

'Do not even whisper it to Polly,' he added lightly, 'nor to your magic quilt!'

She smiled, but was disquieted.

'I will start with the lady who set these events in train. Alice Brakespear.'

Imogen's mouth opened in a noiseless 'Oh!' This she had not expected.

'I'll wager,' said Timothy, 'that you thought I was going to caution you about Haraldstone and the friends you have made there, as she has done? Well, you are mistaken. Now, my dear, although we are all very fond of Alice and she has many sterling qualities, would you agree that her vision is somewhat limited?'

Imogen remembered Alice's golden head bent over the imagination game all those years ago, stolidly transforming a line into a five-barred gate. She nodded.

'She loves you dearly, but your unpredictable choices, your lack of religious commitment, and your addiction to Crazy Hats do not fit in with her idea of a godly life, and since she cannot understand this side of your character she wishes to improve it. Are you with me?'

We'll sort you out and put you on the right road.

'I'm with you.'

'On the other hand, a handsome man of some charisma, dedicated to the care of underprivileged youngsters, is undoubtedly godly.'

This man, Imogen, is the nearest thing to a saint that you are likely to meet.

'And when he also turns out to be a regular church-goer who believes in old-fashioned discipline and expresses a horror of witchcraft, she realizes that he is just the good angel to correct your faults. I speak, of course, of Philip Gregory.'

Apprehension crawled under Imogen's skin.

Timothy communed with his whisky.

'I have been wondering how much to tell you,' he said slowly. 'I wish to forearm you but not to frighten you – to tell you enough but not too much. Let me give you a brief sketch of Philip Gregory.'

Another pause.

'He was born, as they say, with a silver spoon in his mouth. He is greatly gifted, understandably ambitious and hard-working. But he is also a highly sensual man as well as a vain one, and he is morally weak – a dangerous combination. In the right circumstances, with wise guidance, he could be honoured and illustrious, and he once had the chance of all that. But he fouled – I use the word quite deliberately – fouled it up.

'You remember, Imogen, when Christ was in the wilderness and the Devil tempted him with the world?'

She nodded, and sipped courage.

'Christ refused the offer. Given the same opportunity, Philip would have accepted so quickly that even the Devil would have been astonished!'

She managed a wan quirk of the lips at this mild joke.

'Philip had everything most men would desire: an excellent post with splendid prospects, a beautiful wife, a lovely home, many friends and universal esteem. But being a gourmet of the flesh he sought ever more subtle savours and sensations. His lovely and loving wife Kay bore with several infidelities – the last and most fatal of which was Edith Wyse.'

Imogen's startled face was his reward.

'Kay Gregory died one weekend when Philip was away at an educational conference. She was found on a Sunday morning, lying in her nightgown on the kitchen floor with her head in the gas oven. She had taken every precaution to make sure that the job was done properly and that she would not be discovered until it was too late. She had left no note, but her doctor testified that she had been suffering from depression, and he had prescribed tranquillizers. The verdict was suicide while of unsound mind.

'But Kay was well loved and had good friends, in whom she had confided her fears about the affair with Edith. And in losing his wife Philip also lost his defence, because Kay had shielded his infidelities. Whispers about him now became open talk. And a new whisper crept in – that Kay had been murdered to make way for Edith.' His eyebrows were eloquent. 'There was no evidence of this, and Philip's solicitor quelled further rumours. However, the damage was done and the groundswell of local feeling made his position untenable. He resigned his post and put some hundreds of miles between himself and the tragedy. And as *you* have found, my dear, distance does not change the person, merely the circumstances.

'Philip arrived in Langesby carrying a burden of guilt that required him to enter a long period of atonement if he were to heal himself. To be fair to him, I imagine that he began his work here with that in mind, because he has a gift for dealing with young people, a pleasing manner, a sense of humour, and a remnant of honour and conscience – whereas *Edith –*' he pronounced her name as if it were an expletive – '*Edith* has none of these qualities. I would hazard a guess that he neither invited her nor wished to

219

see her again, but she followed him to Langesby, bought herself an elegant house in Church Street and made herself necessary to him. Between them they built up the admired institution which is known as Prospect House – though that is another tale.'

He ruminated over his malt whisky.

'His reputation once more began to shine. His desire to be reinstated in the eyes of society grew. And Edith, who loves power above all else, had become a political force in Langesby. So last year she made quite a creditable effort to wangle him on to the honours list.' He gave a little chuckle. 'But I defeated her.'

'*You* defeated her?' Imogen cried.

'That must not be known, of course,' he warned her.

'I'll be as silent as the grave,' said Imogen miserably, and wished she had chosen a livelier image.

'Of course you will,' he replied firmly.

He observed Imogen's rigid posture and empty glass.

'Come,' he coaxed her, 'have another drink.'

Returning with his own glass replenished, as well as hers, he said, 'And that, my dear, is their story in a nutshell. Now, to your part in its future.

'I think that Philip may have fallen a little in love with you, and seen in you a chance to begin again, to shed Edith and to redeem himself. Like our excellent friend Alice, he probably thinks you should marry him, forget Crazy Hats, tell Edith to go about her business, and lead a worthy life with him thereafter.'

Imogen opened her mouth to protest, but his upraised hand silenced her.

'That you have your doubts of him, I know, but you are also strongly attracted to him and that is dangerous. Do not be careless in your relations with this man. I promise you that if you were to give yourself up to him the relationship would founder, and at unthinkable cost to yourself, because Philip has no moral stamina and Edith would not allow it – or you – to prosper.

'I will say no more of her than this, for the present. No one is her friend, and I know of none, saving myself perhaps, who would dare to be her enemy. The only chink in that black armour of hers is Philip.'

Imogen was endeavouring to remain steadfast.

'How do you know all this?' she asked.

He was bland, fluent, scholarly.

'An academic training is an excellent thing, my dear. It teaches one to be continually curious, and also how to satisfy that curiosity. I have done a vast amount of research into Edith's past since she appeared on the Langesby scene. I researched Philip's past in the same way. At first, his seemed more sensational. Later, Edith's proved to be far more riveting – but enough of that for now.'

Afraid that her teeth would chatter, Imogen held her jaw muscles rigid.

'Do you always investigate newcomers to Langesby?' she demanded. 'Did you investigate me?'

He affected astonishment.

'Good heavens, no. How would I find time to do all that and pursue the rest of my many concerns? Naturally, I am intrigued when anyone of consequence hoves into view,' and he made her a courtly little bow, 'but only when I feel they are dangerous do I pay such particular attention to them.'

Picturing him like a stout old spider, vigilant at the centre of the Langesby web, ready to trap any fly that threatened its safety, she blurted out, 'Why? Why do you? Why should you? Why *you*?'

His eyelids were half-closed. Beneath them his gaze was penetrating. After a moment or so he said lightly, 'I dare say some might call me an interfering old busybody, and who is to say they are not right?'

His tone, and the manner in which he rose and walked away, signified the end of the conversation. He picked up the heavy book from the desk and turned to her.

'I have a copy here of a series of lectures which I gave to the Langesby Magical Arts several years ago. You may find it of some interest.'

His twinkling smile told her that he knew that she had already looked through it, knew about her connection with the witches of Haraldstone, knew things about her which she possibly did not know herself.

Confused, she accepted the book and thanked him. 'I'll take good care of it,' she promised. 'When would you like it back?' She wondered when she would find the hours to read and absorb all that esoteric information.

'Oh! Some time. No hurry. I have other copies. The time will dictate itself,' said Timothy. 'And speaking of time, Mrs Housam will scold me dreadfully for keeping you here so late. Allow me the very great pleasure of driving you home.'

Her bedroom was as cold as the North Country spring, and she allowed Polly to creep between the duvet and the quilt, and nestle down, purring.

In sleep, the Tree of Life rose before her, dominating the open landscape. Naked, she walked forward to embrace it. The light poured down on her, dappling the leaves and her flesh as she climbed from branch to branch, shining so radiantly that she had to stop and shield her eyes.

And woke, with her arm protecting her from the morning sun which had penetrated a gap between the curtains.

TWENTY-FOUR

Philip's letter headed the correspondence page of the *Chronicle*.

Dear Sir,

Though genuinely sympathetic with the plight of the mentally retarded and afflicted, I feel that I must underline the risks involved in allowing them to roam freely in the community. It is absolutely essential that the health authorities ensure proper care and control of these unfortunates, for their sakes as well as our own.

Only this week we had an incident on our premises where one such person, who had previously been turned away for watching our girls at recreation, climbed over the wall. His reason may have been harmless, such as a childlike desire to join in the game, but our youngsters are especially vulnerable. Luckily, he was apprehended and returned home – with, I hasten to add, humour, goodwill and understanding.

I have no wish to add to the burden of his carer, for in our own small community I know the personal cost of looking after the underprivileged. My criticism is directed at the health authorities who released him, and I should like to draw their attention to this particular circumstance and ask them to judge the possible consequences.

Suppose our premises, instead of being well guarded and constantly inspected, had been an open playground or common? Suppose the man's intention – which again I stress was most probably quite harmless – had been of another sort? In brief, if Langesby suffers a tragedy of the kind so often and so well publicized in the national press, who will be to blame? Knowing the difficulties of present-day public finance and administration, there are no easy answers to these questions, but they must surely be asked and even more carefully considered?

Yours faithfully,

Philip Gregory, Director of Prospect House, Home for Young Offenders

★   ★   ★

The Brakespears walked together in the vicarage garden in earnest conversation. They linked arms. Their mood and tone were intimate. At the end of the lawn the two lilac trees, one purple, one white, had decided to brave any late frost. Their scent, suffocatingly sweet and sharp, hung on the evening air.

'Delicious!' Alice cried, momentarily uplifted. Then, returning to the point of discussion, 'Oh, but I do wish Phil hadn't brought this into the open. Although I can't fault the way he's dealt with it – no names mentioned, no accusations made – still, I wish he had talked it over with us before making such a public pronouncement. Poor Mary will be dreadfully upset. But how can she watch a grown man every minute of the day, and look after them both and manage the house and the land, at her age? And that poor creature, Stephen, is not to blame either. What is there for him in the way of occupation or amusement or company of his own age, out at Howgill? No, he is not to blame, and nor is she, and yet they have been put under public scrutiny, and who knows where it will end?'

The lilac and the air of a late April evening were not completely wasted on Hal, and his answer was delivered in a milder tone than usual.

'No, it's not their fault, but he should never have been released in the first place. Mary is too old to look after him. I'm afraid he must go back.'

Alice's face was apprehensive. She foresaw the next step.

'And yet I'm sure he meant no harm, my dear, I think, as Phil suggests, that he simply wanted to join in the game, as a child would.'

'Yes, but this child has a man's body, and some of Phil's girls are sexually experienced. The situation could develop in a number of undesirable ways. No, Stephen must be properly supervised, and the sooner we can put the case before the authorities the better. But first of all, one of us must persuade Mary that this is the right solution.'

'Oh dear!' Alice said, to herself rather than to him.

'I'll do it if you feel you can't,' Hal said, 'but I would rather it were done as diplomatically as possible, and diplomacy is not my strong suit.'

Alice said, as she had known she would, 'I will try.'

He picked up her plump little hand, kissed it, and retained it in his. Abruptly, he said, 'I shall fight Stephen's cause energetically, but I have the feeling that in the end it may not help him – and won't do me much good either.'

Alice compressed her lips and nodded.

Frowning at the lilac without seeing it, Hal said, 'I don't like these undercurrents. Something is brewing which I don't comprehend, and over which I have no control.' Almost in apology, he told her, 'If it's what I suspect, we may be packed off again.'

Alice answered on a sigh.

'Yes, I realize that. But I lost the place I liked best a long time ago. If we have to leave St Oswald's it will be sad, and if we left in disgrace it would be terrible, but in the end it will only be another move, not a heartbreak.'

Hearing the fullness in her voice he looked at her attentively.

'You're thinking about the Gloucestershire parish?'

She nodded because she could not speak.

He bowed his head, and pursed his lips.

He said, 'Poor Alice, you deserved an easier life. You set foot on a rough road when you married me.'

Still unable to answer him, she squeezed his fingers to show that she did not regret her decision.

Yet she felt unable to tackle Mary Proctor by herself, and persuaded Imogen to give up her Tuesday afternoon, which was half-closing day in Haraldstone, in order to accompany her.

Annoyed with herself and circumstances outside her control, Imogen trailed palely behind, hoping to help, fearing to hinder, dreading Mary's reaction.

The door of Howgill House opened suddenly, as if they had been long expected, but just as quickly Alice spoke in a light, bright tone.

'Here we are again, Mary. You know Imogen, of course? I picked her up in Haraldstone to spend the afternoon with me, and as we were just passing I thought we might look in on you for a few minutes.'

'Come on in,' said Mary grimly. 'I know what this is all about. Just passing indeed. Never in this world. You're do-gooding again, Mrs Brakespear. I did warn you against it.'

'Unfortunately,' said Alice, caught out, 'it is my task in life.'

They greeted Stephen, who was sitting staring into the fire-grate, shoulders hunched, smoking a pungent cigarette. The room was warm and close, and the acrid smell dominated the subtler scents of apples and herbs and baking.

'You'd best sit down,' said Mary.

But they lingered by the door, feeling unwelcome.

Taking no further notice of them, Mary pursed her lips, folded her hands in her apron, and stood by her son, looking down on him.

'Do you see what you've brought me to?' she asked. 'Fetching other people in to tell me how to run my life!'

She filled the kettle at the cold tap, brushed past him, and banged it down on the black-leaded range. Over her shoulder she said to her visitors, 'Well, I can tell you that it won't happen again!'

Alice and Imogen hovered awkwardly while Mary explained herself.

'I was a bit tired that afternoon and I must have dozed off. Mind you' – nodding at Stephen – 'I gave him his tablets after dinner, so he should have been dozy too.'

She turned to her callers now, raising thick grey eyebrows, nodding significantly at her son's bent head, indicating that they should observe the effect of her words upon him.

'But I'm not daft.' More loudly: 'I know what he's up to!'

Stephen, who had been the image of apathy, now sat up, alert and shifty.

'I'm a trained nurse,' Mary continued in the same register. 'He can't fool me. I know every trick in the book.'

He was listening in apprehension, cigarette held nervously between two stained fingers.

'I'll bet a shilling to a halfpenny that he never swallowed them. Just kept them in his mouth and then spat them into his hand when I wasn't looking,' she said.

In his terror, Stephen dropped the cigarette on the rag rug and rescued it at the expense of his fingers. His mouth trembled. He whimpered quietly to himself.

'I'm sure he's very sorry and won't do it again,' said Alice, distressed.

But Mary was intent on truth and justice rather than fudging and forgiveness. She spooned Nescafé into four cups with such emphasis that Imogen feared it would be too strong to drink.

'Well, pull up two chairs and sit down, both of you,' Mary ordered. 'I'm going to sit in my rocking chair, opposite that bad lad, so I can keep an eye on him.'

'Oh dear. I'm sure he didn't mean to upset anyone,' Alice cried, for the friendly atmosphere she had hoped to create was being destroyed.

'Rubbish! Of course he meant it,' said Mary, downright. 'He knew very well what he was doing. And he'd have got away with it, too, if he hadn't been caught climbing over the wall.'

Stephen put his head in his hands and snivelled.

'And of all the walls he could have chosen,' cried Mary, enraged, 'it had to be *that* one. Oh, the *gentleman* was very civil when he brought him back,' her tone was bitter when she spoke of Philip, 'but it didn't stop him writing to the *Chronicle* about it, did it? And nobody warned me. So everybody was gossiping before I'd had time to open the paper. How do you think I felt about that?'

Stephen threw back his head and howled with remorse.

'Oh, poor thing!' said Alice. 'He hasn't enough to do here, you see, Mary. And you haven't the energy to watch him and look after him all day.' She plunged, since she was not allowed to wade carefully in. 'Mary dear, don't you think it would be better for both of you if we persuaded Bethesda to take him back?'

'No, I don't! He's my son. He may be a bad lad but he's all I've got.'

Stephen wailed, 'I wasn't bad, Mother, I was just watching. And the gentleman didn't say I was bad. He laughed about it. He comes and talks to me when we go to the Hall. The others don't. Mr Gregory's my friend.'

Mary's face registered disbelief, suspicion and fear.

'Is he, indeed? Funny sort of friend, bringing you home and then talking to the *Chronicle* behind our backs.'

Stephen sought among the rubble of his mind for an explanation. 'But he likes me,' he offered, watching his mother with painful attention. 'He smiles at me when he talks.'

Imogen could see Philip's smile, frank and true, and the way he would run one hand through his hair while he chatted, and how he would charm this simple-minded listener.

Mary's silence conveyed disgust beyond words.

Imogen sipped her coffee, in spite of its taste, rather than draw attention to herself, and saw Alice doing likewise.

'Smile?' Mary cried, when she could master her voice. 'I should think he did smile – to see a silly lad making a fool of himself, watching those girls. Whatever were you thinking of?'

It was obvious to everyone present, but Stephen lowered his eyes lest they should guess. One hand strayed towards his trouser crotch in remembrance, but Mary's tone arrested it.

'And you can stop that nonsense!'

The hand fell away. He covered his face again, and rocked to and fro, to and fro: a child in disgrace.

Alice said hurriedly, 'I really think we should go now, Mary. I won't bring this subject up again, but if you change your mind, or would like to talk it over, you know where we are. I'm sorry. I seem to have done everything wrong again. I didn't mean to upset poor Stephen. I was only . . .'

She did not finish her sentence, fearing another stinging rebuke. She set down her cup, and Imogen was glad to follow suit. They rose together, but Mary made no move to show them out. Her anger was draining away, leaving the lined map of her face colourless and composed. She sat forward, frowning with thought, old shoulders bowed, old knees spread, old hands folded in the lap of her clean print apron. Then she looked up at them, quick and shrewd, and spoke with rough good humour, nodding at the coffee.

'I don't blame you for leaving it, I've got a heavy hand when my temper's up.'

Distressed at the thought of seeming to scorn her hospitality as well as upsetting her, Alice protested, 'My dear, we didn't come to impose upon you.'

But Mary looked away again, preoccupied with her own thoughts.

'We must be what we are, and do what we have to do,' she said finally. 'We can't help that. Like you say, Mrs Brakespear, it's our task in life.'

Perceiving her change of tone, Stephen peeped through his fingers and then dared to lower his hands. He watched and listened intently.

Mary rocked to and fro, eyes on the dale beyond the kitchen window, thinking aloud.

'I'm an obstinate old woman, and I've got a sharp tongue, but I know the truth when I hear it and I don't want to be selfish. I can't get about like I used to. And the ointment isn't doing my legs any good.' She looked up at them fiercely. 'But I shall manage somehow. I always have.'

She brooded. Alice and Imogen exchanged glances of understanding and sat down again.

'I know,' said Mary with compassion, 'that this poor lad is no more than ninepence in the shilling, but he's got feelings the same as anybody else. Like you say, he hasn't enough to do. I dare say they had a lot of games at Bethesda, billiards and that. And woodwork classes. And company – of a sort.'

Stephen was regarding her closely. She made a costly personal decision. Her eyes shone with unshed tears, but her chin would have taken on the world. She said reproachfully, 'And we talk about him, and across him, and make arrangements for him, without so much as saying a word to him directly.'

Alice and Imogen, made aware of this, felt both guilty and exasperated. Mary turned to Stephen and asked him outright.

'Do you want to go back, love? You shall if you want. I'll come and see you like I used to, and fetch you presents. Just the same.'

'Of course we can't make any promises,' Alice was beginning. 'It will take time and patience. But my husband is very persuasive.'

That's not the word I would have used, Imogen thought.

Neither mother nor son was listening. He was on his knees, head in Mary's lap, sobbing his refusal.

'No, I don't want to. I want to stay here. I want . . .' His mind could not encompass the idea, but strove to do so. '. . . it's my home and nobody else's. I want − to get up when I like − and eat what I like − and do what I like . . .' He hastened to reassure Mary in muffled abjection. 'I won't do nothing *you* don't like. I'll be good, Mam. I'll be a good lad.'

He lifted his smeared face and looked vaguely round. Something else, he felt was needed. These two fine ladies would want a more sophisticated reason. He rummaged mentally. He remembered that his mother let him lock up the house at night. There was a phrase she used then, which pleased him and made him feel important.

'Besides,' Stephen said slowly, 'I have to look after her.' He savoured the phrase. 'I'm the Man of the House.'

Mary looked up at them. She had triumphed, though it was a sorry victory.

Alice said, 'We'll go now, Mary. I'm sorry to have troubled you.'

They left them together: he with his head in her lap, the prodigal returned; she stroking his hair, reprieved for a little longer.

TWENTY-FIVE

So long had Langesbydale been gripped by a hard winter and a reluctant spring that the milder weather took Imogen by surprise. She became aware that she could slip out of bed each morning without shivering; that the cold did not strike through her bare feet; that her breakfast china was not chilly to touch; that the air was warm and silky, and even the oldest and wisest trees were beginning to unfurl their buds.

On a mid-May Sunday, standing alone on top of Haraldstone Hill, hands in the pockets of Fred's navy blue blazer, she saw that the harsh stronghold of the countryside had been transformed into rolling green downs and wooded valleys. The villages and towns were no longer huddled in bleak hollows for refuge, but spread out prettily like toys on display. And the sky meditated over all, blue and deep, with light, passing thoughts of clouds.

Now her flesh, quiescent in early widowhood, too stunned by loss to feel, was being warmed and softened by remembrance of pleasures past, stirring at the thought of pleasures to come. She called up Fred: a natural and perceptive lover. Despite Timothy's verdict she considered Philip, who hinted at more sophisticated delights. The one had gone, the other carried a high price tag. But the fresh life in her was searching for someone, something, and must be appeased somehow.

'I'll tell you what it is,' said Sadie that evening, setting down the quilt she was stitching, lifting her breasts absent-mindedly, staring ahead of her, 'it's time for a new man. I wonder where I'll find one?'

'I don't know,' said Imogen, creating a gold organdie *fantaisie*, concealing a smile. 'How do you start? Usually, that is.'

'Well, usually, I perform a good old-fashioned magic ritual.'

'None of your rats' bane and frogs' tongues, I hope?'

'Facetiousness does not become you,' said Sadie. 'Always remember that you're the romantic type. Never spoil the image.'

'What image might that be?'

'The dark lady of mystery,' said Sadie promptly.

'And what's your image?'

'An ageing Nell Gwyn.'

'Yours sounds more fun.'

Sadie sighed. 'Yes, but not so romantic. None of your chivalrous devotion and long summer nights. I have to make do with a randy man and a quick lay. Any old how, do you want to know how I get a man or don't you?'

'I do indeed. You never know when I might need the information.'

Her expression was demure, her tone solemn, but amusement was only just around the corner.

Sadie looked at her severely, and said, 'The true rite involves a mandrake root, but as they don't grow here I use white bryony instead. It has to be performed at a certain time of day and month before sunrise, when the moon's waxing and you can see the Pleiades in the sky – which can be difficult in bad weather. You dig up the root, saying, "Blessed be this Earth, this root, this night' – and take it home and trim it so that it looks like the man you fancy, and name it with his name and rebury it. Preferably in a churchyard or a crossroads. That can be awkward, because they're public places, so I use my window-box.'

Imogen's eyes were drawn to the petunias on the sill outside.

'I mix a libation of milk and water and a few drops of blood – *my* blood,' she said as her listener's eyes widened, 'make the mark of a cross on the topsoil with a silver spoon (it needn't be a spoon, but it has to be something silver) and pour it over, saying another incantation. Then I keep the root watered until the next lunar cycle begins, dig it up again, speak certain words over it, dry it out . . . oh well, I won't go into all the details. It's quite complicated. There's another spell called the Magic Rose which is simpler and more poetic. You might prefer that one.'

Imogen said, 'Sadie, are you serious?'

'Of course I'm serious.'

'You mean to tell me that you get up in the dead of night—'

'An hour before sunrise.'

'. . . in the dark, anyway, grab a garden spade and torch, and go out to dig up a substitute mandrake root?'

'You think it's funny, don't you?' Sadie said. 'But it works. Well, in my case I may have to perform the ritual more than once, of course, probably because I'm getting on a bit. Witches are the same as other women, you know. They have fewer chances as they get older.'

'Still, this – spell – does work eventually?'

'Oh yes,' said Sadie, 'but as the proverb says, never wish for what you want because you might get it. I got Arnold last time, and he was more trouble than he was worth – though sexy. Very sexy. Always at it. In fact, to put it bluntly, I don't think he knew who he was poking, anyone would have done. Which does tend to put a girl off. Us women like love-making to be personal, don't we?'

'Indeed we do,' Imogen murmured blandly.

'Anyway, I felt that his approach lacked feeling, so I got rid of him. I don't think he minded losing me in particular but he was a bit fed up until he found someone else – or she found him.'

'He sounds ravishing,' Imogen said, tongue in cheek. 'I can't wait to cast a spell and find an Arnold!'

'And now you're being saucy,' Sadie remarked amiably. 'Why would you need a spell? Spoiled for choice is what I'd have said in your case.'

Imogen set down her *fantaisie*, half-made.

'I'm only joking,' she said, suddenly sad. 'I don't want to put a spell on anyone I can think of. I've lost the man I wanted.'

They sat in silence, contemplating their inner worlds, needlework neglected.

'You need to forget yourself for a bit,' said Sadie finally, observing her. 'How about joining us witches on the thirteenth? It's a full moon and we're holding a special meeting.'

'On Haraldstone Hill again?' Uncertainly.

'Well, where would you like to hold it? In Langesby District Park? You entered into the spirit of the occasion last time, and don't deny it. You and Jinny danced like a couple of dervishes.'

'But I'm beginning to feel very embarrassed about hopping from one religious culture to the other. I celebrated Easter Sunday with the Brakespears at St Oswald's Church. Sympathetic to all and committed to none – that's my problem.'

'So you're a seeker?' Sadie said magnanimously. 'You haven't made your mind up yet? But us Haraldstone witches are all very fond of you, and we thought you contributed a little something extra to our meeting. Anyway, please yourself. It was only a suggestion.'

Her tone changed. She said, 'Incidentally, I shall be leading us this time. Mary Proctor doesn't feel up to it. She's under considerable pressure at the moment, and it's reflected in her general health. In our ceremony we shall be giving her strength and healing.' She paused and thought for a few moments. 'And confounding her enemies.'

Imogen was unpleasantly startled.

'Cursing them?'

'No, no, no,' said Sadie, shocked. 'That would be dangerous. Curses can rebound – especially if the enemies are powerful. Best leave that sort of thing alone. No, no. We shall be invoking protection against them.'

The smell of blackcurrant tea and peppermint mingled with the usual scents in the kitchen at Howgill. Mary was rubbing a home-made ointment into her leg, and Stephen was watching a game show on the television, when George knocked on the door.

'You'll have to wait a minute, whoever you are!' Mary called, with her usual asperity. 'Calling at this time of night, when I'm soaking my feet.'

'It's only me,' George called back cheerfully, understanding her.

'It's our George!' Stephen cried, transformed.

Mary's tone changed, became indulgent, mocking.

'Well, if it's George what are you standing out there for? The door isn't locked. Lift the latch and come on in.'

'It's our George,' Stephen repeated unnecessarily. 'It's our George, Mother.'

'I know it's George. I'm not soft. Hush your noise,' said Mary, good-humoured, 'and give me that towel, so's I can dry my feet. If you'd got a ha'path of common sense you'd have let him in yourself. And switch that rubbish off.'

Stephen's mind could not cope with more than one thing at once, and the game show continued at full blast while he jumped up to paw this visitor.

'How are you doing, Stevie?' George said, hugging him, patting his back.

He looked over Stephen's head at Mary. 'They tell me you're not feeling so well,' he said to her. 'Here, lad,' to his half-brother, 'I've brought you something. Go and sit down with it, will you?'

'And give me that towel, and switch that noise off. Do you hear me?' Mary ordered him. Then, to George, 'I never knew how much trash there was on the television until this lad came home.'

Stephen did not hear her, fully occupied with his bag of chocolate caramels. George strode over to the television and dismissed the game show, picked up the hand towel and gave it to Mary.

'I shouldn't think *you're* what they call a couch potato, are you?' she asked, and began to dry one foot.

He pulled up a chair and sat down, watching her and smiling.

'No, I'm not. I haven't even got a television.'

'Why not? There's some good programmes on,' said Mary, revived by his presence, prepared to have an argument. 'You needn't buy one. You can rent it.'

'I haven't the time to spare. Now never mind all that,' he said firmly, as she showed signs of pursuing the subject. 'I haven't come here to talk about renting a television, and I can't stop long. I've come to see *you*. What's wrong with you? Out with it, and none of your nonsense.'

Stephen's head lifted at this challenge. His eyes glinted for a moment in admiration of George's daring. Then the chocolate caramels repossessed him.

Mary said peaceably, 'I've got a bit of a cold, that's all. Who's been tattling to you? Alice Brakespear?'

Keeping his own counsel, George answered, 'You've no need to ask who. There's plenty of talk in Langesby. You've only got to kick one and the rest will limp.'

She grinned appreciation of that comment.

'I've brought you some brandy,' said George. 'If you can't take it neat then mix it with water. It'll pick you up.' He drew a half-bottle of enticing gold liquid from his jacket pocket.

'I'm not against brandy,' said Mary. 'I just can't stretch my purse that far.'

He put up his hand pacifically.

'I know. And you've only to ask me if you want anything – but you won't.'

'No, that's right,' said Mary, understood. 'I shan't. Well, thank you, George. I'll put a spoonful in my tea at bedtime.'

'I've got twelve caramels,' said Stephen. 'I can count.'

Mary and George exchanged a look which did not need to be translated into words.

'By God, you're hoeing a hard row,' said George in a lower tone. 'Are you sure it's for the best?'

She nodded.

'Then I'll say no more. Is there anything wrong with you apart from a cold?'

She hesitated, but had been carrying her trouble alone and was glad to share it. She stuck out her right leg.

'I've got a sore or two that won't heal.' The truth said, she hastened to adulterate it. 'But it's nothing that a good ointment won't cure.'

George was not a medical expert, but he was concerned by the look of the leg. 'There's three of them and they're ulcers,' he observed.

'You needn't tell me they're ulcers!' Mary cried, enraged. 'I'm a trained nurse.'

'Well, *as* a trained nurse, don't you think it'd be a good idea to get a doctor to look at them? Or go to the hospital for a check-up?' He was undeterred.

She did not meet his eyes, but said defiantly, 'I don't like doctors. I've always looked after myself. And the hospital hasn't time for check-ups. It's only a few ulcers. At my age I'm bound to have something wrong with me. I've made up a good ointment. I keep putting it on.'

Avoiding his gaze, she dried her other foot.

'I don't like it,' said George decidedly. 'You're here alone – no, don't give me that nonsense about Stevie, you know very well what I mean, he lives in a world of his own.'

Stephen had taken advantage of their conversation by switching on the television and turning the sound down so they wouldn't notice. He was sucking caramels blissfully, absorbed in the game show. George continued forcibly.

'You're here alone, with too much to do and too much responsibility. I know that most of it's your own fault because you're so bloody obstinate, but you're my mother and I care about you. I can make an appointment for you at any surgery you fancy, and take you there and back, and look after Stevie. But I want a doctor to see that leg – and I want you to tell him about your cold, and anything else that's not right. You're run down – and I know why.'

She seized on this excuse.

'Yes, I'm run down. That's all it is. It's been a long winter. I need a tonic. I'll make one up.'

He surveyed her with love and exasperation.

'If you won't meet me halfway I'll get a doctor myself and come round her with him.'

Her eyes flashed outrage and astonishment.

'You wouldn't dare.'

'Oh yes, I would,' said George. 'Make no mistake. Now do you want to fight about it, or are you going to be sensible?'

Mary pursed her mouth until it was a thin line stitched with wrinkles. She brooded first on the glowing coals and then on her adult child sucking caramels, with a trickle of chocolate on his chin. But when she looked up her eyes were as light and clear as a summer day.

'You're a good lad,' she said. 'And you do remind me of him.'

George's face and tone were gentle.

'My father?'

She nodded, then brooded again. She spoke softly to the coals.

'If he'd wanted to stay with me I'd have moved heaven and earth to keep him. But he didn't, so I let him go. He was a loner, like you.'

George sat, hands between his knees, smiling at her, loving her.

'But life can be a marvellous thing,' Mary continued, in a tone that few had heard. 'What it takes with one hand it gives back with the other, and I'm grateful for that.'

She smiled back at him now.

'I'll see Dr Whitely, if it'll please you,' she said. 'I don't mind him as much as the others. But I can tell you now that he won't be able to do any more for me than I'm doing for myself – if as much.'

George slapped his knees in relief and victory. He rose, and so did her voice.

'I suppose you're going now, aren't you?' Mary accused him. 'Oh yes, I thought so. Once you've got your own way you're off – just like your father.'

'Ah, but the difference between him and me is that I'll be back again tomorrow,' said George. He smiled, and kissed her cheek.

TWENTY-SIX

Thursday

The letter in the *Langesby Chronicle* had been tucked in the middle of the 'Dear Editor' column, between two innocuous epistles, as if Derek Bryant hoped it might escape notice.

Dear Sir,

With regard to the correspondence of previous weeks, I believe that the vicar of St Oswald's should be allowed to make his own decisions about church affairs, but I do dispute anyone's right to monopolize the church hall, which has so far been a community centre devoted to general use.

For the past two months an unknown amateur group, named 'Peele's Players' has been using the hall on Mondays and Thursdays, for rehearsals of an obscure Elizabethan farce which they intend to perform during Langesby Fair week. Unlike ordinary mortals, they pay no rent, and extensive alterations and decorations are taking place, also free of charge, because the present building did not come up to their requirements. Furthermore, the hall will be closed for some days before the fair, so that a special stage can be erected. I can only conclude that witchcraft does exist in our midst, and that the Reverend Harold Brakespear is under some sort of spell!

Considering that our own established and highly respected Langesby Dramatic Society will be performing *Love on the Dole* at the town hall throughout the festival, as a superior local attraction, one would have thought 'Peele's Players' effort superfluous – if not impertinent. It is also worth remarking that the members of our dramatic society are all Langesby citizens who intend to donate half their profit to the civic fund, while 'Peele's Players' are mostly strangers who have refused to contribute anything at all.

In view of this farcical situation I am going to make a suggestion for the future, namely that Langesby uses its Fair Fund to build a Community Centre and leaves the church hall to its own devices.

I am not afraid to sign my name, nor to discuss this matter with the Reverend Brakespear any time he wishes.

Yours etc.

John Breerton, Councillor

George's regular appearance at rehearsal showed sheer dedication to the play. He was there as decorator of the hall, improving their environment weekly, for Hal had extorted free undercoat, emulsion and gloss paint from a Langesby shop. He was there as stage improviser and designer, with materials again produced by Hal's obedient volunteers. He kept Stephen occupied while Mary acted. And most chivalrous of all, he carried Delia the heroine on his pillion and delivered her without fail every Monday and Thursday. But tonight he came as a messenger of bad tidings, with Imogen in the front seat of the van and an exultant Stephen sitting among the tools in the back.

'Incapacitated, you say? My dear fellow, I am extremely sorry to hear that, Timothy said.

His sympathy came first, but concern followed quickly.

'What on earth are we to do?' he asked himself. 'Only a month away, and not a substitute in sight. Did this happen suddenly, George?'

'No. She's been soldiering on for quite a while, saying nothing, but I took her to Dr Whitely on Friday. He's making an appointment for her at the hospital, and he says she's to rest the leg as much as she can. She's none too pleased about that, but to tell you the truth, there's no chance of doing much else. She can't put her foot to the ground without pain.'

Timothy looked into George's warm brown eyes, which were also suffering.

'My dear fellow . . .' putting a hand on his shoulder. 'I do understand, believe me I remember the effect my mother's illness had on me . . .' He also remembered that no one was officially supposed to know about the relationship, and patted George's shoulder instead of speaking further. 'Oh, we shall manage somehow. Never fear,' he said stoutly. 'But how is she coping with Stephen?' He looked askance at George's companion who was sitting on his usual chair, rolling a cigarette and smiling to himself.

'Well, I'm sleeping at Howgill House for the time being and doing what I can for them both. Alice is looking for people who'll have him in turns during the day, and help Mary out. Meanwhile I take him round with me in the van. It slows me down, but he likes being with me and I can deal with him. Poor lad, he thinks it's all an adventure! And the vicar is writing to Bethesda, and using Mary's state of health as a persuader to get Stevie taken back. She's creating merry hell about that, too.' He laughed, but the laughter hurt because all this was hard on him.

'Yet you and I know that Bethesda would be much the best solution for everyone, and as soon as possible,' said Timothy earnestly. 'Let us hope that Hal succeeds. Unfortunately, the official wheels tend to turn slowly.'

'Oh, he'll give them an extra spin or two,' George remarked, and grinned in recollection. 'And his spins count.'

'A bonnie fighter!' Timothy agreed, and put one finger on his lips, thinking. 'Well, well, I must break the news to the cast, and someone will have to read Mary's part while I look round for a replacement. Curious, how one problem inevitably brings a series of others in its wake. We have a particularly busy and fragmented evening ahead of us. Sadie Whicker has rifled my dressing-up box, and is coming to do fittings, and Milia Godden is bringing her designs and taking measurements. On top of that, Philip's youngsters will be here for the first time.'

He patted George's shoulder again.

'We shall miss Mary sorely, but we must manage somehow. Let us hope that the hospital can get her back on her feet again in time for the production. Give her my most respectful regards, and the company's united good wishes for a speedy recovery. I will keep in touch with her.'

He hurried away.

Imogen was sitting quietly on the edge of the platform, waiting until they finished their conversation. Now she came forward.

'Who's going to take Mrs Proctor to hospital?' she asked.

George was harassed.

'It's a funny thing,' he said at random, 'but you've only got to suggest something to Mary for her to take against it. Alice Brakespear offered, and she won't hear of it.'

Imogen was not surprised. Something in Mary spoke to something in herself. Neither of them wanted to be under Alice's benevolent tyranny.

She said, 'I'd arrange to take her. If she would let me.'

He was too troubled to thank her properly.

'How can you? You don't know what day or time it will be. You've got a business to run and it's close to the big season.'

'It can only take a morning or an afternoon. Sadie would keep an eye on the shop for a few hours – particularly as it's for Mrs Proctor's sake. Your mother isn't close to me but, on the other hand, she's not against me. You could say she sees me as neutral territory. Also, she's proud and she wants someone who's not going to trespass on her privacy. I shan't trespass, and she knows that. In fact, we know each other very well, considering that we know each other hardly at all. I think you'll find she doesn't mind the idea of me.'

George relaxed into a smile, and Imogen smiled back, glad to see him looking more like his usual self.

'I'd call that low cunning on your part!' he said, joking.

'Low cunning is my survival kit,' she replied.

'It's very good of you. I thank you with all my heart.'

'Oh, you're more than welcome. You were kind to me when I most needed it. And you've been kind to Fred, too. Appreciating his toys and selling them.'

The evening which had begun on such a disastrous note continued to deteriorate. Sadie and Milia Godden arrived together with costumes and materials: the one flourishing a measuring tape, chalk and purple pin-cushion; the other brandishing a folio of sketches. Immediately they commandeered George, who was forced to supply a folding table, two chairs and two screens and rig up a makeshift clothes shop at the back of the hall. Nor were they prepared to fit in with Timothy's schedule, but insisted on the respect that was due to them both as voluntary unpaid workers and professionals. The rehearsal must be, as it were, pinned down and cut out to their pattern rather than his.

With an exasperated Timothy before them and two formidable ladies behind them, Peele's Players had an arduous evening ahead, and Mary's absence posed yet another difficulty. Apart from the loss of her as Gammer Madge, she had taken charge of refreshments and been responsible for bringing supplies. Now the larder was bare, the shops shut. It seemed that even a reviving beverage was to be dashed for their lips. But, as Timothy threw up his arms and exclaimed at still another unexpected catastrophe, Imogen stepped into the breach.

'No, no, it's all right. Alice will lend us tea and biscuits. I can pop along to the vicarage and get them. And I'll do the refreshments.'

'I'll help you,' said Deirdre.

'That would be most kind,' Timothy said, momentarily appeased.

He clapped his hands.

'It's 7.30, everyone. Sacrapant isn't here yet, so we have no magician and no chorus. Delia is going abegging and Delia's lover is being fitted for his costume – you will be some time yet, I take it ladies?' They assented.

'Hm, hm. We'll have a comedy scene to cheer us all up. Lampriscus and his pot of honey! Lampriscus, Erestus, Corebus and Huanebango on stage, if you please.'

By the side of George's ladder, George's new assistant was slopping equal quantities of emulsion on his overalls and the wall.

'I do think,' Timothy murmured to the fates, aggrieved, 'that we might have been spared the presence of Stephen!'

This was not to be the worst of his problems.

Philip arrived late, full of apologies, with nine clean docile youngsters, followed by an uninvited guest, who showed her teeth at the assembled company by way of introduction.

'My dear Edith,' said Timothy, appalled, 'to what do we owe this delightful surprise?'

As if in echo to his dismay Ian yelped as Sadie stuck a pin in his leg.

'Sorry, dear,' said Sadie, but her eyes were on Edith.

'I can leave at once, of course, if I'm not wanted,' said Edith, bridling, 'but I came on an errand of mercy.'

'An errand of mercy?' Timothy repeated, in disbelief.

Philip was looking particularly handsome and open-faced.

'A last-minute decision,' he explained, smiling. 'Edith understands that Mrs Proctor is ill, and suggested she might help out this evening.'

George, on the top step of the ladder, had stopped painting and turned towards them, brush poised.

'But how could you know about Mrs Proctor? I've only just heard the news myself,' said Timothy mystified.

Imogen, returning at that moment with a borrowed basket full of borrowed goods, was unpleasantly affected by the group from Prospect House. There was a regimental stillness about the youngsters, a suppressed eagerness about the adults that froze her. She remained by the swing doors, observing Timothy's polite consternation, the expressionless faces of Sadie and Milia, the watchfulness of George.

Edith replied with chilling playfulness, 'Elementary, my dear Timothy! A friend of mine told me that Mrs Proctor was in Dr Whitely's surgery on Friday, and I was looking out of my window when Mr Hobbs arrived with Stephen Proctor and what's-her-name in his van. So I put two and two together. Poor Mrs Proctor is not well. I thought, and will be away this evening.'

Timothy partly recovered himself, narrowed his eyes and smiled.

'How very far-sighted of you,' he said.

Something about his tone and smile disturbed Edith.

'Of course, if you have an understudy already?' she suggested.

'As you may possibly know,' said Timothy, glancing at Philip, 'this is a large cast and some are already doubling parts. We have, as yet, no understudy for Gammer Madge.'

He, too, was worried, though he still smiled. And Edith was not so sure of her position either, because she made a point of recommending herself.

'I have had acting experience, you know.'

'I know you have. With the Langesby Dramatic Society. When you first came here. I remember you as a powerful Hedda Gabler. They must have been sorry to lose you. But then, the opportunities in a local dramatic society are limited, and committee work offers greater scope for your many talents.'

'I simply hadn't enough time to do both.'

Timothy's voice was softest silk.

'Then it is undoubtedly kind of you to find time for us,' And he waited.

Imogen was reminded of a chess tournament, with each player thinking out possible moves ahead. The tension between the two protagonists had affected the whole company and put a stop to the decorating. They all listened in silence.

Not knowing what was expected of her, Edith said, 'I'm always ready to help out my friends in an emergency. You need an understudy and I don't mind learning the part. It isn't a big part and I'm a quick learner.'

At this reply, as if she had told him what he wanted to know, Timothy became all affability and pushed forward a pawn.

'I hesitate to ask so much of you. I don't think that will be necessary. Mrs Proctor should be back in two or three weeks.'

Edith took it.

'The play opens next month. Aren't you cutting it rather fine? Supposing Mrs Proctor doesn't come back in time? Who could you find at the last minute?'

He shrugged. 'There you have me!'

She gave a little laugh and said, 'Well, if you don't want me I'll go home.'

He gave a wonderful performance of a man who bows to the inevitable. He came forward and took both her hands in his.

'My dear Edith, it would help us immensely if you would be kind enough to read the part this evening. Forgive my half-hearted reception of your generous offer, but the news of Mrs Proctor has been somewhat devastating.' He began his usual amiable fussing. 'And now let us make you feel at home. Mrs Proctor most thoughtfully sent her script . . .'

Philip had wandered over to the decorators to bestow sympathy on George and seek information.

'Terribly sorry to hear that,' he was saying. 'Please give her my best wishes, and Edith's too, of course . . .'

Stephen stood worshipfully before him: a dog who has found a new master. Emulsion dripped from the brush in his emulsioned hand.

'You're my friend,' he said.

Philip smiled on him: the essence of good-natured understanding.

'I am indeed,' he said. 'I see that you're helping George tonight.'

Stephen nodded.

'Well, I think he's very lucky to have you. I'm sure you'll do an excellent job,' Philip said, and gave him a kindly pat on the back before he walked away.

Dazzled, Stephen turned to his half-brother.

'He's my friend, George,' he said.

'Oh, is he?' said George. 'I should watch that brush if I were you, or we shall have to clean the floorboards as well as your overalls.'

It was the strangest rehearsal any of them had ever attended. The wardrobe experts effaced themselves, drawing in players who happened to be idle, releasing them when they were needed; taking down measurements, trying on costumes, with the minimum of conversation and interruption. Peele's Players, word-perfect by now and inclined to argue their case, were unusually submissive, absorbing Timothy's criticisms and following up his suggestions without comment. Delia succumbed to a more than usually magnetic Scrapant. And Edith brought forth her own version of Gammer Madge. She was surprisingly good.

'Quite a new approach to the part,' Timothy observed wryly. 'A sophisticated Gammer with undercurrents. One feels, given a chance, that she might tell us a darker tale than this one.'

Poison in 'the pudding of her own making', Imogen thought.

Timothy cleared his throat. 'You read well, Edith. Thank you.'

He turned to Philip's contingent, who had been sitting in the middle of the hall, watching the proceedings. Four boys and five girls, they were aged between twelve and fifteen, all wearing bright cotton shirts, blue jeans and sneakers. Apart from a quality of inertness, they looked like any other Langesby youngsters.

'We have already been introduced to these splendid young people who have offered to be our chorus, and now we must spend the next hour integrating them into the play.' He beamed on them. 'Would you all like to come forward?'

They did not move. They looked at Philip for orders. There was an uncomfortable moment. Then Philip laughed.

'Come on, you dozy lot!' he said in teasing tones. 'Dr Rowley is in charge here, so you do what he says – briskly and cheerfully, if possible.'

They jumped up at once and stood in a line before Timothy, heads well up, hands clasped behind their backs, as if on parade.

'I think,' he said mildly, observing them over his spectacles, 'that we need to loosen up a little. Please will the company leave the stage and take a break while our young friends do a few exercises? As the chorus will be sitting for a long period a warm-up will help them.' He turned to Philip with exaggerated courtesy. 'Do I have your permission, my dear fellow?'

Philip's smile did not falter. He gave permission lightly, with a hint of amusement, so that everyone would know that Timothy was being ridiculous.

Undeterred, Timothy pulled off the cashmere sweater that was part of his producer's outfit, revealing a stout torso clad in a scarlet shirt. He marshalled them on to the area which would be the apron stage, but for the moment was marked out with chalk.

'Form a circle round me. Give yourselves plenty of space to hop about. I want you to turn into frogs.'

They stared at him woodenly.

'Do as I do,' Timothy ordered, and squatted with surprising agility.

They obeyed, more slowly.

'Now hop on the spot. Up – and then down. That's right. Now a little faster. Up. Down. Up. Down. Up. Down. Now rest.'

He had hopped with them. Stiff smiles appeared on their faces.

'Quite right! It's supposed to be fun,' he said, straightening up, unabashed. 'Now as I'm a great deal older than you, I'm retiring, but you are to go on being frogs. Listen to me carefully and do as I say.'

He produced a whistle from his trouser pocket.

'When I blow this whistle you start. When I blow it again you stop and rest. Do you understand?' Silence. 'Do you understand?' Louder.

The authority in his voice forced out a dutiful chorus of 'Yes, sir.'

'I'm relieved to hear it. I thought you had no voices for the moment,' said Timothy, smiling. 'Now back in your places. Ready? When I blow the whistle all frogs hop round in a circle!'

This time their movement were more lively. Walking round the edge of the stage area, giving orders, blowing his whistle, Timothy made them hop faster, slower, making long or short leaps, form squares, triangles and figure eights, cross lines, race each other. Inevitably there were clashes, stumbles and falls of a harmless nature. Their inhibitions vanished. At each accident the boys shouted, the girls shrieked; even laughter was heard. At last they sat cross-legged on the floor, breathing heavily, grinning at one another, while Timothy praised them.

His sphere of influence removed, Philip had been sitting, arms folded, his brightness overcast. But he laughed and clapped with the rest of the company when the exercises were over.

'And now, everyone,' Timothy cried triumphantly, 'in the time that is left to us, I should like you to take the play from the beginning while I show our vivacious young friends how to mime.' He raised his voice to address Sadie and Milia: 'Do you ladies need my three clowns or will you make do – which would be *greatly* obliging – with Delia and Venelia?'

Sadie's mouth was full of pins, and her present victim seemed to have suffered from quite a few. She motioned Milia to answer for them both.

'Yes, we can make do for now, Dr Rowley,' Milia announced in a sonorous voice, 'but we shall need to come to at least two more sessions. There is a great deal of work to be done here.'

Sadie disposed of her pins and stabbed them into a fat black purple cushion. 'A lot more than we bargained for!' she warned him.

'Of course. Of course.' Pacifically. 'We are entirely at your disposal and eternally grateful. Perhaps the three of us can meet at my house later in the week, in order to discuss mutually beneficial arrangements. Meanwhile . . . ?'

'Meanwhile,' said Sadie, always practical, 'we'll have Delia first – and then she can make the tea while we're fitting Venelia.'

To the Editor

Dear Sir,

May I once again beg the hospitality of your columns, this time in reply to Mr Breerton's charges against me?

Firstly, the church hall is owned by St Oswald's, and as its steward I have the authority to let it to whom I please and decorate it as I wish. Some much-needed painting and refurbishment is at present being carried out, which will be enjoyed not only by the audience and players of this production but by all future users. The materials have been donated, and the labour is voluntary.

Secondly, Langesby citizens still have primary use of the hall, so I would not describe a theatre company taking two of the less popular evenings in the week as 'commandeering'.

Thirdly, the play is being produced and directed by Dr Timothy Rowley, who was born and bred and still lives in the district of Langesby, and needs no introduction from me. 'Peele's Players' is his private company, which he has brought together for the sole purpose of giving this play. The members are actors and actresses whom he has chosen for their talents rather than their residential qualifications. Many of them are old friends from his past productions.

Fourthly, *The Old Wives' Tale* is not a farce, it is an original Elizabethan comedy of considerable distinction, by a playwright on whom Dr Rowley has written a highly praised thesis.

Fifthly, the reason that 'Peele's Players' are not contributing to the Civic Fund, and that they have free use of the church hall, is because they are giving every penny to the restoration of St Oswald's Church – a gesture that the town council might well consider when they count their gains from the Langesby Fair.

I remain, sir, yours sincerely,

Harold Brakespear, Vicar of St Oswald's

TWENTY-SEVEN

Full Moon

The ground was dry, the air clear, the moon ripe as a cheese. On top of Haraldstone Hill the seven women laid down their accoutrements and stood quietly, getting their breath back. Behind them the Listeners communed with each other against a night sky.

Walking away from the group Imogen went to her favourite mother and child, clasped her arms round them and leaned her forehead against their cool gritstone strength. This time no pangs of conscience, religious or otherwise, assailed her. She was content to join the healing ceremony, and had made her contribution in the form of an image of Mary Proctor.

'That figure would look far more lifelike in modelling wax,' she had said to Sadie, who was fashioning a crude likeness from a peg doll.

'I dare say it would, Clever Clogs,' Sadie had replied, 'and if you want to do it you're welcome to try. But this is only a symbol, and it's the intention that counts, not the appearance.'

'The first time I met Mrs Proctor she reminded Alice that good intentions paved the road to hell.'

'You know very well what I mean.'

'Shape with loving care and stitch with loving kindness?'

'That's the ticket.'

So Imogen spent two precious evenings modelling Mary's spare erect figure and indomitable face in wax, teasing out realistic hair from white and sandy-brown wool, copying her best black dress and painting shiny black shoes on her feet.

'Well, I'm blessed! That's Mary to the life!' Sadie said. 'You could earn a living at this sort of thing, you know.'

Imogen said mischievously, 'Supplying wax images for witches' ceremonies?'

'I'm talking about making dolls and dressing them.'

'I can just see the advertisement: *Life-like figures made to order. Stabbing pins supplied free. Results guaranteed. Only genuine covens need apply.* Do witches pay well, by the way?'

'And now you're being cheeky!'

Gravely, Sadie marked a twelve-foot circle inside the stones with the ritual knife, and then drew an imaginary circle in the air above it.

'Let this be a boundary between the world of gods and that of men,' she said.

To north, south, east and west of the circle, tall candles flickered in their sconces. In its centre, a white silk square painted with runes, by Milia, was spread over a small table that acted as an altar. On it stood a slim silver vase of flowers, supplied by Erica; a bunch of dried herbs from Jinny; a stick of incense in a brass holder from Beth; and a carved figure of Ceres the Earth Goddess, courtesy of George.

One by one the witches slashed the air to enter the invisible circle, redrawing it behind them. At a signal from Sadie, Imogen walked forward and placed the image of Mary Proctor on the altar. Then they all joined hands and began to pace round, chanting softly, 'Isis, Ceridwen, Astarte.' Pace and words quickened. 'Is-is, Cer-id-wen, As-tar-te.' Faster and faster.

'Runn-ing and chant-ing and heal-ing,' ran through Imogen's head. 'Runn-ing and chant-ing and heal-ing.'

'Isis, Ceridwen, Astarte, Isis, Ceridwen, Astarte.'

Sadie's hand signalled them to stop. In the silence, motionless, they concentrated on a prearranged image: Mary within a magic circle of protection, healed and whole.

On the altar the wax image lay, hands folded across its best black dress, painted eyes starting at the night sky, black shoes glittering in the moonlight.

Mentally Imogen drew and redrew the circle round Mary, smoothed out the wrinkles, unknitted the doughty brow, relaxed the stern mouth, took away care, poured light into the old body.

They were all very quiet and peaceful together. The women and the listeners, and the little doll on the altar.

Fire in the cauldron. Wine drunk. Bread broken and eaten. Smiles and quiet conversation. The deep warmth of companionship. The subtler warmth of moral satisfaction. A good job well done.

Jinny jumped up. 'I'm going to dance!' she cried, and began to pull off her clothes and throw them anywhere.

'So am I!' Imogen cried, and undressed so quickly that she and Jinny

250

stood side by side, naked and laughing, before the others could make up their minds.

'It's all right for you two,' said Sadie, looking dolefully at small pert breasts, narrow waists and tight buttocks, 'but some of us older ones need to cover up rather than take off. I warn you, I'm not a pretty sight. Still, here goes.'

And yet, Imogen thought, amazed, as they revealed themselves, each of them possessed their own beauty. The full-bodied maturity of Milia, the lean athleticism of Erica, the heavy splendour of Beth, the jolly curves and bounces of Sadie, the plump delights of Deirdre.

One by one the women emerged from their clothes, pale and soft-fleshed, peeled peaches against the slithering flames and flickering lights, dancing beneath a contemplative moon. Arms outstretched or flung above their heads, they gave themselves alternately to the cool night and the warm currents of fire.

A thrill in her back, a warning note in her head, were totally intuitive. 'There's someone watching us!' Imogen shrieked, and froze.

The flash caught her turning round, hair swirling, while the others still leaped and tossed their limbs in abandon. As the women scattered with cries of confusion, the camera continued to flash and click.

The main photograph on the feature page of a national Sunday newspaper was a picture of naked women of various ages, shapes and sizes, dancing round a fire. The witch nearest the camera had been caught in mid-flight. Fortunately for her, the face was in shadow, but the long slim body and long black hair suggested that she was young and desirable. Around it were displayed views of Langesby Town Hall decked out with flags for the Silver Jubilee of 1935 and bearing the caption *Historic Fair*; Langesbydale in the evening with the stone circle silhouetted against the skyline, entitled *Witches' Meeting Place*; and a sunlit snapshot of the Catwalk with the sinister pun *Witch Crafts*? The headline declared:

The Haraldstone Witches Ride Again!

The North Country market town of Langesby could hardly be described as well-known, and even fewer people will have heard of Haraldstone, a former industrial village some miles away in Langesbydale, but you are about to hear much of both places. Next month the town will be celebrating the fourth centenary of its fair charter with a week of festivities, and the quality crafts shops in Haraldstone are likely to attract customers out of sheer curiosity.

Langesbydale has long been noted for its witches. At one time covens proliferated, but the most important of these was centred in Haraldstone and governed by one of an ancient tribe of witches, a descendant of whom still lives in the dale today.

Traditions die hard, and Langesby has recently been suffering from a series of incidents which hint that the Old Religion is reviving. The Reverend Harold Brakespear, vicar of St Oswald's Church in Langesby, had his altar defiled by celebration of a Black Mass some weeks ago, and his attempts to pass off the affair as a nasty joke provoked bitter and widespread comment in the local press. On the other hand, the vicar is not popular in all quarters, and my sceptical mind was inclined to agree with him.

This situation was further exacerbated by his connection with an unknown group of amateurs called 'Peele's Players' who are performing a weird Elizabethan folk tale at the church hall during the Fair Week. News that he gave them priority over everyone else, asked no rent, and redecorated the hall at their request, brought forth the jocular suggestion that the Reverend Harold was bewitched. The real reason was more prosaic. Apparently the company was formed, with the blessing of the vicar, for the sole purpose of making money. All profits will be handed over to the Church Fund. So much for the civic spirit – and for witchcraft!

I pride myself, however, on keeping an open mind. So when I was told that certain rituals would take place on Haraldstone Hill this month, at full moon, I went there with a photographer and witnessed a genuine witches' sabbath.

In the moonlit stone circle a group of women, with the aid of various props which included a savage-looking knife, invoked the powers of evil. Moving round and round in a circle, chanting, they concentrated on a doll-like image that lay on the altar. Having put a curse on their victim they lit a fire, flung off their clothes, and danced in triumph round the flames. What will happen to this person is beyond the knowledge or imagination of your correspondent, but the seriousness of the rite, and the abandonment with which they celebrated its conclusion, suggested the worst. It also confounds the opinion of the Reverend Harold, who apparently described the Haraldstone witches as harmless middle-aged women making fools of themselves!

Langesby begins its civic celebrations next month, in great expectations and tremendous style. The main street will be decorated, a fairground erected, and market stall holders will wear sixteenth-century costumes. Various entertainments are provided throughout the week, beginning with a carnival procession, floats and stilt-walkers. At one end of the town the official Dramatic Society will be giving their usual worthy performance of a worthy play, in this case *Love on the Dole*. At the other end 'Peele's Players' will be up to their Elizabethan tricks. And somewhere in the midst of these secular frolics, the Reverend Harold is setting up a religious ceremony to bless the newly cast tenor bell due to arrive at St Oswald's Church.

There is a rumour that he personally borrowed a considerable sum of money to complete this five-year task in time for the fair, and is hoping to recuperate it by means of donations and the charitable efforts of 'Peele's Players'. Meanwhile, down at the town hall, they are a trifle peeved because they think that money made through Langesby Fair should be rendered up to Langesby.

Despite these warring factions I am sure that visitors will enjoy themselves. And the most exciting event of all may be provided by the Haraldstone Witches – cooking up fresh devilment to confound everybody's plans! Roll up! Roll up!

'We have asked you all to come here,' said Hal, pouring generous portions of sherry, whisky and gin, 'to see if we can shed any light on this disgraceful business. Help yourselves to ginger ale, tonic and so on.'

Alice, coming in too late with a bottle of acid white and another of pungent red, said, 'Oh!' And then, 'If anyone would rather have a glass of wine?'

Their smiles were deprecating. They clutched their tumblers thankfully to their chests and shook their heads.

'I'm sure Imogen would prefer . . .' Alice began.

Imogen had already taken a surreptitious and necessary gulp of neat gin.

'Ice, then?' Alice asked, defeated.

'Yes, my dear, we should like some ice,' said Hal, and added, 'if it's not too much trouble.'

Behind the terror and shame that had enveloped her since Sunday, Imogen's knowing imp whispered, 'Hal's feeling guilty.'

Taking courage from this inner rascal she managed to look round the familiar circle in a semblance of normality.

Who guesses it was me? she was wondering.

Philip? He was avoiding her eyes. Edith? Amused and faintly contemptuous, but then she always was. Timothy? Keeping his own counsel. George? He gave her a friendly nod. Yes, George would know, and would not condemn. Alice and Hal? Their belief in her was a blindfold, and she felt guilty, not of what she had done but of deceiving them.

'Has everyone got a drink?' Hal asked. 'Good!'

He settled down in his armchair with a generous slug of whisky and a squirt of soda. On the table beside him lay a copy of the newspaper folded open at the feature page. Imogen was yet again made miserably aware of herself as a blur of pale flesh and dark hair turning towards the camera, and wished she could curl up, foetus-fashion, and hide away until the scandal blew over. Alice was walking pensively round the room, diluting their drinks with ice cubes. Hal waited until she poured a glass of wine for herself and sipped it cautiously. He began on a sombre note.

'I must confess that I didn't take this witchcraft business seriously enough.'

They were silent, each of them having a different view of the situation.

Alice, who was visibly upset, burst out, 'I did try to warn you, as far back as January . . .' and stopped, because Imogen and George lived in Haraldstone. She amended her protest. 'I tried to tell you certain things I'd heard.'

'Well, that's old history,' Hal said quietly, 'and we can't do anything about it now.' He indicated the newspaper. 'What does concern me is the personal information which this journalist has collected. I believed that only my intimate friends knew about the loan – and my opinion of the Haraldstone witches. And who put him on to this meeting in the first place? Last week I should have laid the blame on my civic enemies, but I doubt that they have this sort of knowledge. Can any of you shed any light on the matter?'

The men looked round at each other, ready to give their opinion but anxious not to be the first to speak. Edith was waiting for some opportunity that had not so far presented itself. Then Timothy's seniority prevailed.

He said, 'I believe, my dear Hal, that this is far graver than you imagine. There is undoubtedly a serious attempt to discredit you by the Langesby officials whom you have annoyed and frustrated. But in this case they are simply taking advantage of an attack which is coming from quite a different direction. We all know what they hope to gain by your downfall – namely a new vicar who resembles your predecessor, and who will allow St Oswald's to crumble away peacefully without bothering them. Although that constitutes a major crisis for you, I would describe it as a minor problem compared to the aims of the real troublemakers.

'I have no specific knowledge who or what or how many they are –

let us simply call them the *Opposition*. I suggest that the Opposition informed this journalist about the meeting – and it is worth noting that they had information about the witches as well as yourself. But I should most strongly advise you not to reproach or question the journalist or his editor, because they will – quite properly – refuse to reveal their source. Moreover, they are not the culprits but the dupes.

'Briefly then, though this sounds ridiculously melodramatic, I believe that the Opposition is a centre, or would-be centre, of black witchcraft which hopes to infiltrate Langesby and the dale with its own peculiar brand of evil.'

As they stared at him, astounded, he drawled, 'I am, as you know, not entirely ignorant on the subject of magic, but I approach the subject as a mere scholar and I am not infallible. If my supposition is wrong then I shall be delighted. If I am right then we are in graver trouble than any but the *cognoscenti* can realize.'

In the silence that followed Hal swallowed the last of his whisky, got up and poured himself another. They watched him, nursing their own empty tumblers.

Alice said in a small voice, 'Do you happen to know who the Haraldstone witches are cursing?'

It was evident that she had her suspicions. Her eyes were on her husband who, suddenly alerted to this new peril, paused and looked enquiringly at Timothy.

'I'm sure they were not cursing anyone, my dear. I suspect that the journalist's impression was influenced beforehand,' said Timothy. 'But as I am not privy to the counsels of the Haraldstone coven, and was not there at the time, I can only offer a reasoned judgement. These Haraldstone witches are delightfully white – *Do as thou wilt and harm no one* as they say – and their leader, a descendant of the original witches, is in poor health at the moment. I should think they were conducting a ritual of healing on her behalf.'

Alice said in a small voice, 'You don't mean Mary Proctor, surely?'

'Yes, my dear, I do. Mary Proctor is your genuine article,' he said, looking very hard at Edith, who looked away.

Alice was alarmed and stammering.

'But you said – more than once – when Edith was making insinuating remarks – you said Mary wasn't a witch . . .'

'No, no. I said no such thing, my dear. I turned Edith's comments aside by saying that Mrs Proctor was an admirable woman and we all respected her – which is true. I would never deny that Mary was a witch because

I know her to be one.' He added, 'Normally, I should not dream of revealing such information, but these are perilous times and only the truth will do.'

Hal was watching him with a frown of concentration, neither condemning nor agreeing with this point of view; but Alice was at sea and floundering wildly.

'Know her to be a witch? Surely, you can't be serious?'

'I take a broad view of people's beliefs, and she is the follower of a far older religion than yours, my dear. Indeed, St Oswald's Church is built on a pagan foundation, and the Christian Church has taken over many of the pagan festivals and renamed them.'

Alice was metaphorically struck to the ground, but Hal held up his Christian shield, and stood fast.

'Mary Proctor's practices and beliefs may seem questionable to you,' said Timothy, 'but her morality is beyond reproach. If you need proof of that then may I remind you of the touching story you once told us? Where would you have been in those early, difficult days without the care and goodwill of Mary Proctor?'

Alice murmured into her glass of sour wine, 'I don't know. I can't tell. It's all beyond me. What in heaven's name is happening to us?'

Timothy left her to her thoughts and addressed himself to Hal.

'I should be more sorry than I can say if this knowledge damaged any friendship with Mary, but we must all know where we stand.'

Hal made a gesture of appreciation.

Edith was watching and listening. Imogen said nothing. George sat, head bent, hands clasped between his knees. Philip spoke up soberly.

'Like Hal, I've tended to discount local gossip, but if the matter is as serious as Tim says then we can't sit on the fence. Even friendships must be sacrificed.'

Searching for culprits, Alice addressed George directly.

'Did *you* know about this, George?'

Her tone was that of a headmistress, catching a pupil smoking behind the gymnasium. His head jerked up, but his reply was tranquil and monosyllabic.

'Yes. Of course I did.' The truth caught him up. 'She's my mother. Of course I knew. And it doesn't make any difference.'

'But you're a bell-ringer. The captain of the tower,' Alice cried. 'How could you do that to us?'

Hal roused himself.

'Don't be ridiculous, Alice. George hasn't done anything at all.'

Edith said impatiently, for she wanted to hear more. 'Let's get back to the point, shall we?'

She was the touchpaper needed to set Alice alight.

'This *is* the point,' Alice cried, jumping up and confronting them. 'Hal and I have been working for St Oswald's for five hard yards, in good faith, and doing our best by everybody, and suddenly we find out that nothing is what it seemed and everyone is against us. We thought that Mary and George were our good friends.'

Timothy put up his hand to check the flow of words, spoke soothingly to her.

'My dear Alice, they still are, and you have many good friends in Langesby who all wish you well. It is your enemies with whom you should be concerned.'

She was only half listening. Her world had lost its bearings.

'Enemies? I'm not even sure who my friends are, at this moment.'

She swung round on Imogen, who had been hoping that she might go unnoticed, and wishing that Hal would offer her another gin.

'What about you, Imogen? Are you my friend, or have they corrupted you, too?'

'I think . . .' Timothy murmured, lifting his eyebrows at Hal, who nodded and came over to his wife and put his arm round her shoulders.

'Alice,' he said softly, 'come along, my dear, and let's get you to bed. You're upset and exhausted with this wretched business . . .'

But she thrust away his arm and demanded the truth.

'Imogen, did *you* know that Mary Proctor was a witch?'

Everyone's attention was transferred to the young pale woman, twisting her empty tumbler between her hands. For an eternity of seconds Imogen did not reply.

Then she said, 'Yes.'

The long chase was over at last. She volunteered the information that Alice was about to demand.

'I know the other witches, too, and I took part in the meeting the other night. Timothy was right. It wasn't a ritual curse, it was a healing ceremony. The image on the altar was of Mary Proctor, and I made it.' She looked directly at Alice and said, 'But I *am* your friend, and I always have been. Nothing alters that.'

Alice put her face in her hands and began to cry softly.

Hal said, 'If you'll all excuse us, I think Alice should rest.'

Timothy answered for them all.

'Yes, of course, my dear fellow. We'll see ourselves out. Come along

257

everyone. Good-night, both of you. Take care. By the by, my housekeeper always recommends hot milk and honey for a sound night's sleep. I'll ring you tomorrow, Hal, to find out how Alice is.'

Imogen put down her glass and followed the rest of them, feeling a social leper. As the door of the vicarage closed on them. Timothy was at her elbow, kind, smiling, neutral.

'Would you like me to drive you home?' he offered.

She envisioned the little chat that might ensue, and had neither the stamina to undertake it nor the strength to refuse him. Fortunately, George arrived at that moment, wheeling the old Harley-Davidson round the corner of the house.

'It's a bit out of your way, Tim,' said George, matter-of-factly, 'and I brought the lady, so I'll drive her home. Hop on, Imogen.'

She could not have spoken, so she managed a smile and nodded at Timothy in a friendly manner. Then she straddled the pillion, put her arms round George's waist and her head against his shoulder, and left the rest to him. And George knew exactly what to do. He delivered her safely back to Polly and Crazy Hats, made her a mug of milk and honey, and told her to sleep well.

TWENTY-EIGHT

The arrangements to take Mary to hospital were a problem for everyone but herself.

George could not drive them there. He had Stephen to look after, not enough room in the van, and an eight o'clock start to his day.

Alice's original offer had been refused, and no others would be forthcoming. There was silence between the vicarage and the dale, though tongues tattled and gossip spread all over Langesby.

Transport among the witches was limited. Only three of them had any vehicle at all. Erica owned an old MG that no one else could drive, even if she had allowed them. Sadie had a vast elderly Vauxhall, which she used for travelling to exhibitions and craft fairs, but as she was looking after Crafty Notions and Crazy Hats, while Imogen escorted Mary, that was out of the question. This left Deirdre, who obligingly cancelled a blow-dry and a manicure in order to take them there. And as no one knew how long they would be Timothy gave gracious permission to ring him at any time, and promised to collect them shortly afterwards.

Mary, having caused her friends so much trouble, was now gracious.

'That's very kind of him,' she said, 'but then, Dr Rowley was always a gentleman – and his mother was a lady. She wouldn't have used any liniment for her rheumatism but mine.'

She was sitting with George, Stephen and Imogen in the kitchen at Howgill, discussing details and drinking tea.

'And you're a good lass,' Mary said to Imogen, the Haraldstone exile, 'and so is Sadie, for helping out. I know you've got both businesses to run. You're all good people and you won't lose by it, I promise you.'

What treasure might accrue to them as a result of their efforts Imogen could not guess, but in that moment she felt sure that a rich reward awaited her.

★　　★　　★

'There seem to be a lot of people waiting,' said Mary suspiciously, leaning on two walking sticks and peering along the row of hard wooden chairs. 'What time did you say my appointment was?'

'Ten-fifteen, Mrs Proctor.'

'And what time is it now?'

'Ten o'clock.'

'Right. We'll sit here.'

She sat down suddenly and heavily next to a small timid man of indeterminate age, and stuck one of the sticks just under his right leg. Imogen took the other before she could inflict it on anyone else. The small man shrank away to give her more room. His hands perpetually clasped and unclasped, his smile was a rictus, his body a frail shell in which he would have hidden if he could. Immediately Mary spotted a natural victim, and pounced. She addressed him directly.

'And what time's *your* appointment, may I ask?'

His head tried to poke itself back into the shelter of his collar. He swallowed and hastened to answer her.

'Nine-fifteen, Missis.'

'I knew it,' Mary said to the high white ceiling. 'They're running late already. Mark my words, we'll be here until dinnertime at this rate.' She chewed an invisible cud. 'I don't suppose they do a cup of tea, do they?' She turned on the small man. 'They used to have a trolley at one time.'

He wrung his hands and grinned like death.

'I'll ask,' said Imogen, and smiled at a passing nurse. 'Excuse me, but is there anywhere we can get a cup of tea?'

The girl was high-coloured, full-bosomed, and brassy with good health. She spoke imperiously, as if sick people were a lower order.

'There's a refreshment room on this floor, but I'm afraid you can't leave your seat while you're waiting for an appointment.'

'Oh, I see,' said Imogen, accepting the edict.

But Mary cried aggressively, 'What do you mean – *can't leave my seat?* Suppose I want to go to the toilet?'

'You'll find the toilets at the end of the hall,' said the nurse briskly, moving on.

'Just – one – moment!' Mary commanded, holding up a forefinger. Her tone and the gesture made the nurse pause. Mary lowered her finger, and spoke in her most forthright manner.

'Are you – as I strongly suspect – running late?'

'Not as far as I know . . .'

At this moment Mary's obliging demon caused another nurse to pop her head out of a consulting room, calling, 'Mrs Carsby? Doctor will see you now.'

The middle-aged woman by Imogen's side rose. She was a stout, homely person wearing a navyblue coat and a paisley headscarf. Mary, judging her to be a sensible body in the same social category as herself, addressed her in friendly tones.

'You'll excuse me for asking, but could you tell me the time of your appointment?'

'Nine o'clock,' said the woman, and added with a sigh, 'I thought, with it being so early, that I'd be seen straight away. And I've got my Tesco shopping to do yet.'

The hands of the clock on the wall were pointing to ten.

'Thank you very much,' Mary said. She turned on the nurse. 'So I shall be here for the next hour.' She could not forbear from adding, 'At the very least. Just give me one good reason why I can't go away for a cup of tea?'

'Regulations,' said the nurse brusquely, tossing her head, 'and I'm afraid there's nothing I can do about it.'

Mary's eyes turned a dense, mean green.

'You could mend your manners for a start,' she said frankly. 'You're very rude.'

Here an unexpected ally in the queue said, 'Aye, you're right about that, Missis. I come here every week, and doctor's never on time, and th'hospital's full of snotty young bitches as treats you like muck.'

'Ex-actly,' said Mary.

The nurse's complexion turned a deeper shade of rose.

'I'm afraid I can't deal with individual complaints,' she said. 'You must refer those to the proper authority.'

'Oh, I shall,' said Mary deliberately. '*And* I know who to go to.'

'Excuse me, nurse,' said Imogen, attempting a compromise, 'but I brought this lady here, and I have no appointment. Am I allowed to leave *my* seat?'

The nurse was reluctant to yield and answered grudgingly.

'Oh yes. You're a visitor and that's different. You'll find the refreshment room down the second corridor on the left.'

'Perhaps I could bring Mrs Proctor a cup of tea?' Imogen suggested hopefully.

'I'm afraid that's not allowed,' the nurse was glad to say.

'You're afraid of a lot of things,' said Mary roundly, 'and the way this place is run nowadays I'm not surprised.'

Here a number of other rebels joined in with personal reminiscences.

'I'm afraid,' said the nurse, in retreat, 'that I can't help you, and I'm needed elsewhere.' After her mauling she departed with some shreds of dignity.

'They say,' one of the rebels remarked, 'that you'd best not come here to die. The nurses give you a hard time, and if you're not quick enough then the doctors finish you off.'

But Mary had had enough mutiny for the moment, and turned on this ally.

'Stuff and nonsense!' she cried. 'I was trained in this hospital sixty years ago, and there isn't a better one in the country. That girl might be impudent but the standard of nursing is excellent, and our doctors were never murderers.'

Having now made enemies of both staff and fellow sufferers, she sat back satisfied, prepared to take on the rest of the world if need be. But her tone, when she spoke to Imogen, was warm and intimate.

'You go and get yourself a cup of tea,' she advised. 'We'll be here a long time, or my name isn't Mary Proctor.'

'No, no,' said Imogen. 'I'm not thirsty. I'll sit with you.' She remembered George's suggestion for such an emergency, and brought out the latest copy of the *Langesby Chronicle*. 'Would you like to read the paper?'

'No, I would not,' said Mary ungratefully, 'but if I have to wait here all morning then I'll be writing a letter to the *Chronicle* that will be worth reading. In the meantime I'm watching that clock!'

She was summoned at half-past eleven.

'Are you a relative of Mrs Proctor?' the doctor asked Imogen, as they entered together. 'No? Then, if you don't mind, I'd rather you waited outside. We'll call you if necessary.'

Mary looked suddenly so old, with her wild sandy-white hair and defensive stance, that Imogen feared to leave her.

'Are you sure you'll be all right?' she asked.

'Don't be so soft. Of course I'll be all right,' Mary answered. She faced her new adversary doughtily. 'And let me tell you this, young man, doctor or no doctor – I will *not* be patronized.'

He was undoubtedly young in years, but evidently old in wisdom. He smiled disarmingly. He seated Mary down, removed her sticks to a safe place, took her by the hand and gave it a friendly little shake.

'I've been hearing about you, Mrs Proctor. I believe you've brought two generations of Langesbydalers into the world.'

'Yes I have.' Unbending a very little.

'In that case, you know far more than I do,' he said engagingly, 'but as my job depends on it, would you permit me to give you a general examination?'

'I'm a professional,' said Mary, unbending a little more. 'I know what's needed.'

'Then shall you and I look into this little problem together?'

'If you like,' said Mary, reluctant.

'I think,' said the doctor, smiling very wide, holding the door open for Imogen, 'that Mrs Proctor and I understand each other.'

His nurse, who had heard Mary's exchange with her colleague, whispered to Imogen, 'We'll be half an hour at least, if you'd like a cup of coffee or something.'

They were far longer than that.

The round-faced clock ticked on and on. The young doctor had taken a fancy to Mary, and she, in a begrudging way, to him. From time to time he would appear at Imogen's side to report a progress that would have been comical were it not so puzzling.

'We've been testing for diabetes, and she has some sugar. Nothing to fuss about. Diet will sort that out. But the leg ulcers are rather nasty.'

'We've been testing Mrs Proctor's sight. It is, of course, defective, but no more than one would expect at her age.'

'There seems to be no reason for the dizziness and palpitations she experiences. The heart appears to be sound. Still, I'd like her to have a cardiogram, just to be on the safe side.'

'She looks rather thin and complains of sweating at night and general lassitude, so I'm sending her for a lung X-ray, just to be certain.'

As the hours dragged on, Imogen drank coffee and ate a ham sandwich without appetite, knowing that Mary was being made aware of all her physical disabilities with nothing to sustain her. Occasionally, the old woman was let out to await some further form of examination, and sat quietly, munching her lips, narrowing her eyes, communing with herself silently. Her shoulders became more rounded, her stance less truculent, as if their failure to pinpoint her ailments underlined some diagnosis of her own.

Imogen was afraid to ask if she was all right because evidently she was not and would have dismissed the enquiry with some asperity. Yet at one point she dared to squeeze the old hand next to her.

'Aye,' Mary remarked, allowing this. 'They say that death's the last enemy, but it's not so. Old age is the last enemy. It's hard to be old. You're no use then to yourself or anybody else, and folk can't be bothered with you. All the kind words in the world won't alter that. You'll find out if you live long enough, my lass. And then you'll look back at what you thought was the worst that could happen – and I know you've had your share of sorrow – and you'll know it was nothing, because you had your health and strength and youth. But wait until you're seventy-eight. You'll remember what I said then, and think on.'

Sombrely, Imogen imagined herself at seventy-eight, thinking on.

At four o'clock Mary was taken to the dietician, and weighed on the way in.

The full-bosomed nurse who had confronted them early in the morning was in charge of these scales, and ready for a fresh challenge. She had decided that this difficult patient should be treated in a familiar and playful fashion.

'Oh dear me, Mary. Six pounds underweight. We'll have to do better than this! Haven't you been eating your cornflakes for breakfast, you naughty girl?'

Mary's reply was deliberate.

'Well, you've been eating yours. You must be two stones overweight if you're an ounce. And, since we've not been introduced,' with bitter emphasis, 'I'd thank you to address me as *Mrs Proctor*.'

Alerted by the patient's tone a sister enquired with sinister politeness, 'Is anything wrong, Nurse?'

Confronted by the prospect of attack from both sides, the nurse retreated. 'Oh no, Sister. Mrs Proctor and I were just chatting.'

Momentarily, Mary was placated. But the sight of the dietician, who must have been all of twenty-four years old, aroused further aggression.

'Let me tell you, young lady,' she began, conveying her contempt for juvenile impertinence, 'that I was nursing before you were born, and I know all about diets. If you can sort out a healthier diet than the one I follow then I'll take my hat off to you.'

The girl knew better than to join battle.

'If I could just ask you a few questions, Mrs Proctor . . .'

To all of these Mary responded truthfully but sullenly, further enraged to perceive that the dietician thought she was fibbing. In the end she was presented with a menu which strongly resembled the one to which she was accustomed.

In a final gesture of defiance, she said, 'Well, I shan't gain weight on this, I can tell you. It's what I usually eat!'

Finally released, she said to Imogen, 'We don't ring Dr Rowley just yet. I'm parched and famished, but I wouldn't use that refreshment room if I'd just walked in from the desert. Come on, my lass, and I'll treat us to tea at Fortune's.' This was the most fashionable and expensive tea-room in Langesby, known throughout the county and specially mentioned in the festival brochure.

Imogen said, 'No. Let me treat us. Please. I should like to.'

Mary gave her a long judgmental look, but finding neither pity nor charity in Imogen's face she accepted.

'But I'm warning you,' she said, 'when I say *tea* I mean a good one, and Fortune's isn't cheap!'

'It doesn't matter. I sold two hats yesterday. The sky's the limit.'

Mary linked arms with her and said, 'You can see me across the road. My eyesight isn't what it was and I'm not used to traffic these days.'

Established in the high bright tea-room, under the famous glass dome, surrounded by the elect of Langesby ladies, Imogen ordered cinnamon toast for herself. Mary had a pile of toasted teacakes, a selection of jams and a generous slice of Fortune's celebrated chocolate gâteau. She drank three cups of strong brown Assam tea straight off, ordered another pot, and spread black cherry jam liberally on the top teacake. Her attitude dared Imogen to speak.

Wisely, she chose not to, so Mary offered an explanation.

'They said I must cut out sugar altogether – not that I've got a particularly sweet tooth, though I enjoy a bit of something sweet now and again. But today I'm flying the flag. Do you know what I mean?'

'Yes,' said Imogen, thinking of her nakedness exposed to strange eyes, 'you mean – to hell with the bloody lot of them.'

Mary nodded. She ate for a while in defiance, rather than enjoyment.

Then she said, 'I told George they could do nothing more for me than I'm doing myself. Well, I was right.'

The words were delivered without her usual gusto, and Mary did not speak again. They sat together in sad silence while she finished her banquet.

TWENTY-NINE

'I think,' said Timothy wisely, looking at the steep narrow lane, 'that I'll leave my car here, Mary, if you don't mind. Imogen and I can help you down to the house.'

'Oh, I'm all right on my own, once I get my balance,' said Mary defensively, reaching for her two walking sticks.

The ducks ran to their wire-netting fence to give her a raucous welcome. From the centre chimney smoke was drifting idly into the air. The stream ran softly, talking to itself, willows dipped into the water, and the rowan trees stood sentry. Howgill was a good place to come home to, at the end of a mild June day.

'George will have made up the fire on his way past,' said Mary, stopping for breath, pointing to the chimney smoke with one stick. 'He's a grand lad.'

She ploughed on and then stopped again, alert.

'Someone's here that shouldn't be,' she said, and began to hobble forward.

Imogen's skin prickled. She looked round, but there were no watchful eyes, no hidden presences. 'There's no one here,' she said.

'Then there has been, and they've left a calling card,' said Mary forcefully.

'Stay here, Imogen my dear!' Timothy ordered in a high strained voice, and hurried ahead with Mary.

But Imogen followed.

They stopped a short distance from the door that Mary always kept locked, and she joined them.

The bundle of twigs, perhaps eight inches long, seemed innocuous at first, then Imogen saw that it was neatly trussed with straw at neck, arms, wrists, legs and ankles to represent a figure. Cock's feathers were tucked into its head, the limbs were smeared with a whitish substance, the body clad in rags and stabbed with thorns. A miniature scarecrow, it had been

267

tucked away in a corner of the unused doorway, where it was likely to be overlooked. And this was no childish mischief. There was something vicious in the way it was bound, daubed and pierced, and the iridescent feathers formed a barbarous decoration.

Mary said, 'I knew it,' and sagged on her sticks.

'What is it?' Imogen whispered, hugging her arms to her breasts for comfort. But she guessed what it was, and they did not answer her. Timothy was the first to recover.

'I think,' he said, in his most pedantic manner, 'that we must render this abomination harmless. With your kind permission, Mary, I should like to remove the object and deal with it myself.'

Mary nodded, frowning, lips compressed.

'There is the possibility,' he continued, 'that we may find other calling cards in Haraldstone. Sadie must be warned that any of her group might be visited – and that includes you, Imogen. Well, we shall deal with that contingency shortly.'

He saw that she was frightened and lightened his tone.

'What a good thing I brought you ladies home! I seldom have the opportunity to study these unsavoury offerings at first hand.'

She was cheered but not deceived.

Mary had recovered a little. Gesturing Imogen's help away she drew herself up and began to hobble towards the front door with the aid of her sticks. Over her shoulder she said, 'You can do the running about for me, my lass, and find Dr Rowley whatever he wants.'

Timothy linked Imogen's arm to comfort her, and said, 'I shall need a large sheet of drawing paper, my dear, a stick of charcoal or a thick pencil, and a flat surface on which to produce my safety device.'

The two women sat together at the kitchen table and watched him work. Deep in concentration, he drew a large square, a diamond within the square, a square within the diamond, and a circle within the square. These he divided into sections, which he proceeded to fill with sacred symbols. Finally he printed on either side of the diamond:

NIHIL MALI
CAPIAT ME.

'Nothing evil can harm me,' Imogen said under her breath.

'Exactly!' Timothy said. 'And now, my dear, since you will not do as Alice tells you, and persist in sticking your nose into these strange affairs, you can be my assistant. Mary, may I borrow your fire-tongs? And though you would probably do so anyway, I should like to add the warning that you steep them in salt and water afterwards, and say a few appropriate words over them to purify them. One can't be too careful.'

He looked at her closely.

'You have had a long hard day and are somewhat pale, Mary, which is hardly surprising. Are there any fortifying liquors in the house? Brandy, for instance?'

She nodded towards the corner cupboard.

'Imogen, bring the brandy for Mary, if you please, and mix it as she likes to take it. Then come with me.'

By herself, Imogen would long since have panicked, but her faith in Timothy was now absolute.

Stalking solemnly after him, carrying the fire-tongs and sheet of drawing paper, she said, 'I suppose you've been into all this with the Magical Arts Society? What a thing it is to be knowledgeable – and what a lot there is to learn. I've been reading up your lectures, bit by bit. Goodness me. You must have taken a university degree on the subject. I shall be ages before I—'

'Silence, chatterbox!' Timothy said, with amiable authority. 'Give me the paper and the tongs and stand well away. These things are not to be treated lightly.'

Obediently, she stepped back and watched.

He spread the paper on the ground, lifted the twig figure with a dextrous clip of the tongs and dropped it on to the diagram.

'Good,' said Timothy. 'Now I can put it in the boot of my car and take you to Haraldstone. I'll destroy it when I get home.'

In her imagination, Imogen felt the beast boring evil rays through her back as she sat in the passenger seat.

'Is it truly safe on that piece of paper?' she asked.

'Safe as houses, I promise you. I shall also make sure that your premises are secure before I leave you.'

Imogen said, remembering her companion, 'Oh, but poor Polly's there and if they leave something nasty she won't know what it is. She might be hurt.'

'Polly wouldn't go near such a thing. Have you seen any of Mary's cats around since we got here? No, of course not! They're hiding until the coast is clear. Cats take care of themselves. Don't worry. And I must make sure that George knows about this affair as soon as possible, so that he can keep an eye on her. How I wish she had a telephone. The simple life is a worthy one but it plays the very devil with communications.'

But there was nothing on Imogen's doorstep. Polly greeted Timothy as a friend, and trotted around with him importantly as he inspected every corner of the premises. Afterwards he walked over to Sadie's shop and spent a good half-hour talking to her privately. Finally he reported that all was well on the Haraldstone front, and drove home to dispose of the bane.

But Imogen locked both doors, front and back, closed all the windows, and suspected even the shadows on the stairs until she proved them innocent.

The *Langesby Chronicle* had realized that if it did not keep a sharp eye on Haraldstone and the witches, it might be elbowed out of its own news by the national papers. So when the tale of Mary's calling card was leaked to the editor, he put it on the front page and gave the scoop his own lively interpretation.

WITCHES' CURSE ON DALE DOORSTEP ran the headline. The drift of the story was that a reputed witch had been cursed, and it was suspected that local covens were fighting for supremacy. Mary's name was not revealed, because she refused to be interviewed and the paper could not afford a libel action. But they reproduced the photograph of the witches' dance, by kind permission; the sunlit court of the Catwalk in 1930 which needed no permission at all; and their photographer took a snapshot of Howgill House entitled, 'A peaceful corner of the dale', so that any reader with a modicum of intelligence and a smidgen of curiosity could make the connection.

A shoal of letters descended upon the ambitious head of Derek Bryant and he printed the most controversial. 'A Concerned Christian' raised his sword once again, to be joined in battle by Hal again, and enthusiasts flocked to their separate banners. Pseudonyms abounded, and the subject of witchcraft attracted the usual nutters. Someone calling himself Jack o' the Dale, and purporting to be the high priest of an arcane hermetical order, offered to negotiate a peace between the covens. He and his credentials were immediately attacked on all sides.

By now, those who had been trying to advertise themselves through the Langesby Fair knew that they were on to a winner if they mentioned witches. Foremost among those to take advantage of the situation was the landlord of that male chauvinist preserve the Dancing Witch. Flying in the face of tradition and his regular customers, he decorated his premises inside and out, commissioned a ravishing young naked witch to be painted on the new sign, refurbished the parlour and ladies' cloakroom, and openly welcomed females, families and charabancs to 'this ancient Haraldstone hostelry, the origin of whose mysterious name is lost in the mists of time'.

The national newspapers, at first merely amused by these North Country shenanigans, now began to follow the events with interest, and to comment on the more bizarre. They also resolved to send a reporter and photographer up to the fair on opening day.

Wary of these tasty gobbets of news, Haraldstone itself kept a low profile. In the collective memory of the village, witchcraft and its consequences held an ominous place. At Crossdyke Street Chapel, only a century ago, a word from the pulpit or a whisper among the brethren could lead to victimization of the cruellest kind. Lives had been made wretched by ostracism and niggling daily torments, minds unhinged by fear. Occasionally some poor creature died in dubious circumstances, but the case was always enveloped in a fog of silence through which it glimmered unproven. Earlier than that the records became more shameful still. Women had been openly hunted down with hounds, held under water until they died, hanged in Langesby market-place. Haraldstone knew in its ancestral bones that the subject of witchcraft was not titillating but dark and dangerous. So it went about its business and was careful not draw further attention to itself.

Derek Bryant was not an unprincipled man, but the *Chronicle* was selling more copies than ever before and it was his job to keep the stories going. He had heard some funny rumours about that attractive girl with the hat shop, and as Liz Bagshaw had interviewed Imogen previously he sent her out again, with her notebook and camera. The pretext for the interview would be a feature on 'Craftswomen of the Dale'.

Ms Bagshaw was young and shrewd and would go far. She was also assisted by Imogen's natural modesty.

'But I'm just a newcomer,' Imogen said. 'You really should talk to Sadie Whicker. She runs Crafty Notions just opposite, and she's been here for years.'

Sadie was willing to oblige, and Liz Bagshaw set about her in a friendly, chatty way. She already knew that Imogen was the heroine of *The Old Wives' Tale* and now she discovered that Sadie was the wardrobe mistress, and that other enterprising women who lived nearby were also involved in the production.

'Oh yes, I've heard of Milia Godden,' Liz Bagshaw said, 'though if I may say so – no offence intended and none taken I hope – I don't earn the sort of money that buys her scarves! And you say there are two other ladies in the cast who run their own businesses, who live in Haraldstone?' Storing information. 'Would it be possible to interview them too?'

Obligingly Sadie telephoned them.

'What I'm after, you see,' said Liz, 'is a general profile of talented and independent ladies. The feature is for our Woman's Page, and although most of our readers are tied to the sink and an uninteresting part-time job, they still like to dream. So let's make it really good!'

In this way she rooted out Milia, Deirdre, Jinny and Beth, lined them up on the cobbles with Imogen, Sadie and Erica, and noted that altogether the women numbered seven.

'This is such a quaint little place,' Liz said, with engaging honesty, bringing out her camera, looking round the court. 'Wonderful background. Gorgeous name. I simply must work that name into the title somehow. I know you don't all have shops in here but that won't matter. And I'm sure you'll agree that "The Catwalk" has far more ambience than "The Dale!" '

Sadie saw exactly what she meant.

They were photographed in a group in the courtyard, and given the caption *Catwalk Ladies Make Their Own Kind of Magic!*

Imogen, younger, lovelier and slightly taller than the rest, as well as being photogenic, was the most noticeable.

The feature, given a distinctly feminist slant, made the *Chronicle*'s readers wonder several things. No one could have found fault with Ms Bagshaw's enthusiasm for female ventures, nor the vivacity of her reporting, but the underlying implications disturbed her seven victims, who felt, not without reason, that they had been misled.

Timothy said outright that had he known about the interview he would have advised them against it, that he thought the connections Ms Bagshaw had made between Haraldstone, witchcraft and Peele's Players could not pass unnoticed, and that the whole affair was a great pity.

'As if,' he said reproachfully, 'there were not enough rumours already.'

Mary Proctor ordered Sadie to Howgill House for an interview, and while resting her bad leg and keeping Sadie standing, she castigated her outright.

'I've lived in the dale all my life, and kept my mouth shut. Folk might wag their tongues but they could prove nothing. Then a gasbag from the

Chronicle comes along with a mouthful of flattery and waves a camera at you, and you tell her more in an hour than the rest have got from me in sixty years.'

Nor was this the only censure they incurred.

Mario's delectable restaurant, pride of the Catwalk, whose reputation was known far beyond Haraldstone, had not been mentioned by Ms Bagshaw, nor even used as background in the photograph. The affront to his dignity was immense. From the morning that the article appeared Mario greeted them coldly and avoided conversation. The cost of publicity was proving to be beyond their means.

But the event that disturbed Imogen most was an evening visit from Timothy, unexpected and unannounced.

In a rain of apologies, he cried, 'I shall take up no more than a few moments of your valuable time, my dear, but this is a matter of some importance. I have just spoken with Sadie, who tells me that you are both creator and keeper of the little image used in your healing ceremony. Does it, by chance, bear any personal tokens of Mary? Strands of hair, pieces of genuine clothing, and the like?'

'Oh yes,' said Imogen, with pride. 'I made it properly.'

'Could I possibly see it?'

She brought it to him, wrapped in a cloth to keep it clean.

'A-mazing!' he remarked, as a miniature Mary stared belligerently up at him. 'What a clever young woman you are! Look here, my dear, would you mind terribly if I took care of this?'

Imogen made a little gesture of assent, knowing better than to gainsay him, for his disclosures at the Mount, and the subsequent events, had influenced her profoundly. And yet she had seen and heard much already, and he must know that she had deduced even more, so surely she deserved some sort of explanation?

'A thousand thanks, my dear, as always,' he murmured, preparing to leave.

Imogen said outright, in something of a temper, 'I don't mind your taking the Mary doll if it's necessary, Timothy, but I should like to know why.'

He raised his eyebrows in a pained, polite way which hinted that she should say no more. She refused to oblige him.

'I need to know what's happening,' she said decisively.

'Very well, my dear, you shall,' he said abruptly. His tone conveyed that he would not spare her fears.

'Because Crazy Hats is not a stronghold, and you are not knowledgeable enough to defend it or yourself, this image could be a danger to you, and in the hands of her enemy would be fatal to Mary. It will be safer with me.'

He drew himself up and looked so stern at the prospect of further questions that she hesitated for a moment.

Then, obstinately, sturdily, she heard her voice say, 'But who is Mary's enemy?'

He gave an impatient sigh. She was to be punished for her impertinence.

'I haven't time to go into details with you just now, Imogen, so I will be brief. I thought you would have realized by now that it was Edith – who is also my enemy' – his pause was deliberate – 'and yours.'

The dismay on Imogen's expressive face gratified him.

'My thanks, once again,' said Timothy urbanely. 'Good-night, sweet dreams, and sleep well!'

THIRTY

Outwardly all appeared to be going well with the production, but inwardly nothing was right. There was an undercurrent of strain and disquiet in the company. Mary continued to stay away. Timothy's resourcefulness seemed to have deserted him. And Edith acquired the role of Gammer Madge by default. Still, no one could have disparaged her efforts. She learned her lines quickly and delivered them well, accepted Timothy's direction with unusual forbearance, and solved a problem for Sadie by providing her own costume. But her Madge was dark and wily rather than homely and wise, which subtly altered the mood of the play.

Also, there was a power struggle going on between Philip and Timothy over the direction of the silent chorus. The youngsters did whatever Timothy told them, and had become uncannily clever at interpreting the mood and actions of the players, but sometimes Imogen caught them glancing at Philip as if for different instructions. So far he had remained impassive, yet she felt that at any moment he might countermand an order and they would obey, and then where would their director be? Where, indeed, would any of them be?

And then, as if that were not enough, Timothy had been slightly cool towards her since their little confrontation, and Imogen was torn between resentment and sadness. Her friends were few, and had grown fewer. She could not afford to lose any more. Yet some good came out of this ominous time, providing a degree of freedom and an element of protection.

Imogen's distrust of Philip, combined with her fear of Edith, gave her the courage to fend him off decisively. When George collected her on the Monday evening she was stuffing a bulbous black-necked bottle into a rucksack, along with her manuscript and handbag. She offered no explanation and he asked for none, but being George he observed what happened before the rehearsal began.

As unobtrusively as possible, Imogen went up to Philip and put the bottle into his hands.

'I have a bad conscience about this champagne,' she said, trembling slightly, for Edith was on the watch as usual, 'because I don't intend to meet you again in a private capacity. I'd like us to remain friendly while we're working together, and then for you to forget about me.'

He was puzzled, chagrined, incredulous. Preserving his dignity, he accepted the bottle with a little bow, a little smile. He seemed about to walk away without answering. Then he paused and said quite simply, 'Why?'

Imogen would have liked to explain, to apologize, to smooth the leave-taking, to justify her decision, but she knew that this would give him hope, and her fear of hurting anyone might even lead to a temporary reconciliation. So she stared past his shoulder, straight into the green eyes of the enemy, answered, 'Edith!' turned her back on him, and went.

That same evening, instead of roaring off into the night when he had delivered her home, George asked if he could come in for a cup of coffee. She was so grateful for company that she almost thanked him for asking, then reverted to her usual brand of self-mockery.

'As you know, I haven't quite cracked the art of coffee-making, but I've just invested in a percolator so the Crazy Hats cuisine is looking up.' She added sincerely, 'And you're very welcome.'

He wandered round while she presided anxiously over the new percolator, surveying without comment. Both the range and the narrowness of her daily life were evident in this small room. He admired a hat-in-making under its protective muslin canopy. He studied Fred's photograph and gave him a nod. He made overtures to Polly, who accepted them as her due. And when Imogen brought him a cup of hot light brown liquid he said, 'That looks grand!' though it looked no better than it tasted. Then they circled round the point of his visit.

'Mary's getting better.'

'Oh, I *am* glad.'

'She's feeling able to look after herself, so I'll be moving back to the chapel in the next day or so.'

'Oh, *that's* good.'

'Stevie's still come round with me in the van for part of the day, and sleeping at the chapel, of course. She's not well enough to have him all the time.'

'No, of course not.'

'I was wondering,' said George suddenly, 'whether you'd give me some advice about the scenery and stage props?'

'The scenery and stage props?' She was mystified.

'Yes. I've got ideas of my own, and a few sketches, and I'd like to try them out on you before I take them to Tim. You see, Tim's decided to treat the stage business as a special joke with the audience. For instance, two stage hands dressed as Elizabethan labourers will carry on two stylized plywood trees, set them down, say, "This is the deep dark wood!" shrug their shoulders – and exit. Now that's all very well, but I think he needs more than that . . .'

He was in full flow now, and she listened, smiling at him.

'. . . I see the Well of Life as being silver – Beth Lawler's making the Speaking Heads that rise from it, thank God! – in papier mâché – and the severed head of Sacrapant, so that's a big worry off my shoulders . . .'

He talked on. Imogen reheated the coffee.

'. . . and then I thought that you should have a personal symbol as Delia. Supposing we put you behind a semicircle of white turret, only a couple of feet high, to represent an enchanted tower? If you've got a pencil and some paper handy I'll show you. Thanks. I was wondering if it should be studded with supposedly precious stones . . .'

Imogen said, fetching out a sketching block and soft black pencils, 'Don't tell me. Show me. Let's start again at the beginning.'

At the shop door at midnight, he said, 'The vicar told me I could take Stevie to his Youth Club on Tuesdays and Fridays. I could drop in then for a couple of hours, couldn't I, while I sort it out in my mind?'

'Yes, indeed you could,' she cried.

'And perhaps you can come to the chapel to act as overseer when I start making it all?'

'Yes. Yes, of course I will.'

'Stevie won't be any trouble,' he assured her, 'and you can bring your sewing. I only need a nod and a wink of advice now and again.'

Inwardly she was awash with gratitude. The interview with Philip, and the cost of acting with him afterwards as if nothing was amiss, had exhausted her emotionally. And at the pit of her stomach doubt sat like a small cold toad. She was afraid of something in Philip, and her solitary status made her vulnerable. Her dreams that night would have been dreadful, but for George. And now she knew that he would be living only a few hundred yards away, and that her evenings would be policed, as it were, by his presence, she felt safer.

She noticed, as she locked the door after him, that Sadie closed her bedroom curtains and switched out her light, as if she too had been keeping watch.

At the church hall that Thursday, the prompter was a mere appendage and the players were perfecting their roles, Sadie and Milia had finished the costumes, and Timothy was holding rehearsals in full dress so that everyone would become accustomed to striding about in jerkin, doublet and hose, or managing a long gown. In Imogen's case the skirt was also stiff and wide, and she had to come to terms with a hoop, a corset and a stiffened farthingale.

'Remember that you'll be taking up far more space than usual,' Timothy advised her, 'so make allowances for that, too.'

He took his mug of tea from her tray with formal thanks, sat between Ian and Gerald, and addressed the company in conversational fashion.

'It is marvellous what can be achieved when people work for a common purpose,' he began. 'In an idle moment yesterday I was reckoning up the commercial cost of this production, and including the transformation of the hall it runs into thousands of pounds. Without our donors and volunteers there is simply no way that we could have afforded to pay for it. I happened to mention that fact when I was talking to the Brakespears the other day, and Hal proposes to use it as the basis of a sermon.'

Imogen drew a deep breath, and stirred her coffee. Mary Proctor, being in poor health, was back in Alice's favour. And since George had never been out of favour with Hal and could hardly be ignored, Alice accepted him also, though with reservations. But she had loved Imogen too much, and Hal had cared for her too little, to forgive easily. So the Brakespears were still not on speaking terms, and there seemed no way of reviving the friendship.

'Alice has been an absolute brick,' Timothy continued, 'in contributing her particular talents to our production. She has found a full complement of willing ladies prepared to do refreshments, and sell tickets and programmes. I have invited them all to take tea with me next Sunday, and I know that Mrs Housman will give them a feast to remember. However, I digress. With her usual efficiency Alice has not only organized a rota, she has also made up a reserve list, so that nothing can go wrong.'

Here he touched the wooden seat of his chair superstitiously.

'*Shouldn't* go wrong, at any rate,' said Timothy, correcting himself.

Imogen kept her head down and reflected miserably that the whole of Langesby must have heard about her taking part in the witches' dance, and by this time, thanks to Liz and the *Chronicle*, they could guess who the witches were and possibly recognize her in that first photograph. No one had even hinted at such a thing, but they probably thought about it all the more.

The chorus sat slightly apart from the rest, drinking orangeade and saying nothing, keeping an eye on Philip for instructions. Stephen had edged his chair nearer and nearer to the Prospect House group, and to Philip who was always kind to him.

'Good for Alice!' Philip said amiably, noticing everything, revealing nothing.

'Yes, we must give her a special thank-you, at curtain call on the final night,' Timothy added thoughtfully, 'and persuade her to come on stage with the rest of our splendid helpers, for a well-deserved round of applause . . .'

THIRTY-ONE

The doorbell rang at seven o'clock on a fine June morning, as Imogen was sitting up, stretching and yawning. Half-blind with sleep, she pushed up the sash window and called out, 'I'll be there in a minute!'

Buttoning her cotton housecoat, winding her hair into a topknot and spearing it with tortoiseshell pins, she followed Polly's tail mast down the stairs.

On the ground floor a strained face stared at her through the glass.

'George?' Bemused. 'George! What's wrong?'

'Sorry to wake you up, but I'm in trouble.'

'Come in. Come in.'

'No. I can't stop. Have you seen anything of Stevie?'

She shook her head.

'It was a lost hope anyway,' he said, 'but I have to ask anyone who knows him. He wasn't in his bed when I woke up. I don't know how long he's been gone. All night maybe.'

She thought of the people whom Stephen knew, and why he might visit them.

'We-ll, he's a great walker and it's a lovely day. He could have woken up early and decided to go and see your mother. Or you might try Timothy. Stephen's been pestering him to bring that costume to rehearsal. He might even have felt neighbourly and walked up to Langesby to visit the Brakespears. Or,' – she did not like this idea – 'he could be hanging round Prospect House again.'

George's face lengthened.

'Yes, I'd thought of that. I was afraid of that. But I'll try them all. I'm going to work my way up the dale. I've cancelled my jobs for the morning. Might have to cancel them for the afternoon, too. I shall have to be careful with Mary. She's quick to find out when something's wrong. If she gets in touch with you don't say anything. Don't even say you've seen me.'

He gave Polly a perfunctory rub round the ears as she nosed at his ankles.

'Right,' he said, in a ghost of his usual manner. 'I'd best be off.'

She could think of nothing to say but, 'You'll keep in touch, won't you? Let me know what happens.'

He swallowed, frowned, shifted from one foot to the other, then left her.

Feeling useless and helpless, she called after him, 'Oh George – good luck!'

In the final weeks before the opening of Langesby Fair business was brisk. Whatever Alice might now think of her parchment rose hat, she had sowed the seeds of interest by wearing it to church. And Imogen, reaping the benefit, was selling summer straws as fast as she could trim them. The Misses Richison, with their refurbished headgear, had given her another idea. She had made a bronze velvet cloche and put it in the side window, dominating the usual display, and labelled *For the autumn. Individual colours and styles. Made to order.* Orders were already coming in, and though Crazy Hats would not be making her fortune as yet, she could coast through the winter months on present sales.

That morning she looked after the shop automatically: smiling, talking and advising, but all the time waiting for news. Finally, as she was locking the door at lunchtime, her telephone rang.

His voice sounded distant, muffled.

'Imogen. It's me. George. We've found Stevie.'

His pause was so long that she realized the news was bad, and waited for it without comment. The three words came in a burst.

'He's dead, Imogen.'

Another pause. George was struggling to find words and control.

'What can I do to help?' she asked.

'I – don't know. It's – a police case. They've – taken him away.'

'Is anyone with you?'

'Not now. They have been. Tim's gone off. One of his hunches. The Brakespears came up – trumps. She offered – to tell Mary. But that's – my job.' He added under his breath, 'Hell of a job.' Then stopped, either unable or unwilling to say more.

'I'm free for the next hour,' said Imogen, 'and in any case the shop's pretty quiet on a Monday. If you want something to eat, someone to talk to, moral support of any kind, just say the word.'

He was hesitating.

'I shall understand if you say no, but if you're even *thinking* of saying yes, then here I am, at your service.'

George answered at last, 'I'd be grateful. Glad of you. Can't . . . think straight. Don't know . . . what to say – or do.'

She took charge. To take charge of George, who had always looked after himself and sometimes Imogen as well, was a heady experience.

'Where are you now?' she asked decisively.

'I'm at the Unicorn in Tofthouse. Having a double whisky.'

'Look,' said Imogen, 'I'm about to make a sandwich for myself. I may not be one of the world's great cooks but I create a serious sandwich – even Fred admitted my superiority in that department.'

She paused, to make sure that she was not losing him.

'I can make one for you too, if you like. Why don't you come here first? You don't want to deliver bad news on an empty stomach, do you? And just drinking whisky might fuddle you.'

'I can't eat.'

Silence. She waited. He made a decision. His voice sounded stronger.

'No. I'll go to Howgill now. I don't want the news to reach Mary before I do. I'll come on to your place later. Imogen, if you could just be around?'

'I'll be around.'

She made two plates of sandwiches, covered one with clingfilm and put it in the refrigerator. When she had eaten hers she went down to the shop again, sat and sewed, and waited.

At six o'clock she fed Polly and looked up her party recipe. With frequent references to the text she produced a dish of rice that did not emerge as a glued mass, poached two chicken breasts, and accomplished a lump-free lemon sauce. She dashed round the corner to Hunwick's Supermarket, and bought a respectable bottle of Beaujolais and a tub of Barton's Farmhouse Vanilla, the famous dale ice-cream. She chopped up an apple and a pear, sliced an orange and a banana into a fruit salad, decorated it with six halved green grapes, and laced it with dry Martini. She laid the table with a rich pink cloth and matching napkins.

'Nearly up to your standard!' she told the absent Fred.

He did not reply and she resumed waiting.

George arrived at eight o'clock, famished and exhausted. The supper she had prepared so carefully was eaten automatically, though he thanked her for it more than once, and looked much better afterwards.

Still, Imogen thought, that means I can do it again for him some time when he does notice, and I've had a practice run.

Beleaguered, within and without, she was cheering herself on. Her flippancy had always been a form of reassurance, to herself and others.

She had not questioned George when he arrived. She did not question him now, as he settled into the other armchair and sipped coffee which Fred would have called fairly reasonable. She could wait.

Finally he drew a deep breath and said, 'I think this must be the worst day in my life.'

Only then did she say, 'Tell me about it.'

With a feeling of vindication, for his conscience had tweaked him now and again, Derek Bryant was that moment sketching out the main news feature.

He had been right after all in his suppositions, and the journalist in him could not help thanking God that the *Langesby Chronicle* would reap the benefit of yet another scoop. This story would have the nationals beating on his door. Following the headline, RITUAL SACRIFICE ON HARALD-STONE HILL, the article read:

The body of a man has been found lying in the centre of the notorious Haraldstone Stone Circle, known to be the regular haunt of local witches. It is suspected that he died of an overdose of drugs, but the police have not ruled out the possibility that he was involved in some satanic ritual. No name is being given, at present, but it is believed that the man had been an inmate of the Bethesda Institute, who was released into the community earlier this year.

Readers will remember that Mr Philip Gregory, who runs Prospect House, a Home for Young Offenders, wrote to this paper only a few weeks ago to report a distressing incident that had taken place on his premises, and stressing the dangers attendant upon allowing such unfortunate people their liberty.

The dead man had apparently escaped the custody of his carer, and was reported missing yesterday morning. A search was instituted which at first proved fruitless, but thanks to the inspiration of the desk sergeant, a new light was shed on the matter.

'Recent news of satanic practices made me wonder whether the man had perhaps been enticed away by evildoers and come to harm,' said Sergeant Applecroft. 'I suggested that we visit Haraldstone Hill, and there we found that my suspicions were justified.'

'I am regarding this tragedy very seriously indeed,' Chief Constable Garside told the *Chronicle*. 'We are making extensive inquiries, and the public can rest assured that no stone will be left unturned until the case is solved.'

'How is Mary?' Imogen asked, and the name slipped out naturally though she had previously referred to her as Mrs Proctor.

George said, 'First of all she tore a strip off me, and nothing I said was right. Well, that's only natural, isn't it? Then she sort of shrank into herself, sad to her bones. Wouldn't talk, wouldn't eat, wouldn't drink. Just rocked to and fro in her chair, staring into the fire, with a cat in her lap. I did my best but I was making no headway. Tim had told me to keep in touch. When I couldn't bear the silence any longer I drove to the telephone box at Tofthouse and rang him. And, by God, he's got her dander up. She seems to be saving the sadness for later. Now she's cold and hard and angry as I've never seen her before, and Tim's egging her on for all he's worth.'

'Is he at Howgill now?' Imogen asked, startled.

'Oh yes. I left them hobnobbing together. He turned up at seven o'clock and took over, in that gentlemanly, bullying way he has. Wouldn't take any of her "nos" for an answer. "Leave this to me, George," he said, "and I'll ring you later." I knew that I was neither needed nor wanted so I left him in charge and came here. His housekeeper had sent a picnic basket of food over with him. A complete meal for two, from soup in a thermos flask to a very swish apple tart and a bottle of sweet white wine.'

Intrigued, puzzled, Imogen said, 'But she's supposed to be on a diet.'

George said philosophically, 'Then it's gone to pot tonight.'

He sat up and looked directly at Imogen, as if seeing her for the first time.

'That was a grand supper. I thought you said you couldn't cook.'

'It's my party menu,' said Imogen honestly. 'My solitary culinary achievement so far – apart from grilling and frying. I quite enjoyed doing it, too, though it took a long time. I must learn how to cook a different one later on.'

He laughed for the first time that day, and she smiled at him.

'You're a funny lass!'

'Have some more coffee,' she said. And as she was pouring it, 'I told Fred the meal was almost up to his standard.'

'And what did he say to that?' George asked, quite naturally.

'He didn't say anything. He hasn't spoken to me since November. His last words were, "Yes, come for a walk!" That was just before we set out for Haraldstone and I decided that this was the place for me. From then on – silence. I can't make up my mind whether he was for the idea or against it.'

'I expect he brought you to the right place, and then left you to get on with your life by yourself.'

'You do?' She considered this. 'I'd like to think so.'

'Take my word for it,' said George. 'If he didn't approve he'd say so fast enough.'

Fred's sourest comments flitted through her memory: milestones in her journey from him. Her smile became secret, satisfied.

'You're right,' said Imogen. 'He would.'

They were sitting in peaceable silence, finishing their coffee, when her telephone rang. 'That'll probably be Tim for me,' said George, and he was right.

The conversation was brief, and on his side monosyllabic. At the other end of the line, Timothy was orchestrating this latest development.

George put down the receiver and was silent for a few moments.

Then he said, 'Tim seems to have done the trick, and he's going home, but the day's not over yet. Mary would like to see you, and she wants to see you now.'

He was apologetic. He would never have asked such a favour for himself, but his mother had the right to command an audience at ten o'clock at night.

'I'm sorry if it seems a bit much,' said George, 'and I don't know what it's about, but I can ferry you there and back on the bike. I shouldn't think it'll take long. She must be exhausted by this time.'

For his sake as much as Mary's, Imogen said, as if it were the most natural thing in the world, 'Of course I'll go.'

The evening was mild, the early summer scents sharp and sweet. Light lingered behind the trees and softened the outline of the hills. The road was almost empty, and Imogen, borne along without effort on her part, felt suspended in space and time.

Nothing was as usual. Mary did not call on them to lift the latch and come in. She was waiting in the doorway, leaning on a stick, as George halted the motorbike. Without speaking, she hobbled slowly ahead of them into the kitchen, and motioned them to sit down. She did not offer to make tea. Her black kettle squatted on a cold hob. And she held up one hand as she saw that Imogen was about to offer sympathy.

'There's no need for words,' Mary said, and sat for several moments in silence, staring into the dull grate, gathering strength.

The kitchen had lost its warmth and light and subtle fragrances, its charm and its air of repose. It seemed as old and poor and bruised in spirit as its mistress.

Mary cleared her throat and spoke gruffly but not ungraciously to Imogen.

'I'll not keep you long, my lass, but I need some help from you to put my mind at rest. Fetch a chair over and sit with me.'

'I'll do that,' said George quickly. 'They're heavy.'

Mary's eyebrows lifted at this chivalrous gesture, but she made no comment apart from, 'Put the chair in front of me. Facing me.' And then, 'You can leave us, if you like, George. The television's in the parlour.'

But he had enrolled himself as Imogen's protector, though against what he could not have said.

'The television's never been much in my line,' he replied drily. 'I'll stay, if you don't mind.'

'Nay, I don't mind.' Her tone was weary, almost pettish. 'There's nothing to make a fuss about. But keep still and keep quiet. We shall have to concentrate.' To Imogen she said, 'Give us your hands, my lass.'

Sitting opposite Mary, Imogen stretched out her hands. They were clasped lightly, just enough to make contact between the two women.

'This may take a while,' Mary said, 'but I want you to shut your eyes and empty your mind, and then tell me what you see.'

'What are you after?' George demanded.

His mother flashed round on him.

'No harm, I tell you. She'll come to no harm with me. I know what I'm about. If you can't stop mithering – take yourself off!'

'I'll stay here,' said George, and sat like a monument, watching the one woman, watching over the other.

Mary's face and tone softened as she spoke to Imogen.

'It's all right, my lass. Don't you fret. Sit you quiet for a bit.'

The turbulence of the day, her own apprehension and George's concern had set up a swarm of bees in Imogen's mind. Under the influence of Mary's dry clasp and gentle tone the noise quietened and gradually ceased.

She was in a half-light, as if dawn were about to break or night to fall, and her inner eyes took time to adjust. The place was silent, but still holding the urgency of people who had fled. In the clearing ahead of her a pagan god lay on his back asleep, arms and legs outstretched, head crowned with ivy leaves, face turned away from her.

The desire of Mary to know everything made Imogen come nearer and look more closely at Stephen in his last guise. The shambling gait, the slack lips, the uncertain gaze, had gone. Unhampered by clothes his body emerged as long-limbed and graceful, spare-fleshed. Beneath half-closed lids his eyes glimmered in ecstasy. On his mouth lay the memory of a smile.

She heard Mary's voice, strained with effort to control, crying, 'Did he suffer?'

'No, no,' said Imogen, soothing her, smiling with him.

In herself she knelt beside him and stroked the fair damp hair away from his forehead, but did not touch the wreath of spade-shaped leaves.

'You're having a wonderful time, aren't you?' she asked him, marvelling. Mary's voice tugged at her.

'But before that. Did they torment him? Go back. Go back.'

Imogen was among strangers and totally disorientated. She had been blindfolded. Laughter jeered behind and around her. Hard little hands pushed her. Presences encircled her. Adult voices were directing a game in which she was both object and victim. She began to panic.

'Not you. Him,' cried Mary. 'Him. Him.'

Imogen slipped from herself to Stephen, and the laughter changed, the voices mocked tenderly, enticing him, bent on his delight. There were girls around him, young girls, slender girls, girls as mother-naked as he was, and ready for games he had played only in furtive feverish imagination. Their hands and lips were rich with pleasure. He ran free in pastures that had been forbidden him. They crowned him with ivy and told him he was king, placed a sacramental wafer on his tongue, held a wine chalice to his lips. He drank long and deeply.

They were running away, but only Imogen saw them. In his dream the god sank smiling beneath the earth and would soon become part of it.

'No,' said Imogen. 'He didn't suffer.'

How could she tell his mother that for one night he had been Bacchus?

'He was a child,' said Imogen. 'He thought it was all a game.'

Mary released her and sat back, eyes closed. They sat on with her, tired and silent, and she began to rock meditatively to and fro, to and fro. Gradually her face softened, her fingers relaxed on the chair arms. She opened her eyes and smiled at them.

'I'm going to take Imogen home now,' said George, 'but I'll come back and stop the night.'

'Nay, you needn't. Nobody'll trouble me now. They've done their worst.'

'Then is there anything I can do for you before I go? Should I make a bit of fire for you?'

Mary looked at the lifeless coals accusingly as if they had gone out on purpose.

'Yes, my lad – if you would. I can't think what I was about. Letting it go out like that.'

Neatly, quickly, George re-laid the fire and lit it. He stood up, dusting his hands. 'Are you sure you'll be all right?' he asked.

She nodded.

'I'll drop by tomorrow morning on my way to work.'

She reached up and clasped his arm.

'You're a good lad,' she said. And turning to Imogen. 'And you're a good lass. I thank you both.'

The flames licked and crackled. The kitchen was coming to life. Bottles gleamed, a bowl of fruit glowed like jewels, and a host of delicate scents arose from the hanging herbs.

THIRTY-TWO

Whitechapel

'Recasting a bell is a very special occasion,' said George, looking out of Imogen's living-room window, hands in pockets, talking half to her and half to himself. 'I've seen others done, but they were smaller bells. This is my bell. This is Great Isaac.'

'I remember him,' Imogen replied with suitable gravity.

She had closed the shop ten minutes ago, and was thinking seriously of supper, when George had wandered in with something on his mind.

'There are only two founders nowadays who cast bells,' said George. 'Isaac is being cast at Whitechapel.'

She was wondering how long she could live on Welsh rarebit without imperilling her health; although, she told herself, she was so busy with Crazy Hats and the play that she simply didn't have time to think about shopping for food and cooking it, as well as doing everything else.

'It'll take all day,' George went on. 'Up on the morning train to London, and back on the early evening train to Langesby. So I'll lose a day's work, but it's worth every penny of that, and more.'

Not sure what he wanted of her, Imogen answered positively, 'Of course it is.'

And there again, talk of Welsh rarebit, she bet she had run out of cheese.

'The vicar talked of coming with me at one time,' George continued, 'but I didn't think he'd make it, and sure enough something turned up as it always does with him. So he won't be there.'

'What a pity!' Imogen cried automatically.

Because if she had no cheese it was eggs again, providing she had enough eggs. Oh, this was ridiculous.

He turned round and considered her. He spoke as if the idea had that moment occurred to him, but deception did not come easily to George and his spontaneity sounded forced.

'I was just thinking. The casting takes place next Tuesday. That's half-day closing in Haraldstone.'

'So it is,' Imogen said obediently. In despair, she added, 'George, would you like a gin and tonic? Because it's been quite a day, and I'm gasping for one.'

She had thrown him out of stride.

'Oh. Ah. I suppose you haven't got a beer?'

'No. I'm afraid not. I don't drink beer.'

'Then you go ahead. Don't bother about me. I'm all right.'

He followed her to the kitchenette, and hovered as she mixed a double gin and tonic and opened the refrigerator.

And when she got there the cupboard was bare, Imogen thought. Well, at least she had plenty of ice cubes. She dropped a couple into her glass.

George was right behind her, saying, 'I just wondered if *you* might be interested to see the bell cast and have a day out in London.'

As she turned round and stared at him, bemused by both his invitation and her lack of food, he added, 'It would be my treat – I mean, you'd be my guest and we'd do it in style. Breakfast on the train up. Dinner on the train back. Make it a holiday.' He risked sounding personal. 'I'm not asking you because Hal Brakespear can't come. Normally, I'd go by myself and enjoy it. But I'd like you to be with me when they recast Isaac.'

He had concentrated her mind at last. She remembered the numinous shapes in the twilight of the bell tower. Saw George lay an affectionate hand on the silent giant. Heard him say, 'This is *my* bell.'

The invitation was an honour, the admission of wanting her company a greater honour still.

He added quickly, 'But it's a lot to ask, and I shall understand if you say no.'

She said slowly, 'I'd – oh, I'd love to, George. I'm just thinking about leaving the shop – even for a morning . . .'

'I'd thought of that. Sadie would help you out again, wouldn't she?' Hopefully.

Imogen could picture Sadie's knowing wink, hear the coyness of her acceptance, feel her roguish nudge in the ribs. She winced, and put the image away.

'Yes, I'm sure she would. She grumbled a bit last time, but I think she rather enjoyed it. I'll ask her.'

She basked in his smile, and smiled back.

'Anyway, to hell with the shop,' said Imogen recklessly. 'I can shut it up for the morning and leave a notice, for once. How about, "Closed for today, owing to a special occasion".' She improved on that statement. 'No. "Closed for today, owing to the event of a lifetime"!'

She laughed and he laughed with her, relieved and gratified.

'What are you doing for supper tonight?' he asked, having noticed the emptiness of her refrigerator.

'I'm thinking about it,' she replied guardedly.

'I didn't see much to think about, apart from ice cubes,' said George, grinning, 'so when you've finished your drink why don't we hop on the motorbike and I'll treat us to a Chinese in Langesby?'

Imogen found it strange to return to London now that it was no longer her home, and stranger still to walk on familiar streets in the company of George instead of Fred. There was an air of unreality about the entire expedition which, if she were to be honest, made it even more intoxicating. Anything might happen, nothing mattered. She had felt the same on going abroad for the first time, and speaking a different language in a foreign country. I can say or do as I please, she had thought, and it doesn't matter, because this isn't real, it's a special piece cut out of my life, not subject to time or space. Here I'm set free to be myself.

'It's like a meditation,' she added, to George.

'Ah!' he replied, mystified, but accepted her statement without question. She slipped her arm through his.

'Has anyone ever told you how restful you are?' she asked.

But George was not the man to go into an analysis of his character, or anyone else's for that matter.

So he said, 'No, they haven't. And we want to be there on time. So let's grab a quick cup of coffee, and catch a tube to Whitechapel.'

It was an eighteenth-century building of blackened brick, with an inscription arched over the stone porch: CHURCH BELL FOUNDRY. Going through the door they left the uproar of traffic behind them, and entered the clamour of the workplace.

The craft was ancient, involving skills acquired by years of knowledge and dedication. Casting took place only once a week, and heating the gas furnace took all morning. The process was methodical, leisurely. Around the grey furnace, ministering to it with asbestos-gloved hands, moved men clad in blue boiler suits and leather aprons, their feet and calves protected by thick boots, their faces shielded by visors. From time to time one man opened the door and hooked out slag with a long rod, while another removed the lambent load in a wheelbarrow. There was no ventilation and the air was full of smoke and steam, the smell of sulphur, and a continual hissing and roaring; as if the bells of heaven were being forged in the depths of hell.

By lunchtime a small crowd of some twenty disciples had gathered, to share an occasion which approached the mystical. The onlookers stood in a straggling line at a safe distance, watching the thermometer on the furnace door. Two of them had cameras. They coughed and talked. Against the walls were stacked bell moulds of every weight and size. A smaller bell was being cast that day on the foundry floor, but the thirty-seven hundred-weight mould of Great Isaac, standing shoulder-high to a man, had been lowered into a chamber below the floor at the side of the furnace, to receive its benison of bronze. Then the ladle, resembling a giant bucket, was wheeled forward and placed in a chamber beside it.

'The mould is made in two halves from special clay,' George informed her. 'They bind it with straw and horse manure – you saw that outside? – and make a top and a bottom.'

George had been here before and was at his ease, alight with pleasure. The manager recognized him, nodded and smiled at him. He spoke to the foreman, shook hands with one person, had a few words with another, but did not forget or neglect Imogen, who stood by his side, and the watchers included her in their interest. The atmosphere around them was friendly, curious, respectful. Imogen and George were persons of consequence because Great Isaac was their bell, and his casting would be the highlight of that day.

A bell rang, and chattering ceased. The gas furnace was ready. Its servants opened the gate. The crowd maintained a reverent silence which, quixotic-ally, reminded Imogen of the pause before the bull is let out into the ring. Then a white-hot mixture of molten copper and tin poured forth down the conduit into the bell mould. The walls of the foundry and the visors of the workmen were lit by incandescent red and orange light. Gold sparks spat out in all directions. The smoke plumed up: luminous pink and purple and thick, soft white. Resurrection had begun.

Thinking of the bell's long life, past and future, Imogen said, awed. 'This is history in the making, isn't it?'

And George nodded.

Everyone was talking again. Two workmen were hooking out the slag that floated to the top. For eleven minutes Great Isaac had his fill. Then as he simmered, replete, they directed the stream into the ladle.

'Now they'll cast the smaller bell,' George told her.

They watched the crane carrying its cargo of liquid metal across the foundary floor, steadily and surely. The vast bucket of molten metal hovered over the shape of the bell below, tipped slowly to the correct angle, poured, paused, and poured again until it was full. Then, in the same unhurried dignified fashion, it travelled back and topped up Isaac, who produced a final plume of smoke and a brief firework display.

'That's it.'

'Stop the pour.'

The incandescent light faded. The noise of the furnace died down. Slag was being tipped into barrows and wheeled away.

George drew a deep breath and said, 'I think that's it now.'

The crowd, satisfied, began to break up, to wander round and inspect the premises, to thank those involved and ask questions.

'Yes, that's it,' said George. 'Now he has to cool, and not too quickly.'

'How long does that take?' Imogen asked.

'About twenty-four hours. Then he'll have to be tuned.'

'How long before he's ready?'

'Two or three weeks.'

Imogen said, reluctant to let go of the experience, 'So it's over?'

'It's over for now,' said George, smiling, 'but not over.'

Imogen nodded.

'We can look round their museum,' said George, 'and then find a good pub. I expect you're hungry.'

She nodded again.

'I'll tell you what,' said George. 'Come with me and I'll show you something.'

He ushered her out, and as Imogen emerged into the London day a carillon of twelve bells began ringing the changes. They were mounted in rows by the side of the green door and their sound was bright, clear, joyful. All shall be well, they told her, and all manner of things shall be well.

'Oh, how beautiful!' she cried.

'They work mechanically,' said George, and began to explain.

He liked explaining things, but though she smiled and nodded she was not listening to him but to the bells.

She was still smiling, still hearing them, long after they walked away.

EXORCISM

THIRTY-THREE

In the first week of July the main street of Langesby was being decorated with coloured lights and bunting. Its shops were becoming groves of artificial flowers and evergreen, behind which lay seductive bazaars. Its market-place would be a medieval fairground. Already, the dark, imposing façade of the town hall was almost obliterated by flags, swags, window-boxes and vast potted plants. Just outside it, an opulent noticeboard would soon advertise the opening night of *Love on the Dole* by the Langesby Dramatic Society ('prizewinner in the County Drama Festival of 1994'). Yet this, though much, was not all.

Over the past few months the conventional efforts of the official committee had been overwhelmed by a burst of civic pride and the joys of carnival. At first it was deemed necessary only to decorate Market Street, where the official opening would take place, but then other citizens had put in their claims, foremost of these being the vicar of St Oswald's.

Church Street, Hal said with truth, boasted some of the finest and oldest buildings in Langesby, and as people would be visiting St Oswald's and attending the play in the church hall, surely this part of the town was also worthy of illumination?

His appeal to the *Chronicle* was immediately backed by petitions from the stationmaster at Langesby Junction, the headmaster of Langesby Primary School, the chief librarian, the Medical Officer of Health and other dignitaries: each of whom had an historic grey building and a meritorious service to proclaim. In consequence of their numbers the committee was able, thankfully, to dismiss them all with the one excuse. There was not enough public money to present every institution, however worthy, in gala dress.

'Very well then,' Hal said, addressing himself yet again to the editorial column of the *Chronicle*. 'We at St Oswald's will pay for it ourselves.'

Fired by this spirit, other public bodies followed his example and other citizens decided that their part of the town was worthy of notice. This feeling was made manifest from top to bottom of the community. Some of the poorest streets resolved to give parties on opening day, and it was noted that the more impoverished the venue the more extravagant the preparations promised to be. A myriad ideas and proposals poured forth. A horde of small separate funds was set up to provide personal entertainment and adornment in honour of the festival.

Swept along in the general enthusiasm, the committee, in a weak moment, agreed to a Children's Walk, and then could not refuse a Sunday School Walk, or indeed any walk that suggested itself, so finally they were all amalgamated into one: the Festival Walk, with adults, children and two brass bands. Whereupon dressmakers were deluged with orders for white dresses; Marks & Spencers ran out of boys' white shirts and shorts; shoe shops scoured the country in search of white slippers and sandals; florists, already overwhelmed by public and private orders for the day, agreed to work overtime to produce nosegays, garlands, buttonholes and wreaths of blossom; and the police department groaned at the prospect of further crowd control.

Floats had been organized and created, and were taking up space and making themselves inconvenient in work yards at different parts of the town. The Ram's Head, the Railway Arms, and other official lodgings prepared to overflow; and anyone who possessed spare beds and was prepared to cook breakfasts now advertised for guests. The taxi rank was crammed with cabs, whose drivers hoped that the exertions of this one week would transform magically into a family holiday at Butlin's. Restaurants and cafés vied with each other to present delicious-sounding menus, and many of them rechristened local dishes, to entice the visitors. Old Langesby Sugar Cakes might well have the same ingredients as iced buns but the name made all the difference.

The demand of the town for supplies threatened to drain the county's resources, but Langesby did not care. They were about to show everyone how to celebrate a great occasion in grand style. And by this time their individual projects had cost so much thought and energy that if scandal and tragedy helped to sell the event who were they to cavil at it?

Excitement, and the prospect of increased revenue, had spread down the dale, and Haraldstone among others, though somewhat bruised in spirit, rolled up its sleeves in preparation and made the most of its natural assets.

In the Catwalk, as in Langesby Market Street, Sadie had instituted a competition for the best window. Privately, she and the other women had decided to award the prize to Mario, whose temper would be sweetened by the honour. They did not like to be estranged from him, and an accumulation of unfortunate incidents made it obligatory to do something for him.

Otherwise, Imogen reflected, she really should have won the accolade herself. Her bouquet of hats, each one a personal triumph, sprang on silvery wires from the centre of a green lawn, and she had decorated the billiard cloth ground with hand-made *fantaisies*. So pretty and so imaginative was the décor that she worked herself up into an internal argument about this competition, which was no competition at all, merely a combined female effort to placate male pride.

As if in agreement, two or three early visitors, wandering round the Catwalk that Monday afternoon, now stopped in front of Crazy Hats and were joined by others. Quite a little crowd of them were staring at the display, commenting favourably, and smiling. One hat in particular seemed to excite admiration: all eyes were focused on the same place and some fingers pointed to it. Yet no one came in to try it on.

As the watchers dispersed, Imogen's anticipation faded but her curiosity increased. She came forward to see which creation had captured their fancy, and found that Polly had upstaged her by going to sleep in the window: head resting on a white velvety lily, one paw blissfully needling a crimson satin rose.

THIRTY-FOUR

Monday

The little cloud over their relationship had been dispelled, but Imogen knew that she was completely forgiven when Timothy put one plump white hand on her arm and the other on George's arm, and beamed on them both.

'I know, my dear, that this young man likes to escort you home, but would he allow an elderly admirer to take his place this evening?'

Imogen and George looked at each other simultaneously, with equal suspicion. Timothy being gracious was Timothy at his most insistent.

George said flatly, 'If it's all right with Imogen it's all right with me.'

'Good. Good. Because I have a favour to ask of this dear girl.'

I might have known it, she thought.

So they journeyed home together, and Timothy played the charmer.

'I took the liberty of bringing a bottle with me.'

'You mean, you don't want to drink my coffee?' Imogen asked resignedly.

'What nonsense! You make perfectly good coffee. But, as I said, I have a favour to ask of you and I thought it might seem more acceptable under the influence of alcohol – although I do assure you that my intentions are entirely honourable.'

He glanced at her archly as he said this, and chuckled. But after that he was unusually silent as they drove to Haraldstone, and his expression became sombre.

'Most striking! Quite enchanting!' he cried of her window display, and was especially amiable with Polly, who allowed him to stroke her.

'And how is the love-lorn Philip progressing in his courtship?' he asked, as they mounted the stairs.

'Not at all. I told him two or three weeks ago that we shouldn't be meeting again on personal terms, and he hasn't spoken to me since – except on stage.' She glanced at him sharply. 'Surely you've noticed that?'

For what did he miss?

Timothy murmured, 'I had wondered – yes.'

'And I returned a bottle of champagne he had left behind.'

'A noble gesture – unless you dislike champagne?'

'You must be joking!' she cried, in a tone of disbelief. 'I love champagne.'

'Then observe the results of casting your bread upon the waters.'

He unwrapped the parcel he was carrying, and revealed a dark bulbous-bodied, long-necked bottle clad in a silver freezing wrapper.

'Would you be so kind as to find us two wineglasses?'

Wordless with astonishment, Imogen brought out two champagne glasses from the sideboard, and in her turn surprised Timothy.

'Bless me, how very elegant!'

'They were a wedding present from the staff in the downtown diner where Fred worked,' said Imogen, pleased. 'Just the two of them in a gift box. We only had champagne once a year, on our wedding anniversary, so they've survived intact.'

'You are an amazing young woman. I have always said so. Allow me.'

I know I'm going to be conned, so I may as well enjoy myself, Imogen thought.

Polly settled on the arm of Timothy's chair. They sipped at first in an appreciative silence. Then he topped up their glasses and cleared his throat.

'Now, my dear, do you believe that I have your safety and well-being at heart?'

'Yes,' said Imogen doubtfully.

'Your tone suggests that you have reservations.'

'I know,' said Imogen, choosing her words carefully, 'that you mean well by me, but I also know that you have more important issues at stake. And this isn't a normal situation, is it? Fine feelings go overboard when you're adrift in a lifeboat.'

He looked at her long and hard, and with respect.

She added in earnest, 'I should never have come to Haraldstone. I'm out of my depth. But I'm committed now. So ask your favour, and I'll do it if I can.'

He was avuncular, benevolent, twinkling so brightly that Polly nudged his hand with her head to remind him that her chin was available for chosen friends.

'Oh come, come. It's not as frightful as all that. How dramatic you are! I was only going to ask you to show a little kindness to Philip.'

She was apprehensive and he hurried to add, 'Not to compromise yourself in any way, simply to turn his thoughts in your direction.'

He saw that this would not do either, and spoke frankly. 'Imogen. I need Edith's attention temporarily diverted.'

She was just as frank.

'You mean you want to use me as a cat's paw?'

'That is putting it rather baldly, but I understand your reaction.'

He was silent for a while, judging where to start.

'You have, no doubt, observed a great change in the company since Edith and the chorus arrived?'

She was deeply afraid, and fear made her vehement.

'Yes. She and they are bad, bad news. Why did you let them take over?'

His tone was stern.

'They have not taken over. They have been *allowed* in.'

Imogen subsided.

'The youngsters have no powers of their own. They are merely being used. But there is a real power struggle going on at the moment between Edith and Mary Proctor. Fortunately, for her sake and ours, Mary is a wise old woman and extremely tough, but she is not invincible, and Edith has dealt her a terrible wound through her afflicted son.'

Imogen said in a small voice, 'Edith killed Stephen?' and held out her glass at the same moment that Timothy proffered the bottle.

'Oh, I don't think she intended to *kill* him. It isn't convenient to be connected to dead bodies – and Edith has a few lying around. I think that she meant him to be found on Haraldstone Hill, under the influence of drugs, apparently after a witches' meeting. Then he would certainly be locked up. Unfortunately, they either dosed him too high or he reacted badly.'

'They?'

'Oh, Philip was certainly involved – as on the previous occasion.'

'You're saying that his wife didn't commit suicide?'

'No, I am saying that he was morally responsible for her death. I believe Kay Gregory was persuaded, tricked or coerced, by whatever despicable means Edith chose, to take her own life – and Philip pretended not to know what was going on.'

Imogen's throat constricted.

'Drink your champagne,' said Timothy. 'It will soften the loathsome outlines of this tale. So, morally speaking, the pair of them murdered Kay Gregory, but murder kills far more than its victim. Edith's motive was clear. She wanted to marry and possess Philip, to make a king and rule from behind the throne. But Philip had no motive. He was simply a victim of his lust. And I would guess that his infatuation with Edith died with

Kay, because he refused to become her private property. But people like Edith do not let go. She had lost the power of the flesh, but she captured the darker side of his imagination. And now we come to the heart of the matter.

'In following Philip here Edith found herself in an old stronghold of witches which had dwindled to a few harmless women, who practised healing and worshipped the old religion – and a group of congenial old buffers who met once a month in Langesby to discuss esoteric subjects. Small fry, in her opinion, content with little. Hence her contempt for the Haraldstone witches and her scornful dismissal of our Magical Arts Society.

'Edith is highly gifted, and from the moment she realized her own powers she began to exploit them. What age would she be, do you suppose? Fiftyish? Then let us say that for the past thirty years she has pursued her studies of witchcraft assiduously. I discovered that she had joined various covens, at one time or another, but always moved on. I would guess that her frequent changes of group were caused by her abrasive personality and fixed ideas. Edith has to rule wherever she goes, and there is not nearly as much black magic practised as people suppose. So I expect when they saw what she was, and where she was heading, they quietly got rid of her. And I think she came to the conclusion that the only coven worth joining was her own.

'I would guess that her aim is to form a group of which she would be the head, and to revive black witchcraft in the dale. I would also guess that she is further corrupting that sinister crew of young delinquents at Prospect House. Whether Philip is privy to her inmost counsels I do not know, but he is certainly assisting her, and apart from unfortunate accidents such as the death of Stephen Proctor, and the occasional scream from his conscience, I would say that on the whole he is enjoying himself.'

Imogen stared into her empty glass.

'If it were only Philip,' said Timothy musing, 'I should have concluded this business long since. I have sufficient evidence to send him to prison and break up that little den of iniquity he has founded, but I have not yet nailed – to slip into the vernacular – his partner in crime. And she is far more important.

'What I fear most about Edith is her arrogance – and her ignorance of the forces she could set in motion. You see, my dear, when you deal with evil you must keep a tight hand on it, partly because it can turn against you, mostly because it attracts further evil. Edith has considerable talent, but she is not omnipotent.' Here he gave a little sniff. 'She is not even in the first rank of practitioners. So she could prepare the ground for herself, only to be supplanted by someone or something far more powerful. Then heaven – or hell – knows what would happen.'

They sat together in silence for a while. He roused himself, divided the rest of the champagne scrupulously between them, and spoke briskly.

'So we really must put a stop to it. I have a few surprises up my sleeve for that unhallowed couple. I plan the first one for the final rehearsal on Friday. And that is why I need – why I beg – your help.'

What were you about, letting me in for this? Imogen asked the absent Fred. *Why couldn't you have spoken up earlier?*

Seemingly as conversant with her inner life as with her outer mode, Timothy said. 'How can you know why you are here, or what is in store for you? You can't see the reasons yet, my dear. You must walk on to the end of the road.'

Lifting her head, Imogen said simply, 'Yes, I understand that, but I'm not a brave or adventurous person, and I'm very much afraid of letting you down.'

His countenance was rubicund. His smile was confident.

'Nonsense,' said Timothy. 'You don't know yourself. A crisis such as this will bring forth a strength you never knew you possessed.'

As she remained uncomforted, he added, 'You will astonish yourself, Imogen.'

She gave a despairing little laugh and said, 'I can't refuse. But I don't like it.'

'You may rest assured,' said Timothy, 'that I wouldn't send you into a lion's den without keeping an eye on both you and the lion. And what I am asking you to do is quite simple. Could you, I wonder, after rehearsal on Thursday, invite Philip round here for a drink on the following evening?'

The thought chilled her.

She protested, 'But how can I do that when I've told him I don't want to see him any more?'

'By exerting your considerable charm, and hinting at a change of mind. It is supposedly a woman's prerogative after all, and beneath those satanic trappings Philip is a conventional man.'

She was unconvinced.

'Yes, but how do I deal with him when I've got him here?'

'Oh, you won't have to deal with him at all,' Timothy said surprisingly. 'The invitation will not be taken up. I simply need to have Philip full of anticipation, and Edith seething and preoccupied with him, for twenty-four hours. You are the best and most obvious person to do that.'

He made a steeple of his fingers, and contemplated it.

He said complacently, 'I believe I have thought of everything.'

In the silence that followed his departure Imogen asked aloud, 'Oh, Fred, where are you?'

But Fred did not reply.

THIRTY-FIVE

Tuesday

'Imogen? It's George! Sorry to disturb you so early but I have to be off in a couple of minutes. I need to get my jobs finished by lunchtime. I meant to remind you at the weekend – but things have been a bit hectic recently, and then last night the maestro whisked you off in his limousine, so we didn't get a chance to talk. You have remembered about this afternoon, haven't you?'

Imogen, half-awake, put a hand to her distracted head. She had slept fitfully, dreamed dreadfully, and was rehearsing a 'get lost' speech to Timothy which she knew she would never deliver. She evaded the question as gracefully as she could.

'George, I can't even remember my own name these days, until someone mentions it, and I'm never at my best first thing in the morning . . .'

'They're delivering Isaac around three o'clock this afternoon . . .'

Oh Lord, to have forgotten that!

'. . . and the vicar's giving a special lesson and blessing the bell. It's only short ceremony, but you said you'd like to see it if you could – and – Imogen, talk about casting being the event of a lifetime, this is another. My last job is in Tofthouse, so I can pick you up at one o'clock and take you out for a pub lunch.'

She was wide awake.

'Oh, how wonderful! You can count on me. But it's my turn for hospitality. George, you'll never believe it, but I've learned how to make really good coffee. The secret is to put in twice as much coffee as I usually do, and add a pinch of salt. I read it up in Fred's cookery book and tried it out on myself. It was a revelation. And I'll make delicious sandwiches – even Fred admired my sandwiches – and we can have a quick lunch here.'

'Would these be your famous ice-cube sandwiches?' George asked.

She heard the smile in his voice and smiled back.

'No, they would not. Home-baked ham from the delicatessen,

local-grown salad stuff from the greengrocer, and French bread from the baker's. I might even treat us to a cake from the *pâtisserie* if you're polite. Any objections?'

'Only abject apologies, from a kneeling posture,' said George. 'Be seeing you!'

Imogen dressed quickly, breakfasted briefly, completed her chores at high speed, was not surprised by the emptiness of her larder, and wrote out a long shopping list. By nine o'clock, basket on arm, she was in Crafty Notions, where Sadie rocked to and fro in her chair, nursing Tarquin.

'Sadie – will you be an absolute angel and watch over the shop until ten while I do some serious shopping?'

Sadie rolled her eyes and spoke mockingly to the sprawling black cat.

'One of the gentleman friends is coming to lunch, Tarquin!'

'You must be a witch to know that!' Imogen replied, mocking in her turn.

'No. Just logical. You wouldn't bother to do serious shopping for yourself, and if he was coming to supper you could shop this afternoon . . .'

'Not only a witch but a detective!'

'I don't miss much. I saw Daddy bringing you home last night, with a bottle under one arm. And everyone's talking about you and Philip on stage – and speculating what happens off-stage. So who's the flavour of the month?'

'Don't be ridiculous, Sadie. It's only George.'

'Oh, it's only George, Tarquin,' Sadie told the purring monster. 'He's no trouble at all, is George. Just needs a day out in London now and again.'

'Sadie, you didn't really mind, did you?'

'I know I'll be glad when you're married and settled down.' She addressed the cat again, in pretended horror, 'But what am I saying, Tarquin? You and I will be running both establishments while Madame has a winter honeymoon.'

'Sadie, you're not truly cross with me, are you?'

'Oh, be off with you and do your blessed shopping!' Sadie said, grinning.

Imogen paused at the door.

'Why a winter honeymoon?' she asked, interested.

'Even you wouldn't ask me to run both shops until the season's over!'

Imogen's smile became as secret and complacent as that of the cat. 'Has anyone ever told you that you're artful?' she asked.

*   *   *

Citizens of Langesby had been alerted by the *Chronicle* the previous Friday, and by Hal Brakespear twice on Sunday, that Tuesday was Bell Day, and a small crowd of St Oswald's faithful had already gathered in front of the church when George and Imogen arrived. As captain of the tower George was immediately brought forward, greeted and questioned; while Imogen, being neither bell-ringer, church attender nor Langesby citizen, was left in the background. But she had always enjoyed the role of observer.

By any standards this was a splendid summer day. By northern standards it could only be described as a right bobby-dazzler. She felt the heat of the sun on her bare arms, closed her eyes against its brilliance, moved under the shade of a yew tree growing over the wall, and leaned against the cool mossy stones, content to wait. Gradually the crowd swelled to twice its original size. Men and women walking past on their way to somewhere else, stopped to ask what was going on, and loitered for a while, hoping to catch the moment of arrival. Three o'clock chimed. So did a quarter and a half-past. A group of young mothers and two house-husbands, who had just collected their toddlers from the primary school nearby, joined the throng, and excitement mounted.

At twenty minutes to four a large green lorry turned the corner from Market Street, followed by a scarlet mobile crane.

George shouted, 'Here they are!'

There was a little flurry of *hurrahs!* from the youngest members of the group, and a burst of comment and laughter from everyone else. Then silence as they watched the heavy vehicles approach. Church Street, in the old quarter of Langesby, had long since been banned to transporters, and this open breach of public regulations added considerable zest to the occasion.

A few yards away, the vehicle stopped. Both drivers got down and George walked towards them. They went into consultation. Everyone listened intently.

'You should have come first,' said George to the mobile crane drive. 'I told your boss to send you up Church *Road*, not Church *Street*. We need you in front of the lych-gate, and the bell lorry behind you, in reverse.'

The drivers grumbled about faulty directions and the narrowness of the street.

'I'll see you right,' said George; 'no need to worry.'

At this moment a haulage truck appeared, preventing the others from moving at all, and George went up to the cabin to deliver a polite reprimand.

'You shouldn't turn in here, mate. Didn't you see the sign?'

The driver's tone was indignant, misunderstood. He cocked his thumb towards the other two vehicles.

'Well, what about *them*, mate? *They're* here.'

'They're supposed to be here.'

'I followed *them*, see.' Injured. 'Thought they was on the same route.'

'Where are you headed for? Sheffield? Well, go sharp right when we've got you out and keep straight on. It's only three miles to the motorway and it's well signposted. What the hell's happening now?' A busy blue van hooted imperiously from behind the truck. 'Oh sod it! The television camera crew. That's all I needed. Wait a minute!' He turned to the haulage truck driver. 'What's your name, mate? Joe? Just hang in there, Joe. I'll be back. Now, you mates. Yes, I know who you are, *Northern News*. We weren't expecting you until five o'clock. You can see what's happening here. You'll have to go back and come up Church Road. Right? Right!' Returning. 'We'll deal with you first, Joe.'

In a louder voice, to the crowd: 'I'll need a couple of helpers here. We'll have to reverse them all. We can use the side lane near Mrs Horsefield's house.'

Immediately two fathers willingly unloaded their offspring and joined him. Together they began to reposition the lorry and mobile crane and send the truck about its business.

'Back, back, back! Stop! Now hard over right! Stop! Forward! Hard over left.'

Eventually, reluctantly, Joe the intruder disappeared down the street and headed for Sheffield, while the other two gravely lumbered through their paces. The crowd scattered to make way for the mobile crane, and reformed at a safe distance, blocking the entrance to Church Road and the camera crew. The elation was increasing, and as the green lorry reversed slowly towards them and they saw Isaac sitting in massive dignity in the back, they gave him three cheers.

Meanwhile, the sight of the great bell, the forty-ton crane and the excited crowd had proved too much for the Sheffield driver. At the final roundabout before the motorway Joe changed his mind. Twenty minutes later he nosed his lorry round the corner of Church Street to see if the coast was clear, sidled forward, and reversed into Mrs Horsefield's lane. Unobserved, he switched off the engine, and strolled forward, hands in pockets and casually whistling, to gatecrash the party.

'Back, everybody! Stand well back!' George cried, as the ninety-foot jib swung out sedately and hovered over the open roof of the truck. Eager

312

hands guided the iron hook. Eager voices directed the crane driver. Gulliver was being steadied by his Lilliputian attendants as he rose. In a minute or two, up came thirty-seven hundredweight of bronze bell, to be lifted clear into the summer air.

The children jumped up and down, squealing with pleasure, shouting for joy.

Portentously, Isaac sailed across the road, over the lych-gate, above the churchyard and its quiet sleepers, was lowered by degrees, and brought to rest on a stout pallet of wood covered with old carpets, in front of the bell tower. Here, his minions removed the straps, and the crane swung gracefully away, its task done.

The television crew took pride of place and had right of way. The crowd surged forward and re-formed in a half-circle around them and the tower. Standing on the church wall or perched on marble monuments, amateur photographers with camcorders and cameras recorded the event.

By this time, Joe the truck driver had given up all pretence to anonymity, rolled up his sleeves, and was standing shoulder to shoulder with two other men, attempting to push the bell through the doorway.

'Right lads,' said George. 'One. Two. Three. Shove!'

Isaac's clapper chimed a protest. He deigned to inch forward.

Two V-cuts had been made in the base of the door uprights to accommodate the flare of the bell, but they saw now that these would not be deep enough. Under George's direction, two more men came forward with club hammers and chisels, to chip away the stone.

'Excuse me,' said a man's voice at his side. 'Mr – er – Hobbs, isn't it?'

George glanced at him abstractedly, and said, 'Yes. Can you stand clear?' For the work ahead of them was onerous and required all their strength and concentration. The man gave a short self-important cough.

'I am the chief reporter from the *Chronicle*, Mr Hobbs.'

He paused, to allow this honour to be digested.

George said patiently, 'Well, could you come back later? I'm busy right now. All right, lads. And again. One. Two. Three. Shove!'

Isaac was moving forward another inch or so, protesting.

'And again. A long strong one this time, lads. One, two, three . . . and IN!'

The cheer from the onlookers was cut short and changed to an *ah!* of regret as Isaac, on the lip of the threshold, jangled triumphantly back on to his pallet.

'All right, lads, take it easy for a minute,' said George.

The men stood back, wiping their hands on the sides of their trousers, drew breath, then again screwed up their faces, clenched their teeth, set their strength against the weight of the bell, sweated, strained.

'And a one, and a two, and a three – hurray!'

Isaac was there despite himself. He sat on the floor of the tower while his minions prepared to bind him with chains, and bring him up by means of rope and pulley. Above him all the hatches had been laid open so that he could rise up to the sunlit belfry unhindered. Inch by inch they would haul him, watch and guide him, for two long hard hours until he was safely home.

'. . . and may the voice of this bell glorify the resurrection of the Lord at Easter, ring out good tidings of great joy at Christmas, ring in the hopes and vows of each New Year, and summon the faithful to service for generations to come. I baptize you in the name of the Father, the Son and the Holy Ghost . . .'

Isaac was no longer tainted by the world. He had changed his secular birth for ecclesiastical status. And now the bell-hanger from the foundry was about to strike the first note. It came deep and sweet and clear, sending out waves of after-sound, just as a fine wine leaves an aftertaste on the palate.

'Tuned to C Sharp!' the expert told anyone who wanted to know.

But no one cared. They had heard Great Isaac chime. Their heads were still humming with gold, remembering.

314

THIRTY-SIX

Thursday

In accordance with Timothy's instructions, Imogen's invitation to Philip was openly conveyed at the end of rehearsal, within sight and hearing of Edith. Unfortunately, Philip's response was not the one that Timothy had anticipated.

'My dear Imogen, I'm afraid I can't.'

He interpreted her dismay as chagrin and was quick to explain. Drawing her to one side he lowered his voice confidentially.

'I would cancel any engagement for your sake, but it's Edith's birthday on Friday and I've arranged a little party for her at Prospect House.'

'Oh, I see,' said Imogen, wondering what to do next.

'Another evening, perhaps?'

'Yes. Yes, of course.'

She looked round for help, but none was forthcoming. Timothy was already going out through the door, surrounded by a group of his old pupils and talking animatedly. To insist on speaking to him now would seem very odd.

'Are you expecting George to take you home?' Philip asked.

'Oh, no. Not tonight. There's a meeting with the bell-ringers at the vicarage. Deirdre and Jon are giving me a lift home. I must be going.'

He was puzzled by her anxiety.

'And you have plans for this evening?'

She could not think fast enough.

'No, I'm not doing anything. But I don't want to keep them waiting.'

'Then if that's all you're bothered about, let *me* drive you back.'

Her excuses were as confused and ineffectual as herself.

'But I was planning an early night. I'm low on coffee. And I've run out of gin.'

He smiled at her persuasively.

'I can pick up a bottle of wine on the way, and I promise to be gone by eleven.'

Timothy had impressed secrecy upon her, so she could not confide in Deirdre, but she could give her a hint that would filter through to the witches. Philip was not a favourite with the Haraldstone clique.

In a high, tight voice, she cried, 'I must tell them I don't need a lift.'

She sped away before he could protest, but Philip would not have protested. He was smiling when she left him, and still smiling when she came back, slightly forlorn, for she had to give the message to Jon, and could not make it as explicit to him as to his wife.

Edith was with Philip, saying, in a tone that she did not trouble to lower as Imogen approached, '. . . I only hope she enjoys travelling back in a minibus full of delinquents. And don't expect me to come and babysit for you at a moment's notice. You'll have to manage them as best you can without me.'

Imogen froze, thinking of the nine automatons, the clean institution with its unclean atmosphere, of Stephen in his amorous death. She pictured herself captured, raped, dead or left for dead, sprawled like a rag doll on Haraldstone Hill. But if such an event was intended then surely Edith would be supervising it, and with relish, whereas Philip was plainly bent on excluding her.

I think that Philip may have fallen a little in love with you, and seen in you a chance to begin again, to shed Edith and to redeem himself, Timothy had said.

She could only hope he was right.

'That won't be a problem,' Philip was answering easily. 'At least let us drop you off at your place.'

This was open provocation, and Edith took it as such.

'There is no need to *drop me off*, as you put it. I am perfectly capable of a short walk to the end of Church Street. But here comes what's-her-name. Pray don't allow me to delay your rendezvous.'

Her ice-green gaze, had it been a spear, would have impaled Imogen on the spot. Edith turned her back on the interloper and walked away.

Philip made no comment on either her remarks or her abrupt exit. He put his arm round Imogen's shoulders.

'And now for an evening at Crazy Hats!' he said. 'Do you know, I still have that champagne at home? I'll pick it up when we deliver the youngsters.'

She still suffered some nasty moments when they drew up in front of Prospect House, but Philip decanted his nine silent passengers and came out brandishing a familiar black bottle. The surge of relief when she realized that he truly meant to take her back to Haraldstone was followed by fresh apprehension. For she must play this game without rules or guidance, and she was on her own. Timothy had overlooked an important point.

So here they were: he, tanned, handsome and triumphant; she pale and inwardly petrified. Shut in the bedroom, Polly was going berserk.

'At last!' Philip cried, as the champagne cork soared to the ceiling. 'I began to think that this bottle was under some sort of spell,' and he glanced at her mischievously: 'destined to remain forever unopened.'

As always, her body responded and her spirit shrank back.

She said stupidly, 'I seem to be drinking champagne all the time these days.'

He paused for a moment, and asked, 'With other fervent male admirers?'

'No, no,' Mentally slapping herself. 'I'm exaggerating as usual,' she lied splendidly. 'It was only one time, and not real champagne, anyway, Sadie treated me to a glass of Babycham at the Dancing Witch.'

She recollected that he didn't like Sadie, and mention of witches could be unfortunate. But Philip smiled and said nothing. He poured skilfully, wasting not a drop.

'To you!' he said, raising his glass. 'And to us!'

'Well, let's sit down and make ourselves comfortable,' Imogen cried airily. She sensed an ambiguity about this statement as well. I can't say the right thing this evening, she thought.

They sat opposite each other, sipping, watching.

He said, 'There's a lot to talk about. When we've finished this off I can get another bottle.'

'But it's past ten o'clock,' Imogen protested, looking at the clock on the mantelshelf. 'The off-licence will be closed soon.'

'Oh, I'm not dependent on off-licences. The evening's young yet,' said Philip, sitting back and smiling at her. 'I know a club in Langesby which will harbour us all night, and serve us breakfast if necessary.'

The prospect stretched out in front of her: a long road ending in a cul-de-sac.

You may rest assured, Timothy had said, *that I wouldn't send you into a lion's den without keeping an eye on both you and the lion.*

But that had been arranged for Friday and this was Thursday. It was all very well for Timothy to sit, secret and spider-like, at the centre of his web, but he was not the only spinner. I might be caught by accident, along with the other flies, she thought. And though he would be genuinely sorry, I should be sorrier still. When this is over, she promised herself, I shall leave the dale.

How she was to move, with barely a year of her lease expired, no capital and no means of selling a new business in a recession, she could not explain, but the idea of being in control of her destiny was comforting.

The first glass soothed her nerves.

I can manage, she thought, making conversation about the play.

The second glass set her tongue free, and Philip plied her with questions which were light and unimportant and delightful to answer. She heard herself being entertaining and was full of self-approval, but the approval felt hollow. She was temporizing, praying for Sadie to ring the doorbell, for Timothy to telephone, for George to drop in on his way home and say good-night. None of these things happened. At one point she walked over to the window on a pretext and looked out. The court was unlit and silent, devoid even of its silky, slinking cats.

At his ease, Philip poured the last of the champagne into their glasses and changed the mood of the occasion.

'I have never told you, by the by, how much I admired you the last time we met at the Brakespears',' he said. 'To stand up in the vicarage, and admit that you consorted with witches, takes more than usual courage.'

She made a sober answer.

'That's kind of you, but it's something I'd like to forget.'

And lest he thought that this compliment should cloud her judgement, she added, 'I'm surprised you should praise me for it. I distinctly remember your saying on that occasion that if matters were as serious as Tim believed, even friendships must be sacrificed.'

She was proud of herself, though fearful.

Philip's smile broadened. He made no attempt to explain or defend himself. 'What an astonishing memory you have!' he said carelessly. 'So I did.'

His confidence worried her. She hurried to set herself right.

'In any case I'm not a witch. I may have joined in the dance.' She corrected herself: 'I *did* join in the dance.' She expanded. 'In fact that wasn't the only ritual I've attended. Mind you, I was drawn into the first by accident . . .'

She stopped herself. I'm becoming a garrulous twit, she thought. she finished by saying defiantly, '. . . but I'm not a witch.'

He had been smiling and listening. Now he came over to her, took the glass away and set it down gently, clasped her hands and pulled her to her feet.

Imogen could think of nothing more subtle to say than, 'I don't want you to make love to me.'

'My dear girl, I wouldn't dream of it, without your express permission.'

He was eroding her self-image. In contrast to Philip's humorous composure her own behaviour seemed churlish and gauche.

'Listen to me,' he said, holding her elbows and giving them a friendly little shake. 'The witchcraft I abhor has nothing to do with your charming folk dance in the moonlight. I'm talking about black and midnight hags brewing up horrors – the genuine article, as Edith would say. And I disagree with you on one point, Imogen. You most certainly are a witch – and in the loveliest sense. You enchanted me the moment I saw you.'

They stood face to face but he made no move to come closer, and she found herself wishing he would. His voice and eyes mesmerized her. His hands were warm and firm.

'Shall we find more champagne?' he asked.

She had not yet recovered her equilibrium but was approaching it.

'No, thank you. And night clubs are not in my line either.'

He was at his most disarming. Holding her lightly, listening to her responsive body, wooing her hostile mind.

'I was only trying to impress you,' he said, almost shamefaced. 'I've never been there. In fact, I suspect that it might be rather dull.'

Imogen giggled with relief, and he grinned. He gave her a final little shake and released her. His tone became brotherly, reassuring.

'So you don't want any more to drink, and you don't want to go to a night club, and you don't want me to make love to you. Shall I take you for a drive?'

Immediately a door in her mind slapped shut. No. The thought of the claustrophobic minibus, with Philip in command of it, worried her.

'Then let's stay here.' His tone was patient, understanding.

Yet she was also afraid of being trapped in this small room, and Polly's helpless squalls and scrabbling did not reassure her.

'Whatever you like,' he said. 'Whatever suits you.'

Half of her was saying, 'Oh, don't be paranoid. He's only courting you.' The other half said, 'Leave a loophole.'

She glanced at the clock. Giving George time for cocoa at the vicarage and a good-night call on Mary, he was bound to be coming back from Howgill on his motorbike within the next half-hour.

'I need to talk to you,' Philip said earnestly. 'There are matters I must sort out, must explain. I want to make things right with you before we go any further.'

His forbearance made her caution seem ridiculous. And yet, the silent village, the long empty road.

She walked over to the window again, pretending to study the weather. Nothing. No one. She made an effort to sound friendly and natural.

'In that case, as it's a lovely night, let's stroll along the road as far as Tofthouse and back. We can talk on the way.' In an effort to assert herself, she added, 'And then you must go, Philip, because I'm tired and I need my sleep.'

His face lightened. He hurried to place her summer shawl about her shoulders. His touch was fire. Her heart was ice.

'I'll just let Polly out,' she said hurriedly.

Equally hurriedly, Philip said, 'Then I'll wait downstairs for you.'

THIRTY-SEVEN

Outside, the moon was high and bright, the air mild, the country tranquil. Neither of them spoke for a few minutes, finding their pace, matching their walk. She shrank away, but Philip sensed that she did not want him to touch her and kept his distance. Just outside the village, near the side lane that led to Haraldstone Hill, he stopped and spoke earnestly.

'Imogen, I know that you've had your doubts about us, and I'm more grateful than I can say for being given a second chance. So I want to put my cards on the table and tell you what I have in mind.'

He drew a deep breath and said the unexpected in formal fashion.

'I should like to ask you to marry me.'

As her startled face turned to his he put up one hand.

'No, don't say anything yet. Before we go any further I have some confessions to make.'

She suffered a savage twinge of conscience. She had not given him another chance at all. They were only here together because of Timothy's machinations. And whereas he was being open with her she was only mollifying him until George arrived. She felt she owed him an honest refusal.

'No, Philip, I must stop you before *you* go any further. Philip, I do appreciate the offer, but . . .'

But what? Make it good!

'I like my independence – and I'm – I'm not thinking of marrying again yet.'

Why yet?

Fearing that this might give him future hope she amended the statement.

'To be quite truthful, although I admire your – your good works – I could never cope with Prospect House as a way of life. It's simply not me.'

He looked at her as if seeing her true nature at last. His stance, his expression, even his clothes were heavy with disappointment. She should have been shocked and sorry for him, but there was something so theatrical, so insincere about the whole effect as to alarm her deeply.

Surely he never expected me to say yes? she thought. Not on all the past evidence. Not on one flimsy excuse of a reunion. So why is he doing this?

'I'm sorry, truly sorry,' she said hastily, 'and — and please don't confess anything, because it wouldn't be right for me to hear it.'

And I don't want to know. I'd be horrified to know.

His tone was that of a man who had trusted and been betrayed.

'Edith told me you were playing the tease. I didn't believe her.'

Imogen was not prepared to put up with this, and defended herself stiffly.

'In the first place Edith's opinion of me is bound to be prejudiced. In the second place, far from playing the tease, I have done my best to keep you at arm's length. But I don't want to quarrel with you, so, under the circumstances, I think we should finish this conversation and go back.'

His face frightened her, not because of the moods it reflected so express-ively but because he was playing a part, for reasons she could not fathom. The stage directions in his mind were almost readable: *Instant shock. Slow recognition. Rising disgust. Growing indignation. Outright rage.*

'How can you say that? You've encouraged me to hope. You were the one who asked me over tomorrow evening . . .'

This was the last of several straws and she was furious.

In her mind she shouted, Damn and blast you, Timothy Rowley!

He maundered on.

'You've accepted everything I offered — dinner at Mario's, flowers, notes, champagne . . .'

She was no longer sorry for him, nor careful of him.

'Only because you wouldn't take no for an answer. Only because my stupid good manners wouldn't allow me to tell you to get lost from the beginning!'

Does not hear her, his mind read. His voice followed the directions obediently. She was talking to an automaton.

'. . . and we've been making love at rehearsals for months. Anyone would tell you that. It's a company joke.'

She saw then that in some curious way he had convinced himself.

A little in love with you, ran through her mind.

She willed her anger down and spoke more gently.

'But rehearsals aren't real life! Philip, the play is only a play.'

She pressed her hands together, pleading for him to come back. She looked into eyes that would not see.

'Philip. Please. Please listen to me.'

His stage directions read, *Addresses her with sorrowful reproach.*

'Can you deny that you weren't attracted to me — strongly attracted to me? Can you say that you were pretending?'

She was silent, wondering how to tell the truth without feeding his resentment. And his directions were running on regardless.

Speaks with contempt.

'You know very well that you were. So what exactly did you want of me?'

Declares judgement upon her.

'I thought you were different, but you're no better than the rest of them. I treat you like a queen and you behave like a slut.'

So that's it, she thought. He needs to give himself an excuse.

His metamorphosis was complete. He caught hold of her and shook her until her teeth chattered. His yelping laugh was without humour or kindness.

'You bitch!'

Her shawl slithered down on to her arms and slipped away, forming a pale pool on the grass. She opened her mouth to call, to scream, and he punched her in the stomach. As she doubled over, holding herself, coughing and retching, he grasped her shoulders and turned her roughly round. Systematically, he tugged and tore out her hairpins, talking himself into a righteous frenzy.

'You've been a very naughty girl, Imogen, and you have to be punished. I've always tried to please you, to give you what I thought you wanted. But you wouldn't respond to me in the right way, would you? Well, now we know what you were really after we must make sure you get it.'

This is how he talks to them when the doors are locked against the world. She thought, sickened. This is what happens at Prospect House.

Her hair fell in a long silky sheath. He wound it tightly round his left hand and jerked her head back. He locked one arm behind her. Still struggling for breath, Imogen flailed weakly with the other arm but could not reach him, and he laughed. Stage directions continued to float through from his mind to hers.

Speaks softly, with menace.

He put his lips close to her face.

'You seem to be fond of playing games with the girls. Now let's see how you manage a man. Keep quiet and march!'

He hustled her into the lane that led to Haraldstone Hill.

He stopped here on purpose, she thought, stricken. Whatever I did, wherever we were, he meant to corner me.

She had only just recovered her breath and her throat was dry. He held her head at such an angle that she could make only inarticulate sounds of protest, and he kept a painful hold on arm and hair, giving both an agonizing tug when she stumbled or attempted to cry out.

As they started up the slope she heard the distant burr of the Harley-Davidson riding the road from Howgill. If only he had been a few minutes earlier. Her heart hammered with terror and despair. The sound grew to a muffled roar and then diminished. Silence. George passed by.

She dared not believe that she was entirely at Philip's mercy. Surely, she thought, there must be courting couples around, night-strollers – somebody? But superstition clung to the hill, as to the village. No one ventured there at night.

They stumbled into the ring of standing stones and paused.

'I'm going to hit you very hard if you move or scream,' he said factually, 'and there's no one to hear us. So stand still and do as you're told.'

He released her, stood apart and smoothed her hair, smiling at her.

'I believe you like dancing naked in the moonlight,' he said conversationally, 'and I always believe in women doing what pleases them. That way we both enjoy ourselves. So let's see you play Salome. None of your countrified skipping around. I want oriental seduction. Take your clothes off and dance for me.'

She was cold with fear and humiliation. She endeavoured to counsel herself.

If you're ever attacked, Fred had said. *Kick the bugger hard and run harder!*

She had been the best runner in her house at school, but that was a long time ago. Could she move fast enough to kick this man and make a break for freedom?

'Don't think of doing *anything!*' Philip warned her softly.

He uttered no threats but she heard them in his voice. That they were nameless made them more horrifying. His teeth and eyes gleamed.

'Take off your clothes!'

She stood numb and dumb. He laughed to himself.

'I've often wondered what you were. I thought there might be a wanton under that chaste exterior, but it is an innocent after all.'

He muttered a litany that evidently accompanied this sort of event, dwelling on punishment, and she wondered how she was going to survive.

He walked forward and slapped her face experimentally. The slap was not hard, just a preliminary insult. His expression was not cruel. He was simply interested in her reaction. She was a subject for sexual investigation.

The slap woke her up, roused her anger, overrode her fear, made her think. She decided to play the innocent for all she was worth. She put her head in her hands and sobbed, watching him between her fingers.

He liked this, and began to ask her questions. Would she do what he wanted?

She shook her head from side to side and wailed as if she had lost her reason.

He laughed again, and said, 'I think you would, Imogen. Yes, I can see you would. Will you be a good girl?'

She had no idea what he was going to do next but she realized that he could hardly be absorbed in this game and on guard at the same time.

She wailed again and begged him to let her go.

He stood over her and ordered her again to take off her clothes. She became hysterical in her refusal. Her disobedience added to his enjoyment. He muttered another tedious recital, put his hand in the neck of her cotton dress and ripped it open.

'Step out of it! Quickly!'

Making as much noise and fuss as possible, Imogen stepped out of her dress.

'Take the rest off!' he commanded.

As she hesitated he raised his fist. She knew she must keep her wits and senses about her so that she could seize any opportunity. She obeyed him. After all, she thought despairingly, a lace brassière and a pair of hip pants were not going to protect her from anything.

'And your sandals. You're not going anywhere!'

She regretted the loss of her sandals. Running in naked feet would not be easy.

He glanced round him, frowning. He was missing certain props which Haraldstone Hill could not provide. No ropes, no sticks. The ground was bare of stones; the branches of the nearest bushes too far away. The Listeners offered nothing but themselves.

He stood, fists on hips, legs apart, lord of all he surveyed, including his victim, who cowered, whimpering, before him. He looked away again, thinking.

And she was gone. Dodging between the Listeners, skimming over the tussocks, flying on the wings of a nightmare. Running, running, running. Her heart hammering, blood singing in her ears.

In a few seconds he was after her, laughing and shouting, stimulated by the chase. His legs were longer. He was catching up.

She heard Alice's voice crying in her ears, 'Come on, Imogen! You can make it! Run for the house, Imogen! Run for the house!'

She was a girl again. She played a schoolgirl's trick. In a split second as she sensed his presence close behind her she stopped short, stepped aside and stuck out her foot.

Philip stumbled over it and sprawled on the grass, momentarily winded.

Slyboots! Timothy remarked in her ear.

Kick the bugger and run! cried Fred urgently.

She drove her heel as hard as she could between Philip's outstretched legs. Heard him shout with pain. And ran. And ran. And ran into another rapist – whom she flailed with her fists, screaming all the while, 'I'll kill you, too. I'll kill you all. If I die for it I'll kill you.'

'Here, steady on!' George said, putting his arms round her. 'Steady on, my lass. It's only me.'

She rested against him, drawing deep sobbing breaths, listening to a different story.

'I knew something was wrong,' said George. 'I called in at Crazy Hats on my way back from Mary's, and the place was black as pitch and old Polly was raising hell. Then Sadie ran across, hearing the motorbike, and said she'd been late home and Deirdre had been ringing her, to say that Philip had brought you back from rehearsal and you didn't seem happy about it. She was getting the girls together for a search party, but I told her to leave it to me. I saw the minibus parked in a side-street, and I guessed that you'd gone for a walk with him, along the Langesby road, hoping I might turn up. So I set off in that direction, and found your shawl on the ground at Hill Lane. Here, let me wrap it round you.'

Imogen was laughing and sobbing and talking, and George listened, stroking her hair, soothing her, throwing in the occasional comment.

'Philip? Oh yes. A right Jekyll and Hyde, that one, and bent as a hairpin. No need to worry about him. He'll have slunk off by now, with his tail between his legs. No, I won't say anything – and he certainly won't. I'd like to finish him off but I'll leave that to Tim Rowley. There's a lot happening, my lass. You'll see the start of it tomorrow night. I can't say more – even to you. But I'm going to have quite a few words with Tim.' Grimly: 'Letting you in for this lot . . .'

★   ★   ★

326

Imogen became aware of herself in relation to him, and covered her breasts with her arms, but the gesture was purely formal. She had been physically aroused by the night, the place, the over- and undertones, and the subsequent struggle. Her body had drawn the line at consorting with a murderer and abuser, but remained open for further and more acceptable offers. Still, there were conventions to be observed. Her eyes begged George not to notice her nakedness, and his own were cast down in answer. In truth, now that the hero had rescued the heroine, he was at a loss what to do with her. He knew, naturally, what he would like to do, but felt it would be inappropriate, and perhaps unacceptable.

Fortunately, nature had no such fine feelings. Here were two people who had long been drawn to each other. Liking, respect and friendship were fine things, but as far as nature was concerned they were mere accessories to the fact. Only the mutual attraction mattered. Both woman and man had been awakened by what went before, now they were left alone in a place where they were unlikely to be disturbed: the one naked, the other dressed, and both ready.

George's erection was troubling him. He strove to conquer it by collecting up the loved one's clothes and coming forward to proffer them to her. It was a fatal mistake on his part. They were too close for either of their comforts.

Imogen sobbed just once more, whether in supplication or invitation no one could have known, and he clasped her in his arms again to console her.

She said unnecessarily, 'Oh, hold me!'

George answered, taking care that she should not notice his condition. 'I'm here now. No need to fret.'

For some reason he was taking off his clothes instead of helping her on with hers, and Imogen said, 'Yes, that's right!'

He felt very lean and beautiful, flesh to flesh, and she moved beneath him so that he would have no trouble in penetrating her.

Then they went at it, as George himself would have said, hammer and tongs.

'Oh God!' George whispered, into her small soft breasts, 'I didn't mean to do that. You'll think there's nobody you can trust.'

But Imogen answered tenderly, in mockery, borrowing her words from Delia's speech, 'Not so, good sir, for you are by!'

And they both laughed.

He moved further up, cradling her shoulders in both hands. The springy grass was a magnificent mattress. They were prepared to try it out all night.

He said, 'Imogen, it wasn't just opportunity. I've wanted to – for a long time. But I didn't want to admit it.'

She answered from deep in her satisfied female self, 'I know. I've wanted to, as well. For a long time. And I didn't want to admit it, either.'

His voice changed. He said, 'The back of your shoulder feels rough. Did he . . . ?'

'No,' said Imogen, drowsily stretching. 'Those are Polly's claw marks. It's a sign of her affection.'

He meant to kiss the scars gently, but had another impulse.

'It's been a long time,' said George in apology, mounting her again.

'Be my guest!' she replied, engaging with him.

Much later, they went back to the shop. Holding an indignant Polly to her shoulder and crooning to her as they mounted the stairs, Imogen still floated on bliss, for George slept by her side, and in her early dreams, as she climbed lightly from branch to branch of the Tree of Life, whichever branch she landed on – there again was George.

But towards morning the darker memories came to the surface, and she dreamed that she was being driven through the night to an unknown destination. The man at the wheel neither spoke nor looked at her, only drove faster and faster, lips compressed, eyes on the road ahead. Terrified that they would crash, she begged him to go slower, pleaded with him to stop. He turned a cold white face toward her, devoid of humanity. She clutched his arm and it began to disintegrate. Nuts and bolts flew all over the place and she saw that he was made of metal: a mechanical man, driving a vehicle at a speed far beyond its powers. They were both beyond control. Knowing that nothing could save her, she battered at the windscreen of her nightmare and screamed and screamed.

Sitting at the breakfast table with a solicitous George and a subdued Polly, unable to eat, drinking tea that could not warm her, teeth chattering in her head, she reached an inevitable conclusion.

Dialling Timothy's number, she blurted out, 'It's Imogen. Philip Gregory came here last night and tried to rape me. I can't see him again. I can't go through with the play.'

THIRTY-EIGHT

Friday

Peele's Players must have bolted their high teas or made do with a quick snack, because everyone was there by seven o'clock, as Timothy had requested. The maestro and George arrived a little late, linking the arms of a pale but resolute Imogen. The day had been an arduous one, on themselves and others who were inevitably drawn into a critical situation. Sadie Whicker took care of both shops. Mary Proctor healed and counselled the victim privately. Mrs Housam provided a picnic basket lunch for everyone, and a substantial afternoon tea. And George pronounced a judgement on Timothy, which was humbly accepted. But in the end they all delivered the heroine of the play more or less on time, and more or less in her right mind.

Others had also endured a harrowing day. Philip, knowing very well who Imogen's champions were, had expected an unwelcome visit from Timothy, George, or the police. Venturing out to the rehearsal at last, skulking in the wings, with Edith simmering at his side, he again looked for retribution and found none.

Imogen was born away to the dressing room by Sadie. George called for silence. And Timothy stepped forth, addressing them in his airiest fashion.

'Good evening, Players! My apologies for keeping you all waiting, but our charming Delia was taken ill today. Fortunately, being a courageous and resilient person, she has overcome her malaise, but if she seems less vivacious than usual that is the reason. She would like to sit quietly by herself between stage appearances. Pray respect her need for rest and privacy.'

Murmurs of sympathy and understanding.

He hurried away to encourage the convalescent.

'Philip and Edith don't know which way the cat is going to jump – which was exactly what I wanted – and everyone thinks you're wonderful, my dear.'

Imogen cheered up slightly.

'Did you know it was Edith's birthday today?' she asked.

Timothy chuckled.

'Is it, indeed? How fortunate that I happen to have a gift for her.'

And he bustled off, exultant.

Dressed in her Elizabethan finery, Imogen went to sit in Stephen's old chair at the back of the hall. Now and then a head turned in her direction, someone nodded encouragement or smiled commiseration; otherwise they left her alone as Timothy had requested, and gradually her mood changed.

It was difficult not to be caught up in the general tension and exhilaration. For three months the company had laboured hard and long, and at last were on the eve of achievement. Backstage, Sadie and Milia acted as dressers, ready to make any last-minute alterations. On stage, George orchestrated his assistants. Across the buzz of general conversation, questions were called, orders given. The men strutted about. The women swept to and fro. Until the clack, clack, clack of Timothy's palms and his sonorous voice brought them to attention.

'Before we begin, I have some astonishing news to impart.'

Their silence was absolute. He made a courtly gesture towards Edith.

'First of all, my dear Edith, we must thank you from the bottom of our hearts for stepping into the breach so promptly and splendidly, and taking on the role of Gammer Madge while Mary was afflicted.'

She was uncertain whether to smile or not. He turned to his company.

'I am sure you will all agree that Edith has cast new light on this part, and conducted herself so skilfully and well that we have been able to work round and with her, and there has been no hitch in the rehearsals. I know we all thank her for helping out at a crucial time, and say, "Well done!" '

His tone demanded the murmurs of agreement which they gave, though everyone was puzzled. Edith smiled no longer.

'But, as my dear grandmama used to say, it is the *unexpected* that always happens. I was informed only today by Mary Proctor that, despite her ailments and the tragic loss she suffered recently, she now feels able to return to us. She will play the part of Gammer Madge after all!'

A babble of astonishment and disbelief was followed by a spontaneous burst of applause as George entered the hall with Mary Proctor on his arm. They stood together for a few moments, as he presented her to the company. Then he stepped aside, and left her to receive her ovation.

The events of the past weeks had heaped years on Mary, and she looked old age incarnate. But she held herself almost as erect as ever, though needing the assistance of a stout ash walking stick. And she was dressed in the original costume, provided by Timothy.

Appearing among them, as if by magic, she was Gammer Madge in person: in a frilled white cap, with a black fringed shawl crossed over her chest, a white apron round her russet brown skirt, and beneath it all her own black wool stockings and immaculately polished black-strapped shoes.

Formerly, she had kept her fellow actors at a distance. They had admired her and been slightly afraid of her. But in her absence affection and appreciation had grown. She had left them as a respected senior member of the cast. She returned to them a beloved heroine.

In perfect unison, Antic, Frolic and Fantastic stepped forward, swept off their feathered hats and bowed low. And after them, with mingled laughter and homage, curtsies and bows, the company followed. Even Sadie and Milia darted from the wings and dared to give Mary a welcoming hug. Finally Timothy strode through the ranks of his company to make his obeisance and kiss her hand.

Mary's eyes shone more brightly and her doughty chin quivered. Then she recovered herself and took them all to task.

'I don't know about *The Old Wives' Tale*,' she declared roundly, 'I should call this *Much Ado About Nothing*!'

They all laughed.

'It's very good of you all. I appreciate it, and I thank you sincerely,' said Mary. She added, 'But if this is supposed to be a dress rehearsal we'd best get on with it, hadn't we?'

Timothy had not forgotten Edith, merely been diverted by events. He had a little gift ready for her, and a little speech prepared.

'George, could you please . . . ?' he begged.

George roared through cupped hands, 'Quiet, everybody!' And they were quiet.

Timothy turned towards the deposed one, taking a tissue-wrapped package from his pocket, and was beginning, 'My dear Edith, this is a small—'

Edith turned her back on him and walked out.

Timothy said, 'Ah!' and then, 'Dear me!' and there was a brief embarrassed silence. Everyone looked covertly at Edith's friend and partner.

Philip was noticeably subdued. His youngsters stayed together in their usual huddle, looking to him for a lead, but he stayed incommunicative. He was in a difficult position: suspecting much but able to prove nothing. The timing of this announcement and its abruptness were, he was sure, deliberate; and beneath it all lay much that was unknown or unspoken.

Furthermore, Edith was his ally. Yet he could prove nothing, and officially she had taken the role on the understanding that this was a temporary measure. To walk out after her would be childish and unjustified. And yet, and yet . . . So he remained uncertain. And while he hesitated Timothy came over to him, to protest concern.

'I'm afraid this must have come as something of a blow to Edith,' he said apologetically, 'and I'm sorry about that. But I do hope you will convey our warmest gratitude to her, and this small token of our appreciation – inadequate but sincere – for her sterling support over the past weeks.'

Philip's lips were stiff and pale. He said automatically, 'That's very kind of you. I'm sure she'll understand.' He did not know how to translate the walk-out.

'Her reaction was quite natural,' Timothy explained, and his voice was benevolence itself. 'She has put her heart and soul into the part and such a *bouleversement* is hard to take.'

Lest this give Philip an excuse, he added, 'I did, if you remember, point out when she first made her generous offer that it would most probably be a temporary measure – but no doubt in the heat of the moment she has forgotten that.'

He cleared his throat and became affable, shrewd.

'However, I do assure you that her goodwill shall not go unheeded. On the last night we shall make public and particular mention of her splendid work. And I do hope, my dear fellow, that by then you will have managed to smooth things over and persuaded her to take a bow with the rest of us, on stage?'

Philip's reply still sounded mechanical, as if he were reading a prepared speech out loud.

'Yes, certainly. Oh, I'm sure she will. It's just that she's – very highly strung, very sensitive. And, as you say, the news came as a personal disappointment. But of course, she will be delighted that Mrs Proctor is well enough to take the part, and when she's got over the initial shock she won't mind a bit.' He rallied to her banner. 'Edith is, above all else, a good sport.'

Timothy's eyes narrowed. His smile widened.

'Of course she is. Of course she is. As well as being a close friend and invaluable assistant to yourself. I do realize,' he continued, 'that you may well be feeling some chagrin on her behalf, but I hope, my dear fellow, that this will not in any way threaten your commitment to the play?'

Philip still looked irresolute. Timothy became humble, his argument more convoluted, his flattery more fulsome.

'Setting aside the fact that your youngsters are an integral part of the production, *you* are the linchpin. I had good reason for begging you to take part in the first place. You see – if I am to come clean, as they say – you possess a personal power that conveys itself to the audience. If you were to desert us . . .' As Philip's frown deepened, and his doubts increased, Timothy hurried on: '. . . for reasons of personal loyalty which would be *perfectly* understandable, we should find ourselves in a painful position. I don't say that the play would be cancelled, because I have some small reputation to uphold, and I could not allow that. The show would assuredly go on – but with a decided loss of . . . what shall I say? Panache? Magnetism? No, even more than that. A lack of *authority*.'

Edith's dominion had implanted seeds of rebellion in her lover and disciple, Her self-confidence threatened his self-esteem. Her power rendered him impotent. And in Philip admiration warred with resentment. Timothy had made him aware that he was a man in his own right, a separate and powerful force with which to be reckoned. He knew he had panache and magnetism, but the word *authority* came far sweeter to his ears, for this he had sometimes doubted. And Timothy's tone suggested that women, however clever and worthy of gratitude, should be loved and honoured but kept in their place. Their subordinate place.

Perceptibly, Philip straightened up, became his handsomest smiling self, and apparently in full control of the situation.

'My dear Tim!' he said, speaking almost with a hint of condescension. 'There was never any question of my giving up the part or withdrawing the youngsters, out of pique or anything of that sort. That would be unthinkable. Naturally, I am concerned for Edith and devoted to her. But I'm sure I can persuade her to take the broader view.'

'Certainly you can. You lighten my heart! Dear, dear Edith! Well, well, well,' said Timothy benevolently, patting Philip's sleeve, the slippery black silk sleeve of Sacrapant that shimmered with gold runes. 'Shall we make a start?'

His voice asked permission. His eyebrows asked Philip if he might call his flock to heel, and Philip obeyed cheerfully.

'In your places, chorus!'

Heeding the tone of command, his acolytes scrambled to obey him.

'A word in your ear, my dear,' said Timothy, as Imogen emerged from the ladies' dressing room at the end of the evening.

She had been wooed by Sacrapant with less than his usual zest, had responded likewise, and was feeling tired, cross, childish and ill-used.

Her 'Yes, Tim?' was haughty.

'I do understand how you feel about my shortcomings,' he said graciously, 'and when the show is over you may beat me over the head with my own cricket bat, but bear with me for the moment. I say this solely for your own good.'

'Oh, *everyone* knows what's good for me!' Imogen said bitterly. 'I just can't help wondering why I always end up in a mess in spite of their advice!'

He lifted one hand, to silence her, to apologize.

'I must speak briefly because I don't want to draw undue attention to us,' he said. 'Edith has swept off in high dudgeon, which bodes no good to anyone. Mary and I will be first in the firing line, and there will be others, but I suspect that you come high on her list. So for the next twenty-four hours keep an eye on yourself and your premises.

'If you find anything of the sort we found at Mary's house, you are to leave whatever it is strictly alone and telephone me at once, at any hour of the day or night. Is that understood?'

She nodded sombrely.

In a louder voice, he said unctuously, 'Good! Good! I knew, my dear Imogen, that you wouldn't mind my mentioning that little matter.' He gave her a jaunty wave, and hurried off to speak to someone else.

When it's all over I *shall* leave Haraldstone, Imogen told herself.

This inner voice was that of a mother, such as Alice had been. Unlike Imogen it differentiated sharply between good and bad, knew which side it was on, stuck to the rules and the place in life to which God had chosen to call it, and did not seek to venture beyond its elected boundaries. Consequently, it knew not only where it was but where it was likely to be in ten years' time. Within reason, it could have mapped its life out from start to finish and not been far wrong. And now that it found Imogen in a tight corner, through every fault of her own, the voice knew exactly how she should behave, and told her so.

'There's still a reasonable amount of capital left. Your Uncle Martin made sure of that. So the best thing you can do is to confide in him (up to a point) and then follow his advice to the letter. Put your business up for sale. It should fetch something. You might, with luck and Uncle Martin's good management, break even. At worst you can go and live with him for a few months, or even a year, while you sort yourself out. Actually, that's quite a good idea. You can shed your responsibilities, pull yourself together, make your hats and sell them to shops just as you used to do. And he'll be glad of a little company. He's been lonely since Aunt

Ethel died. Then, when everything is cleared up and you know exactly where you stand, you can look around and try again – but *judiciously*, this time.

'So there is a way out, and if you use your common sense you'll do as I say.'

Imogen surfaced into the present, aware of George looming up in front of her, saying, 'I've told Tim that *I'm* taking you home.'

The voice had forgotten to include George in its master plan, and the implications of his presence flustered Imogen. So she found herself on the pillion of the Harley-Davidson, speeding along the road to Haraldstone as usual.

Too much had happened over the last twenty-four hours. She needed time to absorb it all, time by herself. Not, she reflected furiously and unfairly, some man taking advantage of the situation.

Arriving at the shop door George naturally expected to be invited in, but by this time Imogen needed to punish someone. He was the nearest, and the dearest.

She dismounted in a dignified manner.

'Thank you very much,' she said formally, and then with some imperiousness. 'Are you taking me to the hall tomorrow evening?'

George was neither slow nor unperceptive. His look and his retort were direct.

'Why shouldn't I?'

He was supposed to say 'What's wrong?' so that she could tell him at length. Instead, she had to improvise a reason.

'Oh, I just thought you might be staying up in Langesby after work, you see. Being busy with the stage and the lighting.'

'That's all organized. It's simply routine work from now on.'

He was not being helpful.

She added, 'I can always get a lift from someone else if I have to.'

George refused to be provoked. His answer was crisp.

'Look, Imogen, if you don't want me to pick you up I won't.'

She now had to find a way back.

'Oh no. I'll see you tomorrow. Thanks for the lift. Good-night!' And she became preoccupied in fitting the key into the lock.

'Right you are,' said George carelessly. 'About a quarter-past six then?'

He wheeled the cycle round and revved the engine.

But he had no right to do this to her, Imogen thought, no right to accept her snubs without question. He knew damned well that something was wrong and he ought to find out what it was. Imogen wanted a blazing row, during which she could tell him exactly how she felt, and why, and preferably blame him for it. He would apologize and promise not to upset her again. And after that they could make up the quarrel, and make love.

Realizing that this was not to be, she could have stamped with temper. Over the noise of the engine she shouted, 'By the way, I shan't be staying here when the play's over. I've decided to leave the dale for good.'

Without so much as turning his head, he shouted back, 'I don't blame you!' then swung round the corner, and roared off down the road.

Which left matters exactly as they were.

'Don't even so much as *mew!*' she warned Polly, bouncing into the shop and slamming the door.

When at length she managed to go to sleep, a double gin and a long single-sided argument later, she was restless, ready to wake at the slightest sound: cats in the court, the inward monologue of an old building, an aeroplane passing over, a solitary car on the solitary road, mice in the walls. The night was warm and close, but she was afraid to open the window lest something apart from air drifted in. There was stealth on the stairs and they creaked. Half a dozen times she sat up in bed, having dreamed dreadfully or heard Timothy's voice raised in warning. Then, just as she was drifting off again, Polly demanded to be let out.

Shivering with apprehension, Imogen switched on the light and opened the bedroom door. She carried a heavy torch to find the way downstairs, but also to act as a weapon in case of an intruder. Every moment that it searched the waiting shadows was sheer terror. Ahead of her, unconcerned, trotted the busy backside of Polly, tail upright.

In the shop, dimly gleaming with ghostly hats, she let the cat out and peered into the court. Nothing and no one, apart from the moon illuminating windows and cobbles.

Until she saw that a wide-brimmed straw hat on the floor of the window was askew, and beneath the brim peeped the top of something crowned with dark artificial hair.

Immobilized, Imogen backed away. Her heart was suffocating her throat. Her face was stiff, her hands slippery on the torch. Keeping her eyes on the object, she felt for the telephone and dialled Timothy Rowley's number. And as she waited, she prayed that the thing would not suddenly come to life and move, that Polly would stay outside in safety, that Tim would not mind being woken in the early hours of the morning.

A man's voice, deep, sleepy and apprehensive, said, 'George Hobbs speaking. Who is that?'

'Oh God, I've dialled the wrong number!' she said to herself in despair.

George's voice was suddenly alert.

'Is that you, Imogen? What's up?'

She was almost crying with fear and anger.

'I'm sorry, George. I wanted Timothy. I've got – something – under a hat in my front window. I'm sorry. I must get Timothy.'

Wait five minutes and I'll be round,' said George.

'But you mustn't. You can't. Tim's got to come. He's the only one who knows how to deal with it.'

'You need moral support,' said George. 'Stay where you are until I get there. We'll both phone him when I've seen it.'

Imogen put down the receiver and sat behind the counter, watching the coarse hair poking from under the fine straw curve. And at that moment Polly clawed at the door and demanded to be let in. Refused, she trotted round to the window and scrabbled frantically on that instead.

Afraid lest the cat rouse whatever it was, Imogen sidled towards the door, opened and shut it in three seconds, grabbed Polly, and stood outside, hugging her, enduring the probing claws and dribbles of delight, and waiting for George.

He was as prosaic as usual, despite wearing a tracksuit over his pyjamas, and breathing quickly because he had sprinted from Chapel Street to the Catwalk.

'You haven't locked yourself out, have you?' he asked.

She shook her head, wordless with shock, and gave the door a gentle push to show him.

'Right. Where is it?'

She followed him into the shop and pointed to the hair beneath the hat.

'No, keep away from it! Don't touch it!' she shrieked, as he leaned forward.

He smiled at her benignly, lifted the brim, and brought out a hand-brush.

'Oh!' Imogen said, totally deflated.

She plumped down on the window dais and began to cry into Polly's neck. George sat down by her, saying kindly, 'It's a mistake that anyone could make in the circumstances. You're under a lot of strain at the moment.'

Polly was wriggling crossly out of Imogen's embrace.

'That's right, Polly,' said George, but without rancour, knowing that cats will always be cats. 'Take care of Number One. It doesn't matter how upset she is, don't let her wet your fur!'

He eased Imogen carefully to her feet, put a long arm round her, and began to walk her up the stairs, soothing her all the way.

'What you need is a good stiff drink, or a nice hot one – whatever you feel like. I'll make it for you. And then I'll search the premises to make sure it's all clear. But' – watching the cat bustle ahead of them – 'I should think everything is hunky-dory – otherwise old Polly would have cleared off and left you to face the music by yourself. That's what I call a good friend!'

A phantom giggle bubbled up inside Imogen. She began to feel better.

'But to make such a fool of myself twice in one night,' she said later, sipping a hot gin noggin. 'First the wrong telephone number and then the wrong idea!'

'It's understandable,' said George. 'And I'd like to think that you meant to call me, even if you did think you were phoning Tim.'

She glanced at him shyly, and veered away from the direction that their conversation was taking.

'I can't think what I was about, leaving the brush there. But I was in such a tizzy this morning. Probably I was tidying the window when the telephone or the doorbell rang. And then Timothy and you and Sadie came round, and I went to pieces and forgot all about it. Yes, that was probably what happened.'

George said, keeping to the point, 'You were in a right royal rage with me this evening. What was that for?'

'Oh!' She consulted her glass for a while, wondering how to explain.

'You see, I like to go my own way, and I hate people telling me what I ought to do,' she began, 'and since I came here I've been pulled between Timothy and Philip and the Brakespears until I felt like screaming. Last night was the worst ever, and I wanted to crawl away and die, but Tim still had to patch me up and push me on stage this evening. And then you brought me home and I thought – well, I thought – well, I just wanted to be left alone.'

She glanced at him self-consciously, and he was smiling at her.

'You thought I'd used you?' he asked.

She coloured up and shook her head.

'So you weren't blaming *me* for anything?'

'I wasn't blaming you at all,' said Imogen, 'but I'd had a bad time and

I wanted to make somebody pay for it, and you happened to be there.'

'Oh, well, that's all right then,' said George cheerfully. 'I can understand that. So we've sorted ourselves out?'

She nodded, and bent her head in contemplation, and he thought how lovely she was, with her long dark hair and pensive face.

'Don't you think,' said George carefully, 'that as I'm here, and as you've had a bad time, and as we've both got a big day tomorrow and need our sleep, that I'd better stay with you?' As she lifted her head, surprised and hopeful, he said quickly, 'I can kip down here in the living room.'

She thought through the next stumbling sentences on both their parts, and saved them both a lot of time and nonsense.

'We can sleep together,' she said. 'I've got a double bed – and a magic quilt.'

'I'll just nip back and lock up,' said George.

THIRTY-NINE

And the crisis was all nothing, all forgotten, when George drove up on his motorbike at six o'clock the following evening, and found her locking the shop.

'All right, then?' George asked, meaning many things.

She saluted him: thumbs up.

They were together in a bright-eyed, eager-spirited adventure. She thought how pleasing he looked, as he smiled within and without.

'I do like lean brown silent men,' she said, teasing him.

'That's good,' said George. 'And I like long, slim, dark women. What do you think about that?'

'We make a good couple,' said Imogen, mounting the pillion. 'No, George, don't go for half a minute. There's plenty of time. How's Mary?'

'Fine.' He frowned slightly. 'Well, as fine as Mary can be. You know what she's like. Ready for anything and raring to go. But the spirit's stronger than the flesh. I'll feel easier in my mind when this week's over. I wish,' said George, 'that I could make her take life easy, but how do you persuade Boadicea to retire?'

'You can't. It's much more exciting to whip up the horses and charge off in your chariot to give the Romans what for!'

She put her arms round his waist and laid her cheek against his. She could feel him smiling.

'Tonight's the night,' she said. 'And, oh I *am* looking forward to it! I'll bet Timothy's at his best and worst. Shall we join him?'

'Off we jolly well go!' said George, and roared out of the Catwalk.

Any cloud from the previous evening had been dispelled by elation. The first to be dressed and made up, Imogen, encased in her fine stiff gown, stood slightly apart from the rest and took on the role of spectator, marvelling at the bustle and splendour of the event.

Backstage was mayhem, with everyone playing a heightened version either of themselves or their character. Between the two makeshift dressing rooms darted Sadie and Milia: hauling at corset or bodice strings, adjusting the angle of a man's hat, fluffing up a feather, setting a ruff, tugging a sword belt into place, standing back to give a final critical look at each creation, followed by a swift appreciative nod.

The scene shifters, plainly dressed in green jerkins and orange tights, inspected their plywood charges, and checked their elaborate list of exits and entrances.

Out front, Alice's workforce had assembled early in readiness. A table had been set up at the far end of the hall, supplied with a roll of shocking pink tickets and a blue striped pudding basin full of small change. Behind it sat two buxom members of Alice's workforce, chatting to the programme ladies. They wore smart pleated silky skirts and jackets, lapel brooches and diamanté earrings, to distinguish them from the casual summer-clad audience.

In the kitchen the refreshment ladies, practically attired in short-sleeved cotton dresses and white aprons, were setting out cups, saucers and glasses, emptying packets of biscuits on to plates, and filling the giant urn with water. Crates of soft drinks and bottles of squash stood in one corner.

On stage, unusually smart in cream linen trousers and a maroon shirt, George orchestrated his assistants. They were drawing down the blinds to shut out the June evening, lighting up the hall, transforming it into a private theatre.

Here, there and everywhere strode Timothy, portly and resplendent in full evening dress, raising everyone's spirits. His eyes sparkled with good-will. His tongue was eloquent, his smile frequent. Seeing his Delia watching everything from the shadow of the wings, he came forward to voice his admiration of her beauty, and to kiss her pale jewelled fingers.

Hal and Alice were the first to arrive, and caused quite a commotion on the ticket table when they tried to pay. Both ladies refused their money outright in the name of the management, and playfully called upon Timothy to endorse this decision. Which he did: escorting the Brakespears with much ceremony to the reserved seats in the stalls, commanding two free programmes for them, and leaving them with a reverent little bow.

They sat together, pleased and smiling, and Alice began to look round and talk animatedly. From her observation post Imogen watched with a sharp sense of loss. She could not hear what Alice was saying, but her gestures and expression conveyed astonishment and delight. This was not surprising. The metamorphosis of the church hall was remarkable.

Then Alice, pointing out the backcloth, espied the spectator in the wings and stopped and stared. Hal, who had not been listening to his wife, was now alerted by her unexpected silence. He followed her stricken gaze, frowned, looked away again, and studied his programme assiduously. But Alice, as if drawn by an invisible thread, rose from her seat, walked forward to the very edge of the apron stage, and called Imogen's name. Reluctantly, the outcast came forth.

Delia's dress was Milia's triumph. It had been modelled on one worn by Queen Elizabeth I fifteen years before the play was originally performed – but who was to know that, apart from a costume expert? By the side of Doreen Yarwood's illustration had been written, '*White gown – embroidered sprig pattern in gold & colours – gold frog fastenings, centre front – green and gold embroidered mantle – white lining – lace-edged ruff at neck & wrists. Gold. Jewelled collar & head-dress – gloves – feather fan – pearl necklace.*' And with a minuscule budget and maximum imagination, enterprise and skill, Milia had concocted a dazzling imitation.

Alice saw with wonder, as Imogen approached, that while the illusion faded the brilliance of its creator increased. This sort of magic could only fill her with admiration. She fingered the modest stuff of Delia's dress almost in awe and paid a little flurry of compliments to Milia's ingenuity. She had meant only to be civil and to keep her distance, but looking up at Imogen's face she said what she felt rather than what she intended.

'How lovely you are, my dear.'

She spoke from the heart, and Imogen answered from hers.

'So are you, Alice.'

Neither of them said anything else.

Alice stood on tiptoe. Imogen bent down. Each touched the other's cheek with their lips, and then, like sleepwalkers, turned away.

Various important strangers were now being guided by Timothy to the reserved seats. He beamed and gleamed as he shook or kissed hands with each arrival or put a friendly arm round their shoulders. They all had an air of importance, and were well pleased with themselves and him. As soon as the greetings were over, the official photographer was pressed into service, and took a number of group and single photographs. Behind him hovered a self-conscious young man with a camera, and a self-confident, high-coloured young woman.

She now introduced herself and her associate to Timothy, who received them with polite affability, presented her to no one, delegated her to the third row of the stalls and bore the photographer away. Holed but unsinkable, Ms Bagshaw occupied herself by recognizing illustrious names and faces and writing them down in her notebook. And, sure enough, there was a sprinkling of newsmen from far bigger papers than the *Chronicle*, who all knew each other and were evidently hoping for the worst.

The trickle of people had become a flow. Neither worthiness of cause nor excellence of production could have fetched in so many. A fair number came out of interest in Timothy's work, devotion to Elizabethan scholarship, friendship or loyalty. But the majority had paid for their seats gladly and were now staring round greedily, because the newspapers said that Langesbydale was riddled with witchcraft, that a mysterious death and obscene practices had taken place, that the play had aroused fierce local controversy, and anything at all might happen. So, at considerable trouble and expense, they had taken buses and trains or driven themselves to Langesby, in the hope that they might be scared out of their wits with no harm to themselves.

By twenty-past seven all seats had been sold, and latecomers were buying tickets for the second performance.

'Are we all ready, Players?' Timothy asked.

Yes, they were ready, in their Elizabethan pomp and finery. Lines and moves learned. Hearts beating faster than usual. All eyes on their director.

'Dim the house lights.'

An expectant hush descended on the audience, who disappeared into an artificial twilight while the apron stage became as bright as day. A pause.

Timothy lifted one finger, and nine youngsters ran on to the boards, turned nine perfect somersaults, jumped up and bowed to the spectators. They wore black tights and jerseys. Made up as mimes, their eyes were the only living thing in a white mask of a face. They sat cross-legged round the sides of the stage and became motionless and expressionless.

A round of applause.

'Good!' Timothy said to himself, and gave a nod to the scene shifters.

The two men were also actors, and their huffing, puffing and muttering were all part of the effect. Carefully they placed their painted plywood trees on the marked squares, stared at each other, stared at the trees, said disbelievingly. 'This is the deep dark wood!' shrugged and marched off.

A ripple of amusement.

Timothy held up his finger for a requisite five seconds, then nodded to the three waiting comedians.

On ran Antic, Frolic and Fantastic, and stopped centre stage, laughing and pointing at the audience, amazed to see a hall full of people. Remembering their manners, they nudged each other, swept off their feathered hats and bowed low.

Then Antic said, swaggering forward, 'How now, fellow Frolic! What, all amort?'

And the play had begun.

Timothy was proud of his comic characters. Over the past months he had trained them to walk a tightrope between comedy and farce, until they could balance beautifully.

'With just a hint of the old music hall,' he had said. 'Involve your audience!'

So Clunch the blacksmith came to the front of the stage and faced the spectators, arms akimbo, saying, 'Hark! This is Ball, my dog, that bids you all welcome in his own language.'

Meanwhile the two scene shifters, silent and unobtrusive this time, had been creating Clunch's cottage. Behind him rose the arch of a doorway covered with paper roses. Beyond that a wooden table and chairs, plaster food, pewter mugs and wooden platters, and a painted plywood hearth and fire.

His wink at them, his kick at the invisible hound, had raised a laugh, but when he knocked on the arch and cried, 'Open door, Madge; take in guests!' a hum of interest ran through the house, followed by a sudden hush as she hobbled on with the aid of a stick.

For they had all heard about Mary Proctor, her strange practices and her great loss. And there was a spatter of sympathetic applause as they realized that her stick was a necessary aid.

Composedly, Mary waited until they were quiet before her forthright North Country voice reached every corner of the theatre.

'Welcome, Clunch, and good fellows all' – including the watchers with a hospitable gesture – 'Come on, sit down: here is a piece of cheese, and a pudding of my own making . . .'

As the play moved on, the ingenuity of direction and the professionalism of the players became apparent. An Elizabethan audience was expected to imagine a change of scene, but Timothy had brought in scenery and stage hands as part of the story. There were several: A Wood. Madge's cottage. The Cross. Sacrapant's study and dining hall. Sacrapant's cell. A Churchyard. The Well of Life. The Inn. The actors moved from one to the other and back again, and none of the scenes was long. Backstage, Sadie and

Milia stood ready with simple changes of costume for those who had to double up roles. So timing was crucial.

George's special effects were a tremendous success. The first Speaking Head was greeted with applause when it rose from the Well of Life. But when Zantippa broke her pitcher on it, and thunder and lightning leaped and crackled all over the auditorium, they fairly let themselves go.

In fact they had slipped into a music hall or pantomime mood from the beginning, responding openly and delightedly to the players. Haunebango, with his two-handed sword, was such a favourite that he received a round of applause whenever he came on.

'Tone it down just a little, my dears,' Timothy advised his company mildly. 'This is more than a joyful romp.'

His mainstay was Gammer Madge, who had been placed in a chair at the back of the stage, knobbed hands on knobbed stick. Aware that trouble could be brewing, she kept a sharp eye on the proceedings. And when Delia's first appearance was greeted by calls and wolf whistles from a young and boisterous quarter of the house, the old beldam rose from her chair, shook her stick, and cried, 'That's enough!'

The audience laughed. For a moment Imogen panicked, afraid that she could not recreate the mood, but was saved by those she most feared.

The chorus had shown talent from the outset. This evening they surpassed themselves. When Gammer Madge issued her unauthorized warning they turned their heads to the audience and put their hands over their mouths in horror.

Then Sacrapant held his arms wide, from which flowed the black silk sleeves painted with gold runes, and said in his most caressing tones, 'How now, fair Delia! Where have you been?'

So she drifted into what she called her Sacrapant-mode, answering him from her spell of enchantment. And the audience settled down to be enchanted by her.

Returning to the wings, hand in hand with her sorcerer, she whispered to the watchful Timothy, 'Weren't the chorus amazing?'

'Positively inspired!' Timothy answered, and gave Philip a long cool look.

'We've been rehearsing at home as well as here,' said the sorcerer defensively.

Timothy's eyes returned to the stage.

'That was not rehearsed,' he remarked. 'Ah! You're on again, my dear fellow!'

To Imogen he said almost absently, 'Oh yes. Something's afoot. But from what quarter will it come, one wonders?'

George's thunder and lightning once more made the audience cower and shriek, and then laugh at themselves. Silence fell as Sacrapant stood forth, the embodiment of evil, and his forefinger cast Delia's two brothers to the ground.

'Watch this, and you'll see what I mean,' said Timothy, without looking at Imogen.

The Furies, played by Deirdre and Jinny, their other costumes covered with black cloaks and hoods, ran shrieking on to the stage. Usually, the chorus hid their eyes and swayed in terror. But now they shrieked and grinned with the Furies and swayed in menace. The effect was electric, and at its centre stood Philip smiling; satanic and resplendent. A hush descended on the house.

'Now do you see him?' Timothy asked.

Gazing straight ahead, Imogen replied through stiff lips, 'You underestimate me. I have always known him.'

The Furies screamed back into the wings, dragging the bodies of Delia's brothers. Since the young women were not as strong as the young men, the stage hands ran out and helped them.

The moment passed. A prosaic sense of order and ordinariness prevailed. And on came Delia's handsome young lover, sighing for his mistress, to be followed a couple of speeches later by four comedians, all playing heavily for laughs.

The goose that had walked over Imogen's grave walked no longer.

The audience had loved Huanebango. Now they transferred their allegiance to the Ghost of Jack. His pallor and white costume were almost phosphorescent and it was evident to them that the man was a phantom. Yet everyone on stage persisted in dealing with him as with a living person, which was both annoying and intriguing.

'Can't you see he's a ghost?' yelled one lad from the auditorium.

Gammer Madge rose from her chair and lifted her stick, but before she could speak the audience chanted delightedly, 'That's enough!' and laughed at their own wit. The chorus once more turned their heads towards the offender, and placed their hands over their mouths in mock horror.

Liz Bagshaw had ceased to look for faults and was laughing and calling out with the rest of them. But Timothy's underlip lengthened and he drew a deep breath through his nostrils, and continued to watch the auditorium, the stage and the players.

The Well of Life was given an ovation. The Speaking Head with Ears of Corn and the second Head full of Gold gained a cheer apiece. The play built up to its climax, and Sacrapant's downfall was imminent.

The Ghost of Jack stuffed wool into the ears of Eumenides, Delia's lover, saying, '. . . you shall not be enticed with his enchanting speeches . . . and so, master, sit still, for I must to the conjurer.' Exit.

On stage, the lone figure of Eumenides sat as if made of stone. Beyond him, Gammer Madge seemed to have gone to sleep in her chair. The atmosphere was as brittle as glass. One sound, Imogen felt, and everything would splinter.

Timothy's expression was grim, but he was still in charge. He held Philip back in the wings for a few seconds to increase the tension, before giving him a smart tap on the shoulder.

Sacrapant whirled on like a dervish and confronted the audience, head high, arms outstretched, the gold runes shimmering and swirling on his sleeves and gown. There was a burst of applause. He smiled and signalled them to be silent. Then he lifted his sword and nodded to his minions.

At this point the chorus had been instructed to bow their heads and shield their eyes against the horror of the coming event. But now they sat up, and began to sway slowly from side to side, and to chant softly, monotonously, 'Sac-ra-pant! Sac-ra-pant! Sac-ra-pant!' as if he were a celebrity to be honoured.

The magician should have been seeing his doom, but he made no effort to continue with the part. He kissed the blade of the sword, held it high, stood like a general at the head of his regiment, and smiled.

Imogen crept close to Timothy and clutched his arm.

'He's missed that cue deliberately, damn him. Never mind. Go on now, Ghost of Jack!' Timothy whispered sharply.

But Jack stood in the wings as if transfixed. Around him other members of the cast were also immobilized.

The chant had turned to a long low humming: soporofic, bonding. The audience stared and listened, as entranced as the players.

'On, Jack!' Timothy commanded aloud.

Jack opened his mouth, and closed it. No one moved or spoke. Only Timothy remained in control, with Imogen, conscious of what was happening, holding on to the lifeline of his arm.

The arm stiffened, sensing danger, and suddenly Imogen saw Edith Wyse standing in the wings opposite. The pale green eyes flickered with malice, and Imogen closed hers, turned her head away and clung to Timothy.

He concentrated his powers like a beam of light. The woman opposite dissolved them in darkness. Again he poured out light, and again she consigned it to oblivion.

Under her breath Imogen was whispering a strange mixed litany of prayers, culled from years of seeking. Through her mind floated sacred symbols, talismans, amulets, charms, tags, quotations. She grabbed at each for safety, and lost it, grabbed again. Up floated *Nihil mali capiat me*. She made a mantra of it, while seeking something stronger, whispering over and over again, 'nihil mali capiat me, nihil mali capiat me.' She was in the midst of evil, suffocating in the terror of it. Beneath her fingers she could feel Timothy pouring out his strength, and a pinpoint of valour lit inside her. Instead of drawing courage from him she began to add her strength to his. She dared to loosen one hand and put it out to touch the person nearest to her.

It was Jinny in her role as Venelia. Imogen's fingers recognized the frizz of hair, slid to the motionless shoulder, travelled down the marble arm, gripped the stiff fingers and felt them move. The long slow awakening had begun. With infinite leisure, Jinny reached out to Deirdre. Deirdre found Sadie. Sadie reached Milia.

Daring still more, Imogen took Jinny's fingers and gave them her place on Timothy's arm. Keeping in touch with the chain of women she made her way to the far end of the stage, seized Milia and reached out to clasp Gammer Madge's cold knobbled hand.

'What?' Mary grunted, as if emerging from a catnap. 'Oh!' Comprehending.

She became one end of the chain and Timothy the other. Together they set their wills against Edith.

On stage, Sacrapant's stance wavered.

From the back of the hall came delicate sounds and movements. The doors swung softly out and fell to again. In the front row of the stalls Imogen could see Hal and Alice: she with her mouth slightly open, a puzzled little frown on her forehead, he labouring and gasping, like man coming to the surface after a deep plunge. But all the rest were mesmerized.

The resonant voice of the tenor bell struck Imogen painfully, swept through her body and limbs, possessed her. The command welled out musically, beautifully, reverberating, disappearing into a blissful nothing. And then again. Boom. The deep sweet note of C sharp rang out, welled forth, and was restated. Over and over again. Dong. Dong. Dong. Thirty-seven hundredweight of Great Isaac, and the strong brown hands of George, were tearing through the invisible web spun by Edith and Philip.

Dong. The actors drew breath and stirred.

Dong. Hal rose in his seat: a prophet about to come to judgement.

Dong. The chain of hands gave each other a little squeeze, and slipped away.

Dong. Edith had gone, and Sacrapant's sword arm fell to his side.

Dong. The chorus, obeying a different authority, bent their heads and shielded their eyes because Timothy had said so. Sacrapant was doomed.

Dong. Timothy said, in his dry way, 'Clunch! Run over to the bell tower, will you, like a good fellow, and tell George that's enough. Oh – and give him my compliments and thanks.'

Amusement was rippling through the audience. They were making faces at the noise, putting their hands over their ears, laughing.

Dong. Alice tugged Hal's sleeve and he sat down again, for once embarrassed.

Dong. The last sound travelled out into infinity. Do-o-o-on-n-n-g-g-g.

They all listened, and listened. But it had gone.

Imogen thought: And there was silence in heaven for the space of half an hour.

The silence was not to be so long.

Timothy drew a deep breath and signalled the prompter, who, finding herself needed for the first time, fairly hissed at Philip. 'How now! What man art thou?'

From a personal abyss, Sacrapant delivered his lines in a hoarse deep voice that riveted the audience.

'. . . Then Sacrapant, thou art betrayed.'

Timothy said, unmoved. 'You're on, Ghost of Jack.'

As the wreath was torn from Sacrapant's head, and the sword wrested from his hand, the sorcerer delivered his own epitaph.

'He in whose life his acts have been so foul, now in his death to hell descends his soul.'

He became a pool of black and gold silk, spreadeagled on the floor of the stage, and the chorus moaned softly, and huddled over their knees, arms outstretched, as Timothy had told them.

'Excellent,' he murmured, as if nothing had happened.

While Delia's lover was digging at the foot of a green plywood hill with a silver plywood spade to find the magician's light, the scene shifters wheeled on a curtained recess, and Imogen slipped in behind it, waiting to be discovered.

She sat at peace, eyes closed, hands placed palm upwards in her lap.

She heard Eumenides wind his horn to summon the madwoman. She heard a faint tinkle as Venelia broke the magic glass, and a murmur of 'A-a-ah!' from the audience as Sacrapant's light, the source of his power, was extinguished.

The Ghost of Jack was saying, '. . . and now, master, to the lady that you have so long looked for.'

He drew the curtain aside, and Imogen, opening her eyes, saw Fred.

Her lips moved soundlessly over his name.

He gave her a wink and a nod, as if to say, 'All's well!' and became the Ghost of Jack again.

She stretched out her hands to bring him back, and they were clasped by her stage lover. Imogen stared at him like a sleepwalker, rudely awakened.

'God speed, fair maid, sitting alone – there is once!' Eumenides cried.

She remained dazed.

'God speed, fair maid – there is twice!' A little louder.

Feeling she was overdoing her response, he cried loudest of all, 'God speed, fair maid – that is thrice!' and emphasized the *thrice*.

The prompter opened her mouth in readiness for a second crisis, but Imogen had made the crossing and was Delia once again.

She smiled most beautifully, saying, 'Not so, good sir, for you are by.'

It was all over. Gammer Madge gave her final speech, though she needed assistance to get out of her chair, and the unobtrusive support of Frolic and Fantastic, with a hand beneath each elbow. They continued to support her as the company took their bows.

Timothy had arranged for all the ladies to receive Elizabethan-style nosegays, but Imogen was also given twelve flame-red roses from George, and several home-grown bouquets with messages from esoteric gentlemen who hoped to make a closer acquaintance. There was even a bunch of drooping wild flowers wrapped in an old copy of the *Chronicle* and signed 'Jack o' the Dale.' At which, fraught by the tensions and emotions of the performance, she could have laughed and cried together.

The acclaim was all that the company could have wished. The audience demanded three curtain calls and gave personal ovations to their favourite characters and to the chorus. Gammer Madge had to be reinstated in her chair at one point, and this gained a particularly warm round of clapping and affectionate shouts of 'That's enough!'

But it seemed that nothing was enough for them. They wanted to see and thank everyone. Timothy was brought on first, beaming and bowing, and extending his hand to include George. They clapped George heartily, though they did not really know who he was nor what he had achieved,

351

but no one minded. They called for the Talking Heads, which were brought on by their creator, Beth Lawler. Even Hal and Alice were fetched from the stalls and lauded. Last of all the ticket and programme sellers and the refreshment ladies trooped on, and squeezed into the throng.

As George said to Timothy, 'It's a good thing we built this apron stage. We'd never have got everyone on the other!'

Throughout the long acclamation, Philip, as white and exhausted as Mary, behaved with perfect precision, rather like a clockwork doll that had been wound up. And stopped quite suddenly when it was over, sitting apart from the rest of the company with his head in his hands.

Of Edith there was nothing to be seen.

'Exceptionally well done, Players!' Timothy cried, as the hall emptied and the doors were closed. 'Now we have exactly half an hour before the second performance. So I advise you all to rest and relax as best you can.'

He too was pale and tired, shaken with emotion and effort, but he walked over to Philip and stood looking down on him. The look was steely, the manner light and affable.

'You must be exhausted, my dear fellow, after that astonishing performance. Do you feel fit enough to carry on?'

Philip lifted his head in some surprise.

'Oh yes. Certainly. In any event,' and something of his old friendly mockery returned, 'you'd be hard pressed if I said no, wouldn't you?'

'I should be extremely *sorry*,' said Timothy, smiling, 'but since the scare with Gammer Madge I have made quite sure of having understudies for the major roles.'

Philip's mockery faded. He looked old. He sounded wooden.

'Do I understand that you have an understudy for *my* part?'

'Oh yes. I can at a pinch supply another chorus,' Timothy lied.

He added with deliberate playfulness, 'And we, too, have been rehearsing at home.'

FORTY

There could never again be a performance as strange and marvellous as the first, but Peele's Players' reputation was made by it, and would rest upon it ever after. A long queue had formed outside the church hall for the second show. Again people had to be turned away, and tickets were now being sold for evenings in the following week. In various local pubs, reporters from the *Chronicle* and more illustrious or notorious newspapers were discussing the experience and would later be in the throes of hyperbole as they described it.

At the other end of the town Langesby Dramatic Society was acting its heart out to a row of civic dignitaries and a half-empty theatre.

The final curtain call had been taken, the last members of the audience were trooping out, the kitchen was being tidied up and the ticket table cleared, when Timothy came backstage and clapped his hands for silence.

'A word with you, Players. I know that the hour is late and you must be exhausted after your labours, but we can all lie long abed tomorrow.'

George and Imogen clasped their hands in a silent promise to each other to share that bed.

'I know there was talk of our having a convivial noggin this evening at the Ram's Head, but when I mentioned this to my housekeeper she became very fierce indeed, and informed me that this was no way to celebrate a great occasion.'

He beamed round as they laughed.

'She was, as always, quite right. So I am inviting you all to the Mount for some rather good wine and a cold collation – in the preparation of which, I do assure you, Mrs Housman has surpassed herself.'

They all conveyed surprise and delight at his announcement, though rumours of this reception had been circulating for the past week, and everyone had brought festive clothes for the event.

Mary Proctor spoke up, white and weary.

'I shan't come a-partying, Dr Rowley, if you'll excuse me. Thanking you just the same. I'll be best off at home – if Sadie will kindly take me back.'

Timothy bowed over her hand and kissed it, voicing his regret.

With a shadow of his former assurance, Philip said, 'Sad though it is, I'm afraid you must count us out too. I think these youngsters have had enough excitement for one evening, and I promised Mrs Slater we'd be home before eleven.'

Timothy purred, 'We shall miss you, but we do understand.'

The rest of the company hastened to change from costumes to gala dress, and to crowd into the cars lined along Church Street.

George said to Imogen, 'I'll join you later. I'm going along with Sadie. I'm a bit worried about Mary. I want to make sure that she's all right.'

Timothy was beside them, twinkling on both.

'Then I shall take care of this lovely lady in your absence.'

George said drily, 'Yes, you do that, Tim.'

A remark that was not lost on Timothy, though he remained unruffled.

Peele's Players' previous meal had been a rapid snack, and they did Mrs Housam's banquet justice. Timothy moved among them, full of hospitable persuasion. And over them all presided the portrait of his mother in her prime. She twisted her long pale rope of pearls in long pale fingers, and looked down on her son's triumph with enigmatic eyes.

Imogen was in her element. Glass in hand, she wandered from group to group, smiling, talking, listening to the mood of the party. She was happy again, secure again, in love. The phantoms of the night had receded. Edith had been sent away; Philip subjugated. All would be well. Meanwhile she could eat, drink and rejoice in peace. As if to set the seal on that moment, Alice and Hal walked in smiling from the summer night, holding out their arms to embrace her, and behind them came George, with thoughts for no one but herself.

'Alice, sparkling wine for you, to match the sparkle in your eyes!' Timothy cried. 'Hal, you would rather have whisky, wouldn't you?'

He poured a generous measure into a cut-glass tumbler.

'Rather a promising start, don't you think? The reviews should be satisfactory. And if the local and county papers give us their blessing, and the nationals spread the word, we should be able to repay your loan and the interest, and have enough left over for a bottle of beer – which we shall give to George' – patting him on the back.

'George, you would prefer beer to wine, would you not? Yes, I thought so. I laid in a rather special local steam beer for you. Help yourself, my friend.'

'All this and a new peal of bells,' cried Alice, turning to her husband, laughing. She meant: we shall stay here after all. There won't be any trouble after all.

She addressed her host:

'What a pity that Philip couldn't come. We thought he was quite amazing – but so was the chorus. It must have taken hours to train them. Goodness, how hard you have all worked.'

'Oh, Philip thought – quite rightly in my opinion – that his youngsters needed a good night's sleep after their exertions,' Timothy answered smoothly.

Alice sighed. 'He's totally absorbed in those unfortunate young people. Perhaps a little too much so, I think, at times.'

'I think you may well be right,' Relishing his irony.

'And we should have liked to congratulate Mary, too. Wasn't she wonderful? So full of homely wisdom and humour – though we thought she looked very frail and tired at the end.'

'Mary's as tough as her ash stick!' Timothy reassured her. There was a subdued radiance about him, as of a man fulfilled.

'Dear Mary,' said Alice. 'I must visit her soon. And now for a word with my darling Imogen – oh, didn't she make a lovely heroine? Do you know, I positively shed a tear or two when she woke up and looked round so sweetly and sadly. Just as if she had seen a vision and couldn't tear herself away from it. So talented. Imogen dear, Imogen, I was just saying . . .'

'This is absolutely fascinating,' Imogen whispered, meeting up with Timothy at the buffet table. 'Hal and Alice don't know what happened.'

He fixed her with his bland, affable gaze.

'Why?' he asked gently. 'What did happen?'

'You know! When the play stopped and we formed a ring of power against Edith. Oh, I haven't been obvious about it, but I sort of hinted about the lapse in time, expecting a response, and I didn't get one. Was everyone mesmerized?'

'My dear Imogen,' said Timothy in his most avuncular tones, 'I believe I have had reason in the past to comment on a certain charming romanticism in you. There was indeed a slight hitch in the proceedings when Philip forgot to give his cue to the Ghost of Jack. Fortunately our prompter was on the ball and I don't think anyone noticed.'

She stared at him incredulously, and he smiled back.

'What about the bell-ringing?' Imogen asked mutinously.

'An imaginative gesture on George's part – who would have thought it of him?'

She opened her mouth to argue, and closed it.

'Are you sure you wouldn't like some more wine?' Timothy asked, in a tone so benevolent that it hinted she had drunk enough already.

'Yes, I would, please,' said Imogen, stubborn to the last.

Smiling still, he filled her glass, but as she was about to walk away, stiff with displeasure, he put one hand on her arm to detain her. He spoke in confidence.

'I don't mean to hurt or estrange you, my dear, so I will put it more plainly. This is not a subject for casual conversation, and the business is not yet over. So keep that frivolous tongue of yours in check.'

Imogen lowered her voice in response to his.

'But you won. Edith's gone.'

'I won, as you put it, a major battle, but the war is not yet over. She has simply retired for the moment to plan a final confrontation.' As Imogen's face reflected her dismay, he said. 'Her concern is with me, not with you and the others, and I shall be ready for her. Besides' – in a kindly tone – 'you have your protector. George is a man of great strength and natural wisdom. Now, do you feel better? Or are you still cross with me?'

Imogen leaned forward and planted a smiling kiss on his cheek.

'What a witch you are,' Timothy said. 'Be off with you, and enjoy the party!'

Hal's congratulations to George began with an accusation.

'You didn't tell *me* you were going to toll the tenor bell!'

'It was a last-minute decision,' said George mildly, smiling into his steam beer. 'I hadn't time to ask you, I'm afraid. But I shan't do it again. It was an idea that would only work once.'

FORTY-ONE

There is magic in a theatre at night. The silence holds remembrance of applause. One performance has ended, but another is about to begin. The seats are ready for the next audience. The empty stage awaits its actors.

While Imogen and George drowsed in rapture, and Peele's Players dreamed on their laurels, and Langesby Dramatic Society salved its wounds in sleep, the enemy launched its final offensive. And nine fire-makers, clad in black wool caps, jerseys and tights, flitted noiselessly forth to change the course of many lives.

This was not the first time that they had entered a building at night to play malignant games; not the first time their mentors had planned a campaign, instructed and coached them, driven them there and brought them safely home again. The element of danger and discovery heightened their exhilaration. The thought of entertainments afterwards, pleasurable or otherwise, aroused the depths of their imagination, but even more titillating was the thrill of wreaking havoc. In desecration and violence they could avenge a young lifetime of resentment against all forms of authority, including those who at present imprisoned them.

In her dream Imogen climbed upwards, from branch to branch of the Tree of Life, to escape Edith who was trying to burn it down. Smoke rose to suffocate her. The air was hot, and thick with fumes. Her eyes smarted and she could neither see nor breathe properly. A red-gold light flickered through the leaves, and she heard the dull roar of the fire eating its way towards her, the crack and spit of burning wood, the crash of falling branches.

Imogen woke up screaming, 'Fire! Fire! Fire!' and George was holding her and saying, 'It's all right. It's all right. It's all right.'

She rested against him for a minute or so, while the sights and sounds and smells receded.

'You were having a bad dream,' said George, comforting her.

But Imogen pulled away from him and scrambled out of bed.

'No. Oh no. That was a real dream. The Tree was burning down. It means that something's wrong. We must get up and find out. We must drive all along the dale and make sure that everyone and everything is all right.'

'You're not serious!'

'Please, oh please, George.'

'It's ten-past two in the morning, Imogen.'

She turned a pale relentless face on him.

'I dreamed true,' she insisted. 'I dreamed true. I shall go on foot if I have to.'

He shrugged his shoulders, and reached for his trousers, muttering to himself. 'And who am I to argue? The son of a witch!'

Imogen was dressing rapidly, distractedly, saying, 'Where have I put my shoulder bag? I've got everything in that shoulder bag. I'd survive in the Gobi desert with that shoulder bag . . .'

And George said, 'Keys. Keys. Best take all my keys. You never know.'

In the Catwalk and through Haraldstone everyone slept on undisturbed, and the dale was peaceful, dark and hushed as they sped along the road to Langesby. Though Imogen could still feel the resonance of an inner alarm, she began to be assailed by doubts, and she knew that George was humouring rather than believing in her. Then, as if in affirmation, the kitchen window lit up at Howgill.

She tapped his shoulder and called in his ear, 'Mary's awake.' And lest he be concerned, she added with a new authority, 'No, don't stop. She's not ill. It means that she knows, too, George.'

Now they were both certain.

'Right!' he said, and rode on.

The Mount was in darkness, though Timothy could have been keeping a dimmed vigil on his own account. But as they passed the gates of Prospect House Imogen glimpsed bright windows.

'They're awake and up to something.'

He nodded. They were both thinking of Stephen crowned with ivy leaves.

The centre of Langesby was empty and silent, but as they turned the corner into Church Street Imogen saw that a light shone into the back garden of Edith's elegant house, and Philip's minibus was parked in Mrs

Horsefield's lane. Yet everything else seemed as usual. The school stood four square in its playground and St Oswald's reared up, black and dignified. Then George came to a slithering halt in front of the lych-gate and pointed down the lane. The church hall had lost its bleak grey air and behind its windows flickered a roseate glow.

'Bloody hell!' said George, and went into action.

'You phone the fire brigade, the Brakespears and Tim Rowley. I'll ring Isaac. And let's be sharp about it!'

Oh God, oh God! (Why am I bothering God again?) Hurry up, hurry up! Imogen prayed, as she stamped her feet impatiently, and spelled out details to an operator with a composed voice and a taste for precision.

'Yes, Church Street. The church hall. And please hurry!'

She sorted out her small change and dialled the vicarage.

'Is that you, Hal? This is Imogen . . .'

So what's happened to George? she wondered, as the great bell remained silent.

As he ran round to the vestry door two figures in black flitted swiftly past him. He was not fast enough for one, but brought the other down in a flying tackle.

'Now then,' George cried, forcing a face to the gravel and an arm behind its back, 'who are you, and what are you up to?'

He pulled off the black wool cap and was given his answer. The face turned round and spat at him.

'So it's one of you lot, you murderous little buggers!' George said between his teeth, and fought down the murder in himself. At that moment he could have broken the boy's neck and enjoyed doing it.

'Get up!' he said savagely.

The youngster came up snarling and George shook him in a frenzy of rage, because he needed to do three things at once: to hold the fire-maker, to put out any fire he had started, and to sound the alarm. He made up his mind.

'March!' he said, and pushed his captive forward into the church.

A pile of soaked rags lay along the base of the carved rood-screen, and the fire was beginning its meal with relish. George assessed the situation.

That'll keep for a bit, he decided.

For this was not a shabby old tinderbox of a church hall but solid wood and stone which would take a while to consume.

Anyway, it better had, he thought, less confident.

In the tower room, he swung the lad round and gave him a deep, hard punch in the stomach, and an uppercut to the jaw.

'And you'll keep for a bit, too,' he remarked with some satisfaction, rubbing his knuckles.

He pushed the unconscious body under the wooden seat against the wall, and laid hold of Isaac's rope.

Imogen dialled Timothy Rowley's number and waited, drumming her fingers. St Oswald's clock chimed four quarters and three ominous notes. In the mirror of the telephone kiosk she saw a faint blush behind the stained-glass windows.

At that moment Great Isaac began to toll a sonorous alarm.

Within minutes every sash window but one was thrown up, and residents ran out in their night-clothes. Less than a hundred yards away, as if on cue, the hall windows burst open and spewed forth flames, causing shrieks, exclamations of horror and a jumble of orders.

'Phone 999. Water! Someone fetch water. No, don't go near it. It's dangerous. Look at the way it's blazing up. Has anyone called the fire brigade?'

'Yes, I have,' Imogen cried at the top of her voice, tumbling out of the kiosk. 'I have. And I think the church is on fire too, and George is up in the bell tower . . .'

They neither heard nor listened, though several ran back in again to jam the local switchboard with emergency calls. Others, preoccupied by the inferno down the lane, were already staggering out with brimming buckets.

But there is usually a retired military officer living in these quiet residential backwaters, and Imogen recognized the stance of one, even in his dressing-gown. Unlike the rest, he had realized that the hall was beyond their power to control, and was considering what to do. She ran to him and tugged his sleeve.

'Please listen. I have rung the fire brigade. But there's more than one fire. I think they've just set light to the church, too. Look! And my friend George is trapped in there, tolling the bell.'

The colonel saw possibilities in this second conflagration. 'Leave it to me, my dear,' he said magnificently.

Then he stood forth and gave voice, forbidding anyone but his wife to ring 999 until it answered, forming an orderly line of water-bearers, and commanding two men to break the church door down with axes.

'Oh no, stop!' Imogen cried, running after them. 'The vestry door will be open.'

But they had already done some damage before she could make them listen, what with the resonant notes of Great Isaac and the street full of fear and noise.

'It's those damned witches, I'll be bound. I say burn and hang every one of them!' the colonel was shouting.

The mood of the crowd was with him, and news of the fire was spreading as rapidly as the flames.

Up Church Lane strode Hal Brakespear, wearing a tracksuit over his pyjamas. On either side of him strode his two sons, similarly clothed, and as grim-faced as their father. Behind them hurried a distracted Alice, pulling a weatherbeaten raincoat over her nightgown and calling to her husband and sons, 'Hal, Julian, Matthew, wait for me!' and varying this with, 'Hal, do be careful!' But they pretended not to hear. So, having no more breath left to prevail upon them, she attempted to quicken her pace and button the coat at the same time.

Alerted, Timothy bustled forth from the Mount, followed by his house-keeper. Even in the direst situation his courtesy did not fail him. From behind the wheel of his limousine he issued polite requests.

'Forgive me for robbing you of your sleep, Mrs Housam, particularly after your recent and most deeply appreciated exertions, but would you be kind enough to stay up and keep an eye on the premises until my return? Lock all the doors and windows, and if you see or hear anything unusual ring the police. But first and foremost take care of yourself. Your life is more valuable than bricks and mortar.'

Having seen him drive off, she set a tray of refreshments ready for his homecoming before making herself a pot of tea. Then she sat up in her padded dressing-gown, neat grey pigtail hanging down her back, waiting and watching.

In the bell tower, George stopped tolling, and rested, and drew breath. He was at peace with himself again. He touched the arsonist with the toe of his trainer and felt him stir; walked over to the glass partition and looked down into the body of the church. While the blaze of the hall lit up the sky round Langesby, its citizens were busy dousing St Oswald's eighteenth-century rood-screen and everything around it, treading mud and water into the carpet on the aisle, and doing more damage than the fire, until three fire engines clanged into Church Street, and turned the place into a muddle of rubber hosepipes. They were followed almost immediately by two flashing police cars. And now buckets were replaced by powerful jets, and policemen were asking questions.

George could see but not hear what they were saying. A military gentleman in a Jaeger dressing-gown acted as spokesman for the residents. And pushing her way through the throng came Imogen. She was pointing to the tower room, speaking volubly. He saw the shape of his name on her lips, watched the movements of her mouth with love. His joy, as he heard her coming up the stairs, was supreme.

At Howgill, Mary had woken on Imogen's scream, but the house was silent and tranquil. Since her illness George had brought her bed down to the sitting room, so that she could live on one level. Slowly she sat up and listened, eyes closed. Flames leaped and fluttered like banners from place to place. Wood crackled, roared, fell into ash. Heat seared and overpowered. Water soared and steamed.

'It's near the end,' said Mary. 'I must make ready.'

She lit a candle and reached for her grey wool shawl, wrapped herself in it, sat on the side of the bed and looked all round the room she had known for over half a century. The broad hearth was swept clean, and a tall stonewear jug full of dried flowers stood in the empty fire-basket. The furniture had been built to withstand generations of children, and every picture, rug and cushion represented some mood, event or portion of time in her life.

She reached for her ash stick, and limped into the kitchen. She could hear the faint but unmistakable sound of the Harley-Davidson in the distance.

'I must let her know I'm awake,' Mary said aloud, and switched on the light.

George's motorbike roared past.

'It's their job now,' she said. 'I've done mine.'

There was still a little fire in the grate. She raked and fed it skilfully, put the kettle on to boil, sat in her chair rocking, to and fro. The cat had produced another litter of kittens the previous month, and slept curled round four miniature versions of herself and the black tom from the Hill Farmhouse. Mary looked lovingly at them, and again at all the familiar objects of her daily life.

'In a minute,' she said, 'I'll put the box of papers out for George, and then he'll know where to find everything.'

★   ★   ★

'Ah, my dear Imogen,' Timothy said, as she hugged him, in sympathy. 'How good of you to find me.'

He was standing at the front of the crowd, watching a dream die. In his beige polo-necked sweater and cinnamon checked trousers he looked like a grieving Tweedledum.

'Heartbreaking, heartbreaking,' he said, and his voice was full. 'What a cruel end to such a fine beginning!'

'Does this finish us?' she asked quietly.

'Yes. Oh yes.' A long-drawn sigh. 'Hal, of course, will not admit defeat, and has suggested that Peele's Players perform in a borrowed marquee on the vicarage lawn or a travelling wagon round the town. One must set such nonsense down to his state of shock. As I told him, there is simply no way that we can carry on. This was never intended to be an outdoor production, and all our props are burned to a cinder. Costumes, scenery, the wonderful Talking Heads that were so much admired. When one considers the time, care and skill that went into every aspect of the play, the sheer dedication of everyone concerned . . .'

Imogen kissed his cheek, and said, 'There is one good item of news. I came to tell you that George caught one of Philip's little mob in the act, and handed him over to the police. And we can give evidence that Philip's minibus was parked in Horsefield's lane. So they can piece the story together.'

Timothy roused himself.

'Given time, and the material I shall put at their disposal, yes. Meanwhile there are two devils and eight imps on the loose, with precious little to lose.'

He sighed again.

'Well, well. There is nothing any of us can do here, apart from mourn our loss – and that, at the present time, would be pure self-indulgence. I think we should leave the good Brakespears to come to terms with their personal disaster, and go home to safeguard our own premises.'

'I've been talking to Hal and Alice. This will be hard on them,' Imogen said.

'Yes, indeed. As well as incurring displeasure in certain quarters, Hal will be left with a debt that he cannot honour, a damaged church, and a ruined hall. I fear it will be end of him in Langesby. A great pity. A great man.'

Brows furrowed, he roved a mental landscape.

'There will be much to do. I must compose a notice to be printed in all the local papers, and telephone members of the cast to spread the sad tidings. One hesitates to burden Alice with the task of informing helpers that their services will no longer be required, and yet the work will keep her mind off her troubles. And I must hold a committee meeting tomorrow evening at the Mount, to discuss how we return money for tickets that have been sold – and so on and so forth. Eight o'clock might be a convenient time for everyone, don't you think . . .'

He turned to Imogen. His tone changed. His expression became gentle.

'Have I ever told you, my dear, that you remind me very much of a girl I used to know at Cambridge, many years ago? She played the part of Delia in my student production of *The Old Wives' Tale*. The play, of course, was not the achievement of last night, which had nearly half a century of experience behind it, but it was a commendable effort and I had hoped for much from it. More, evidently, than I had a right to hope. Ah, well. That is old history.'

He was silent for so long, musing, that Imogen asked softly, 'What happened?'

He spoke in a dry, matter-of-fact tone.

'The lady married her Sacrapant, my dear. He was a great charmer, but did not, I fear, make her happy.'

He returned to the present, became brisk and businesslike.

'Take my advice, Imogen. Find that young man of yours and go home.'

FORTY-TWO

Shadows in the Catwalk stirred and came to life. The crash of glass woke Tarquin, who lifted his head, listened and sniffed the air. His ears pricked up. The tip of his tail quivered as he tuned in to disaster. A second crash, close to home, brought him in one leap from chair to floor. His lips drew away from his teeth. He backed off hissing. Then took the stairs in leaps to scrabble and howl at Sadie's bedroom door.

Flames made glittering reflections in the Silver Shop.

In the window of Crafty Notions the summer bridal throw became a sheet of gold.

In Crazy Hats, half a dozen flowery creations blazed on silver stems.

The *pâtisserie* was guiltless of witchcraft, but had rented work-space to Milia Godden on the first floor, so shared her fate.

Back to Nature and Jon and Deirdre were alight.

The fire-makers' list was short and they worked their way rapidly and efficiently through it in couples. One smashed the window, the other lobbed a home-made bottle bomb into the premises of known witches, or their accomplices, and Crossdyke Street Chapel received its share. Luck and skill and speed all played a part in this magnificent game, and the victims were scarcely awake by the time their attackers had gone. Then luck ran out at Beth Lawler's cottage on the far edge of the village.

The two artists were advocates of simple living, and their lack of electricity was a source of pride rather than inconvenience. Nor did they ever lock their doors, for they had nothing with which to tempt modern burglars. So Frank Hedges, suffering from insomnia, had come downstairs to make himself a mug of cocoa, and was about to light a candle when two black figures flitted into the yard. A burly man, he was nevertheless quick and light on his feet, and he ran outside even as they launched an attack on the scullery window, and banged their heads together before they could turn round. Then he bawled for Beth, who bound them up in various lengths of ethnic material, while he smothered the fire.

The rest ran to the minibus which was waiting in a farm lane. None of them knew what had happened to the others, but the village was now astir and they could not afford to wait for stragglers. So they drove off into the open country, leaving Haraldstone to burn.

Dawn was breaking as George and Imogen rode home, keeping watch all the way. At Prospect House Imogen caught a glimpse of the minibus in the driveway, and called in George's ear, 'They're back!' He nodded.

The Mount looked as usual, though their glances were perfunctory because Timothy would take care of his own property. But at Howgill George slowed to a stop. A thin trickle of smoke from Mary's chimney, and a light in the kitchen window, suggested that all was well, but he was uneasy.

'I wish I could be in two places at once,' he said.

'Well, you can't, but if there's any trouble at Haraldstone you're the one to deal with it, so drop me off here and I'll stay with Mary. You can come back for me as soon as you know that everything's all right.'

He hesitated, disliking the idea, so Imogen made up his mind for him, dismounted and gave him a kiss.

'Off you go!' she said. 'And, George – make sure that Polly's safe.'

Then she walked down the lane to tell Mary the news.

The blush of early morning concealed the blush of fire, but George could smell the smoke and hear the noise of crisis as he reached the crossroads, and he fairly roared up the main street in his anxiety.

Haraldstone had risen to the occasion. Its residents might not themselves be witches but most could claim, or volubly disclaim, a witch in their ancestry. Besides, Langesby and the world tended to lump them all together, so they stuck together. They might not be many, but the community spirit was strong. When Sadie ran into the middle of the Catwalk in her Indian cotton sari and screeched aloud for help she did not lack it. Mario was first on the scene but not the last. By the time George arrived the whole village was out with hosepipes, sand and buckets, all but one of the fires had been contained, and they were damping everything down.

'Oh, my God!' he groaned, at the crazy remains dripping on charred stems, the sodden green velvet ground and trodden *fantasies*. 'Imogen will go spare! What's happened to Polly?'

'She shot out when we were hosing the shop-front down and I haven't seen her since,' said Sadie. 'All the cats have disappeared, including Tarquin. And you've got more to worry about than Polly. The chapel's well alight, and they can't get it under control, but the fire brigade should be here any minute now.' She shrieked after him, 'Your van's safe. Jack Helme and Bill Hunwick broke into it and released the handbrake, and rolled it into Crossdyke Lane . . .'

The flames licking round the last and finest of Fred's toys had disturbed the mechanism of *Mr Rumbleton's Residence*, and like some latter-day Beau Geste the owner was making a final stand: bobbing up at each window of his house in turn, firing on the enemy.

FORTY-THREE

'I've been keeping watch for you,' Mary said.

She was sitting back in her chair, which had ceased to rock, colourless to the lips. At intervals through the night she had completed certain tasks which she deemed to be necessary. She was fully dressed in her Sunday clothes, even to the mirror-polished shoes. On the kitchen table a tray was stacked high with her best tea set. Six of everything, flowery, gilt-rimmed, complete with jugs, sugar bowl, slop bowl and teapot, only seen so far through the window of a corner cupboard. Beside it stood a cardboard shoe-box and a pile of school exercise books tied with a faded chocolate box ribbon.

'I brewed the tea a while back.' Mary said. 'It might have gone cold.'

Imogen noted the lax hands and waxen skin, and in her growing wisdom knew that she must make no comment, but act as if everything was normal.

So she said lightly, 'George sends his love and he'll be along soon.'

'It's not over yet,' Mary said.

Imogen made an imaginative leap.

'No,' she replied. 'That's why he couldn't come in with me. Do you want to know what's happened so far?'

'It's not necessary,' said Mary, 'and I'm a bit on the tired side.'

Imogen felt the teapot, which was barely warm, and emptied it. She raked the fire and mended it, filled the kettle and set it on one side of the hob.

'There's no time for that,' said Mary. She pointed to the chair opposite. 'Sit there and listen to me.'

She dozed off for a few minutes. When she spoke again she picked up an idle, conversational thread.

'My mother bought me that teaset from the auctioneer at Langesby Market, just before the second world war. It started off at two guineas, and he knocked it down to thirty shillings. That was a lot of money then. You could fetch a family up on thirty shillings a week.' She paused. 'I never let the children touch it, and there's a not a piece chipped or broken. It must be worth a bonny penny now. When you and George get married I'll give it to you as a wedding present!'

Her attention wandered to the hearth, where the kittens had woken and were busy suckling, their spindles of tails trembling in ecstasy.

'The cat needs three drops of cod–liver oil in a teaspoon of milk once a day until they're weaned. Find them good homes, but don't part with that black one and don't have him castrated. He's the best of the litter. He'll make a fine tomcat. I thought you and George might like him.'

And how would Polly take that? Imogen wondered, but did not demur.

'In the box on the table,' Mary continued, 'are all my papers, set in order. They're for George. I've left everything to George. You'll both need a home to live in and you'll find a good one here. If the others come making a fuss you can tell them it's all legal and witnessed, and send them about their business.'

She looked all round the room and traced a pattern on the arm of the rocking chair with her fingers.

'It's a grand house, is Howgill. My father bought it for me when I married Dick Proctor, and did it up. I had one of the first bathrooms in the dale. Father was always one to speak his mind. Like me. When he handed me the deeds he said, "These are in your name, Mary, and keep them that way. You'll need a good house, because Dick won't make a good husband."'

She paused and nodded.

'And he was right,' she said, and traced another pattern.

She began again.

'Those notebooks are for you. They're the work of a lifetime. Recipes for brews and tinctures, oils and salves. Healing. Some rituals. Simple magic. You can tell George I've given the notebooks to you, but don't talk about them or show them to anyone. Keep them hidden, and keep them to yourself.'

She seemed to doze again for a while, then her eyes opened green and wide, her voice grew stronger.

'That scorpion shouldn't call up fire,' she cried vehemently. 'She can only sting herself to death.'

She glared at Imogen.

'Mind that *you* never call up powers that you can't control. Remember you're the servant, not the master. Harm no one!'

Her voice and expression softened.

'You'll be all right,' said Mary graciously. 'You've got a lot to learn, but you have the gift. Given time, you'll take my place in the dale. I didn't get this far in five minutes, you know. It took years. You might go further yet, and study high magic with Dr Rowley. He's more than he seems. Do you understand me?'

Imogen said, 'Yes. I understand you.'

Mary nodded. Her face changed.

'I should have liked to see George,' she said, 'but I'm grateful for what I've had.' Then she smiled across at Imogen and said, 'Come and sit by me, love.' And closed her eyes.

They sat together tranquilly, Imogen's warm young hand over Mary's cold one, until the sun rose on another lovely summer day. And she wished she could have shared Fred's death in this way, setting the past in order, making good the present, providing for the future. But his bright spirit had been snuffed out in an instant on a rainy day, because he was inventing a new toy and crossed the London street without looking.

FORTY-FOUR

Mysterious Fire Destroys Church Hall

In the early hours of Sunday morning, after a performance of *The Old Wives' Tale* that will long be remembered, St Oswald's church hall in Langesby was burned to the ground and the church itself suffered minor damage. Other fires were started in the dale and the police arrested three suspects. They are now conducting a wider investigation into this and other incidents, which they feel might be related. At the moment they are not divulging names, but the Chief Constable said that this had nothing to do with so-called witches, and that a lot of harm had been caused by malicious gossip.

There will be a great deal of sympathy for Dr Timothy Rowley and his talented company, known as 'Peele's Players', who have been forced to abandon the play. 'We have lost everything!' Dr Rowley said. 'There is simply no way of carrying on.' Tickets had already been sold for performances during the Festival Week, and these will be returned on application to the address below.

Proceeds from the play were to be donated to St Oswald's Church, whose vicar and congregation have worked so hard and long to raise funds to repair the bell tower and restore a full peal of bells. The Reverend Harold Brakespear would not disclose how much money is still owing on a loan they obtained, but was confident that his parishioners would support him, and said they were not defeated.

The Langesby Dramatic Society has also sent a message of sympathy to Dr Rowley and Peele's Players. 'We were deeply shocked and horrified to hear the news,' said their producer. Their play *Love on the Dole* will be performed nightly all this week at the town hall.

Death of Prominent Langesby Citizen

The death is announced of Mrs Edith Wyse, who for some years had been one of the town's most dedicated and public-spirited citizens. A highly respected member of local committees, and well known for her voluntary work, she was a keen supporter of the home for young offenders run by Mr Philip Gregory. He was not available for comment, but a member of staff at Prospect House said they were all deeply shocked. The body was found by a neighbour, and it is thought that Mrs Wyse died of heart failure. She will be much missed in Langesby. A full obituary appears on page 6.

'I'm not surprised they've hushed it up,' said one Church Street neighbour to another. 'Mrs Horsefield's still in shock. She was the one who found her – well, found whatever it was. She says she'll never forget it as long as she lives!' Then she mouthed, 'Spontaneous combustion. And there was no fire around her,' she continued. 'Apparently they just burn up by themselves. Peculiar, isn't it?'

FORTY-FIVE

'No breakfast, lunch or tea for me tomorrow, Mrs Housam,' said Timothy, laying aside his copy of the *Chronicle*. 'I propose to spend the day in meditation. I should be greatly obliged if you would observe the usual procedure. I am not to be disturbed unless it is absolutely necessary – and that I leave to your good sense. You may expect to see me some time in the evening, when a sandwich and a glass of wine will suffice.'

Bathed, shaven, and anointed with a sweet-smelling oil, Timothy padded back into his bedroom and donned a black silk kimono. He brought out two keys from a hidden drawer in his cabinet, stood for a while, rubbing them with his forefinger thoughtfully, and mounted the stairs to the top floor in a leisurely fashion to his inner sanctum. There he switched on the light, and locked the door behind him.

The walls and windows were covered with a rich dark silk drapery which hung in heavy shimmering folds from a starry blue ceiling to a black and white mosaic floor, in which were set the four cardinal points of the compass. The only piece of furniture was an antique oak chest containing ritual implements. This he unlocked with the smaller key and transformed into an altar.

From left to right he laid out a wooden pentacle covered with green silk; a crystal; an incense burner; a jar of ungent; and a single yellow rose in a silver vase, which he had borrowed from the sitting room.

Beneath this he placed an elaborate picture of the Tree of Life, the ritual card and the correspondences chart. On an orange cloth he stood a brass Georgian gong and a candle in a brass candlestick; and to the side of them a small sword of tempered steel, on whose blade were engraved names of power, and a hazel wand wrapped in red silk.

At the north point of the compass he placed a little rock picked up many years previously from a Welsh cromlech. At the south a beeswax candle. At the east a glass of consecrated water. At the west a sprig of dried mistletoe.

With a piece of chalk he drew a Triangle of Art in the east to confine any elemental being that he conjured up. He lit the candles and the incense and switched out the electric light.

Finally he drew a circle round himself and began a cabbalistic master ritual to create harmony and peace.

In the silent candlelit room thin spirals of smoke ascended, bearing fragrant scents of aloes wood, cinnamon, saffron, myrrh and cloves.

AFTERWORD

FORTY-SIX

Imogen was branching out in all directions. The purchase of a small car promised to give her future mobility, and George was teaching her to drive it, with an occasional loss of temper on both sides and a consequent making up and making love afterwards. Meanwhile she had invested in a sturdy second-hand bicycle, and arrived at the vicarage that Tuesday afternoon with cold rosy cheeks.

'How well you look!' cried Alice, embracing her. 'And what a lovely day for cycling. Yes, leave it in the porch. It will be quite safe. Come in, come in.'

Their friendship, though as warm as ever, was now conducted on diplomatic lines. There were subjects that Alice could broach easily and with pleasure. Such as *How do you like living in Howgill House? Tell me about your driving lessons. Have you finished redecorating Crazy Hats?* and *Is Polly getting on any better with the kitten?*

Subjects on which she lighted briefly, civilly, and then departed. Such as *And how is dear George?*

Because it was whispered that Imogen and George had taken a pagan vow on Haraldstone Hill, in the company of a group of witches, before setting the legal seal of approval on it at Langesby Register Office. She chose not to believe the rumour, though admitting that Imogen had given rise to this sort of gossip in the past. While Hal, secretly relieved that he did not have to refuse them a church wedding, adopted a philosophical attitude, which was frustrating.

For Imogen's part she never mentioned Philip, and skirted any subjects that might remind Alice how wrong she had been about him. And neither of them, in mute agreement, ever spoke of Edith.

So Alice said, 'I've made sure that we're by ourselves for an hour or two. Vera has 'done and dusted', as she puts it, and gone home. And you and I are going to toast crumpets in front of the parlour fire for a treat – just as we used to do in my room at Scarliff, all those years ago – and eat a good old-fashioned tea, and then I have something rather important to tell you. Well, more than one important thing – but let's hear your news first.'

Autumn came early in the dale, and yet, Imogen thought, sitting in front of a bright fire, taking tea with Alice, she did not regret the passing of summer. She felt at home when frost stiffened the morning grass, ice crackled on the pond, dry drifts of leaves lay in the lanes, the trees became stark and the landscape bared its noble bones. She said so.

'Oh, I knew instinctively,' said Alice, cutting into a substantial fruit cake, 'that you would like it here. You're a northerner by nature. I'm a southerner, of course. Perhaps that's why . . . Yes, Langesby is a town full of character, and the dale is lovely, still unspoiled. And despite all the scandal and grief in the summer' – lifting her chin and smiling at Providence – 'everything has turned out for the best, as it always does.'

'Does it?' Imogen wondered aloud, thinking of all the evil in the world.

Alice's blue eyes were a testament to her faith.

'Certainly it does.' She paused, frowning. 'Of course, sometimes it takes a while,' she admitted, 'and people seem to suffer unnecessarily, but in the end good must prevail or there is no point to life – no point at all.' She checked herself. 'Heavens above, here I am, giving you a sermon instead of our news!'

She braced herself to deliver it as cheerfully as possible.

'Of course, you know that the last few months have been very unsettled for us, but I couldn't say anything until the arrangements were made. We shall be leaving Langesby early in January.'

'Oh, my dear Alice,' said Imogen, sorry for the parting, sorrier for her.

'At least we shall end on a high note. We can celebrate Christmas here, one last time, and you may be sure we'll make it an occasion to remember.'

Imogen said helplessly, 'Alice, I'm so . . . How could they? After all the . . .' But Alice was plunging into explanations, putting her husband's case in the best possible light.

'Oh, there's no disgrace attached to the move. Langesby was only an interim appointment, anyway. And the Bishop doesn't blame Hal personally – though this wretched business has put the Church to a great deal of trouble and expense.'

She cleared her throat and began again.

'As you probably know, the Church is in financial difficulties at the moment, so I'm afraid there's no question of rebuilding the hall. And they're not prepared to spend any more on the church itself. Well, one must be practical. It would cost a fortune to restore it, and the congregation isn't large enough to warrant the expense. It was dwindling long before Hal came, and now, with the – the Prospect House people gone, the numbers have been further depleted . . .' She faltered for a moment, lost in her own account.

'But,' she cried, trying a new tack, 'they congratulated Hal on the restoration of the bell tower and his work with underprivileged youngsters. In fact the Bishop said that he felt the poor and deprived were Hal's true vocation, and his work in this field was far too valuable to be wasted . . .'

'Absolutely right!' Imogen offered, seeing that her friend was adrift again. 'And surely that's the central message of Christianity?'

Heartened. Alice continued. 'That's exactly what I said to Hal. And this will be a new experience which will stretch us both.' Less cheerfully, she added, 'I can't say that I would *choose* a London parish – and such a deprived area – but if that is where we are needed then we shall go gladly. Gladly.'

'They're lucky to have you, and I hope they appreciate it,' said Imogen tartly.

Alice sighed. She had not yet unburdened her mind.

'Fortunately, the move will hardly affect the boys – simply a change of place in the vacations. And though it sounds selfish, I'm so thankful that they're away at school, because otherwise they would be contending with a poor environment and bad influences and temptation on every side, not to speak of drugs and violence – and at such impressionable ages.'

Imogen supplied the reassurance Alice wanted.

'But the greatest security any youngster can have is a loving family and a good home, and you and Hal provide that. Far more influential than the world outside.'

Where there was evil in waiting and good did not always prevail.

'Yes,' Alice answered, comforted. 'Yes, you're right. You were always a good, wise friend, Imogen.'

She brightened. 'But I have some nice news, too.'

Her face was pink. 'It makes me feel rather silly, at my age, to be having a final fling at maternity. But there it is!' Laughing. 'Next March. God willing.' Her expression wavered only for a moment before being brought back in line. 'We should be well settled in our new home by then,' she told life optimistically.

'My dear Alice,' Imogen said in awe and compassion.

For her friend would cope with this as well as all her other responsibilities: many times daunted, never completely dashed, always ready to meet the next challenge.

'Alice,' Imogen said, 'I hope heaven does exist, because you certainly deserve it.'

She came round to the other side of the table, and hugged the fair plump shoulders, and dropped a kiss on the barley-coloured crown of hair; she could have cried for her, but that would have been unpardonable. So again she said what her friend would like to hear.

'Oh, but how lovely for you to have a late baby! The boys will be so thrilled. I can just see Julian and Matthew spoiling a little sister like mad. And she'll wrap Hal round her smallest finger. Alice, how wonderful!'

'Of course, we don't know it will be a girl,' said Alice.

'It *must* be a girl,' said Imogen, very positive. 'She has to inherit the doll's house.'

'A boy would be just as welcome,' Alice replied untruthfully. 'It will be fun to do all the baby business again. Even Hal's pleased. I thought he might feel it was a bit much, on top of everything else, but he looks upon it as a token of our faith in the future. And he fusses over me like a mother hen – when he's here.'

Her mood softened further.

'I must have put down a root or two in Langesby, without knowing it. It will be hard to leave our friends. I shall even miss this mausoleum of a house. And for all its faults and problems, St Oswald's church has character – don't you think?'

'Oh yes,' Imogen lied, for she thought it very ugly. 'Yes, tremendous character.'

Alice's valiant spirit shuddered a little.

'But in a strange house, in a strange city, just at first, I know I shall feel lost without Vera. I said to Hal, "If only we could take Vera with us!" But of course she's a daleswoman. She would never leave here.'

'You'll find another Vera,' said Imogen, buoying her up.

'I suppose it would be too much to hope that there'll be another Mary Proctor,' said Alice wistfully. 'I mean, as a midwife and friend, not a . . .' Reading Imogen's expression she added quickly, 'but God comprehends all. I'm sure she rests in peace and her sins are forgiven her.'

It was the first false note she had struck, and Imogen answered for Mary's sake, as dry as dust. 'If God can comprehend everything what is there to forgive?'

They were on the brink of a chasm which Alice presently bridged.

'Mary was a good woman, and that's what really matters.'

The short silence that followed was an undeclared truce. They sat in harmony, half drowsing in the warmth of the fire.

Then Alice, leaning forward to pat her hand, said, 'I shall miss you most of all, Imogen. Still, distance is not important. We shall keep in touch, as we always have done. We shall write to each other. We shall both have so much news. You must come and stay with us . . .'

For a while, perhaps, Imogen realized. She could not tell Alice that the course of their friendship was run, because this would not be acceptable. So she fled from the truth on the wings of fantasy.

'It *has* to be a girl. I can't make hats for a boy. I see it all quite clearly, Frilled cotton caps at first, then winter bonnets and summer straws . . .' Becoming animated, 'And when she grows up – oh, Alice – think of her wedding!'

For the first time in months Alice laughed.